There was no warning, not one single sound to put him on guard. There was just the one flash of bright light and, right there in front of him, a face staring intently into his, so close that he could look into the silver-grey eyes and feel the cool breath on his cheek.

Then darkness closed in again.

Sweat breaking out on his cold flesh and his heart in his throat, Josse fought for control. His body remembered its training even while his horror-struck mind was in shock and he was on his feet, sword in hand, lunging forward out of the shelter, before he knew it. Then his voice came back and he shouted in a great roar, 'Who's there? Show yourself!'

Nerve endings tingling as he subconsciously awaited the blow, he twisted from side to side, his sword making great deadly sweeps in a wide arc in front of him. 'Show yourself!'

He waited, listening.

There was nothing.

Presently the rain began to fall again.

About the author

Alys Clare is a history enthusiast who has written many novels under a different name. Alys Clare lives in Kent, where the Hawkenlye mysteries are set. You can reach her on her website www.alysclare.com

ALYS CLARE

Whiter than the Lily

HODDER

First published in Great Britain in 2004 by Hodder and Stoughton
A division of Hodder Headline
This edition published in 2005

A Hodder paperback

6

A CIP catalogue record for this title is
available from the British Library

ISBN 978 0 340 83112 0

Typeset in Plantin Light by Palimpsest Book Production Limited,
Polmont, Stirlingshire

Printed and bound by
Mackays of Chatham Ltd, Chatham, Kent

Hodder Headline's policy is to use papers that are natural,
renewable and recyclable products and made from wood grown
in sustainable forests. The logging and manufacturing processes
are expected to conform to the environmental regulations
of the country of origin.

Hodder and Stoughton Ltd
A division of Hodder Headline
338 Euston Road
London NW1 3BH

For Richard, beloved companion on
Romney Marsh 810 years later

Rosa rubicundior,
lilio candidior,
omnibus formosior,
semper in te glorior!

Redder than the rose,
whiter than the lily,
most lovely of all and
forever my pride!

Carmina Burana:
cantiones profanae

(Author's translation)

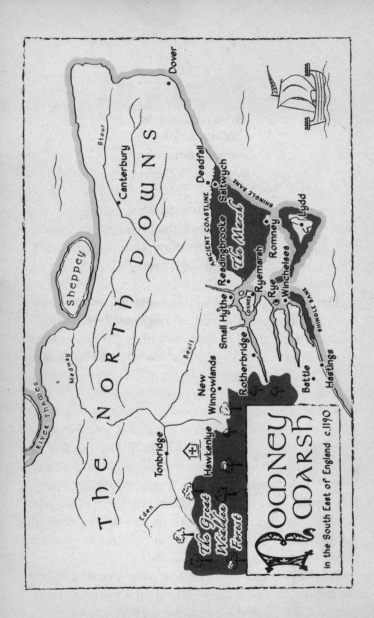

Romney Marsh in the South East of England c.1190

Dover

Stour

Canterbury

The North Downs

Sheppey

Medway

RIVER THAMES

Eden

Bewl

Tonbridge

Hawkenlye

The Great Wealden Forest

New Winnowlands

Rotherbridge

Small Hythe

Deadfall

Saltwych

Reedingbrooke

ANCIENT COASTLINE

The Marsh

SHINGLE BANK

Lydd

Romney

Ryemarsh

Rye

Winchelsea

OXNEY

SHINGLE BANK

Battle

Hastings

The walled garden lay as if stunned under the hot May sunshine. After an indifferent spring, it seemed that Nature was eager to make up for lost time and, since the middle of the month, the weather had been dry and unseasonably hot.

The grass was dotted with daisies and, at a distance from the sheltering group of apple and nut trees in the far corner, three or four fairy rings made a pattern of darker green on the lawn's brightness. Herbs and flowers grew abundantly in the beds. Predominant among the lilies, pansies, poppies, sage, lavender and thyme were the tall stems of rue, its yellow flowers brought early into bloom by the sun and pushing their way vigorously up to the light. Roses climbed in profusion over the southern and westward walls, their bright pink flowers giving a fragrance to the warm, still air. Wormwood and yarrow, southernwood and bramble competed for space in the hedge beyond the nut trees; in the shade of the hedge, in its own marked-off space, grew mandrake.

Between the herb beds, narrow paths wound through the grass. On the furthest path stood a young woman. She had just picked a rose and, holding it to her face, her eyes were closed in pleasure as she breathed in the scent.

She was tall, slim and fair, so fair that, in the bright light, her skin appeared white. Her hair, too, was almost white; a blonde so pale that it resembled ripe flax. She had thrown back the veil that she usually wore to shield her face from the sun and now the faintest blush of pink was beginning to colour her cheeks. She was dressed in silk, expensive, heavy silk, imported from France and acquired, at considerable cost, from a merchant in Romney. The silk was the palest pink of an opening bindweed flower and – not in the least by accident – it exactly matched the soft colour in the girl's smooth skin.

Graceful, rapt, eyes still closed, she was beautiful.

So beautiful, thought the old man watching her from a window above, that she puts the flowers to shame. Who has need of a garden, if he can but gaze on one such as she?

He put up a hand to rub at his eyes. His sight troubled him constantly, although he did not care to admit it. Until quite recently, it had only been close things that he could not see well but now he was also beginning to have difficulty with his long sight. The rubbing did not help; in fact, he realised, it had made matters worse. Letting his hand fall into his lap, he leaned forward in his chair, narrowed his eyes to fierce slits and resumed his intent study. Concentrating very hard, he fixed his watering eyes on her.

Still holding the rose in one long, pale hand, she was moving along the path now. Then, in a swift, supple movement that made the watching man catch his breath, she bent down to pick some small flower from the grass. A daisy, he thought, wishing he could see. Or perhaps a violet. Yes, probably a violet, and she was going to prepare for him some of those sweetmeats made from violets steeped in honey that he enjoyed so much.

Ah, but how he loved her! Loved her for the care she took of him, for the store of remedies for his many ailments that she seemed to keep within that sleek head. Loved her for her affectionate nature and her playful ways, she who made him laugh sometimes like the boy he wished with all his heart that he still were.

She was patient with him, aye, patient and loving. When they lay in their bed and he reached for her, his wife, she had ways of making his old flesh respond and rouse itself. But, despite the small caressing hands, the regular addition of rosemary to his food and the testicle-shaped beans beneath his pillow, it was becoming steadily more difficult to reach any sort of satisfaction, for himself or for her. He worried ceaselessly that her youth and her ardour might tire of his efforts.

Besides that worry there was another. He prayed daily for a child and, as well he knew, so did she. Their intimacies were usually of a nature for her to conceive – not always, but surely with sufficient frequency – and there had been times when she believed herself to be carrying his child. But on each occasion – there had been no more than three – at the moon's turning she had begun to bleed. The loss from her womb had been accompanied by quiet and heartbreaking tears from her beautiful blue eyes, tears which had set off his own so that, balked of parenthood, they wept together and found some small comfort in each other as they did so.

I would give her the world, he mused, staring down at her as, leaving the path, her small feet in their calf-leather slippers lightly crossed the grass. The world, aye, and everything in it. I *do* give her anything she asks of me, not that she asks for much, bless her loving heart.

But I cannot give her a child.

He felt the familiar grief overtake him. He had reached down his hand to her belly and the soft hair of her groin that morning; heartened by a good night's sleep and aroused by the warmth of her bottom pressed into his stomach as she slept, he had woken with his blood pounding. But she had gently taken hold of his wrist and whispered, 'No, my dearest love, for my courses are beginning.'

They had tried not to dwell on it, tried not to let it spoil the bright day. And, after all, were not the spring and the early summer times of hope?

She must have felt his gaze on her. Perhaps, he thought fondly, close to my heart as she is, she senses my distress.

For, reaching the corner of the garden where two walls met and a low door gave access to a little hut, suddenly she stopped, turned and, looking straight up at him, gave him a sweet smile and blew him a kiss.

For a long time he went on staring at the space

where she had stood for that brief moment. Then, as the summer scents and the heat from the sunny garden steadily pervaded the room, slowly his eyelids began to droop. Settling himself more comfortably in his high-backed chair, resting his grey head on the small lavender-scented cushion that she had made for him, he slept.

Down in the little hut, the young woman was busy. She loved it in there, where the walls smelt of cut wood and the reed thatch of the roof housed small and usually unseen creatures whose soft rustlings and sudden brisk movements provided cheerful company for her as she worked.

The hut had been built with its back to the bricks of the walled garden, in the driest place that could be found. It had two little windows in its outward-facing side and, on sunny days, the shutters were always fastened back to allow a good circulation of air. Positioned out of the prevailing south-westerly wind and in the shade of the high wall, the temperature inside the hut remained fairly constant; the girl had stipulated the necessity for this when she had given her orders regarding the hut's construction.

It was the place where she dried and stored her herbs and where she prepared her simples and potions.

Along the rear wall was a wide wooden workbench, on which she laid out her herbs after picking. She had recently been gathering rosemary, eager to collect some of the plant's first potent flowering, and the air inside the small space still smelt sweetly of the herb. Above the bench, several wooden poles had been fastened lengthways under the hut's roof and from them hung bunches of herbs in the process of drying. On shelves at the end of the hut were a great many stone jars, neatly sealed with wax so as to keep out all air and moisture.

She was skilled in herb lore and knew exactly what she was doing.

Now, staring down with unfocused eyes at the empty workbench waiting for her to begin, she ran through in her mind what she would need.

She had forgotten something.

Swiftly she left the hut, went back through the low doorway and emerged into the garden. She looked first up at the window, watching the sleeping face of her husband for some moments before moving on. Assuring herself that he really was asleep and could not see her, she then let her eyes roam all around the garden.

Nobody was about. Nobody was watching.

Turning to her goal, she ran across the grass and, working carefully but as quickly as she could, collected the missing ingredient.

Back inside the hut, she chanted softly under her breath as her hands cut, chopped and tore. Sometimes she reached for another tool – the mortar and pestle for crushing, the flask of freshly collected spring water to dilute – and, always, her practised hands knew exactly where to go without her having to remove her eyes from her potion to look and direct them.

In time, she had finished. Finished, at least, all that

she could do today. One final element had still to be added but she could not do that until the Moon had moved from Scorpio into Sagittarius – the last ingredient must be gathered with the Moon in a Fire sign, for then it would give the necessary heat – and there was a good fall of dew.

In two nights' time, she thought calmly. I shall rise naked from my bed and slip out in the dark hours before dawn.

It was something that she did quite frequently. She did not think that her husband knew, for she timed her absences to coincide with his deepest sleep. She shared much of her life and her thoughts with him but some things she needed to do alone.

She covered her potion with a moist cloth, then put a stone lid on the pot and tied it into place. Then she put it right at the back of the top shelf.

She looked around the little hut as she wiped and dried her hands. Everything was clean and tidy, just as she liked it. Satisfied, she fastened the door and, with a light step, set off for the house.

I

Josse d'Acquin, riding out in a new tunic to visit his neighbour Brice of Rotherbridge, reflected that it was good to be alive on a hot summer's morning with the prospect of a good dinner ahead of him.

The invitation had come as quite a surprise. Josse and Brice had been on politely friendly terms since their first acquaintance four years ago, but the relationship could not have been called close. Then, a few days back when Josse and his man Will had got themselves thoroughly hot, sweaty and filthy supervising the unblocking of a ditch, Brice's manservant had arrived with the summons.

Josse was ashamed of having been caught in such a state. He had intended only to stand above the ditch and supervise his small and singularly dull-witted working party, only somehow he had found himself down in the mud and the sludge showing them what he wanted them to do. Will, clambering reluctantly down beside his master, had sucked at his teeth in disapproval. 'Aye, man, I know what you think and I'll thank you not to make that disgusting noise at me!' Josse had hissed at him.

But Will knew from long experience that his master's bark was a great deal worse than his all but non-existent bite. He continued his tutting and sucking, adding a not quite inaudible commentary along the lines of 'T'ain't right for 'im to dig along o' the likes of them, t'ain't good for discipline,' sentiments which, although Josse might have agreed with them, were hardly helping matters.

Josse's embarrassment at having Brice's long-nosed manservant stare down at him in disdain had prompted him to purchase the new tunic, as if to show that he *could* look smart – and scrupulously clean – if he wanted to. The tunic was of dark forest-green velvet, came to just below his knees and flared out in generous folds at the hem. He had been assured that it was cut in the latest fashion. It had certainly cost enough, especially when he had allowed the merchant to persuade him into buying matching gloves and a hat shaped rather like a turban. Josse was not at all sure about the hat.

The landscape was changing now as he left the High Weald behind and approached the marshland. Brice's manor was partly on the high ridge-top land – the manor house was on an elevation overlooking a wide creek – but most of his acres were down on the levels. It was widely believed that he had earned a small fortune in wool.

Drawing rein, Josse paused for a moment to look out at the view below him. He was further upstream along the same creek that flowed past Brice's manor house and now, with the tide going out, the small water course was a mere trickle, its sides slick with wet mud which erupted occasionally into bubbles that exploded with a soft pop and a brief but noisome whiff of marsh gas.

On the far side of the creek was a low bank, beyond which the ground fell away into a wide marshy valley. Flat and fairly featureless – unless one counted the softly-coloured patchwork of little fields, the few small, stunted trees and the sheep – it ended in a rise of the land some two or three miles away. On that higher ground, Josse worked out, trying to get his bearings, would be the villages of Northeham and, further east on the low cliffs above Rye Bay, Peasmarsh and Iden.

Rousing himself from his contemplation of the serene scene before him – it really was a lovely day and the wide marshlands looked their best in the strong sunshine – Josse clucked to Horace and turned for Brice of Rotherbridge's manor house.

The courtyard was shaded by a brake of willow and alder trees growing alongside and, peering ahead into the cool gloom, Josse called out to announce his arrival. After a moment there was the sound of hurrying feet and Brice's young servant came out of the stables.

'Morning, Sir Josse,' the lad said, grinning up at Josse.

'Good morning – er—' What was the lad's name? Josse tried to remember. The boy had grown in four years almost to manhood but the lank hair, low forehead and broken front tooth were unmistakable. Still, the smile of welcome seemed genuine and, as he responded, suddenly Josse recalled the lad's name. 'Ossie!' he exclaimed triumphantly.

'Aye, that's right, sir,' Ossie said, the grin widening. 'I'll take your horse, will I, sir? There's cool water in the stable and I'll give him a bit of a rub down, seeing as how he's got himself into a sweat.'

'Aye, I'd be grateful,' Josse said, dismounting. 'Warm day, eh, Ossie?'

'That it is, sir,' Ossie said with a dramatic sigh, as if warm weather were one of the plagues of Egypt. 'Dare say we'll be paying for it afore long.' He stared glumly at Josse, then said, 'Go on inside, sir. You know the way? Master'll be waiting for you.'

Josse crossed the yard and went up the steps into the hall. As Ossie had said, Brice was waiting for him and, as Josse approached, he quickly rose from his seat on a bench beside the wide hearth and hurried to greet him.

Studying him, Josse reflected that four years had, if anything, made the man look younger rather than older. Of course, four years back he had recently lost his wife and he had been, Josse reminded himself, carrying a heavy burden of guilt over her death. It had been a difficult time for both men and the residue of awkwardness, Josse had sometimes reflected, probably accounted for why the two of them had kept their distance from one another. Still, Josse was here now, a welcomed guest in Brice's house, and perhaps this unexpected invitation was Brice's way of saying that he too regretted the lack of closeness between them and wanted to put matters right.

Josse studied Brice as his host held out a mug of cool ale. The dark brown hair showed not a trace of grey, the tanned face was smooth and unlined and there was a hint of laughter in the brown eyes. Brice held himself well and his broad-shouldered frame was clad in fine linen and a richly bordered burgundy tunic that looked even more costly than Josse's.

He looked, Josse concluded, raising his cup in response to Brice's courteous toast to 'old friends well met once more', like a man in his prime. And, moreover – just what *was* it about him? Something in his expression . . . aye, there was definitely some suppressed excitement in those eyes. He looked like a man treasuring some thrilling secret thought.

The conversation flowed for a while over mundane topics – the weather, the health of Brice's sheep, the steadily rising price of wool. And presently, as conversations always did just then, it turned to the King.

'He is in good heart, they say,' Brice remarked. 'Although, given the circumstances, it is hard to see how that can be.' His handsome face took on an expression of extreme indignation. 'A Christian king, God's own anointed one, to be a prisoner! Ah, Josse, the humiliation!'

'I think we can be assured that now he is a prisoner in name only,' Josse replied. 'Since that traitorous rogue Leopold of Austria handed him over to the Emperor back in March, it's said that his situation has steadily improved. The latest reports suggest that he is treated more as an honoured guest than a prisoner. Why, he holds court and conducts his business almost as if he were in his own strong-hold!'

Brice waved a hand impatiently. 'Aye, so they say, but he's not *free*, man, is he?'

Josse had to acknowledge that this was true. 'His health has improved,' he offered. 'He's enjoying his food and drink again and he has even been hunting on more than one occasion, and that will build up his strength for sure.'

As if he had not heard, Brice said, 'And what of us here in England? Eh? Kingless, rudderless, with that clever brother of his scheming to sit on our Richard's throne!'

'The Queen is on her guard,' Josse said. 'She knows John as well as anybody and she will do what is necessary to protect Richard's interests.' Both men knew, without Josse having to stipulate, that he spoke of King Richard's mother and not his wife. 'Back at Easter, she increased the guard on the coast and those Flemish mercenaries that John had hired received a tougher welcome than they'd bargained for. And she's made the King's men renew their oaths of fealty.'

'What use will that be if he does not return? If – God forbid! – we have to have his brother in his place?'

'We can do no better than hearken to the King's own words. You recall? When they told him of John's scheming, he said that his brother wasn't the man to conquer a country if anyone offered him the slightest resistance. King Richard does not fear his brother, Brice, so we should not either.'

'But we are here and he is far away,' Brice said

lugubriously. Then, fixing Josse with angry dark eyes, he added softly, 'And now we're going to have to find one hundred thousand silver marks to get him back.'

'Aye, I know,' Josse said heavily. 'They say it's twice England's annual revenue.'

'Will it be raised?'

'Aye,' Josse said, with more confidence than he felt. 'Queen Eleanor will see to it that it is.'

'We've already been bled white to pay for the Crusade.' Brice, as if aware that his words might be regarded by some as next door to treason, spoke in a voice little above a whisper. 'Now it's a quarter of our annual income from every one of us!'

'Not everyone,' Josse protested. 'The poor are only obliged to give what they can.'

Brice said something that Josse did not quite hear, which, given his allegiance to King Richard, he felt was probably just as well.

There was silence in the hall for some time. After discussing matters of such gravity, Josse thought, it was somehow not right to try to turn the talk to a more personal level. All the same, he was still very intrigued to know why he had been invited and even more so to find out just what it was that was making Brice pace restlessly as if his lean body contained too much nervous energy for him to be still. Before he could think of a way to satisfy his curiosity, a stout woman with a neat white cap over her grey hair and a crisp apron covering her brown gown bustled in and told them that dinner was ready.

Brice, acknowledging the brusque announcement

with a smile, said lazily, 'You remember Mathild, Josse?'

'Indeed I do,' he replied. If the woman's food is as good as her ale, he thought cheerfully, then I'm in for a treat.

The meal was excellent. Mathild, who had a light hand with a pastry crust, served a hot pork pasty that was flavoured with some spice that Josse thought he recognised but could not place. Whatever it was, he hadn't tasted it since he had attended the court of the Poitevins and it was a rare pleasure to encounter it again. He and Brice took their time, eating their fill of the savoury dishes. In addition to the pork pasty there was a tartlet of chopped meat in a cheese, egg and milk sauce; white fish in wine sauce flavoured with onions and spices; and a sort of solid pottage that Josse thought consisted mainly of peas. Then Mathild brought in sops-in-wine – generous pieces of her own sweet cake in a mixture of wine, milk and almonds – and her spice sauce once more tantalised Josse's taste buds with all but forgotten delights. He detected ginger . . . and cinnamon . . . and perhaps a touch of clove? . . . and then, with a smile and some earnest words of praise to Mathild, he passed up his platter for more.

'Aye,' Brice said, finally pushing himself back from the table and easing a thumb inside his belt, 'she may lack a certain finesse in her manners, my old Mathild, but she's the best cook I've ever come across. More wine?'

Accepting another refill, Josse was thinking just what a pleasant way this was to spend a lazy sunny day when, draining his own cup, Brice sat up straight and said, 'When you're done, Josse, there's someone I want you to meet. You may know of him. His manor is not far from here – an hour's ride, certainly no more, even if we go very gently – and the day will be growing cooler soon.'

'Someone you wish me to meet?' Josse echoed stupidly, trying to focus his drowsy thoughts. 'But—'

'I should have explained,' Brice said with a swift apologetic smile. 'Only – well, I thought to surprise you.'

Just as Josse was reflecting on the odd comment, Brice corrected himself. 'That is to say, I did not quite know how to say, come and dine with me and then we will ride out to introduce you to my friends, so I said nothing.'

Finishing his wine and reluctantly getting to his feet, Josse could not help but wonder what was so difficult about that.

The afternoon was indeed a shade cooler as Brice and Josse rode off from Rotherbridge. Brice kept to the higher ground and this, besides keeping their horses' hooves out of the mud, also gave the men the benefit of the shade of the willows that grew on the top of the creek bank. As they rode, Josse observed how the narrow creek down on their right was steadily widening. Well, he thought, the water course itself is not increasing very much in size, it's more that the valley through which it flows is broader now. He was about to make some comment to his companion when Brice turned in his saddle and said, 'We have to descend here. We're heading over there' – he pointed across the creek to the higher land on the far side – 'and this is the best way across.'

With a grunt of acknowledgement, Josse clicked to Horace and followed Brice as he rode carefully down the bank. He understood why Brice had chosen to cross here and not higher up, where the creek was narrower; here the sides of the bank were far less steep. And soon he had to admit that Brice knew exactly what he was about. Leading the way confidently towards what appeared to be a dangerously wet and boggy stretch of ground – the sort of place, Josse thought anxiously, where a man and his horse might flounder to a dreadful death – it became apparent as they drew nearer that a narrow path crossed the water. It was not continuous but interspersed in places with firm stepping-stones and, clearly, it would be covered at high tide. As he followed Brice across, Josse had the sudden thought that only a man who made this journey frequently would know his way so well.

The manor house to which Brice took him was pleasantly situated towards the east end of the Isle of Oxney. Beyond it the land fell away towards Rye Bay and, to the rear, it was sheltered by a thick band of woodland. The house was not new – no sign here of alterations and additions of the sort that both Josse and Brice had made to their dwellings – and it blended in so beautifully with its surroundings that it almost looked as if it had stood there, back to the woods, face to the water, for ever.

Shaking away that whimsical thought, Josse realised that Brice was speaking to him and he urged his horse forward. 'Eh? What did you say?' he asked.

'I was informing you of the name of our host,' Brice repeated. 'Behold, Josse, the home of Ambrose Ryemarsh.' He was, Josse noticed, straining forward, eyes narrowed, as if eager for the first glimpse of the house and its occupant. And, as the two of them rode into the courtyard, it seemed that someone had been looking out for them. At the top of the flight of steps that led up to the wide doors, standing open in welcome, was a powerfully-built grey-haired man. Peering down at them, his head straining forward on the sinewy neck like a turtle's from its shell, he called out, 'Brice? Is that you? And there are two of you – you bring your friend?'

'Aye, Ambrose, it's me,' Brice called back. 'And yes, Josse d'Acquin is with me. Wait while we attend to the horses, then we will come up.'

As if waiting for the moment, a young lad came running from the stable block and, with a brief nod of greeting, took charge of Josse's and Brice's mounts. Josse heard Brice give a couple of nervous coughs as he pulled at his tunic and arranged its folds and then they climbed the steps and entered the house.

Ambrose Ryemarsh entertained with a lavish hand. Although Josse had eaten well with Brice, the savoury and sweet delicacies daintily laid out on salvers in the cool hall tempted him to start all over again. With no effort at all he ate two venison pasties with cherry sauce, a small, sweet custard tart flavoured with bay leaf and lemon, and a frothy baked apple studded with dried fruit and flavoured with ginger. There was white wine to drink, and somehow whoever had charge of Ambrose's household had contrived to keep it chilled. Josse had not tasted anything so delicious since he had left France.

The conversation flowed easily but inconsequentially. Josse, still curious as to just what this visit was for, waited patiently.

Then three things happened at once.

There was the sound of light footsteps in the passage outside. Brice's head spun round and, for the split second that Josse was able to observe him, his face wore a strangely excited, expectant look. Then, noticing Josse's eyes on him, he replaced it with an expression of bland disinterest. Which he still wore when the hanging over the doorway was pulled back with a soft swish and a woman entered the hall.

Ambrose got up from his tall chair and held out both hands. The woman walked swiftly over to him and put her own hands in his. Then she leaned towards him and tenderly kissed his face, smiling up at him as she did so.

Ambrose, turning towards Josse, said, 'This is my wife. Galiena, my sweet, I present to you Josse d'Acquin.'

Rising to greet her, swiftly Josse studied her, taking in her appearance. She was tall and slender, the cornflower-blue silk gown fitting her well and showing off the high, round breasts and the narrow waist. Her pale hair was braided into two thick plaits, coiled up on either side of her face. Over her hair she wore a small veil, held in place by a chaplet of flowers. Her eyes were as deep a blue as her gown and her rosy lips were parted in a generous smile.

She was, Josse recognised, a beauty. She was also very young: no more, he guessed, than seventeen or eighteen.

And Ambrose was a man well into, if not actually past, middle age.

Trying to put his tumbling thoughts aside, Josse bowed over the small, cool hand that she held out to him and said, 'It is a great pleasure, lady, to meet you.'

Galiena laughed softly, squeezing Josse's hand as if she knew exactly what he was thinking and was acknowledging his reaction. Then, turning so as to include Brice, she said, 'You have taken refreshment, my lords? My husband has been looking after you?'

'Aye, indeed he has,' Josse hurried to say. 'Wine of a quality I have not tasted these many years. And kept so cool!'

He heard his own words and felt a hot flush of embarrassment flood through him. For one thing, praising Ambrose's wine so lavishly was hardly tactful to Brice, who earlier had entertained him almost as well. For another, he was gushing like a boy and, until he had encountered Galiena, he would have said he had left boyhood far behind.

She seemed to pick up his discomfiture. Without looking at him – for which he was extremely grateful as he was quite sure his face was scarlet – she glided back to Ambrose, pulled up a stool and sat down at his feet. Then, turning to Brice, she said, 'Now, Brice, what news of Rotherbridge? Have Mathild and Robert resolved their quarrel? And did you give Ossie the clove paste for his tooth?'

As Brice replied, Josse studied his face. There was no sign now of that flash of tension that had briefly lit up his handsome features; he sat on a bench close to Galiena and, for all that his expression revealed, could have been chatting to an elderly aunt.

I was wrong, Josse told himself firmly. There is nothing there but friendship. I was wrong.

And yet . . .

But Ambrose was addressing him. 'More wine, Josse?' he said. 'I rejoice that it is to your liking and it does but heat up, standing there on the table.' He raised a hand in a firm gesture that suggested Ambrose was used to giving orders and having them obeyed. 'Fetch it over here and we shall both fill our cups!'

Josse did as he was commanded. As he bent to pour wine into Ambrose's cup, Ambrose said softly in his ear, 'Come and walk outside with me, sir. I would speak with you on a matter of some delicacy.'

Then, standing up, he said aloud, 'Sir Josse, let us leave these two to their gossiping!' He shot a tender glance at his wife as she cried out in mock-protest. 'Take a turn with me out in the sunshine,' he continued, 'and I will show you how Galiena has turned a wilderness into the prettiest garden in England.'

Taking hold of Josse's sleeve in a surprisingly strong grip, Ambrose bore his guest out of the hall.

'The garden is hidden away on the far side of the house, where from the higher ground we look down over the valley,' he said as he ushered Josse along a path bordered with rose bushes. 'Along here . . . wait . . . there! What do you say? Am I not rightly proud of what my wife has accomplished?'

Josse stood and stared. He knew nothing about gardens, his only limited experience being with the Hawkenlye herb garden so carefully tended by Sister Tiphaine. And, back in his own manor, Will and his woman grew vegetables in a muddy plot behind their small cottage. However, neither Will nor the Hawkenlye herbalist had the inclination or the time to grow plants merely for their beauty.

Whereas here, that seemed to have been the main consideration.

His eyes ran over the clipped grass, the rich brown earth of the beds, the spinney of nut and fruit trees. Then he looked again at the flowers and did not think he had ever in his life seen so many different colours, shapes and textures all in one place.

Ambrose, he sensed, was eagerly waiting for his opinion. 'It is a paradise,' he said eventually. 'A true Eden. Your wife has made each flower surpass itself in its loveliness.'

'Ah, and the garden is not merely decorative!'

Ambrose had taken hold of Josse's sleeve again and was propelling him down one of the paths that led out across the grass. 'She grows herbs, you see.' He paused, sniffing deeply. 'Look, here is rue, there is rosemary, there garlic, there . . . oh, I forget its name, something she uses in one of her special concoctions. She does tell me, she always explains what she is growing and for what purpose, but my concentration is apt to lapse and I forget.' He gave a faint sigh. 'I do not like to ask her too often to repeat herself since it can only serve to remind her of the reason for my forgetfulness.' He turned his face towards Josse. 'She is beautiful, is she not?'

'Aye, she is,' Josse said quietly.

'And, as doubtless was your first thought on seeing her, young enough to be my granddaughter.'

'Ah, no!' Josse protested, feeling himself redden again. 'I thought only . . .' He could not summon up a lie, and, his flush deepening, he fell silent.

Misunderstanding him, Ambrose smiled faintly and, looking away, said, 'Well, perhaps not quite my granddaughter. But, for sure, my daughter.'

'She – er, it is clear that she cares for you lovingly and tenderly,' Josse said. Since that was true – or so he believed, on such brief acquaintance – he said it with conviction. He felt his hot face begin to cool down.

'She does, she does.' Ambrose sighed again, more deeply. 'As do I for her. I love her, Josse, and it is my greatest wish to make her happy.'

'She seems happy to me,' Josse said. 'She has the

air of a contented woman.' That, too, he believed to be the truth.

But Ambrose, turning to face him and fixing him with faded hazel eyes, said sadly, 'But Galiena is clever at dissimulation. She wishes me to believe that I satisfy her in every respect. She does not like me to think that she sorrows and therefore she pretends that she is happy, with not a care in the world.'

Josse was beginning to dread what might be coming. 'She – er, she has a beautiful home and a loving husband,' he said, wishing himself anywhere but there in the sunny garden and apparently about to hear some highly intimate confidences. 'Many women would give much to be so comfortably situated.'

'Aye, that is what she, too, says.' Ambrose lowered his eyes. 'Yet that, sir, is *all* she has. We live very quietly here. I do not care for company and, save for Brice and, today, yourself' – he gave an acknowledging nod in Josse's vague direction – 'we have few other visitors other than family. And indeed I am often from home when there is business to attend to or when I am summoned to court. Life with a man who now prefers the peaceful country life is, I fear, dull for Galiena. How *can* she be satisfied with it?' He breathed deeply once or twice, keeping his head down, then, as if he had been gathering his courage, abruptly raised his eyes towards Josse again and said rapidly, 'Sir Josse, I need your help. Brice tells me that you are acquainted with the good sisters at Hawkenlye Abbey?'

'I – er, aye, that I am.' The sudden change of tack

had totally confused Josse and he stumbled over his response.

'Then tell me, if you will, are they skilled in women's matters?'

Women's matters. Oh, God's boots, Josse thought frantically, it's even worse that I feared! 'Er – they have a highly competent infirmarer,' he hedged. 'There are many dedicated nursing sisters and there's Sister Tiphaine, she's the herbalist.'

'They treat women for their *personal* problems?' Ambrose persisted, and the heavy emphasis on *personal* made Josse blush anew.

'Um – hmph – er –'

But Ambrose, lost in his own deep distress, seemed unaware of Josse's extreme discomfiture. 'She is a herbalist herself, my Galiena,' he muttered. 'She has tried everything she can think of. Even what I believe are quite desperate remedies.' The anguished expression making him look even older, he went on, 'I see her at night, you see. Oh, she thinks that she does not disturb me, that I sleep blissfully on when she creeps out of my bed. But I awake, sir, always I awake. I perceive her sudden absence, even if I am deeply asleep. And I go to the window, from which I can look down on the garden, and I watch as she enacts her rites. Only often she conceals herself, you understand, she slips away to where I can no longer see her. It is easily done.' He sighed. Staring out over the garden, dropping to a whisper, he said, 'Naked under the moonlight she is, her lovely body so pale and white. So beautiful. *So* beautiful.'

Suddenly he seemed to recall to whom he was speaking. The intensity left his haggard face and, laughing briefly, Ambrose said, 'Josse, I am sorry. In my desperation, I forgot myself. You arrive here as an unsuspecting guest then all of a sudden your host drags you off alone and starts raving about matters more suited to a private discussion between a lady and her bedchamber maid. You must be quite horrified!'

Since horrified did not begin to describe it, Josse merely grunted.

'What I am asking you,' Ambrose went on, his voice calmer now, 'is whether the Hawkenlye nuns can help my wife. Help both of us, indeed, for it is my wish as much as it is hers.'

Light dawned on Josse, suddenly and totally. Old husband, young wife, and a large, wealthy household whose quiet peace was undisturbed by a child's shrieks of laughter or a baby's cry.

He opened his mouth to speak, but as he did so Ambrose forestalled him. 'Galiena is barren, Sir Josse,' he said quietly. 'And I want more than anything in the world to grant her heart's desire and give her a child.'

2

'You reassure me, Josse. I had no wish to raise my wife's hopes if there *was* no hope, but now I believe I shall make the suggestion to her.'

Ambrose and Josse had walked all around the garden. Josse had answered the older man's questions about the Hawkenlye community as fully as he could, and at last Ambrose seemed to accept that Josse could not be regarded as any sort of an authority on that highly embarrassing subject of women's matters. With a chuckle, Ambrose said he would wait until he could address his questions to the proper person – Josse had told him that the infirmarer was called Sister Euphemia, which Ambrose had committed to memory – and he promised not to badger Josse any more.

As they set off back towards the house, the soft summer sounds punctuated by the tap of their footsteps on the path, Josse suddenly exclaimed, 'We are forgetting the waters!'

'The waters?' There was a note of query in Ambrose's tone.

'Aye, the precious healing waters, down in the Vale.' Confident that this was a type of cure that anyone

could discuss without the hot flush of embarrassment, Josse hurried to explain. 'There is a spring at
Hawkenlye – you have not heard tell of it? The holy
water has worked many a miracle.'

'I am not entirely sure that I believe in miracles,'
Ambrose said. 'Sir Josse, I would risk a further confidence, if you permit?' Screwed-up eyes peering at
Josse's dubious face, he gave a shout of laughter and
said, 'Not that sort of confidence, man! Did I not just
give you my word? No. What I was about to say was
this. We have prayed, Galiena and I, aye, and fasted.
Confessed our sins and done penance, quite extreme
in my case. The priest tells us that Galiena's failure
to conceive is a mark of God's disfavour and that a
sincere and heartfelt repentance will restore to us the
Lord's grace. So we pray, and tell our beads, and I
submitted myself to a hair shirt and no clean linen for a
month.' He shuddered. 'Believe me, Josse, to I who am
probably over-particular, my own stench and the crawl
of lice on my skin were worse torments than the rough
scratch of horsehair. And all for naught!' Anger flashed
in the stern face and, for a moment, Josse caught a
glimpse of the authority and the force that must have
surged in Ambrose when he was in his prime. 'All for
naught,' he repeated more softly, 'for my poor lassie
goes on bleeding regularly each month.'

Feeling that the gentle Hawkenlye monks had somehow been included in Ambrose's rant against the
priesthood, Josse felt obliged to speak up for them.
'There is nothing of that at Hawkenlye,' he said firmly.
'For one thing, the monks are loving and only too

aware that people go to them in trouble. They wish always to help if they can and they do not judge. For another, the Abbess of Hawkenlye would not permit such heavy-handed measures as you describe.'

'The Abbess. Aye, I have heard tell of her.' Ambrose shot Josse an assessing look. 'What is your opinion of her?'

An image of Helewise swam into Josse's mind. In it she was laughing at something he had just said, her wide mouth smiling and her grey eyes under the well-marked brows regarding him affectionately. But then the image changed and, drawn up to her full imposing height, she stood in her severe habit glaring at some wrong-doer, authority in every inch of her.

'What is my opinion of her?' Josse muttered. 'Sir, I do not believe myself fit to have one. But I will say this: she is a good woman, honourable, hard-working, devout.' Meeting Ambrose's narrowed eyes, he said, 'Bring your wife to Hawkenlye and meet her. Experience for yourselves the love and charity of her nuns and at least try the healing waters. They will do you good, I believe, and the monks will make you welcome.'

For a few moments Ambrose studied him in silence. Then he said, 'I will do as you suggest. Let us return to the hall and I shall tell Galiena.'

Josse found it difficult to look Galiena in the face after what her husband had been telling him about her. Still discomfited by her beauty, he heard Ambrose's words running through his head, over and over again. *I watch*

*her as she enacts her rites. Naked under the moonlight, her
lovely body so pale and white.*

Although he knew it was not his fault, he felt
guilty.

Trying to be as unobtrusive as possible, he listened
to the talk flowing between the other three. Ambrose
had already announced that he and Galiena would
make the journey to Hawkenlye and take the cure and
Galiena had seemed genuinely delighted. Ambrose,
muttering to her, had seemed to be cautioning her
against unreasonable optimism, which Josse thought
was wise. Reflecting on what the two of them might
make of Hawkenlye – and, indeed, what Hawkenlye
might make of them – he allowed his attention to
wander.

But then Galiena's excited voice broke into his
reverie.

'. . . no reason why we should not go straight away!'
she was saying. 'Is there, Sir Josse?' He leaped to
attention.

'Er – what was that?'

Smiling, she repeated herself. 'I was saying, we
could set out straight away. First thing in the morning,
perhaps. Unless we have to give notice that we are
coming?' The delicate eyebrows were raised in query.

'No, folks usually just turn up,' he said. 'But – do
you not need to make preparations for the journey?
There must surely be some small comforts you will
wish to pack up and take with you.'

The blue eyes met his. 'Do poor peasants with a
sick child bring such comforts?' she asked coolly.

'No, of course not,' he replied.

'Then what need have we of such things?' Still staring at him, she seemed to notice that her words had stung. 'I am sorry, Sir Josse,' she said, much more kindly. 'I meant no criticism.' Now she was smiling. 'I am very anxious to be on our way and I fear that my mood affects my speech. I did not mean to offend.'

'Neither did I,' he assured her.

'We may set out in the morning, then?' she asked again. 'It is truly in order to arrive without prior warning?'

'Indeed it is,' he said.

'Then we shall do so!' she exclaimed, leaping up and clapping her hands.

But Ambrose was frowning. 'Galiena, I cannot set out from home at a moment's notice,' he said. 'There are matters that I must attend to, orders and instructions I must leave with our people here.' He glanced over in Josse's direction and said quietly, 'The ransom, you know. I have already given as much as I had immediately at my disposal and I have pledged what more I can. I am anxious to have this second sum ready as soon as possible, for without doubt the Queen's newly appointed council will soon send out their officers. To think of the King out there, imprisoned among strangers . . .' With a shudder he broke off, as if further contemplation of the King's situation were just too painful.

Instantly Galiena was contrite. 'My love, of course!' She flew to his side and took his hand. 'In my eagerness I did not stop to think. I know how very important this matter is to you – indeed, to all of us – and I allowed my own preoccupation to take precedence. Forgive me.'

Any brief annoyance that Ambrose might have felt was washed away; fleetingly Josse reflected that she certainly seemed to know how to keep her husband happy.

Then Brice spoke, his interjection coming as a surprise since he had kept silent for a while. 'May I suggest that the lady Galiena goes on ahead to Hawkenlye?' he said. 'Unless, lady, there are arrangements that you also must make before setting out?'

'None that I cannot see to this evening,' she replied. 'Oh, but I think it's a splendid idea!' She turned to Ambrose. 'Do you not agree, dearest?'

Ambrose studied her vivacious face for a moment. Then he said, 'I am not happy for you to travel unescorted, Galiena. Will you not wait, so that we may ride out together?'

Her face fell. 'Oh – if you wish it, my lord.' She gave him a brave smile. 'Only I feel that we have just been given hope and I do not believe I can bear to postpone my departure, even by a day. But it must be as you command.' She hung her head.

Ambrose, clearly uncomfortable at being cast in the role of unreasonable and dictatorial husband, tried to justify himself. 'There is much that I have to see to,' he said, 'and surely another couple of days will make no difference?'

'No,' Galiena whispered. It was amazing, Josse thought, just how much emotion a woman could put into that one short word.

'I would be happy to escort the lady as far as my own manor of New Winnowlands,' he heard himself offer. 'I wish that I could take you all the way to Hawkenlye' – he turned to Galiena, catching the full force of her delighted smile of gratitude – 'but, like my lord Ambrose here, I too have matters that must be attended to without delay.' It was not, he well knew, going to be a light matter to give away a quarter of his income for Richard's ransom, but he also knew that, as Richard's man, he must set an example and have his contribution ready and waiting as soon as it was demanded. 'Perhaps one or two of your household might be spared to ride with your lady on to Hawkenlye?' He looked enquiringly at Ambrose.

'I suppose that is possible,' the older man said grudgingly. 'Galiena's personal maid has no role here if her mistress is absent, so she at least could be of the party and not be missed.' Catching a sudden tension in Galiena, Josse shot her a glance; there was an expression of distaste on her face. Does the lady not care for her maid? he wondered. Then, assuming that her adoring husband allows her free choice in the appointment of her servants, why not dismiss the woman and find another? Strange!

Galiena had not spoken and now, with her head lowered, her face was hidden.

'Dickon can ride with you,' Ambrose said decisively after a few moments. 'My young stable boy,' he said, turning briefly to Josse. 'He'll see you and Aebba safe into the nuns' care, then ride home to report to me. I will join you at Hawkenlye as soon as I am able.'

Nobody answered straight away; it was as if they were all silently acknowledging Ambrose's right to order matters as he saw fit, without comment or protest from anyone else. Then Josse cleared his throat and said, 'We shall meet at the Abbey in due course, then, my lord, since I am eager to speak to the Abbess concerning the – concerning this business that presses on us all.'

Galiena shot him a quick smile. Ambrose, who appeared not to see, merely nodded and said, 'Very well. Let us pray that all our purposes there will meet with success.'

Josse was offered hospitality at Ryemarsh overnight, which he accepted. There was little point in riding away only to have to return in the morning to escort Galiena to New Winnowlands. He took a bite of supper with his host and hostess early in the evening – Brice had already left for home – and soon after they had eaten, Ambrose and Galiena retired to their own chamber.

Josse went out into the soft twilight to take a last turn around Galiena's garden. Bats were flying, swooping in elaborate circles as they pounced on blundering insects. Up above the darkening sky was clear, still faintly tinged with a deep orange band of light in the west. In the east the stars were appearing; Josse let his eyes roam around the sky until he found the great summer constellation that men called the Swan. The scent of flowers was strong; Josse, his head reeling, felt as if he had drunk strong wine.

He turned back towards the house and, making his

way up a narrow stair, settled down in the luxury of Ambrose's guest chamber. He stood at the window as he unfastened his tunic, looking out over the starlit garden. All was quiet, all was still. But – what was that? Peering into the night, he saw a movement in the shadows and watched as a cloaked figure slipped light-footed away from the house.

Despite his curiosity, Josse turned his back on the window and strode resolutely across to the bed. If Galiena chose to have one more attempt to bring about through her own efforts the thing that she and her husband so dearly wanted, then that was entirely up to her. Josse had no right either to pass judgement or, far more importantly, to spy on her. Fighting to banish the seductive images from his mind – *naked under the moonlight* – he screwed up his eyes and violently shook his head.

There were crisp linen sheets on his soft bed and, as he moved, they rustled and gave off a faint scent of lavender. Well fed, with the taste of his host's excellent wine still in his mouth, he was warm and comfortable. Soon he was sound asleep.

Dickon was waiting for them in the courtyard in the morning; it was he who had greeted Josse and Brice on their arrival the previous day. He was a sturdy young man who looked, Josse thought, as if he could handle himself in a fight. He had the horses groomed and ready, with Galiena's and her maid's small packs attached to their mounts' saddles, when the party came out of the hall. Galiena was sombrely dressed in a light travelling cloak of dark blue wool, its deep hood pulled up over her white veil and all but hiding her face. She looked pale, as if she had not slept well, and she seemed tense. There is much at stake for her in this, Josse thought compassionately. He watched as Ambrose helped her into the saddle; the older man said something quietly to her and she gave him a brief smile.

The maid, Aebba, turned out to be a dour woman in early middle age. Like her mistress, she too looked as if she had not slept well, or perhaps the sour, disgruntled expression was the one that she usually wore. She was tall and strongly built, with a pallid and slightly greasy complexion. Her hair was completely hidden by a linen veil that was arranged so as to shade her face and a close-fitting wimple covered her chin and throat. Her eyes – of a shade somewhere between ice blue and palest green – were the most colourless that Josse had ever seen. She did not speak as she mounted her mare and settled herself, save to order Dickon curtly to adjust her stirrups.

When the party was ready and farewells had been said, Josse glanced at Dickon, nodded briefly and led the way out of the courtyard and off on the road to New Winnowlands.

The morning was fine and sunny. They reached Josse's manor in good time and he managed to persuade Galiena to step into the house and take some refreshments; Will's Ella, silent and shy as ever, worked her usual magic and had cups of cool wine and a platter of warm, spiced cakes ready in next to no time. Aebba was offered the same courtesy but, with a brief shake of her head, she declined. Will was sent out to Dickon, left holding the horses, with a flagon of ale and a hunk of bread and cheese.

Then Josse saw the party on their way.

Standing beside Galiena as she sat on her horse, he sensed her nervousness. 'Do not fear, my lady,' he said quietly, for her alone to hear. 'They are good people at Hawkenlye and will do their best to help you.'

'But if I should fail!' she said, her voice anguished.

'Do not dwell on that,' he advised. 'Keep hope strong, for often that is the way to bring about what it is you desire.'

Fleetingly the tension left her white face and she smiled at him. 'What a sound fellow you are, Josse d'Acquin,' she murmured. Then, lightly touching her heels to her horse's sides, she rode straight-backed out of the yard.

Leaving Josse with the distinct but surely mistaken impression that she had been flirting with him.

3

Helewise, Abbess of Hawkenlye, was absorbed in one of the great leather-bound ledgers in which the Abbey's financial records were carefully detailed. In company with every other monastic foundation in the land, Hawkenlye was going to have to give up its wealth to go towards King Richard's ransom; Helewise was in the middle of preparing an inventory of the Abbey's assets.

It was neither a charitable nor a loyal thought, but she could not help but be extremely grateful that Hawkenlye enjoyed the patronage of Queen Eleanor. The Queen might be more eager than anyone else to see the ransom collected and paid over and her favourite son released, but, as Helewise well knew, Hawkenlye was special to the Queen. Had she not taken a personal interest in its construction and dedication, searching out the best craftsmen that France and England could produce to ensure that the Abbey would be memorable in its beauty? Had she not bestowed as her own personal gift – or so they said – the Abbey's greatest treasure, the walrus ivory carving of the dead Christ in the arms of Joseph of Arimathea?

It was possible, Helewise acknowledged, that the Queen would demand the return of her gift so that it might be sold for the ransom. But somehow it did not seem likely.

Wishful thinking, Helewise told herself sternly, returning to her ledger. That's what *that* is. And if we are commanded to give up our treasures, then we shall do so willingly for the King's sake.

Queen Eleanor had visited Hawkenlye in April. The first desperate anxiety over her captive son had abated; she had recently received a letter from him in which he assured her that he was well and content. He also revealed that he had established a friendly and affectionate relationship with the Emperor, and he expressed his deep gratitude to his mother for her endeavours on his behalf. Eleanor, who had previously been beside herself with worry, had been bombarding the frail and elderly Pope Celestine with impassioned letters demanding that he do something to help the great Lionheart. Frustratingly, Celestine had yet to answer; he was, according to the Queen, shaking in his papal shoes at the prospect of performing any action that might offend the Emperor and so, in Eleanor's own words, he had 'taken the coward's way and decided to do nothing'.

The encouraging message from Richard, together with the great comfort of actually being able to do something herself towards his release, had combined to make the Queen feel a great deal more positive, and it was in this mood that Hawkenlye had received her.

'I shall set up a council,' she had informed Helewise,

striding to and fro across the best guest chamber and ticking off points on her long, elegant, fingers. A huge emerald caught the light and glinted on her forefinger. 'That is my priority, to ensure the help of good men to collect the money. The Earl of Arundel, the Earl of Sussex, Richard Fitznigel, Bishop of London – oh yes, and that handsome fellow Hubert Walter shall be at their head, which is only his due as our new Archbishop of Canterbury.'

'They say he is a great man,' Helewise commented. 'His diplomacy, his wide experience and his vast intelligence will be needed in this enterprise.'

'Indeed they will,' the Queen agreed. She fixed intent eyes on Helewise. 'But we shall not fail, Helewise.'

'I know, my lady,' Helewise murmured. 'I know.'

The Queen's restlessness had made that visit a less than restorative one for the old lady, Helewise thought now. Usually when Eleanor came to Hawkenlye, Helewise tried to spoil her a little; give her some much-needed time to herself, provide her with one or two books and make sure that, when the Queen requested it, the great Abbey church was empty for her private prayer. The nuns and monks, too, joined in the cosseting, appearing silently to leave little gifts outside Eleanor's door. A posy of sweet smelling flowers. A jug of cool wine on a hot day. A phial of the precious holy water from the Vale.

But a woman like Eleanor of Aquitaine did not pause to rest, even for an hour, when her favourite son needed her help.

With a sigh, Helewise went back to her ledger.

Picking up her quill, she tried once again to reconcile the revenues from the Abbey's sheep pastures down on Romney Marsh; she had done the long sum three times and each time arrived at a different result . . .

There was silence in her room for some time. Then, just as she gave a soft exclamation of pleasure – the sum had at last seemed to come out right – there was a tap on her door.

'Come in!' she said cheerfully, putting down her quill.

The door opened a crack and the round-eyed face of Sister Anne peered around it. She looked, Helewise noticed, faintly surprised. As well she might – Helewise smiled to herself – since it was rumoured among the nuns that Helewise disliked working on the accounts books. Sister Anne had probably been expecting a less cordial reception.

'What can I do for you, Sister Anne?' Helewise asked kindly.

'I didn't want to interrupt you, my lady Abbess,' Sister Anne said, sidling into the room, 'not when you're so busy, but—'

'I am not busy at this precise moment,' Helewise remarked. Pleasure at the sum finally done was still making her smile but, nevertheless, there was more work to do and she knew from long experience that her patience would soon begin to wear thin. Dear Sister Anne was an amiable soul but not blessed with either swiftness of thought or any fine judgement of another's mood.

'Well, it's like this, see,' Sister Anne began. 'Sister

Ursel was called to the gates a while ago and she sent you a message. She said it's not really urgent but she knows you like to be kept informed, and she did think it a little strange, what with the young lady *being* so young, if you see what I mean, and well-dressed and that, mounted on a lovely mare with saddle and bridle new-like and—'

'What was Sister Ursel's message?' Helewise felt her jaw begin to clench.

'Oh, didn't I say?'

'No.' The monosyllable sounded more like a bark than a word and Helewise hastily stitched a wide smile on to her face. 'I don't believe you did, Sister.'

Sister Anne squared her shoulders as befitted a courier with tidings to impart, frowned in concentration as she brought to mind the details of her message and declared, 'There's a young lady arrived. Says she's called Galiena and is wife to Ambrose Ryemarsh. She asks to see the nursing nuns and so Sister Ursel's taken her to the infirmary.'

Trying to follow the porteress's reasoning – Sister Ursel did not usually feel it necessary to report to the Abbess every new arrival who came seeking help – Helewise said, 'And this Galiena Ryemarsh is a lady of quality, Sister Anne?' Perhaps the young woman's elevated station was the reason for Sister Ursel's action.

'Oh, yes, without a doubt. I saw her with my own eyes and I can certainly attest to that.' Sister Anne nodded violently as if to emphasise her words.

'Ah, I see. The name is not familiar to me but

perhaps I should step across to the infirmary and make the lady's acquaintance.' She frowned, not relishing the interruption.

'Oh, I don't reckon there's any call for that, not unless you feel like it, my lady,' Sister Anne said, giving Helewise an indulgent smile. 'Don't you disturb yourself, not when you've so much to do!'

Losing patience at last, Helewise said, 'Then why are you sent to interrupt my concentration in order to inform me of this arrival, Sister Anne?'

Sister Anne's vapid smile froze on her face. 'Oh – er – um – because of how she arrived!' she stammered.

'Yes?' Helewise restrained the impulse to ask sarcastically, and how did she arrive? Walking on her hands? Dragged on a hurdle? On a wicker chariot and driving a team of wolves?

'She was' – Sister Anne, undeterred by her superior's ill-restrained irritation, paused dramatically – 'alone!'

Helewise made herself work on the ledgers for a little longer, then, since she would soon have to stop in order to attend Vespers, she abandoned her efforts in time to slip across first to the infirmary.

Sister Euphemia came to the door to greet her. 'You'll have been informed of our new arrival, then,' she said quietly, leaning close to her superior. As always, the infirmary was busy and several nuns were hurrying here and there throughout the long room as if keen to finish the present task before the summons to evening prayers.

'Indeed.' Helewise looked around her. 'Is she within?'

'No.' The infirmarer gave her a quick glance. 'She's not sick so there's no need for her to take up a bed among those that are.'

'Then . . .?' Helewise paused.

'Step outside with me, if you will, my lady, and I shall tell you the little that I know.'

Helewise and Sister Euphemia went out through the infirmary's wide doors and turned into the shady cloister outside; the day was still hot and the deep shade was welcome. When they were safely out of earshot of anyone inside the infirmary, Sister Euphemia said, with a brevity that Sister Anne might have done worse than emulate, 'She's called Galiena. She's eighteen, married to a man a good bit older and she wants to be pregnant.'

'Oh!' Momentarily startled, Helewise recovered herself quickly and said, 'And seeks your help?'

'Aye. Seems the young lady is something of a herbalist herself. I took her to see Sister Tiphaine, who was clearly impressed by the remedies that Galiena has already used. She's been treating both herself and her husband, which shows a deal of good sense.'

'Can you help her?' Helewise asked. 'Is there anything you and Sister Tiphaine can suggest that has not already been employed?'

'Reckon there's always another remedy or two worth a try,' the infirmarer replied. 'The lass has agreed that I talk to her at greater length, which I'll do in the morning. *If* I can find the time.' She gave a short sniff, as if to imply that a rich young woman's fancies would certainly not be given preference over more pressing demands. 'Sometimes it's as simple a matter as a couple not knowing what they're meant to do, if you understand me,' she went on. 'I well recall a pair of youngsters I was called to once where the girl was still a virgin.'

'I should have thought that unlikely in this case, since the young lady's husband is older than she and presumably experienced.'

'Aye, so should I, but you never know. I intend to have a look at her while we have our talk. I'll try to discover what their habits are, whether there's any obvious reason why she has failed to conceive.'

'And she, presumably, is happy to be examined and intimately questioned?' It seemed important, Helewise thought, for Galiena to realise what she was letting herself in for.

'I haven't told her yet exactly what the morning's session is going to involve.' Sister Euphemia smiled somewhat grimly. 'But if she wants my help, that's the best way I can start to give it.'

'I see.' There seemed little more to add. 'I shall receive the young woman after Vespers, Sister. Please will you send word to her to present herself in my room at that time?'

'I will, my lady.' The infirmarer gave her Abbess a low bow, then hurried back to her patients.

Helewise sat quietly in her chair, hearing again in her head the peaceful words of the evening prayers. The office of Vespers was one of her favourites and this evening the Abbey church had been wonderfully cool and dark after the heat of the day.

Presently there was a soft footstep outside her partly opened door and a quiet tap sounded. Calling out 'Come in!' Helewise rose to greet her visitor.

Galiena Ryemarsh wore a dove-grey silk gown and was heavily veiled in fine linen, arranged so that the hem fluted prettily but concealingly around her face. A headdress modestly covered her hair. Helewise's first impression was of a woman of fashion dressing as she believed fit when entering – albeit only temporarily – a convent full of nuns.

Her second impression was that Galiena looked older than eighteen.

'You are Galiena?' Helewise asked, although there could hardly be any doubt.

'I am. Thank you for receiving me, Abbess Helewise,' the girl replied.

Resuming her seat, Helewise indicated the low stool that she kept for visitors. 'Please, sit down.'

Galiena did so. She moved, Helewise noticed, gracefully, and the tall, slender body sank down on to the stool in one smooth movement. The long linen veil fell in graceful folds to the floor, pooling with the grey silk of her gown on the worn stones. It was an attractive picture and, had Helewise not realised it was unlikely, she might have thought Galiena had deliberately planned it.

Galiena looked up and Helewise met the bright blue eyes. 'You know why I am here,' the girl said.

'I do. My infirmarer tells me that there are things that she may be able to do to help you and I pray that it will prove so.'

'I pray, too.' The girl's tone was fervent. 'My husband is much older than I am, my lady, and our years together will probably not be as long as either of us would wish, so you see there is some urgency in this matter.'

'But such things have a timing of their own,' Helewise protested mildly. 'Children are not necessarily begotten at our convenience.'

'The remedy must work swiftly. It must!' the girl cried. For a moment a hot pink flush coloured her pale cheeks but then, as if already regretting her hasty words, she said meekly, dropping her head so that her veil hid her face, 'Of course, it is as you say, my lady. God will send us a child in His own good time.'

Or not, Helewise thought, although she did not say it aloud. 'We shall make you comfortable while you are with us,' she said instead. 'You have already been shown your accommodation, I believe, and I trust you find it satisfactory.'

'Oh, yes,' Galiena said. 'The room is somewhat small, but I shall be adequately comfortable.'

'I am delighted to hear it,' Helewise said with slight irony. 'It will be a pleasure to have you as our guest and we shall do our utmost to help you,' she added courteously.

Galiena smiled as if to say, naturally!

Fighting to keep a pleasant expression on her face,

Helewise said, 'I am told that you arrived alone? Was it wise to travel without an escort?'

'I did have an escort,' Galiena said quickly. 'My maid and my husband's stable lad. But it is quite a ride back to Ryemarsh so, as soon as the gates of Hawkenlye were in sight, I dismissed them and sent them on their way.'

'I see.' Helewise frowned. The girl's explanation was perfectly reasonable and, had anyone else given it, Helewise might have been impressed at the selfless motive that had prompted the premature dismissal of the escort. As it was . . .

I am being foolish, Helewise told herself firmly. I am wasting the Lord's precious time on silly fancies.

Getting to her feet, she said, 'I believe that you are to speak with my infirmarer in the morning so, if there is nothing else, I will let you get to your bed.'

Taking the cue, Galiena too rose. 'No, I think I have all that I want,' she said, frowning slightly as if checking through a mental list. 'I will bid you good night, then, my lady.'

She bowed, straightened and turned, then glided out of the room.

Helewise listened to the quiet footsteps receding. For a little while she battled with herself. Then, giving up, she strode over to the open door, closed it rather too forcibly and, safely shut in her room, cried out, 'Well, *really*!'

She returned to her chair and flung herself down. The cheek of the girl! *I think I have all I want*, indeed! As if Helewise had been offering to fetch her a bedtime drink, wash out her personal linen or find her a softer pillow!

She sat fuming for some time. Then, as habits of charity reasserted themselves, she began to regret her outburst. The girl is troubled and upset, she reminded herself. She is clearly quite desperate to give her husband this longed-for child, and why should she not have her wish? The dear Lord knows, enough babies are born to those who do not want them, cannot support them and have little love for them. Is it not something eagerly to be desired, that the healthy young wife of a man of wealth and position conceives and bears a child?

The reasoning was sound enough. Why, then, Helewise asked herself, was she left with the feeling that Galiena Ryemarsh was a determined and ruthless young woman who would stop at nothing to get her own way?

'I am ashamed of myself,' Helewise whispered softly. She stood up, then, falling to her knees, began to pray. With sincere contrition she confessed her lack of charity and the unreasonable way that she had jumped to judge another human being, one, moreover, who had come to Hawkenlye for help. Knowing that these were faults she would have to share with her confessor in due course made her guilt lift slightly; Father Gilbert would view them as gravely as she did and the severity of her penance would probably reflect that. Until she could open her soul to him, she resolved that she would go out of her way to be kind to Galiena.

By acting in charity towards another, the nuns said,

you could override antipathy and even downright dislike. That was why you sometimes observed a sister silently and unobtrusively performing small acts of kindness for one of her fellow nuns; it was never easy, at least to begin with, but very often, with God's grace, it worked.

Helewise sighed. The strength of her reaction against the prospect of doing kind little deeds for Galiena Ryemarsh only went to show how important it was that she start as soon as she could.

4

The next day was as hot as its predecessor. The sun shone down from a cloudless sky and there was no breeze to cool the nuns and monks as they worked through the long hours of toil. To add to the usual daily quota of problems, greater or smaller in nature, a swarm of bees had appeared out of nowhere and settled in the eaves of the stable block. Sister Tiphaine, who knew more about bees than anyone else at Hawkenlye, was trying in vain to keep the nuns calm while she readied a skep for the new swarm, but two of the young postulants had gone too near and one of them had received several stings. From the fuss she was making, Sister Euphemia had been overheard to remark caustically, you would have thought she had been cast into Hell and was being prodded by red-hot pitchforks.

Helewise, making a determined start on her resolve to be kind and generous of heart towards Galiena, offered up a special prayer for the girl at Matins, at Prime and at Tierce. She did not know exactly when Sister Euphemia planned to interview Galiena – the infirmarer had not been specific – and so Helewise sent word to the infirmary asking Sister Euphemia to report to her as soon as there was anything to report.

Sister Euphemia came to see her in the middle of the morning.

Helewise, taking in the expression on Sister Euphemia's face, realised immediately that things had not gone well. Reaching for the jug that stood on her table, she poured out a mug of barley water and handed it to the infirmarer, who took it with an absent nod and downed it in one.

'That's better.' She smacked her lips. 'Thank you, my lady.'

'You looked as if you needed a cool drink,' Helewise observed.

Sister Euphemia grinned briefly. 'It was as obvious as that?'

'It was,' Helewise agreed. 'What has happened, Sister?'

Sister Euphemia sighed and shook her head. 'Precisely nothing, my lady! For all that she clamours for our help, she will not speak to me of intimate matters between herself and her husband. Not a word! And when I suggested I have a look at her, she leapt up and clutched that long veil she wears tightly around her as if I were threatening to strip off her clothes and examine her by force!' Pink in the face at this insult to her professional integrity, Sister Euphemia was momentarily lost for words. Then, in a quieter voice, she added, 'The very idea!'

'Do not distress yourself,' Helewise said soothingly. 'All of us who know your ways treasure your kindness and your tact when – er, when a patient's treatment requires certain intimacies.'

'Thank you, my lady.' Sister Euphemia muttered something to herself then, eyes raised to meet Helewise's, she said, 'I wouldn't have said that young lady was coy, though. I find it strange that she should react to my questions like a timid child.'

'You can never tell,' Helewise remarked. 'Sometimes what we see on the surface masks other, very different emotions.' Remembering her vow to be charitable to Galiena, she went on, 'Perhaps she finds this whole business of trying to conceive rather embarrassing. I mean, she is still young and to have strangers know of – er, of matters usually reserved for the bedchamber, to have people, no matter how well-intentioned, aware that there are difficulties . . .' Floundering, she broke off.

The infirmarer was watching her with a smile. 'Happen you're right, my lady, and I'm grateful to you for reminding me of something I should have thought of for myself. I'm too forthright and well I know it. I meant well, though, and I did stop my questions when she looked so upset. And I'd only got as far as asking her whether her courses came regularly and fully, how frequently her husband lies with her and whether he's still capable of ejaculation!'

Helewise had a moment's genuine sympathy for Galiena. However well intentioned, Sister Euphemia could be formidable when she was seeking out the facts behind a patient's malaise.

'Then I said,' the infirmarer was relating, 'well, my

girl, if you don't want to speak of such things, better hop up on the cot, slip your skirts up and let me have a look at you, and she went so white I thought she was going to faint!' Amazement flooded the honest face all over again as Sister Euphemia described the scene.

'Oh, dear,' Helewise said. 'The thought of an examination genuinely distressed her, then? It was not merely a pretence at delicacy designed to engage your admiration for her refinement?'

Immediately she regretted the words. Sister Euphemia was far too astute to miss their significance; the fact that Helewise should suggest Galiena's modesty was purely to impress the infirmarer reflected all too clearly Helewise's opinion of the girl.

The infirmarer looked at her for a moment. Then she said quietly, 'Don't look so guilty, my lady. The same thought had occurred to me. But aye, that pallor was real, all right. For some reason, the idea of my looking at her private – um, having a look down there put the fear of God in her.'

Helewise, only a little comforted, nodded. 'Well, we must accept the young woman's sensibilities and leave her be,' she said. 'Are you able to offer her any treatment that might help conception? Without knowing more about her – er, her circumstances?'

'Aye,' Sister Euphemia said heavily. 'Aye, there's things we can try. The trouble is, my lady, they may well be the *wrong* things. If I can't pin down exactly what the problem is, then how am I to know how best to treat it? And I cannot identify the precise problem without Galiena's help.'

Helewise remembered suddenly her first impressions of Galiena. 'One thing does occur to me, Sister Euphemia,' she began tentatively. 'Although, when I come to think of it, it is scarcely worth mentioning.'

The infirmarer grinned. 'Why not mention it anyway, my lady?'

Helewise returned the smile. 'It was just that I understood the young lady to be eighteen years old.'

'Aye, that's what she told me.'

'Yet to me she seems older. I cannot say why, exactly, especially when she keeps herself so well covered up. I just wondered if her age might be a factor in her barrenness.'

'She could be a year or so older than she claims,' the infirmarer agreed, 'although I do not think it would make any difference to whether she conceives or not. Why, I've known first-time mothers ten or even fifteen years older than young Galiena! If she were forty, now, *that* might just make things trickier.'

'I did not for a moment think she was as old as that!' Helewise laughed. 'As I said, it wasn't really worth mentioning.' She sighed, then went on: 'If Galiena continues with her attitude, you will just have to manage without the young lady's help and do the best you can, Sister.' She got up, went round her table and, pausing beside the infirmarer, put a hand briefly on her strong right arm. 'As I know you always do,' she added softly.

'Thank you, my lady. I'll get over to Sister Tiphaine and the two of us will get our heads together and see what we can come up with.' She took a deep breath, releasing it noisily and with some force. 'We'll be guessing, like as not, but I suppose that's better than nothing.'

'A great deal better than nothing,' Helewise said encouragingly. Then, with many rather odd thoughts and ideas buzzing in her head, she saw the infirmarer to the door and watched her hasten away.

As the day wound down towards evening, a thin band of cloud puffed up in the west so that, for a time as the sun went down, the perfect sky was shot with stripes of brilliant gold and orange. Helewise, going out of the rear gate of the Abbey on her way down to the Vale, stopped to look and to admire. As she stood in the peace of early evening she reflected that it was the first time she had allowed herself a moment's quiet reflection all day. All week, come to that. Closing her eyes and determined to enjoy it, she breathed in the scent of hot dusty grass. This, she thought, eyes still closed, is a good place.

Then, remembering her promise to visit an elderly pilgrim who, according to Brother Firmin, had not much time left to him to enjoy either Hawkenlye or anywhere else, she opened her eyes, brought her wandering mind back to the present and hastened on her way.

Brother Firmin's old man did indeed look frail. He was propped up on a straw mattress, a mug of holy water by his side and, even from the doorway of the pilgrims' shelter, Helewise could hear the shallow, rasping breathing. She sat down beside him and took one of his thin, age-spotted hands in both of hers.

'Good evening, friend,' she said softly, not sure if the almost-closed eyelids meant he was asleep and not wanting to wake him if he were.

But the old man opened his eyes and, seeing her beside him, gave her a very calm smile.

'You'll be the Abbess Helewise,' he said. 'The old feller said as how you'd come to see me.'

'I am,' she agreed. 'Are my monks making you comfortable?'

'Aye, they are that.' He paused to take a couple of breaths then went on, 'I'm not long for this world, my lady Abbess.'

Sometimes when a sick pilgrim said those words, the very last thing that they wanted, Helewise reflected, was for you to agree with them. Even if it were true, some folk did not have the courage to accept that they were dying and that had to be respected. But this old man, she thought, gazing down at him, was not one of those.

'Have you prepared your soul to meet God?' she asked quietly. 'Do you wish me to send a priest to you?'

The old man smiled his serene smile again. 'I'm ready, my lady. Ready as I'll ever be, that is. I've confessed my sins to the good Father and that old monk has prayed over me. If that's not enough for the dear Lord, then there's no more I can do about it.'

Helewise suppressed a smile of her own; it was unusual to hear someone speak quite in that way of their approaching death. 'And what of your family?' she asked. 'Is there anyone you wish us to contact?'

'No. I'm alone now. Me and my wife were only blessed with the one child and she died when she were five. And my old girl's gone on ahead of me too. I reckon that she'll have my little nook waiting for me when I get to Paradise.' He said it with such conviction that Helewise was moved and, for a moment, could not reply.

Then she said, 'We shall pray for you, that your time in Purgatory is brief and she will not have to wait for too long.'

'Thankee, lady, but it won't make any difference. She'll be ready for me and then we shall be together again.' Tired from the effort of speech, his eyes closed and he let out a faint snore.

Helewise said a brief, silent prayer over his dozing old body and then she straightened up and tiptoed away.

In need of comfort – the old man's simple faith and patient acceptance of his lot had affected her more than she had realised – Helewise made her way to the little shrine that stood over the holy water spring. She opened the door quietly, holding the bunch of keys that hung from her belt close to her skirts to keep it from jangling. She knew only too well from her own experience how irritating it could be to be deep in prayer or meditation only to have some newcomer barge noisily in and disturb the peace.

As she went carefully down the stone steps, she

thought at first that the chapel was empty. But then she noticed a figure crouched on the ground before the statue of the Virgin on her plinth. The figure – Helewise could not tell if it were male or female, young or old – had squeezed into the furthest corner where the light was very dim and seemed to have some sort of covering over the head.

Helewise said a brief apologetic prayer to the Virgin: *I came to seek your comfort, Holy Lady, but in doing so it seems I would be intruding on another's need for privacy, so I will look for you instead in the fields and the clean evening air as I return to the Abbey.* Then, without a further glance at the crouching figure, she left the chapel as quietly as she had entered.

Brother Saul was coming down the path from the Abbey as she ascended it. Ah well, thought Helewise resignedly, if anyone had to interrupt my prayer, I'm glad it's Saul.

She greeted him, smiling at his bent head as he made a low reverence. 'All goes well with you, I trust, Brother Saul?'

'It does, my lady, it does.' He returned her smile. Then, the warm expression fading, he said, 'She's a devout soul, that new visitor, isn't she?'

'The new visitor?' Could he mean Galiena? Surely not, Helewise thought; of all the adjectives that might be employed to describe the lady of Ryemarsh, devout was not the first that sprang to mind.

'Aye.' Saul leaned closer, dropping his voice as if avid gossips lurked in the long grass waiting on his every word. 'That pretty lass as wants to have a baby.'

Ah. So he *did* mean Galiena. Wondering yet again at the mysterious way in which information seeped through the Abbey like water through a sodden sandal, Helewise said softly, 'It is the lady's business, Saul. Hers and her lord's.'

'Aye, that it is, my lady, and I'm sorry I spoke as I did. Only—' Saul's kind, honest face struggled with competing emotions.

'Only what, Saul?' she prompted.

But Saul shook his head and, bidding her good evening, hurried away.

It was not until the next day that Helewise discovered what lay behind that little scene. She went to seek out Galiena – it was, she told herself, high time she spared a moment to see how the young lady had settled in, even if she *was* very busy and didn't really want to. *Especially* because I don't really want to, she reproved herself.

But Galiena was not to be found. The infirmarer shrugged her shoulders and said she hadn't seen her since the early morning when, according to Sister Euphemia, Galiena had informed her that as soon as her preparations were ready, she would take them and be on her way back home. Helewise went next to enquire of Sister Tiphaine, who had all but forgotten who Galiena was. Nobody else seemed to have noticed her about the Abbey. Then Brother Firmin, coming up to inform Helewise that his elderly pilgrim had died in the night, mentioned that the Lady Ryemarsh was in the chapel again and Saul *still* couldn't get in to brush down the steps and it was all very worrying because, as everyone knew, the steps became very slippery if not regularly cleaned and it would be frightful if anyone fell and—

Stopping the old monk in mid-sentence – Brother Firmin had been known to go on for ages if not interrupted – Helewise said, 'You said she is there again, Brother Firmin. She was in the chapel yesterday?'

'Aye, my lady, almost all day! Down on her knees huddled in the darkest corner, veil over her head and face, praying for hours on end! And, although I know I should not speak ill of another when the dear Lord alone knows what goes on in her poor troubled heart to make her shout out so, there was really no call to speak to Saul so unkindly.'

'I see.' It all began to fall into place. 'What happened, Brother Firmin?'

'Well, like I said, Saul was aware that the steps needed a good clean but when he went into the chapel early in the day, there she was a-praying and he didn't like to disturb her with his mop and his bucket. He went back twice more but each time there she was, looking, Saul said, as if she hadn't so much as moved a hair. So finally Saul comes along to find me and he says, Brother Firmin, I can't let it wait any longer, the condition of those steps is on my mind every minute. So I had a bit of a think as to how best to advise him.' Nodding his head, he stared at Helewise as if seeking her approbation.

'You did right, Brother Firmin,' she said encouragingly, wishing that it were not taking quite so long for the old monk to get to the end of his tale. 'It's always best to give a matter proper consideration.' He would not, she was certain, detect the very faint irony. 'And what did you finally suggest?'

'I said, you've got your duties to attend to, Brother Saul, just like the rest of us, and cleaning down those steps is one of them and must not be put off any longer, so just you go in, apologise nicely to the lady for the interruption, roll up your sleeves and get on with it.'

'Quite right, Brother Firmin. It was good advice. And what happened next?'

'Well, my lady, you won't credit it, a soft-spoken, kindly, charitable, understanding lady like yourself, but she shouted at him!' Brother Firmin bridled as he spoke, his thin old face flushing with indignation. 'She cried out, can't you see I want to be alone? Then she said to get out and take his bucket with him!'

'Dear me, how very distressing for poor Saul!' Helewise exclaimed.

'It was, aye, it was,' Firmin agreed. 'Brother Saul isn't used to folks shouting at him, especially not when he's trying to help. Of course, it would have put her off her prayers, having someone cleaning the steps so close to her, but there you are, these jobs must be done.'

'Indeed they must,' Helewise agreed. 'And she stayed in the chapel all day, you say?'

'Aye, and she's back there today!' Brother Firmin's pale old eyes were wide with astonishment. Then, dropping to a whisper, he added, 'If she doesn't get herself with child after all that praying, then I reckon the good Lord must have his reasons agin it!'

'Such things are for God alone to decide,' she said gently. 'We must not speculate, Brother Firmin.'

'No, my lady, of course not, and I wasn't, not really, I just meant—'

'Not to worry,' Helewise said smoothly. 'Thank you for telling me, but let us speak of it no more. Now, about the elderly pilgrim who has just died . . .'

And, for some time more, she and the old monk turned to discussing matters over which she, at least, felt she had rather more control.

I must, she decided later, speak to Galiena. She has come for our help and we are freely giving it – she had checked and Sister Euphemia confirmed that yes, she and the herbalist had made two different remedies for Galiena to take and that they were all but ready – yet she makes no use of that other great solace that we offer to those who are troubled. Yes, she prays alone, or so I am told, but she shows no desire to worship with our community.

To Helewise, who had found when severely tried that the regular offices punctuating the day were her greatest comfort and support, the idea of someone in sore need not attending them was so strange as to be unfathomable. I will find her and invite her to pray with us, she decided. Perhaps she does not realise that it is permitted! The thought, striking all of a sudden, hit Helewise as a likely explanation.

Feeling guilty that she had not made sure Galiena

knew all the relevant details of Abbey life, Helewise
hurried on her way.

Galiena was in the shrine, just as Brother Firmin had
reported. As Helewise quietly descended the steps –
Saul was quite right, they did indeed need a good clean
– the young woman spun round and, from behind the
concealing veil, cried out, 'For the love of God, am
I not to be left alone?' Then, seeing who it was, she
lowered her voice a shade and said rather grudgingly,
'Oh, it's you, Abbess Helewise.'

'Yes,' Helewise agreed. Trying to keep her irritation
under tight control, she said, 'I am told, Galiena, that
you have spent many hours in here on your own.'

'It's allowed, isn't it?' the girl asked truculently.

'Of course,' Helewise said smoothly. 'But, understanding as I do what it is that you pray for, since you
yourself have told me, I wonder if you might rather
join the community in our devotions? You would be
most welcome and, if I did not make this clear to you
when we spoke before, then I am sorry.'

Galiena did not respond for a moment. Her face
was still shaded by the heavy veil and Helewise could
not see her expression. Eventually she spoke.

'I thank you for the invitation, my lady, but I prefer
to be alone.' Her tone, Helewise thought, was a little
strange; almost as if she were having to force herself
to be polite whereas in fact her inclination was quite
otherwise.

But I am being fanciful, Helewise reproved herself.
It is probably just as Sister Euphemia said: this poor

young woman is embarrassed at her inability to conceive and does not wish the world to know that she seeks help. What could be more understandable? And the Lord and his Holy Mother can hear her pleas as well down here in the shrine as up above in the Abbey church.

'As you wish,' she said. Galiena had turned her head slightly and Helewise found herself addressing the girl's veiled cheek. 'We will pray for you,' she added. 'Or, if you prefer that your personal matters are not made public, then I shall intercede on your behalf but in such a way that only God hears.'

Galiena murmured something; it might have been her thanks. But now she was sitting almost with her back to Helewise and it was difficult to be sure.

'The infirmarer tells me that the remedies she and Sister Tiphaine have prepared for you are ready,' Helewise went on. 'I understand that it is your intention to set off for Ryemarsh as soon as you can?'

'Yes,' Galiena said shortly.

'Do you wish me to send someone with you to act as your escort?' Putting that duty upon Brother Saul, or perhaps young Brother Augustus, would mean extra work for the other monks, Helewise reflected, but she could hardly send the young woman off alone.

But Galiena shook her head. 'No need,' she said. 'My maidservant will come for me.'

'How will she know when to come?' Helewise asked, puzzled. 'She surely cannot guess the time that you are ready to start for home and—'

'She'll come,' Galiena repeated, in such a way as

to suggest that she did not wish to continue the conversation. 'And now, my lady Abbess, if I may be excused, I would like to return to my prayers.'

Sensing herself very firmly dismissed, Helewise swallowed her pride – it all but choked her – went back up the slippery steps and out through the door.

5

By the evening of that day, Helewise's resolve to think charitable thoughts about Galiena Ryemarsh and her problems was wearing very thin. Besides her indignation at the way in which the girl had addressed her, she also found herself dwelling on the question of just how Galiena could be so unreasonably certain that her maidservant would come for her. She must surely have sent word somehow, Helewise thought, frowning, but with whom?

The only conclusion that she reached – and she felt it to be a feeble one – was that Galiena had found some departing visitor to the shrine whose way home went close to Ryemarsh and she had paid them to make the detour. She was on the point of setting out to the Vale once more to see if she could verify this assumption when, on going out of her room and into the cloister, she realised that the long June day was at last coming to a close and it was getting dark.

She had been sitting brooding in her room for far longer than she had realised. It was too late now to go asking questions of the monks who would, she was quite sure, have settled down for the night.

As indeed I should have done too, she thought,

yawning hugely and not bothering to put a polite hand in front of her mouth. It was rather nice to be alone and not to have to worry about her manners . . .

Walking slowly across the courtyard towards the dormitory, she reassured herself with the happy thought that Galiena Ryemarsh would probably be leaving Hawkenlye the next day and, with any luck, Helewise would never have to see her again.

Galiena might have wished as fervently as Helewise that an early departure be accomplished. However, it was not to be. Well might the girl have been observed (by Sister Ursel, the porteress, and Sister Martha, who tended the stables) peering anxiously up the road to see if there were any sign of her maidservant coming to escort her home. But the maidservant did not appear. In any case, even had she arrived as early as her mistress began looking out for her, Galiena could not have left with her there and then. The second potion was not yet ready.

It was Sister Tiphaine's fault, if indeed there was a fault. Careful to the point of obsession over her remedies, she had insisted that the last ingredient could not be picked until the planets were in the correct alignment and this had not happened until just before dawn of that day. Then, even having picked, prepared and added the final herb, the mixture had to steep for a certain time. Helewise, sensing Galiena's impatience like an itch on her skin, had sent word to the herbalist suggesting that the remedy might steep even as Galiena bore it back to Ryemarsh. No, my lady

Abbess, came the polite but firm reply. The potion will lose its power if not allowed perfect stillness whilst it matures.

It appeared that the earliest Galiena might set out – assuming either that her woman-servant had arrived or that she would accept Brother Augustus as escort – was midway through the afternoon.

And with that Helewise knew she – and Galiena – must be satisfied. Sister Tiphaine knew what she was doing and it was useless to argue.

Helewise was left with the distinct impression that she herself had received the unwelcome tidings rather better than Galiena. The girl had apparently taken herself off for a walk in the woods. Warned by the well-meaning Sister Anne not to venture off the track that led around the skirts of the Great Forest, Galiena had, according to witnesses, given a flounce of her wide skirts, twitched her veil into place, muttered something that fortunately nobody could make out and marched off.

It is understandable, Helewise kept telling herself. The girl is distraught, homesick, lonely. We – by which she actually meant I – shall just have be patient and kind for a few more hours, then we shall all have our wishes granted and she will be on her way home.

In the late morning, Sister Ursel came hurrying to tell Helewise that there were travellers on the road approaching the Abbey gates.

'Is it Galiena's maidservant?' Helewise asked, trying to keep the hope out of her voice.

'I cannot say, my lady. It is a party of three and, as far as I can tell, consists of a man, well-dressed and well-mounted, a woman and a manservant.'

Oh. It did not sound like a lone woman coming to fetch Galiena. 'Find out who they are and what they wish of us,' she said calmly to the porteress. 'Then report back immediately to me, please.'

Sister Ursel nodded a brief reverence and left.

In the brief period of her absence Helewise did not even try to return to her books. Instead she sat staring at the wall and trying to think kind thoughts.

Sister Ursel reappeared. 'My lord of Ryemarsh is here, my lady,' she said, and the avid curiosity in her eyes belied her deliberately bland tone. 'He says he has come to meet his wife, as they arranged, and that he wishes to take the holy healing waters and pray with her here for a few days.'

Helewise rose slowly to her feet. As they arranged? Why, then, had Galiena not mentioned that Ambrose would be joining her at Hawkenlye? And Galiena wanted to go home, didn't she? It was surely not in her plans to remain at the Abbey, praying and partaking of the waters. Thinking swiftly, she said, 'See to it that the lord Ryemarsh is escorted down to the Vale and ask Brother Firmin to look after him. I will find Galiena and bring her to him there.'

The porteress nodded her understanding and hurried away. Helewise, moving with more deliberation, wondered just how she was going to accomplish her self-appointed mission. The forest was vast and if Galiena had not heeded the warning not to venture within its dark reaches, it was going to be no quick or easy task to locate her . . .

Well, the sooner I start, the sooner I shall succeed, Helewise told herself firmly. Quickening her pace, she set off towards the gate and out along the path to the forest.

Down in the Vale, Ambrose Ryemarsh was still asking for his wife. 'We wish to pray together for the child we both want so much,' he kept saying. 'Also we must both take the waters for they tell me that miracles have happened to those who do so.' He was becoming increasingly breathless and agitated and Brother Firmin, kind-hearted soul that he was, was worried. Urging Ambrose to sit and rest in the shade and take a few sips of the precious water, he caught the eye of young Brother Augustus.

'Gus, I am concerned about our guest,' he whispered. 'Nip up and fetch Sister Euphemia, there's a good lad. I think she ought to have a look at him.'

Gus did as he was ordered, showing a considerable amount of tanned and well-muscled leg as he hitched up his robe and ran off up the path to the Abbey. It was not long before he was back, walking now at the infirmarer's pace and a respectful two paces behind her.

'Where is he?' Sister Euphemia asked Brother Firmin, who had hurried out from the pilgrims' shelter to meet her.

'Over there in the shade.' Brother Firmin pointed to where Ambrose sat with his back to one of the

Vale's fine chestnut trees. A small group of monks stood a few paces off, watching the old man with concern; Ambrose's servant had been left up at the Abbey tending the horses.

Of the woman, there was no sign.

'What ails him?' the infirmarer asked.

'He cannot see, his breath is shallow and he complains of pains in his joints,' Brother Firmin replied. 'But, worse than that, he is troubled in his mind. He is greatly confused and sometimes he does not seem to know where he is – at one moment he was quite lucid, sipping the holy water and asking about the history of the Vale, then suddenly he opened his eyes wide, told me that his groom had run away and then—' Brother Firmin broke off in distress. 'Oh, then, Sister, the poor soul began to weep piteously and cry out aloud for his wife!'

Sister Euphemia nodded, giving the old monk's arm a reassuring pat. 'You were right to send for me, Brother Firmin,' she said. 'Don't worry, I'll look after him. And the Abbess herself has gone in search of his wife, so I'm quite sure that the lord Ambrose will soon have his wish.'

Then, turning all of her formidable concentration on to her patient, she approached Ambrose, sat down on the grass beside him and, taking one of his fretful hands in hers, gently held the cup of water to his lips and encouraged him to drink. Then, her practised and observant eyes studying him, she began quietly to question him.

*   *   *

Helewise's search of the paths up to and around the forest had met with no success. Galiena was nowhere to be found.

Hurrying back to the Abbey, she was coming to the reluctant conclusion that quite a lot of her nuns and monks would have to be taken away from their duties and organised into a search party for the wretched girl. She had a swift look around the Abbey to see if Galiena had found herself a quiet corner within its walls in which to sit out the time until she could depart but, again, there was no sign of her.

Reluctantly Helewise turned for the Vale. She would have to find Brother Saul and instruct him to set about organising the search party. In addition, she realised, she ought to seek out Ambrose Ryemarsh and welcome him with a few well-chosen and reassuring words, which was going to be difficult given that she hadn't been able to locate his wife.

Frowning, she set off down the path that led to the Vale.

She had only gone a few paces when Brother Saul came running after her. Hearing his footsteps, she stopped and waited for him to catch her up.

'Brother Saul?' she greeted him.

'I was looking for you, my lady,' he panted. 'Brother Firmin's got Sister Euphemia to look after the old man – the lord Ryemarsh, I should say – and it seems he's not at all well. Sister Euphemia sent me to inform you that she wants to have him moved up to the infirmary – she says he needs to rest in the cool darkness for a while to see if that'll help him recover his senses.'

'Oh, dear!' Helewise had not appreciated that Ambrose Ryemarsh was sick; was the purpose of his visit, then, more than to take the waters and pray for a child?

'Will it be all right for Sister Euphemia to put the lord Ambrose in the infirmary?' Saul was asking anxiously. 'It's so full at present and strictly speaking the old feller's not really ill, only—'

'Of course it's all right!' Helewise gave Saul a reassuring smile. 'The infirmary is Sister Euphemia's province and I would not dream of questioning her judgement.'

'Aye, my lady,' Saul said, with a smile that seemed to say, course you wouldn't.

They were hurrying on down the path when they saw someone approaching across the short grass over to their left. The figure was tall and strongly built and, until she could make out details of dress, Helewise took it to be a man.

But it was a woman.

Her gown and veil were of dark cloth and she wore a close-fitting linen wimple. Her face was pale, the expression joyless. But it was the eyes that Helewise noticed; wide under pale brows and lashes, they were of the palest green, like thick ice on a pond that is tinged with the colour of what lies beneath.

For some reason, Helewise felt a shudder go up her spine. Rather more curtly than perhaps necessary, she said, 'Yes? Can we help you?'

The woman frowned. Then, in a strangely toneless voice, she said, 'I am Aebba. I serve the lady Galiena.

I am come with the lord her husband to join her here and in time to see her safely back to her home.'

Helewise glanced at Saul to see how he might be responding to this strange woman. He was staring at her intently, a look of puzzlement on his face.

'What were you doing out there in the grass?' Helewise asked, trying to make her voice sound pleasant and non-accusatory.

The woman stared at her for a moment. Then she said, 'I was praying in the Abbey church. For the lady, you know, that what she desires be granted to her. Then I set out to find the Vale, where they tell me the lord Ambrose rests, but I missed the path.'

Helewise was just wondering how anybody with eyes in their head could possibly miss the well-marked path to the Vale when Saul gave a sort of gasp and began, 'But—'

Instantly Aebba stepped on to the path, elbowed Saul out of the way and said curtly, 'I must go to the master. Please show me the way.'

After a brief hesitation, Helewise gave a slight bow and said, 'Certainly. Follow me, please,' and led the way on down the path.

Other than accuse the woman directly of telling untruths, there was little else she could do. Very aware of Saul, walking behind Aebba and muttering softly to himself, she resolved to have a private word with him as soon as it could be arranged.

The moment that Helewise laid eyes on Ambrose she understood Sister Euphemia's concern. The old man lay back against his tree, eyes closed, barely conscious, face pale and with a sheen of sweat. As the infirmarer greeted her and came to stand beside her, Helewise said softly, 'Let us arrange for him to be installed in the infirmary, Sister. I have been unable to locate Galiena but I am sure that she must surely reappear soon – after all, she must realise that her remedies are just about ready for her and she may well be expecting Aebba to have arrived.'

'Aebba?'

Helewise indicated the dour woman standing a few paces off, staring down at Ambrose with an unreadable expression on her face. 'Galiena's serving woman.'

'Ah.' The infirmarer made no further comment.

'Can he walk?' Helewise asked.

'I reckon so, my lady, with help. Saul! Gus!' she called, and immediately the two brothers hurried towards her. 'Help the lord Ambrose to his feet, if you will, and get him up to the infirmary. I'll go on ahead and prepare a bed for him.'

As Saul rushed to obey, Helewise caught at his sleeve. 'Saul?' she said quietly. 'Why did you look so startled when the woman, Aebba, said she had been in the church?'

'Oh, I'm sure I was mistaken, my lady, and that's exactly where she was,' he said instantly.

'You thought you saw her elsewhere?'

'Aye.' Again, the puzzled frown. 'I could have sworn I saw her hurrying away towards the forest.'

Where Galiena went, Helewise thought, thanking Saul and sending him on to help Ambrose. And, since several people seem to have known that's where she ran off to, then it is quite possible that Aebba went to look for her.

And, frowning just as Saul had done, she wondered why.

It was some time before Helewise could go over to the infirmary to see how Ambrose was. A delegation of the Abbey's marshland tenants had arrived while she was in the Vale and she had to see to the receipt and the recording of the money they brought with them as their contribution towards King Richard's ransom. So preoccupied did she become with the visitors, their questions ('Will we have to pay more, my lady? Only it's hard, very hard, on us as are family men to meet these 'ere demands') and their need to gossip ('They do say as how 'e won't be back and that Prince John'll have to be king!) that she all but forgot about the infirmarer's new patient.

Her heart went out to the marshmen. They were the Abbey's tenants and she, as Abbess, had a fair idea of the circumstances of their lives. In common with everyone else in England, they had already had to give more than they could afford to finance the Lionheart's crusade. Although Helewise understood why such an expensive campaign had been necessary, a part of her could not help wondering whether knights, lords and kings with the passion and the thrill of holy war filling their heads and hearts ought not to pause just for a moment to wonder if it was all worth it.

And now King Richard's dreams of glory had come down to this: he was ignominiously imprisoned and his poor struggling people were going to have to reach into all but empty pockets to ransom him. Looking at the faces of the men standing nervously before her now, she pitied them deeply and would have helped them if she could.

But she could not.

She wanted to be able to say that the sum they had delivered today would undoubtedly suffice. She wanted to tell them to go home and work as hard as they could in an attempt to make up what they had been forced to give away. She wanted to reassure them that what they now could put by, from their own increased efforts, would be theirs alone.

But if she gave those reassurances – which were not hers to give – then what if some further calamity occurred? What if King Richard again called upon his people?

It was almost unthinkable, but then the unthinkable did sometimes happen.

When at last she had seen the marshmen on their way, the afternoon was over and it was time for Vespers. As soon as the office was over, she went straight across to the infirmary.

A harassed young nun in a bloodstained apron bowed to her and, in answer to her query, led her along to the small curtained recess where Ambrose lay. Dismissing the nun – Helewise could see she was desperate to get back to whichever patient's blood had flowed out so freely all over her stiff linen apron –

Helewise drew back the curtain slightly and went into the dimly lit recess.

There was a delicious, sweet smell on the air – sniffing, Helewise tried to identify it. Then she looked down at the bed. Ambrose lay with his eyes half-closed, an expression of peace on his face.

For one dreadful heartbeat, Helewise thought he was dead.

But he must have sensed her presence; opening his eyes, he peered up at her and said, 'Galiena?'

She moved quickly forward and took the hand that he held out. It was bony, knotted and misshapen, but the skin felt smooth, almost as if it had been oiled. 'No, my lord, it is Helewise, Abbess of Hawkenlye,' she said softly.

He was squeezing her hand, nodding slightly. 'Aye, I can tell it's not Galiena. I greet you, my lady, and I thank you for your care.'

'Galiena is—' she began, thinking that the best way of telling him that his wife was missing was to come right out with it.

But he said, 'She was here, my lady. Did you see her, my lovely lassie?'

Helewise held back the question that rose to her lips. 'I – er, no.'

Ambrose sighed with pleasure. 'I may not see as well as I did, especially in this dim light, and it was almost as if I saw her in a dream. But I do not need the keen sight of youth to recognise my wife's gentle touch. And I know the smell of the special ointment with which she rubs my sore hands.' Freeing his hand from Helewise's grasp, he held it up side by side with his other hand, as if for her inspection. 'Such pain I had in my joints, my lady, and my Galiena took note and made me a wonderful remedy. She's so clever, such a wise herbalist, and still so young. She knows when I am in pain without my needing to tell her and there she is, by my side, rubbing the precious stuff into my old bones until all the pain is gone! My lady, I have been cared for adequately well by her woman Aebba during Galiena's absence, but it wasn't the same.' He sighed. 'Oh, no. Not the same at all. But the touch of my lovely lassie, ah, that is something to cherish!'

'She has been to tend you? Here?' Helewise asked in surprise.

'Aye, my lady, just now. Why, the ointment is still on my skin! Does it not smell delicious? Good enough to eat!' With a small chuckle, he licked the back of one hand.

'It does indeed,' she agreed.

'I always know my lassie by the sweet smell she carries about her,' Ambrose said, a loving expression on his face. 'She was here, my lady, oh, yes!'

Had he been dreaming? Helewise thought it quite likely. But then it did look as if someone had recently been massaging his hands.

The curtain parted and the infirmarer stepped into the recess. 'My lord Ambrose, how do you feel?' she said, but it seemed that the old man had slipped into a doze.

'He says Galiena was here,' Helewise whispered.

'That she came to massage his hands with her special remedy.'

'Did she?' Sister Euphemia looked doubtful. 'Can't say as I saw her, but then we're rushed off our feet today. And it could have been while most of us were over in the church just now for Vespers.'

'His hands certainly feel as if they have received some sort of treatment,' Helewise said. The infirmarer took up one of the old man's hands and ran a finger over its back, nodding her agreement as she did so. 'But it need not necessarily have been Galiena who administered it,' Helewise concluded.

'My lady, I couldn't say.' The infirmarer looked flustered. 'He's not well, that's for sure.'

'What is the matter with him?'

'He's an old man and his mind's wandering,' Sister Euphemia said baldly. 'In addition he's short of breath, virtually blind and very sleepy.' She shook her head. 'If that young wife of his is serious about conceiving his child, then all I can say is she'd be well advised to hurry up about it.'

'You think. . .' Helewise hesitated. Then, in a barely audible whisper, 'You think he may be dying?'

'He doesn't look any too perky, my lady. But it's always possible that—'

Whatever possibility the infirmarer had in mind was to remain unexpressed. For, interrupting her even as she spoke, there came a terrifying sound from the main body of the infirmary behind them.

It was not a moment for protocol. A nurse before she was a nun, Sister Euphemia responded to the dreadful choking noise by pushing past her superior and setting off at a dash between the curtains and into the infirmary.

Helewise, a pace behind, saw a horrible sight.

Galiena had come bursting into the infirmary and had sunk to her knees on the floor. Her heavy veil was awry – her hair, Helewise noticed distractedly, was beautiful: palest blonde and twined into two thick plaits – and she had torn at the neck of her silk gown, exposing the white flesh of her chest and her rounded upper breasts.

There was a look of extreme terror on her pale face. Her lips were swollen and, as Helewise stared in fascinated horror, a red rash seemed to spread across the girl's throat.

Galiena, it was quite obvious, could not breathe. The rasping, choking noises as she tried to take air into her lungs were quieter now, even as the girl's panic increased. She leaned forward briefly and some liquid came out of her mouth and dribbled on to the floor.

Eyes wide, she stared up at Sister Euphemia, Helewise and the circle of nursing nuns who now stood around her. Sister Euphemia held out her hands to the girl and said something – it might have been an encouragement to sit up straight, so as to let the breath flow more readily into her poor body – but Galiena did not appear to hear.

Then her whole frame convulsed once, twice. She slipped over sideways against Sister Euphemia, who was kneeling down and trying to support her, and then she was still.

After a few moments of absolute silence – the infirmary's patients were too shocked to move, let alone speak – Sister Euphemia said very quietly, 'I'm afraid she's dead.'

6

At New Winnowlands, Josse was engaged in the same sort of task that had been absorbing the Abbess of Hawkenlye. A quarter of his annual income. He had heard the phrase bandied about, had said it himself, but, until this moment when he was actually facing what it meant in the harsh light of day, he had not quite appreciated just what it was going to entail.

Josse was not a wealthy man and his modest estate of New Winnowlands, although well managed and reasonably profitable, was not going to make him one. But he was and always had been a true King's man and, if asked, would have said he'd willingly give all that he had to release Richard from his dishonourable, humiliating captivity and bring him safely home again. However, now that he was having to turn words into action and come up with the money, he was discovering that his feelings were not quite as wholehearted as he had believed them to be. A niggling little thought kept saying, well, the King's got himself into this mess so why should his loyal people have to pay so heavily to get him out of it? Is it really right that we shoulder the burden in this way?

He sat for some time, a deep frown on his rugged

face, allowing rein to this traitorous thought. Then, with a sigh, he picked up his quill and laboriously began to write out figures; writing was not a skill that came readily to him, any more than reading was, which made the task even more unwelcome. But his innermost sentiments would have to remain secret. After all, it was not a question of giving only if you felt you would like to. However you looked at the matter, Josse concluded, paying up was horribly inevitable. There was no point in moaning so he had better get on with it.

When at last he had finished, he felt that he deserved a reward and the first thing that sprang to mind was a visit to Hawkenlye. He had a ready-made excuse – not that he truly felt he needed one – in that he had recommended the nuns' care and skill to Ambrose and Galiena Ryemarsh. And, indeed, he had proposed that they renew their pleasant new acquaintance over at Hawkenlye, hadn't he? The young woman would be there now, he thought, and probably the old husband would have ridden over to join her. Deciding that he would like to see the business through to whatever conclusion it might reach, Josse summoned Ella and asked her to prepare a small pack for him as he was planning a few days' absence from home.

With a brief nod, she turned and put her foot on the first of the short flight of steps leading up to Josse's sleeping chamber. Then, almost as an afterthought, she said, 'Give my respects to the Abbess, sir.'

Josse, wondering how and when he had come to be

so predictable, got up and went to tell Will to fetch Horace from the paddock.

It occurred to him as he set off that Brice of Rotherbridge might like to join the party at Hawkenlye, especially since Brice appeared to be a good friend of the Ryemarshes and to have their interests at heart; had it not after all been he who had introduced Josse to Ambrose and his young wife as one who knew Hawkenlye and its good works? It was only a short detour to Brice's manor and so Josse turned Horace's head and set off to find his neighbour.

Brice was not at home. His stable lad, Ossie, said that the master had set out at first light two days ago and that he was not expected home before nightfall of that day at the earliest. 'Like as not 'e won't be back afore tomorrow, 'e said,' Ossie added. In response to Josse's enquiry about where Brice had gone, Ossie shrugged. ''E didn't say.'

Wondering why Brice's journey to some undisclosed destination should seem sinister, Josse nodded to the lad, set off down the track and told himself not to be fanciful. But against his will he saw again Brice's air of tense expectancy when they sat in Ambrose Ryemarsh's hall. Saw in his mind's eye the suppressed excitement in Brice's handsome face. And, although he tried to stop himself, Josse recalled what he had thought then.

Was he right? Dear Lord, he prayed that he was not.

But, either way, it seemed likely that joining Galiena

and her husband at Hawkenlye promised to answer a few questions.

He did not hurry on his ride to the Abbey. The day had started warm and, as the sun rose higher in the sky, warm became hot and then very hot. In the early afternoon, he found a patch of deep shade in a place where willows grew along a stream bank and, unsaddling Horace, he tethered the horse by the water and threw himself down on the cool grass. Ella had packed bread, a thick slice of her own cured ham, a honey tartlet, a couple of juicy, sweet apples and a flask of ale and, when he had rested for a while, Josse rediscovered his appetite and ate the food hungrily. The ale slipped down almost without his noticing. Then, meaning only to close his eyes for a short time, he fell deeply asleep.

He was woken by a burning sensation in his face. Sitting up with a start, he realised he had been asleep for so long that the sun had moved round and was now shining down full on his head and shoulders. From the feel of his cheeks under his exploratory hands, it looked as if he had given himself a fine case of sunburn.

He knelt by the stream and repeatedly splashed cold water on his face, which gave temporary relief. Horace watched him with mild curiosity. Turning to the horse, Josse said ruefully, 'Well, I can't kneel here with my backside in the air for the remainder of the day. We'd better be on our way to Hawkenlye, old Horace, and pray as we go that the infirmarer has a cure for a flaming, scarlet face.'

* * *

He rode in through the gates of Hawkenlye to tragedy.

The infirmary door was open and, amid the strange hush that seemed to have descended on the Abbey, there came the dreadful sounds of sobbing: deep, harsh, broken, painful sobs that, if he were any judge, were being emitted by a man. Some poor soul has lost a loved one, he thought. Child, wife, mother. Ah well, it was sad but unfortunately not uncommon; even the skills of the nursing nuns could not save everybody. Josse dismounted and led Horace across to the stables, where Sister Martha came out to meet him.

In the clear golden light of the westering sun, he could see that her strong old face was creased with distress.

Reaching out absently to take the horse's reins, she responded briefly to Josse's courteous greeting and then, even as he began to frame the question 'What has happened?' she shook her head and led Horace off inside the stable block.

A sudden terrible fear took hold of Josse. Feeling as if cold fingers had reached inside his chest and were slowly and relentlessly squeezing his heart, he turned and raced for the infirmary.

Bursting inside, he stood on the threshold, trying to look everywhere at once. Where would they have laid her? Would she still be here, or had they taken her to the Abbey church? Oh, dear God, he wept silently, and I never said goodbye to her! Never told her that I –

But just at that moment the hangings around a curtained-off recess at the far end of the infirmary moved slightly, parting as a tall figure passed between them. And walking towards him, her hands held out to him and her face white, came the Abbess.

For an instant his relief was so powerful that he almost embraced her.

No, he told himself firmly. Not that. Never that.

Instead he took hold of her outstretched hands – they were icy cold, even in the heat – and said quietly, 'My lady Abbess, good evening. What has happened here?'

'She's dead!' the Abbess said, her voice unsteady. 'And he – oh, Josse, it breaks my heart to see his pain!'

She was allowing her cool air of authority to slip and he flattered himself that it was perhaps because he, whom he hoped she looked on as an old and trusted friend, had arrived and was in effect offering her a shoulder to lean on. It had, after all, happened before.

But, knowing her as he did, he was aware that she rarely allowed her emotions to break through in front of her nuns. He said very softly, 'My lady, why not step outside with me into the shade of the cloister where, in privacy, you can tell me who has died and why everyone seems so distressed?'

His words brought her instantly to herself. Grabbing her hands back, she tucked them away in the opposite sleeves of her habit, straightened her back, composed her face and said distantly, 'Yes. Follow me, please, Sir Josse.'

Suppressing a smile at her suddenly steely tone, meekly he fell in behind her.

She led the way across to the courtyard off which

opened her own private room and to a far corner of the encircling cloister where, in the shade, there was a stone bench set into the wall. Indicating that he should sit – he did, but then, seeing she was not going to join him on the bench, immediately stood up again – she said, 'A young woman has been with us. Sister Euphemia and Sister Tiphaine have been trying to help her; she wishes to conceive and they have made concoctions to help her.'

'Aye, I—' I know and I sent her here, he was about to say. But the Abbess seemed neither to hear nor acknowledge that he had spoken.

'Her elderly husband came to join her. But—' Her voice broke. She took a deep breath and tried again. 'But she's dead. Just now. She came into the infirmary gasping for breath and Sister Euphemia tried to help her, but it was too late and she died.'

Josse did not know how he managed not to put his arms round her. But it would not have been right, or at least he thought not. She was clearly struggling for control and he would not help her in her efforts by offering kindness. She was in shock, he thought, and probably the best thing for her was to maintain her air of cool authoritative competence.

Whatever the cost.

He said tentatively, 'And it is her husband whom I heard weeping?'

'Yes.' She cleared her throat. 'I was with him when Galiena stumbled in through the door. He's in the infirmary and Sister Euphemia has him under her care.'

'He is sick?' But he had seemed perfectly all right that day Josse had visited him at home. Well, other than being old and almost blind, but neither condition, surely, was one for which the infirmarer could come up with a cure.

'Yes,' the Abbess was saying. 'He – his mind has been wandering and he is very sleepy. Sister Euphemia said—' She broke off, distress clear on her face.

'She said what?' he prompted gently.

'Oh – she didn't think he looked very strong and she said that if Galiena really wanted to have his child she ought not to delay. But it's too late now.'

He knew she was in danger of drowning in emotion. And, recalling the beautiful, lively and affectionate young woman he met that day at Ryemarsh, he could not blame her. But they would achieve nothing if they gave in and sat there howling out their grief. He took a steadying breath and then said in a businesslike manner, 'My lady, I should say straight away that I know of Ambrose and Galiena Ryemarsh. My neighbour, Brice of Rotherbridge, took me to their manor to make their acquaintance. Brice knows, of course, of my contacts with Hawkenlye Abbey and felt that I was the person to answer Ambrose's questions as to whether the sisters here might be able to help Galiena in her wish to bear her husband a child. We spoke together and I urged him to bring his wife here to you. Indeed, I had the pleasure of escorting Galiena and her companions as far as New Winnowlands, from where they came on to Hawkenlye. Ambrose could not set out straight away but was to join Galiena in a few days' time.'

'Which, as you see, he did.' The Abbess frowned. Watching closely, Josse thought that he might have achieved his purpose of turning her mind away from her distress. But then she added, almost under her breath, 'It was strange, then, as indeed I thought at the time, that Galiena did not forewarn us that her husband would be arriving.'

'Eh? What's that?'

She raised her eyes to meet his. For an instant, her sad expression broke into a smile as, apparently for the first time, she looked at him properly. She said, 'Sir Josse! Whatever has happened to your face?'

'I fell asleep in the sun,' he said shortly.

Trying, not very successfully, to suppress a laugh, she said kindly, 'It looks very sore. We must see what Sister Euphemia can provide to alleviate the discomfort. I am sorry, I interrupted you.'

'You were saying that Galiena did not announce that Ambrose would be coming to join her here.'

'That's right. No, she did not.'

'She told nobody?'

The Abbess looked thoughtful. 'She did not tell *me*. I cannot swear that she did not mention it to any other sister but I do not think so, for word would surely have reached me.'

'Hm.' It was his turn to frown, which, he discovered, creased the flesh on his burned forehead and hurt quite a lot. 'Well, maybe she was too busy with her own concerns and simply forgot.'

'She was certainly preoccupied,' the Abbess agreed. 'And, I think, rather embarrassed at the whole procedure of coming here to be treated for her barrenness. As Sister Euphemia pointed out to me, all very understandable.'

Josse wondered if now was the moment to ask the question that he had been wanting to ask ever since the Abbess had told him the news. Studying her, he thought it was as good a time as any. He said quietly, 'My lady, how did Galiena die?'

She stared at him. Then: 'We do not know. Sister Euphemia is even now studying the – er, the body.'

'Was the girl unwell?' he persisted. 'Was there any obvious wound, such as might have been made had she fallen, for example?'

'She was not unwell,' the Abbess said tonelessly. 'She was anxious, distressed even, but not, I think, unwell. As to a wound—' She shrugged. 'Nothing obvious at first glance. No blood on her garments, no twisted limb or bump on the head. Just the swelling of her poor face and the one episode of vomiting, or whatever it was.'

'Vomiting?'

She shook her head impatiently. 'Not exactly that. She opened her mouth and liquid came out. Watery liquid.'

'I see.' It was a silly remark, as he definitely did *not* see. Not with any certainty, at least, although a horrible suspicion was dawning. Hoping that he was doing the right thing and not making a bad matter worse, he said, 'My lady, can it be, do you think, that Galiena was poisoned?'

The Abbess stared at him in silence for a moment.

Then she said, 'It is what I have been dreading. I pray that it is not so, but . . .' She left the sentence unfinished.

'But what else could it be?' he murmured.

'Sister Euphemia has promised to report to me as soon as she has finished,' the Abbess said. 'I fear, Sir Josse, that all we can do is wait.'

They did not have to wait long. But it was not the infirmarer herself who came to find them but Sister Caliste, one of the Abbey's youngest fully professed nuns and a competent and compassionate nurse. She approached, made a graceful obeisance to her superior and greeted Josse with a wide smile. Although she did not speak to him, he read clearly in her expression that she was glad to see him again.

'Sister Euphemia asks me to say that she is ready for you now, my lady,' Sister Caliste said to the Abbess. 'If you both would like to follow me, I will take you to her.'

Josse and the Abbess walked in silence behind the young nun through the cloister and across the courtyard to the infirmary. There Sister Caliste led them along to the left and into a small room leading off the main chamber. In it there was a single, raised cot on which now lay a body covered with a clean white sheet.

Realising that the body was probably naked beneath the linen, Josse stood back. But the Abbess, turning to him, said, 'Please, Sir Josse, come in with me if you will. Your experienced eyes have helped us before and, in truth, this is no time for delicacy.'

Sister Euphemia, overhearing, said, 'Come on in, Sir Josse. The poor lass is decently covered and all I need to show you is her face.'

The Abbess stepped across to stand over the cot and Josse took his place beside her. Sister Caliste remained just inside the door, which she had quietly closed behind her.

Without preamble, the infirmarer said, 'I reckon she was poisoned. There was fluid in her mouth, although I cannot say what it was, and her face had swelled up, especially the lips. I've seen similar symptoms in cases of poison.'

'This fluid you speak of,' Josse said. 'What was it like? Was there undigested matter in it?'

'I looked carefully, but found nothing,' Sister Euphemia replied.

'Strange,' Josse mused.

'Strange?' the Abbess queried.

'Aye, my lady.' Josse glanced across the cot at the infirmarer, who gave a brief nod as if to say, you explain. 'Often when somebody takes poison, the substance causes vomiting as soon as it reaches the stomach. The vomit then can be seen to contain whatever the poison was and also some of whatever else was in the stomach, such as—'

'Yes, thank you, Sir Josse,' the Abbess interrupted, 'I understand.'

'But this is not the case here,' Josse finished.

'No, it's not,' the infirmarer agreed. 'Just that clear, colourless fluid.'

'Could she recently have taken a drink of water?' the Abbess suggested. 'In her distress, she might simply have spat it out.'

Again Josse met Sister Euphemia's eyes. He was quite sure she thought it as unlikely as he did, although both of them were too polite to say so. 'It's possible, my lady,' the infirmarer said.

'But not probable,' the Abbess said with a faint smile. 'I can tell by your tone, Sister.'

The three of them stood in silence around the still figure beneath the sheet. Then Josse said tentatively, 'You mentioned swelling, Sister Euphemia. Might I be allowed to look?'

He wondered even as he spoke whether the two nuns would disapprove of his request but, with a quick gesture, Sister Euphemia twitched back the sheet and said, 'Of course, Sir Josse. Maybe you'll see something I missed.'

She folded the sheet across the dead girl's shoulders, exposing only her face, neck and a little of her chest. And Josse stared down at Galiena Ryemarsh.

His heart turned over with pity at what the poison had done to her. She was still beautiful – the perfect oval of her face and the pleasing symmetry of her bone structure were unchanged. And the abundant, pale blonde hair that he remembered so well had been dressed slightly differently – perhaps by one of the nuns who had helped lay her out? – and now the two thick braids were entwined across the top of the girl's head like a coronet.

Almost unaware of what he did, Josse stretched

out a hand and gently touched them. The infirmarer said softly, 'Her hair was disarrayed. Sister Caliste combed it out and plaited it for her, then arranged it as you see.'

Josse turned to Sister Caliste. 'You did well, Sister,' he said softly. 'I am sure she would have approved.'

But even the most perfect hairstyle in the world could not have distracted the attention for long from the dead girl's mouth. The rosy lips were deathly pale now but, even worse, they were grossly swollen. Around them the white skin bore the residue of a pinkish rash. The lower part of Galiena's face was almost unrecognisable.

With a deep sigh Josse said, 'I have seen enough, Sister.' More than enough, he thought bitterly, for now I shall remember Galiena in death and not as she was in life. He turned away from the cot.

The Abbess murmured something to the infirmarer, who leaned down and carefully replaced the mercifully concealing sheet over the dead girl's ruined face.

Then the infirmarer said, 'My lady, Sir Josse, there is one more thing.'

The Abbess and Josse turned to face her. 'Yes?' the Abbess asked.

Looking straight at her superior, Sister Euphemia said quietly, 'The lass was pregnant. Three or four months gone.'

In the first unbelieving moment, Josse looked at the Abbess. Her face expressionless, she said, 'But Galiena came here because she could not conceive. She cannot have known that already she bore Ambrose's child.'

His own emotions dangerously near to the surface, he watched as the Abbess's face slowly crumpled in distress. 'Oh,' she cried softly, 'oh, and now the poor girl is dead!'

The infirmarer was staring down at Galiena. 'Aye,' she breathed, 'aye. It is a bad day.' She glanced at the Abbess. 'But as to her not knowing, it may well be that she remained ignorant of her condition. With a first pregnancy, many women do not realise until they are some months along and—'

She was interrupted by the sound of hurrying feet outside and by a sudden gasp from Sister Caliste. Still standing just in front of the little room's door, she had been pushed forward by somebody roughly opening it.

All four of them turned to see who had come in.

It was Aebba. Her icy eyes fixed to the sheeted figure on the cot, she said, her low voice almost a growl, 'Is it true? She's dead, then?'

It was the Abbess who spoke. 'I am afraid that she is.'

Josse was watching Aebba. His first impression of her at that meeting at Ryemarsh was that she was a cold and distant woman, uninvolved with those around her. But now her pale face worked as the extremity of her emotion flooded briefly through her.

Puzzled, Josse thought, aye, but different people show their grief in different ways, and I should not judge her when the poor woman's probably in shock. I am wrong. I must be!

Because in that first unguarded reaction to the

dreadful confirmation of the rumour of Galiena's death, the sentiment that Josse thought he had read in her face was not distress but fury.

7

Helewise, who had almost regained control over herself after the infirmarer's poignant revelation, watched Josse staring at Aebba. He looked, she thought, as if something were surprising him. Had he, like her, formed an impression of Galiena's maidservant as an unemotional, even cold woman? If so, no doubt he was taken aback by her dramatic reaction to her young mistress's death.

For a moment, nobody spoke. Then Sister Euphemia said kindly, 'Would you like to see her one last time?'

Wordlessly Aebba nodded.

The infirmarer drew back the sheet again and Aebba stared silently down on Galiena. She stood perfectly still for some time, her face once more an unmoving mask. Then, still without a word, she turned and walked quickly out of the room.

Helewise felt that it was high time she began to act more like the Abbess of Hawkenlye and less like a grieving mourner. After all, she told herself firmly, she had hardly known Galiena and, although the girl's death was undoubtedly a tragedy for her poor husband, it was not one that affected Helewise personally. She said in what she hoped was her usual tone, 'Sister

Euphemia, would you now please prepare the body for burial? Sister Caliste can assist you. In the morning I will send word to Father Gilbert that he will be needed.' Then she nodded briefly to the two nuns and made her way out into the infirmary. Reaching the outer door, she was aware that Josse had followed her.

Once they were in the relative seclusion of the cloister, he spoke. His face still looking worried, he said, 'My lady, this is a strange business, is it not? Can we truly believe that Galiena did not know herself to be pregnant?'

She turned to him. 'What else can we believe?' she asked simply.

He frowned, winced, then said, 'I suppose you are right. Certainly, when I met her at her husband's manor she seemed genuinely thrilled at the thought that Hawkenlye might be the answer to her prayers. I would bet a king's ransom' – he broke off with a wry grin – 'I mean, I would bet much money that she had no idea then that what she so desperately wanted had already happened.'

'Well then, why do you look so doubtful?' She recalled, looking at him now, that she had meant to organise some remedy for his sunburned face; everything else that had happened had driven it out of her head.

He shrugged. 'I don't know. There is something here that I don't understand.'

'What?' she demanded.

He grinned again. 'My lady, do not be so fierce with a man in pain!'

She touched his sleeve briefly. 'I am sorry, Sir Josse. Sister Euphemia is busy, as we both know, but come along with me to Sister Tiphaine, who, I am quite sure, will have some soothing balm for your face.'

The herbalist's little room smelled of lavender and rosemary. As Helewise and Josse entered, she was making something with rose water and the heady fragrance was gradually permeating the air, blending with the background scent so that unconsciously Helewise found herself breathing in deeply, as if to absorb more of the sweet perfume into her body.

'My lady Abbess,' Sister Tiphaine greeted her, bowing somewhat stiffly. 'Sir Josse.' She gave him a wide smile, then immediately reached up a practised hand to a large jar halfway along a shelf behind her. 'I can guess why you have come to see me,' she said as she opened the jar. 'Dab this on your face. It will ease the discomfort and help the skin to mend itself.'

Helewise watched as Josse sniffed at the jar and then gingerly patted a small amount of the contents on his left cheek. 'What is it?' he asked.

'Lavender, mostly,' the herbalist replied. 'Plus a few of my special magic ingredients.'

Helewise was not certain but she thought she saw Sister Tiphaine give Josse a quick wink.

'You have heard the news, Sister?' she enquired.

Sister Tiphaine turned to her, all signs of merriment now gone from her face. 'I have, my lady. And I grieve for the young woman, for all that I cannot say I warmed to her.'

'Didn't you?' Josse sounded amazed. 'But she was a delightful young woman, kind and gentle as well as beautiful!'

Helewise exchanged a glance with the herbalist, who cocked an ironic eyebrow. 'Perhaps, Sir Josse,' she said, 'Galiena was someone who was perceived differently by men and by women, so that your experience of her was necessarily other than Sister Tiphaine's and mine.' It was, she thought, a mild enough comment, in view of the fact that she definitely leaned more towards agreeing with Sister Tiphaine than with Josse. Although it distressed her to think ill of one so recently and so agonisingly dead, her honesty made her accept that she, too, had not warmed to Galiena.

Josse clearly was still not happy. 'But you must agree that she was a good wife and clearly devoted to Ambrose, even though he was so much older than she was!' he protested.

'I had not the advantage of observing them together,' Helewise said. 'Ambrose Ryemarsh arrived only late this morning and at that time Galiena was—' Oh, dear! This was going to be awkward, given that Josse was already seeing mysteries and puzzles where there were none! 'At that time we did not actually know where Galiena was.'

'She had gone missing.' Josse was nodding infuriatingly, as if to say, there! I told you there was something odd about all this!

'Not missing exactly,' Helewise protested. 'She had

set her heart on returning home this morning, only one of the remedies that Sister Tiphaine was preparing for her was not ready.' The herbalist nodded in confirmation. 'Galiena went for a walk in the forest,' Helewise finished.

'The girl was angry,' Sister Tiphaine said. 'She wanted to leave, just as you said, my lady, and she was right put out when I told her she couldn't, not unless she was prepared to risk spoiling the second remedy. She only agreed to wait – and it was a grudging agreement, let me tell you – when I said that some of the mixture's potency would be lost if it were to be disturbed too soon.'

'So she went off for a walk to fill in the time,' Helewise concluded. 'Quite natural, would you not say, Sir Josse?'

'Aye, I might,' he agreed. 'Except that, from what you say, Galiena was planning to hurry back home even as her husband was travelling over here to join her! How do we explain that?'

Helewise frowned. 'You are quite right, Sir Josse,' she said reluctantly. 'I have wondered all along why Galiena did not warn us that Ambrose would be joining her. What possible reason can she have had for her reticence?'

'He's an old man, feeble, all but blind, prone to wandering in his mind,' the herbalist said. 'Or so I hear. Maybe the young lady wished to return home before he set out so as to save him the stress of the journey.'

'That seems likely, and—' Helewise began.

But Josse interrupted. 'I am sorry, my lady, but I do not understand this talk of Ambrose as a doddering dotard!' he exclaimed. 'He's old, aye, and doesn't see too well, I grant you that, but there's nothing wrong with his mind and I would say that he is stronger than many men considerably younger than himself. To say that Galiena wished to spare him the journey here cannot be right! Why, when I last saw him, he was eagerly anticipating it and it was only that he had matters at home to attend to that prevented him riding out with Galiena.'

'Oh,' Helewise said lamely. Then, recovering: 'Sir Josse, it may be that some new ailment has arisen in Ambrose since you last met, for it is certain that now he lies in the infirmary, weak in body and also, I fear, in mind.'

'He has just lost his wife!' Josse protested hotly.

'Yes, I know, and I am more sorry for it than I can say, but he was failing before that.' Trying to find a way to convince him, she said, 'I was with him in the infirmary even as Galiena collapsed. He was vague, disorientated and, I thought, not really able to discern dreaming from wakefulness. Galiena had visited him earlier,' she added, almost as an afterthought. 'Or so he claimed. It was apparently while the nuns were at Vespers, leaving the lay sisters in charge. He said that she had been massaging his hands.'

'He'll be sleeping now,' Sister Tiphaine said calmly. 'I sent over some of my strongest sedative. He'll have some respite from his grief till he wakes.'

Thinking, not without dread, of what she would say

to Ambrose in the morning, Helewise said firmly, 'And we all should sleep soon, too, as soon as Compline is over. Sir Josse, will you join us for the last office of the day? Under the circumstances, I think it would do you good.'

With a nod of acceptance, he followed her out of the herbalist's room and she heard the steady tread of Sister Tiphaine's feet falling in behind him.

Helewise surprised herself by sleeping soundly and, as far as she remembered, dreamlessly. But as she left the Abbey church after Prime, she knew that she could no longer postpone a visit to Ambrose. He might still be sleeping – the coward in her prayed that he was – but all the same she ought to go and check.

Sister Euphemia, greeting her at the door of the infirmary, knew without being told why she had come. 'He sleeps still,' she reported. 'That was a strong draught that Sister Tiphaine selected for him.'

'Send me word immediately he wakes,' Helewise said. 'I wish to be here to answer his questions.'

The infirmarer looked at her shrewdly. 'You think, my lady, that he will seek to lay blame on us?'

'His wife is dead,' Helewise replied neutrally. 'She came to us for help and she died. I do not believe that blame can fairly be laid on us, but he is grieving and grief makes for irrational accusations.' Her thoughts already running to one such accusation, Helewise gave the infirmarer a brief nod and turned to leave.

Then she returned to the church and knelt before the altar lost in one of the most fervent prayers she had offered up in a long time. If what she feared indeed came to pass, she had greater need of God's guarding presence at her side than she had ever had.

She was back in her room when Sister Caliste came to find her. With a deep bow, she said, 'My lady, the lord Ambrose is awake and is asking for you.'

'Thank you, Sister.' Helewise got to her feet. 'Please go and tell him that I am on my way.'

She waited until the young nun had gone, spent a few moments in prayer and then followed her.

Ambrose was out of bed and fully clothed. He wore a long tunic of chestnut brown over what looked like clean linen; he seemed to have had the presence of mind to prepare very carefully for his meeting with her and had, apparently, even had a shave.

He walked towards her up the central aisle of the infirmary and, after a courteous but brief greeting, said, 'My lady Abbess, I would talk privately with you. Let us step outside away from the ears of others' – he glanced over his shoulder at the many occupied cots, some of whose occupants were watching the scene with open-mouthed curiosity – 'and find a quiet corner where we shall not be interrupted.'

She found herself being steered out of the infirmary and into the sunshine. Regaining control – this indeed was a different man from the enfeebled daydreamer of yesterday! – she said firmly, 'Follow me. There is a bench we can use in the shade of the wall over there.'

She led him to the corner where the end of the stable

block overhung the herb garden. There was nobody about; Sister Martha could be heard working in the stables and there was no sign of the herbalist. She indicated that Ambrose should sit and then settled herself beside him.

She was tempted to break the lengthening silence with words of condolence but something made her refrain. Strangely – and surely mistakenly – she was receiving the impression that this was turning into a battle of wills. Well, if that were so, she could keep her peace longer than he could.

Eventually he said, 'My lady Abbess, my wife came here on the recommendation of Sir Josse d'Acquin to ask your help in her efforts to conceive my child. Now she is dead, it seems by poison. What have you to say?'

Helewise had not expected such thinly disguised animosity. She took a steadying breath and then said, 'Galiena asked for our help, as you say. She saw my infirmarer, Sister Euphemia, who offered both to talk to her and to examine her to see if any physical problem could be detected. This Galiena utterly refused. Sister Euphemia then consulted my herbalist, Sister Tiphaine, and they decided that the only thing they could do, not knowing of any specific problem, was to prepare a couple of general remedies that are believed to aid conception. I cannot tell you the details of these, but—'

'Galiena took these herbals?' he demanded.

'I think not,' she replied calmly, trying to ignore her racing heart. 'One was not quite ready and the other, which had already been given to her, seems not to have been drunk from.'

But his expression suggested that he did not believe her. 'My wife was most eager to conceive,' he said coldly. 'I think that, given a remedy that promised to help her in that desire, she could not have resisted the urge to take a dose of it immediately.' There was a pause then: 'I will see it,' he announced.

Bowing her head, Helewise said, 'It is back in Sister Tiphaine's room. Please, come with me.'

They stood up and walked the short distance to the herbalist's hut. Opening the door, Helewise pointed to the workbench, which was empty except for two small bottles.

'This one' – she pointed – 'was not given to Galiena. This one' – she picked up the other bottle and handed it to Ambrose – 'was briefly in her possession.'

Aware of movement behind her, she half-turned. Sister Tiphaine stood in the doorway. Behind her was Sister Euphemia and, at the rear, the tall, broad figure of Josse. Wondering how they had known she was there but, at the same time, hugely grateful for their presence, she turned back to Ambrose.

Intent on the moment, he gave no indication that he had noticed the trio standing behind her. He was holding the first remedy in one hand, staring intently at the stopper. 'Has this been opened?' he demanded.

'I do not know,' Helewise replied. 'Sister Tiphaine? Can you tell?'

Sister Tiphaine took the bottle from Ambrose. Looking at the top, she said, 'I can't say that it has or has not been opened. It might have been.' Then she held the bottle up to the light; the glass was dim and cloudy but by holding it so that the sun shone on it she was able to see the level of the contents. 'Nothing's been taken out of it. Or, if it has, only the smallest amount.'

'Enough to poison my wife,' Ambrose said.

There was a cry of protest, quickly stifled; Helewise thought it came from Sister Euphemia, since Sister Tiphaine, expressionless beside her Abbess, appeared to have been turned to stone.

'The remedy is not poisonous,' Helewise said gently. 'My lord, I understand your need to discover the cause of your wife's tragic death but I would beg you not to make hasty or false accusations.'

'You agree she died of poison?' he demanded, turning pain-filled eyes on her.

'I – it seems likely,' Helewise said.

'Then what else, pray tell me, can it have been?' he shouted.

'I do not know.' She was fighting to keep calm. 'Galiena said she was going to have a walk in the forest so it is possible she picked and ate something – a mushroom, some berries, perhaps – that proved lethal.'

'Hm.' He glared at her and she knew that he did not accept her explanation. She was not sure she blamed him. Then, holding up the bottle, he said, 'Let the herbalist prove that her work is not the source of the poison. She made it, let her drink it.'

Sister Tiphaine held out her hand to take the bottle. But Helewise stopped her.

Taking the bottle from Ambrose, she said quietly, 'It is one thing for the remedy's maker to have confidence in her work but I think you will agree, my lord, that for another to believe in its innocence is a greater test.' Taking out the stopper as she spoke, she added, 'I will drink it myself.'

Again, she sensed that someone behind her was protesting; this time she was sure it was Josse. He did more than make a verbal protest, however; she felt movement and then he was beside her and had taken a tight grip on the hand holding the bottle.

'My lady, is this wise?' he muttered. 'I know what faith you have in your herbalist but could it not be just this once that she has – that there has been—' He broke off.

She turned to him. She could see the anguish in his eyes and she wished she could say something to alleviate it. But in that moment she was Abbess of Hawkenlye and friendships – if friendship described what she and Josse shared – had to be put aside. 'Sir Josse, please let go of my hand,' she ordered.

He gave her one last despairing look that tore at her heart. Then he released her.

Before she had time to change her mind she put the bottle to her lips and took a large sip. She heard Sister Tiphaine gasp and mutter something – it sounded like, 'Go easy! It is strong!' – and then the very powerful taste of whatever it was with which she had just filled her mouth struck her so violently that every other sense temporarily shut down.

She swallowed hastily, feeling the burning sensation

that had begun on her tongue and the inside of her mouth now spread down her gullet. As the first heat subsided, she began to detect some of the elements making up the taste . . . garlic, clearly, and was it onion? Also caraway, wormwood, perhaps – anyway, something very spicy and bitter – and a fruity taste that she thought could be apple . . .

Swallowing again, she emptied her mouth. She was starting to salivate – with a flicker of dread she remembered the clear fluid that had poured from Galiena's mouth – but perhaps it was only the result of having drunk something so strongly and hotly flavoured.

She hoped so. Dear God, she hoped so.

She glanced round at the circle of people watching her. Josse's expression was too hard to bear and quickly she moved on to Sister Tiphaine, whose calm face seemed to say, *Do not worry. All is well.* Sister Euphemia, Helewise noted with an urge to giggle, had put out both arms as if preparing to catch her Abbess as she fell.

Lastly she turned her eyes to Ambrose. To her surprise, he no longer looked either angry or accusing; the expression on his lined old face looked like admiration.

Time passed. Then Sister Euphemia said tentatively, 'How do you feel, my lady?'

'I feel quite well, thank you,' Helewise replied. She felt a burp rise and tried to suppress it. Clearing her throat, she said, 'How long, Sister Tiphaine, would you estimate that a poison would take to work?'

'Hard to say,' Sister Tiphaine said gruffly. 'Depends

what it is. Some take a while, some kill immediately. In most cases, there will be symptoms that develop straight away.'

'As I say,' Helewise remarked sweetly, 'I feel quite well.'

'No burning of the lips and mouth?' Josse asked anxiously.

'None.' She smiled at him.

'No nausea?' Sister Euphemia demanded. 'You don't feel as how you want to be sick?'

'Not at all.'

They waited some more.

Helewise, whose relief was making her feel quite silly, wanted to laugh. They're all waiting to see if I collapse and die, she thought. They can't do anything until either I do or I don't.

Well, I'm not going to. I knew it would be safe and it was.

Straightening her back and squaring her shoulders, she turned to Ambrose. 'It is possible that I may suffer some reaction later,' she said somewhat frostily, 'and if that is the case, I shall certainly tell you.' No – that was absurd. 'You will be informed,' she amended. 'But for now I think that we must begin to look elsewhere for the source of whatever it was that poisoned Galiena.'

8

Josse, weak with what he prayed was not a premature relief, watched the Abbess walk steadily away from the herbalist's hut and back towards the Abbey buildings, Sister Euphemia at her side. She had announced that she must get on with the day's duties and he had overheard her say quietly to Ambrose Ryemarsh that she had already sent word to Father Gilbert, who had promised to come over to Hawkenlye as soon as he could.

Aye, Josse thought. There was the poor girl's burial to be arranged. He watched the old man who, straight-backed, was speaking to Sister Tiphaine. Was he, Josse wondered, apologising for having accused her of poisoning his wife? It was possible.

Then, as the herbalist went back inside her little room and shut the door, Ambrose turned to him. 'Forgive me, Josse, for not having greeted you before now,' he said, giving Josse a quick bow. 'My mind, I am afraid, was on other matters.' He sighed. 'I truly believed that we had the solution to this terrible misfortune, but it seems I was wrong.'

'I think so too, sir,' Josse said gently. 'Of course, it is possible for anyone to make a mistake, but I am of the firm opinion that Sister Tiphaine's scrupulous care and impressive reputation suggest that she is the last person to accuse of accidentally poisoning someone who sought her help.'

He wondered even as he spoke at his choice of the word accidentally; who would deliberately poison a patient?

But, even as he wondered, a frightening possibility occurred to him. Sister Tiphaine would not; he was as sure of that as he was of the sun rising each morning. But someone else might have done. A man, for example, whose mistress had conceived an unplanned child whose existence threatened to turn a pleasant dalliance into something altogether more serious . . .

No. No. The idea followed on a suspicion that had already been developing in his mind but, all the same, surely it was just too far-fetched to be credible.

Shaking his head as if to clear the unpleasant thoughts from his mind, he realised that Ambrose was speaking to him. 'I don't hold you to blame, Josse, for recommending the Hawkenlye nuns,' he said.

'I am glad of it,' Josse replied.

Ambrose gave a great sigh and then, eyeing Josse ruefully, said, 'I should, I suppose, prepare myself to meet this priest who will bury my wife. What say you, Josse? Is he a good man?'

'Aye.'

'Hm.' Ambrose did not look convinced. 'As I said at our last meeting, I have no great respect for the clergy. It is to be hoped that this Father—?'

'Father Gilbert,' Josse supplied.

'—that this Father Gilbert is the exception who will prove that my misgivings do not universally apply.'

'He is a good man,' Josse said. 'He will have been genuinely sorry when told of your wife's death and his prayers for her will be heartfelt.'

Ambrose studied him for a moment. Then: 'Thank you, Josse. Your words comfort me.'

'I am glad of it.'

Ambrose went on studying Josse, who became increasingly uncomfortable under the scrutiny. It was, he imagined, something like a mouse must feel when the kestrel hovers above, fixing it with fierce, unblinking eye.

Breaking the awkward silence – it was awkward for him, anyway – he said, 'Sir? Is there something else you would ask of me?'

'Yes, Josse, indeed there is.' Ambrose paused, then went on, 'I desire greatly to send word to my wife's kinfolk of her death. I would go to their manor myself only I must stay here. I need to be with her while yet I can,' he added in a murmur.

'I understand,' Josse said.

'Also there is the priest to see, and arrangements to discuss.' Ambrose's face darkened into a frown.

'I will ride to break the news to Galiena's family, if that is what you wish of me,' Josse offered.

'Will you?' Again, the fiercely intent look. 'Can I trust you to find the right words, Josse? They are a close and loving family and this will be a bitter blow for them.'

'I can only do my best, but you have my word that

I will try to be gentle and considerate,' Josse said with dignity.

Instantly Ambrose's hand was on his arm. 'I apologise, Josse. I did not mean to imply otherwise. It is merely that in circumstances such as these, when a man longs to perform a delicate task himself, it is hard to entrust it to another.'

Again Josse muttered, 'I understand.'

'You will go, then?' Ambrose appeared to need confirmation.

'Tell me where to go and I will set out straight away.'

In the event, it was not until after the noon meal that Josse set out. The Abbess, informed of the arrangement, gave him a look in which he read both compassion – presumably for the unpleasant task he had taken on himself – and, he thought, a certain admiration. Or perhaps the latter was merely wishful thinking. Either way, he recalled with pleasure that she had said she would keep him in her thoughts until his return and pray that he find the right words with which to inform Galiena's family that she was dead.

The fact that he had found her sitting in her chair and busy working had been immensely reassuring. Aye, it was still just possible that whatever she had drunk from the bottle meant for Galiena might yet work some harm in her but, with every hour that passed, surely that possibility grew less. Or so he fervently hoped.

She came to the stables to see him on his way.

Studying her closely, he perceived a faint flush in her cheeks. 'You are quite well, my lady?' he asked. 'You ate a good dinner? With – er, with no ill effects?'

'I am quite well, Sir Josse,' she agreed, smiling. 'I ate heartily and feel the better for it. My digestion, I assure you, has never been better. Do not worry,' she added kindly, 'I have suffered no hurt. The mystery of what caused Galiena's death is not to be so easily solved.'

'Aye, I fear you are right.' He remembered, against his will, that sudden moment of suspicion. Was it possible she had been poisoned deliberately? But – for surely his instinctive thought was miles from the truth – by whom? And why?

He finished fastening his small pack to Horace's saddle and, unhitching the reins, clucked to the horse to move on out into the sunshine.

'First things first, though,' the Abbess said encouragingly. 'You must complete your mission and I must make arrangements with Father Gilbert. We should bury the poor young woman as soon as we can, I think, for nothing is to be gained by waiting and also there is—' Abruptly she broke off but he was almost certain she had been going to say that there was also the hot weather to consider.

'Aye, my lady,' he said quietly. 'I know.'

She walked beside him as he led Horace to the gate. Then, picking up his dagger and sword from Sister Ursel in the porteress's little room beside the entrance and settling them in their sheaths at his belt, he swung himself up into the saddle and looked down at her.

'Good luck,' she said. 'Return to us soon.'

'I will, God willing.'

The echo of her soft 'Amen' stayed in his ears as he rode away.

Ambrose had given him clear directions for finding his way to the house of Galiena's kin. It lay to the north-east of the Ryemarsh estate and, approaching from Hawkenlye, Josse's quickest route was to cut across country north of Newenden, aiming for the little fledgling settlement of Small Hythe. 'Keep well above the inlet that flows down on its southern side,' Ambrose had said, 'for the stretch of water is tidal and can be treacherous, even when the weather has been dry.' Galiena's family home, he said, was to the north-east of Small Hythe; if necessary, Josse might ask for further directions there since, according to Ambrose, anyone could tell Josse where to find the house.

Galiena's father was called Raelf and his manor was at Readingbrooke. Pressed for further details, Ambrose would only say that Raelf's wife was named Audra and that there were four other daughters all younger than Galiena.

It was to this unsuspecting and, according to Ambrose, close-knit and loving family that Josse was now bound with such terrible news.

Despite the fine weather and the beauties of the June countryside, he could not find the smallest element of pleasure in the day.

He rode into Small Hythe in the late evening. He had not hurried; he had no intention of going on to

Readingbrooke until morning. He had vaguely thought that he would look for somewhere to put up for the night in Small Hythe; it was possible there might be an inn or he could seek out a friendly farmer willing to offer a night's accommodation in exchange for a modest payment. However, as the sun set in rich, burning shades of orange across the perfect, dark blue sky, he changed his mind. For one thing, there was nothing remotely like an inn in the tiny settlement of Small Hythe, which, as far as Josse could see in the fading light, consisted of a few wooden huts along a dried-up, muddy creek. For another thing, he knew he did not want company. All through the journey he had been thinking ahead to his meeting with Galiena's family and somehow his sombre cast of mind did not seem suitable for venturing into a tavern or a farmer's kitchen and making small talk.

No. He would make a private camp somewhere and keep his own company. He had a pair of thick blankets rolled up behind his saddle and it would not be the first time he had slept out of doors. Sister Basilia had made up a package of the best that Hawkenlye's kitchens could offer a traveller and he was already looking forward to tucking into the meats and the sweet pastries. There was also a small flagon of wine and Josse knew from long experience that the cellarer nun, Sister Goodeth, would not have provided for him anything but her best.

He rode slowly along the creek, the last of the setting sun behind him throwing his long shadow on ahead of him. He was on the creek's north bank – it seemed to run almost due west to east – and on his left side, the land rose in gentle folds up to where, to judge from Ambrose's directions, he guessed he would find Readingbrooke.

As he rode on, a new sound on the still air gradually permeated his consciousness. Drawing rein so as to listen, he tried to identify what it was. It grew steadily louder and, with a smile, he recognised what it was.

It was the sound of running water.

Dismounting and walking forward right to the edge of the creek, he looked down. What had appeared to be a dry stream bed with a soggy, muddy bottom was turning, quite quickly, into a narrow river. Gathering together what he knew of the marshlands – which was not much – he realised what had happened. Somewhere a long way off to the south and the east lay the sea. And the tide had turned.

He stood for some time watching the moving water. Looking back along the creek towards Small Hythe, he now noticed that wooden platforms had been constructed, extending out from the northern bank and over the water. Whatever the men of the settlement did there, it must, Josse concluded, depend to a degree on the water.

The sound was comforting. He decided to make his camp somewhere near enough to the creek so that he could continue to hear the water as he settled down for the night. It might just help him to sleep.

He had the soldier's knack of quickly and efficiently making himself comfortable in the field. Turning to his left, leading Horace now, he climbed a short, shallow slope that rose up to the side of a small stream flowing down to meet the creek. Where the slope levelled out, he found a sheltered spot between a length of hawthorn hedge and a gnarled old willow tree. If it should rain in the night – unlikely, Josse thought, since the sky was still clear and what wind there was came from off the land and not up from the south-west – then the thick foliage of the tree would shelter him. And the hawthorn, curving round in an arc from the distant line of the creek, would act as a windbreak if the breeze turned into something more spiteful.

He was not going to find anywhere better so he unsaddled Horace, took off the horse's bridle and, loosely holding a clump of the horse's mane, led him over to the stream, waiting patiently till he had drunk his fill. Then he took a length of rope from his pack and fashioned a rough head collar, fastening the end of the rope to an alder a few paces away along the hedge. Horace, used to such treatment, waited until Josse signalled with a slap on the horse's rump that he was finished, then ambled off and began grazing.

Josse unrolled his blankets and laid out the coarser one on the ground beneath the willow tree. The other one he would use to cover himself. Then, sitting down with his back to the tree's broad trunk, he opened up the neatly tied cloth that contained his supper and began eagerly to eat.

Before he settled for the night he took a last stroll down to the creek. In the hour that had elapsed since he last looked at the water, the level had risen considerably. The water was flowing fast, still busily filling up the creek, and Josse reckoned it must be a few hours yet till high tide. Then there would be that still time before the tide turned and the creek began to empty once more.

Well, he would be asleep by then. Yawning, he turned and walked back to his camp, unbuckling his sword belt as he paced up the slope. It seemed a quiet enough spot but, all the same, he would sleep with his dagger to hand and his sword within easy reach. It did not do to be careless.

He lay under his blanket looking up at the stars. Then, yawning again, he stopped fighting the heaviness in his eyelids and, turning on to his side, was soon asleep.

He was awake and ready for the day by the time there were any signs of activity along the creek at Small Hythe. He had washed his face and hands in the cold water of the little stream, watered Horace and fed him from the supplies brought with him and eaten his own breakfast from the remains of last night's supper. He was ready – or so he hoped – for whatever the day might bring.

He mounted Horace and rode the short distance back to where a group of three older men and a couple of lads had appeared and were standing on the bank staring at him, their mouths open. He wished them good day and the eldest of the men grunted something in reply. He wondered again what work they did in that out-of-the-way place but thought it best not to admit his ignorance by asking. Instead he said, 'Can you tell me the way to Readingbrooke? I wish to speak to Sir Raelf.'

The grunting man, who seemed to be the group's spokesman, said, 'That I can, sir. You follow the north bank a ways, you cross the stream you'll come to in a short while, then you'll take a turn on to your left hand up into the higher ground. Now you'll need to take care there a'cause it's right steep in places, but it's not near so dangerous now it's summer and dry as in winter when it's wet.' He grinned, showing pink gums empty of teeth save one that had worked its way across to the middle of his upper jaw. 'Now, you're with me so far, sir?'

'Aye,' Josse replied.

'Right, then.' The man seemed to be momentarily stuck for inspiration but then, as if recalling where he had got to, he said brightly, 'Then 'tis easy, for you follow the edge of the Hanging Wood till you find a track leading off to your right and, if you follow it right to its end, you'll find yourself at Readingbrooke, can't help it!'

Memorising the instructions, Josse nodded his thanks and, reaching into the soft leather purse on his belt, extracted a couple of coins and lobbed them to the man, who shot out a hand and deftly caught them.

'Much obliged,' the man said, touching the hand that was clenched around the coins to his forehead.

Josse wished the group good day and then, leaving them still staring at him, kicked Horace into a trot and rode away.

*   *   *

He reached Readingbrooke too soon, for he had still not worked out exactly what he was going to say to Galiena's family. But breaking the news would become no easier for waiting so, without pausing for thought, he rode on into the courtyard that opened out before Raelf de Readingbrooke's modest manor house and called out, 'Halloa! Is anybody at home?'

A woman with a sacking apron over a nondescript dark brown gown came out of a building to his right. From the sounds that followed her out, it appeared that it was a dairy and that she had been in the middle of milking.

'Yes?' she said, looking up at him curiously. 'What do you want?'

'I wish to speak to Sir Raelf and his wife,' Josse said.

'Who are you?' she asked.

'Josse d'Acquin.'

She nodded. 'You have the manor at New Winnowlands. You're a King's man, so they say.'

'Aye,' he said, to both statements.

'The master and the mistress are in the solar,' she said, 'together with the girls. Wait here. I'll tell them you wish to see them and I'll send someone out to tend to your horse.'

'Thank you.'

He slipped off Horace's back and, a short time later, a lad of about thirteen came out and shyly took the big horse's reins, leading him off into a shaded corner of the yard where there were tethering rings set in the wall and a large tub of water.

'Give him a drink, if you would,' Josse called after the lad, who nodded.

Then the woman was back and, beckoning to him, she led him up the steps and into the hall, which they crossed to reach another, narrower flight of stairs that circled up to a smaller room on a higher level. The room had wide windows facing south, whose leather hangings were at present fastened back, allowing the sunshine to stream in.

There was a long, narrow table placed in the middle of the room and along each side was a bench. At each end of the table were chairs, beautifully made of pale oak. In the larger chair sat a ruddy-faced, broad-shouldered man aged, Josse thought on first impression, about forty. In the other sat a woman, petite, brown-eyed, perhaps five or six years younger. On the benches sat their four daughters, two to a bench. All four girls were dark-haired like their father and had their mother's round face and ready smile. They were aged, Josse guessed, from about sixteen down to a toddler of three or four. The woman and two of the girls were stitching at fine embroidery; the littlest child was being helped in a simpler piece of work by one of her sisters. The man appeared to be doing nothing except watch his women folk.

At Josse's approach, the man got to his feet – he was quite short in stature – and said, 'I am Raelf de Readingbrooke. We welcome you, Sir Josse d'Acquin, and wonder to what we should ascribe your visit?'

Oh, it was difficult! Turning from the courteously

spoken Raelf to his smiling wife, Josse regretted more than ever the task he had to do. But do it he must; he had made a promise.

He said, 'Sir Raelf, I am afraid that I bring bad news. Perhaps you and I should speak privately . . . ?'

Hurrying forward and grabbing hold of Josse's arm, Raelf said, 'Bad news?'

'It concerns your daughter Galiena,' Josse murmured in his ear.

Raelf muttered something – it might have been, 'Oh, dear God.' Then he said, 'Tell me. What has happened?'

'She is dead,' Josse whispered. 'I am so sorry.'

'Dead.' The colour blanched from Raelf's face. 'Oh, but I cannot believe it. She is young, healthy! You are quite certain that it is she, my Galiena, who has died?' His voice broke on the word.

'Aye,' Josse said. 'I saw her with my own eyes.' He pictured the beautiful face, grossly swollen and distorted in death.

Raelf coughed and cleared his throat. 'How did this happen? How do you, Sir Josse, come to be the bearer of this ill news?'

'She had gone to Hawkenlye Abbey to consult the nuns who tend the sick there. She – it appears that somehow she took poison.'

'Poison! Was this some remedy that she was given?'

Josse could understand the poor man's puzzlement but he knew he must deny that suggestion instantly. 'No, it cannot have been the remedy that affected her for someone else drank of the same substance and she'

– the Abbess's rosy face swam before his mind's eye – 'she is quite well.'

'Then what was it?' Raelf asked plaintively.

'We do not yet know.' Josse spoke gently. 'But we will find out, Sir Raelf, be sure of that.'

Tears were forming in Raelf's dark eyes. Finding it impossible to witness such silent agony, Josse dropped his own eyes. Then Raelf said, 'You say she went for treatment. Do you know for what?'

Josse looked up. 'She – her husband, the lord Ambrose, and she were unable to – er, she found that she could not conceive the child that they both wanted so much. She had tried certain simples that she made herself, I understand, but to no avail. She hoped that the skills of the Hawkenlye infirmarer and herbalist might be more extensive.'

'So she was barren?' Raelf said.

Shrinking from the harsh word, Josse nodded.

'Dear Lord, what irony!' Raelf said with sudden harshness. Then his face crumpled. A sob broke from him as, covering his eyes with his hands, his shoulders began to shake. His wife, who had, Josse now saw, been steadily approaching so that now she stood just behind Raelf, gently touched his arm, at which he turned and bent to bury his face on her shoulder.

Her arms going round him, one hand smoothing and soothing his back as if he were a small, distressed child, Audra de Readingbrooke said softly, 'He will take this hard, Sir Josse, for Galiena was his eldest daughter and he loved her dearly.'

'Aye. I am so sorry,' Josse said inadequately.

Audra smiled faintly. 'Thank you. And thank you, too, for your willingness to bring us such terrible news.'

'Ambrose would have come to tell you himself and indeed he very much wanted to,' Josse said hastily, 'only he remains at Hawkenlye Abbey, where he must make – er, make certain arrangements with the priest and the Abbess concerning – er, concerning her burial.'

'Of course,' said Audra, her eyes bright with tears. 'A dreadful task, for an old man to see his young wife into the ground before him.'

'Aye.'

Sensing his awkwardness, Audra wiped her eyes and said, 'Sir Josse, may I suggest that you leave us for a while? There is much that we would ask you but first we must break the news to the girls' – she gestured behind her to the four daughters sitting with anxious faces at the table – 'and take what comfort we may in one another. Would you be so kind as to wait for us down in the hall? Ask Tilde to fetch you some refreshments. We shall not keep you waiting for long.'

Already stepping gratefully back towards the stair, Josse said, too loudly and too eagerly, 'Take your time, lady, please, take as long as you need!' Catching her understanding glance, he smiled back at her and, more softly, added, 'I'll be waiting when you are ready to talk to me.'

Then, hurrying down the stairs so fast that he all but slipped, he emerged into the cool hall and left the family to their grief.

9

He did not want anything to eat or to drink, although a pretty young maidservant in clean white cap and apron came out from another door in the wide hall and asked him if she could fetch anything for him.

When she had gone, as quietly as she had arrived, he wandered across to the doorway and stood looking out over the woodland and pasture that made up Raelf de Readingbrooke's lands. There was so much to think about – was Galiena poisoned? What could have been the motive? Was there any substance at all to Josse's vague suspicions? – but somehow, here in the house where she had lived, he could not bear to think of her dead. Instead he pictured her happy face that day at Ryemarsh.

And, in time, the tears that he had not yet shed for her formed in his own eyes too.

It was quite a long time later that the family came down from the solar to join him in the hall. It was clear that they had all been weeping and, indeed, the smallest child was still sobbing quietly around the thumb that she had stuck in her mouth for comfort. She stood close to her mother, who from time to time put down a gentle hand to stroke her youngest daughter's smooth brown hair.

Audra summoned the servant girl and spoke in low tones. The girl nodded and disappeared, to return a short time later with a tray laden with bread, cold meats, sauces, a jug of wine and some cups. While this was being set out on the long table at the back of the hall, Josse had a moment to study Galiena's family.

Raelf appeared to be more affected by his eldest daughter's death than any of them, for he made no attempt to help his wife organise the cups and the platters and find benches to sit on. He merely stood to one side frowning in perplexity as if saying to himself, what on earth is all this fuss about? Or, Josse thought, perhaps he always left it to his clearly capable wife to see to everything that occurred within the house. If so, he was not the first man to do so.

His ruddy face was pale now and the short man's stance – shoulders back, chest thrown out, as if proclaiming to the world that, although lacking in inches, he was as good if not better than the next man – had gone. Now Raelf stood slumped, his grief written all over him.

The eldest girl – well, virtually a woman now, Josse conceded, and probably about to follow in her sister's footsteps and find herself a husband – had hurried to help her mother, gently taking the heavier objects from Audra's hands with a smile and a quick word. She was graceful in her movements and modest in her dress and hairstyle; the neck of her gown was cut high and its skirt was widely flaring. Her hair – brown and thick – was coiled at the back of her head and covered with a neat square of snowy-white linen, starched to an impressive stiffness. However, neither cap nor gown could disguise the girl's figure: she was, Josse thought, one of the most voluptuous young women he had had the pleasure of meeting. It would be a lucky man who took her to bed as his wife.

The two other daughters were aged about thirteen and eight and, other than obeying meekly when ordered by their mother to put the benches up to the table, said and did little. Like their sisters, they too were dark-haired, although one had a tinge of auburn in her long plaits.

Audra, Josse realised now, was pregnant. The high waist of her gown and her decorative linen apron concealed her condition to a degree and contrived to make it not apparent when she was standing still. However, in organising the refreshments she had occasionally to stretch across the table, and then the tightening of the garments across her body made the bump plain to see.

Audra was, Josse reckoned, in her early to mid thirties. Her family certainly stretched across a wide age range, for the next child was not yet born and the first had been eighteen years old. So Galiena would have been born when Audra was about fifteen.

It was quite possible. On the other hand, Audra might be older than she looked. Ah well, Josse concluded, it was hardly a concern of his. Watching the round, capable little woman as she issued quiet orders that were instantly obeyed – which earned her Josse's admiration all over again – something, however, was nagging at him . . .

Before he had time to work out what it was, he was summoned to the table and invited to eat. He had not thought himself hungry but, on seeing the spread, he realised that he was. The family served him with impeccable manners, one daughter filling his cup, another breaking bread for him, a third piling his platter with meats and piquant, highly spiced sauces. When everyone had been served, Raelf cleared his throat, closed his eyes and said a simple prayer. Besides giving thanks for the food, he prayed for Galiena and, when he had finished, they all said softly, 'Amen'.

Now that the family were at table, Raelf seemed to take command once more. He said firmly, 'There is a time for grieving, and it will be long and sorrowful for us. But we must also remember the living, especially Sir Josse, who has ridden so far to bring us this dread news, and also my wife, who is in particular need of nourishment.' He met Audra's eyes and they exchanged a smile. 'So, one and all, put aside your sadness and let us eat.'

He picked up his knife, cut himself a good-sized chunk of ham, put it on a piece of bread and, pushing it into his mouth, began to chew. One by one the girls, Audra and Josse followed his example and, for a time, there was silence in the hall other than the normal domestic sounds of a family at their meal.

When the food and drink had been cleared away, Audra told her eldest girl to take her sisters off outside.

'Take them on a wild flower hunt,' she suggested, 'a new ribbon for the one who finds the most.' Then, when the girls had gone, Raelf came to sit beside Josse, and Audra resumed her place at the end of the table.

'Now, if you please, tell us how she died,' Raelf said.

Josse drew breath and said, 'I regret that there is little I can add to what I have already told you. I was taken to meet the lord Ambrose and Galiena by—' No. Perhaps it was better not to mention Brice. 'I was invited to Ryemarsh, I think, because Ambrose knew of my connection with Hawkenlye Abbey and wished to ask my advice. He and Galiena were, as I said, anxious that she should conceive a child and Galiena's own remedies had been ineffective.'

'She was skilled in the use of herbs,' Audra put in. 'It was one of the things we most missed when she wed Ambrose and left us. Although in truth she did not ignore us when she became a wife but was always ready to hurry back to give advice and make up simples for us when we fell sick.'

Raelf nodded. 'Aye, she remained a daughter of the house even though she was mistress of her own,' he said sadly. 'But please, Sir Josse, continue.'

'Er – I told Ambrose that the nuns of Hawkenlye were rightly famed for their care and their skill, and that there was also the precious holy water, renowned for effecting miracles. He decided that he and Galiena should visit the Abbey and she was keen to set out straight away. Ambrose had matters to attend to at Ryemarsh but, because Galiena was so eager, it was arranged that she should ride on ahead with her woman servant and a lad. She was cared for well at Hawkenlye and two preparations were made up for her. She expressed the desire to return home as soon as she could but had to wait because one remedy was not quite ready. While she waited, she passed the time by going for a long walk on the fringes of the forest and, while she was absent, Ambrose arrived. The journey seemed to have affected him and a bed was found for him in the infirmary.'

'What was the matter with him?' Raelf asked.

'Oh – I believe he was exhausted,' Josse said. He could not honestly recall what he had been told. 'Confused, I think.'

Audra looked puzzled. 'It does not sound typical of Ambrose,' she said with a frown. 'He's a strong man still, well able to ride all day without any ill effects.' She looked at Josse, a faint smile replacing the frown. 'We were a little shocked when Galiena expressed her desire to marry a man so much older than herself but, as we came to know him, we understood what she saw in him. He has a sort of power in him, does he not? An air of command.'

'Aye, he does,' Josse agreed. He, too, had been surprised at the news of Ambrose's apparent collapse. Even more so in the light of the fact that he seemed to be quite himself again the next day.

'So, Galiena was out walking and Ambrose in the infirmary,' Raelf resumed. 'Please continue, Sir Josse.'

'The nuns went to the Abbey church for Vespers, leaving a small staff of lay nurses on duty in the infirmary.' He concentrated on remembering the

Abbess's careful account of that crucial time. 'Afterwards, Ambrose said that Galiena had been to see him and that she had massaged his painful hands with some of her special lotion.'

'So she had come back from her walk?' Audra asked.

'It is not certain, my lady,' Josse replied. 'There is some possibility that Ambrose dreamt it. He was, they say, very drowsy. But someone had indeed been treating his hands for the lotion could still be detected on the skin.'

'Nobody else saw her?' Raelf demanded.

'No, unfortunately not. As I say, she could easily have slipped in unobserved while most of the nursing staff were at Vespers.'

'Hm.' Raelf looked thoughtful. 'Then what happened?'

'The Abbess Helewise visited Ambrose and while she was at his bedside Galiena came staggering into the infirmary. She was having difficulty breathing, her face was swollen and she was in great distress. The infirmarer rushed to her aid but it was too late and there was nothing she could do.'

There was silence for a moment. Then Audra whispered, 'Did she suffer much?'

Josse looked at her. 'I am told not, my lady. Whatever overcame her acted swiftly.'

'Was it poison?' Raelf asked, his voice gruff.

'We think so. There was a suggestion that she might have eaten berries or mushrooms in the forest and that one of them contained the deadly toxin that killed her.'

'Impossible,' Audra stated flatly. 'Galiena knew every berry and every type of fungus that is found in the region. Why, one of the first lessons she taught her sisters was how to recognise poisonous plants! Given the rampant curiosity of my four, I've had reason to thank her for it more than once, I can tell you!'

My four. Again something stirred in Josse's mind.

But Raelf interrupted the thought. 'Is that the only explanation that Hawkenlye can offer?' he asked. 'That a woman famous for her herbal skills inadvertently ate a death-cap mushroom or a handful of deadly nightshade berries? I think not.' Then, after the briefest of pauses: 'The sorcerer's berry does not produce its fruit until late summer. And surely the weather has been too dry for the death-cap, which does not normally appear until autumn.'

'Aye,' Josse agreed heavily. He had always doubted the explanation anyway. 'Aye, you're right.'

'There is truly no doubt but that the remedies prepared for her could not have hurt her?' Audra asked.

'None whatever, my lady,' Josse assured her. 'One she had not even been given, the other she probably had not had time to drink from. Just in case she did, someone else sampled it and she took no harm.'

'Who was it? The nun who made it?' Raelf asked with a certain belligerence.

'No,' Josse said quietly. 'It was Abbess Helewise.'

Audra's brown eyes widened. Her husband, who had the grace to look slightly shamefaced, said, 'She has great confidence in her herbalist's work, then.'

'Indeed,' Josse agreed.

The three fell silent. Now that he was not being
called upon to recount the tale of Galiena's death and
that, for the time being anyway, the anxious questions
had ceased, Josse had a moment to make some sense
of the scramble of impressions he had formed. And,
at last, he knew what it was that had been bothering
him. Now all that remained was finding a tactful way
to discover if he was right.

There came the sound of voices and then the four
girls were at the door. Behind them, accompanied
by a grave-faced boy of about nine or ten and a
pretty, bright-eyed girl a little younger, was a woman.
Her smooth face was framed by barbette and light
veil, under which her thick, fair hair was coiled in
plaits around the crown of her head and down over
her ears. She was quite tall and her figure was neat
and slim. In the tumult of all that was going on
about her, the sea-green eyes held an expression of
serenity.

Audra got up to greet her and, in a low voice,
asked her something, in reply to which the woman
nodded, putting her arm round Audra and pulling
her close in a reassuring hug. It was likely, Josse
thought, that Audra had just confirmed that the newcomer had been told the grim news. As they stood
together, the affection between them was apparent
and Josse wondered if they were sisters. Turning to
Josse, Audra said, 'Sir Josse, this is Isabella de Burghay,
my daughters' aunt, and these are her children, Roger
and Marthe.'

Isabella inclined her head gracefully and said,

'Greetings, Sir Josse. You have taken on the unpleasant role of bearer of ill tidings, I understand.'

'Aye, my lady.' He stood up. It was something more than courtesy that prompted the movement; in the back of his mind was forming the thought that, with the arrival of the calm and sensible-looking Isabella de Burghay – she had been introduced as the girls' aunt, so presumably he was right about her being Audra's sister – perhaps he could slip away. The Lord knows, he thought, I'd like to well enough.

Raelf stood up too. Turning to Josse, he said, 'Forgive me if my questions were too blunt and delivered too forcefully, Sir Josse. As my sister-in-law says, yours was not a pleasant task and then, having performed it with such tact and kindness, you were faced with my suspicions and my scepticism.'

'Both of which I understand and for which I readily excuse you,' Josse assured him.

Raelf nodded. Then he said, quietly so that Josse alone would hear, 'You are not going to let it rest, Sir Josse?'

'No.'

'Aye,' Raelf said with a faint smile. 'I know of your reputation and they tell me that you do not give up until you are satisfied.'

Wondering just which of his exploits had reached the ears of the family at Readingbrooke, Josse said, hoping he was not promising more than he could achieve, 'I will do my utmost to find out why your daughter died, Sir Raelf. And when I do, I will come and tell you.'

Raelf looked at him for a moment. Then, with a nod, said, 'Nobody could offer more.'

The women and the girls had gathered together at the far end of the hall, Audra and her sister sitting down. Isabella, obviously a beloved aunt, was cradling the smallest Readingbrooke child on her lap and the second youngest was sitting at her feet. Her son, Josse noticed, was standing on the edge of the group glaring across the hall towards his uncle as if he resented having to stay with the women and longed to be allowed to join the men.

The family needed to be together, he thought, without the presence of outsiders. He said to Raelf, 'It's time I was on my way. If I leave now, I can be at my own house at New Winnowlands before dusk.'

'Of course,' Raelf said at once. 'I am sorry that we have detained you for so long. I will come out to see you on your road.'

Not wishing to disturb the womenfolk, Josse said as they crossed the hall, 'Would you thank your wife for her hospitality and wish her and the ladies goodbye for me?'

Glancing at the group of dark and fair heads all leaning together as the women and girls talked and comforted each other, Raelf said, understanding, 'I will.'

Out in the yard, Horace stood unsaddled. Someone had rubbed him down and watered him and he looked half-asleep. Raelf looked vaguely around for the saddle and then said, 'Jack will have put it away safely somewhere.

Excuse me, Sir Josse, while I seek him out.'

Josse waited, leaning a shoulder comfortably against Horace and absently patting the horse's neck. Hearing light footsteps from behind him, he turned and saw Audra hurrying across the courtyard.

'My lady, I am sorry, I did not wish to disturb you to say goodbye—' he began, but she held up a hand to stop him.

'I wanted to speak to you before you leave, Sir Josse,' she said. The light brown eyes were fixed on his and she added, 'There is more to this than at first it seems, I think.'

Instantly he felt guilty. There was much that he had left out of his account: why had Galiena arrived alone? Why had she not told the Hawkenlye nuns that Ambrose would be joining her there? Why had she been so reluctant to be examined and helped by Sister Euphemia? Why had Josse been so disturbed by Brice's strangely excited behaviour that day at Ryemarsh? And, most crucial of all, why had Galiena gone for treatment for her barrenness when she was already pregnant?

Aware that Audra was studying him closely, he said awkwardly, 'My lady, I am sorry if you feel that I have been less than frank, but—'

Again she stopped him. This time, with a rueful smile, she said, 'Oh, no, Sir Josse. It is not you that I accuse but us.' Then, glancing around as if to ensure that they were alone – Raelf's voice could be heard somewhere inside, calling out, 'Jack! Jack! Where the devil has the lad got to now?' – she said softly, 'There are things that I believe you ought to be told.'

'Ah. Oh.' He did not know what to say.

Her smile deepened fleetingly as if she were amused at his confusion. But then her face straightened and, staring into his eyes, she said, 'You have, I think, drawn some conclusions of your own, for I have observed how you were studying us.'

Deciding to repay her frankness with honesty of his own, he said, 'Aye, my lady. I met Galiena but once, and on that occasion I took note of her appearance. And, truth to tell, I cannot but conclude that she could not have been of the same parentage as your four girls, for there is a uniformity to their appearance that suggests the perpetration of a strong family likeness. In addition, all four resemble their parents. You and Sir Raelf. Also I note that you said Galiena taught *your four*' – he emphasised the words – 'how to distinguish poisonous plants. Finally, madam, I have to say that, had you been Galiena's mother, you would have had to be a very young bride.'

Making a small bow as if in thanks for the implied compliment, Audra said, 'You guess rightly. Raelf was married before but his wife died. Galiena was their child and she was less than a year old when Matilda succumbed to a winter fever. Matilda was never strong, or so I am told, and her poor health caused many problems.'

She was looking at Josse expectantly, as if she thought he might read more into her words than their immediate meaning. 'Ah. I see,' he said, although he was sure he did not.

Audra was still watching him. Suddenly and quite unexpectedly she asked, 'Sir Josse, are you acquainted with Brice of Rotherbridge?'

Shocked, Josse said without pausing to think, 'Aye, lady. He is a neighbour of mine.' Belatedly he added, 'Why do you ask?'

But she shook her head. 'It does not matter. It is of my own family that I would speak. Raelf and I met at Isabella's house – her husband was still alive then but he died eight years later in a hunting accident. Raelf had recently lost his wife and was faced with raising a small, motherless daughter. At first, I admit, my feelings for him were more dutiful than loving and the main impulse in marrying him was because I had fallen for his baby daughter. But love soon followed, Sir Josse, for Raelf is a good man and has been the best husband I could have wished for.'

'I am glad to hear it,' Josse murmured.

'Our own children soon came along,' she continued, a happy, reminiscent smile on her plump face, 'all daughters, as you see. My Emma is soon to be betrothed, but we shall still have Bertha, Alda and little Ewise to love and for my husband to spoil.' She shot a sideways glance at Josse and, blushing faintly, said quietly, 'And soon there will be another baby in the cradle. Perhaps it will be a boy this time.'

Embarrassed, Josse muttered some appropriate sentiments expressing the hope that mother and child would fare well.

She laughed softly, putting a kindly hand on his arm.

'Thank you. Childbed holds no great fears for me any more and I am thankful to say that the good Lord seems to look kindly on my babies and He bestows on them strength and good health.'

'May He continue to do so,' Josse said, and she murmured 'Amen'.

He thought she had finished. He was looking around for Raelf, the stable lad and the missing saddle when she said softly, 'Sir Josse, there is one final thing.'

He turned to her and the grave expression on her face almost made him fearful. 'What is it, my lady?'

She studied him for a moment as if still uncertain whether or not to make this last confidence. Then, apparently making up her mind, she said, 'Raelf's first wife's health was such that she could not conceive. She, however, did not seek a cure for her barrenness for, according to Raelf, she feared pregnancy and childbirth and believed herself insufficiently strong to endure the process.' There was the faintest touch of contempt in Audra's voice, as if the four times proven mother looked down with scornful pity on her feeble and unsatisfying predecessor. 'For her, another solution had to be found,' she went on. 'They decided to adopt a child.'

'Galiena,' Josse said.

'Quite so. Galiena.'

Aye, he thought. It made sense. This unknown, dead Matilda would have had to be tall, pale and blonde to have given birth to Galiena, and even then the girl would have had to favour her mother entirely with nothing inherited from her squat, dark father.

Galiena was adopted. No wonder she looked nothing like the rest of her family.

There were two more questions to ask. Whether or not the answers had any relevance whatsoever to Galiena's death would remain to be seen, but in any case Josse had to know.

He said, 'Who are her real parents? And where did she come from?'

But Audra shook her head. 'I cannot help you with the first question for I do not know.' She frowned. 'I asked Raelf a hundred times back in the early days, for as Galiena grew, her remarkable looks emerged and I was ever most curious as to who had borne her. But Raelf would not tell me.'

'Did he give you any reason?' Josse asked.

'Not really. He used to say that it was for the best if we – and Galiena – put her past behind us. I kept at him for a little longer but then my own babies started arriving and I was too busy to care any more. Galiena was ours, just as my own girls are, and that was that.'

Josse thought back and then said, 'You said you could not answer the first question, my lady.' With his hopes rising, he went on, 'What of the second?'

She smiled. 'I can tell you a place name, nothing more. At least I have always assumed that it is a place name.' She looked doubtful.

'How do you come to know it?' he asked.

'Hm? Oh, I overheard Raelf one day. He was speaking to our priest – it was when my Emma was to be baptised – and Father Luke said something like, you won't be needing any more visits to the Saxon Shore now, Raelf, with one of your own in the cradle!'

'The Saxon Shore?'

'Yes. I believe it means over on the east coast, in the area beyond the Great Marsh. Father Luke said the name of the actual place, too.'

Josse waited an instant, then prompted, 'Aye?'

'Yes. It's a place where the waves and the tides used to lap up against a cliff and where long ago men constructed a fort that overlooked the narrow seas. Only now the fort lies in ruins, the sands have built up and there is marshland where the waters once were.' Audra hesitated. Then, in a whisper, she said, 'It is called Deadfall.'

And, watching her anxious face, he wondered why, as she spoke the name, he should feel as if a cold hand had closed sharp-nailed fingers around his throat.

10

Helewise had not expected that Josse would return from his journey to Galiena's kin the next day; even for one who travelled as quickly as Josse did when need pressed, it would have been asking too much. She would, however, have welcomed his presence at Hawkenlye that day for it was the day they buried Galiena.

It was the third day since the girl's death. The weather continued hot but now there was humidity in the air that spoke of a possibility of storms ahead. Small black biting flies had appeared – clouds of them – and it was not the time of year to leave a dead body unburied.

They interred her in the Abbey's burial ground and, joined by the grieving husband, the servant lad and the woman, Aebba, the Hawkenlye community prayed all together for her soul.

Later, Helewise was sitting alone in her room when there was a knock at the door and, in answer to her quiet 'Come in', Sister Euphemia appeared.

'I hope I am not disturbing you, my lady?' the infirmarer asked.

Since Helewise sat before a table quite empty of ledgers, documents, parchments or anything else, the question was courteous but superfluous. 'Not at all, Sister. I was thinking about Galiena.'

'I have been, too.' Sister Euphemia paused, then, as if only after reflection, went on, 'I've had an idea.'

'Oh, yes?' Helewise looked up into the infirmarer's lined face.

'About how it came to be that she came to us to help her conceive when she was already pregnant.'

'Yes, that's rather what I thought you meant,' Helewise murmured.

'See,' Sister Euphemia said, eagerness creeping into her voice, 'I've been looking at it logically. If a couple that consists of an old man and a young wife have a job getting her with child, then you'd probably jump to the conclusion that the fault lay with the old man. Wouldn't you?'

'Well, you might,' Helewise allowed. 'It would seem the more likely explanation.'

'Exactly! Well, supposing that's what Galiena thought too? She knew a bit about herbs, so we're told, so maybe she also understood the workings of her own body rather better than many young women. She might have known herself to be fit, healthy and regular in her courses and, that being the case, she'd have reckoned that the problem was with her old husband's seed.' Leaning forward confidentially, she said in a whisper, 'They do say the vigour goes out of it when a man comes towards the end of a long, *active* life, if you take my meaning, my lady.'

From the way the infirmarer stressed *active*, Helewise was all too afraid that she did. Banishing firmly from her mind the picture of Ambrose in a succession of beds with a succession of women, bouncing away as if his very life depended on it, she said, 'Indeed, Sister. Do go on.'

'Well, what if this young wife truly wants to have a child, both to please her husband and for her own sake, and decides to take matters into her own hands? She was a comely girl, Galiena, and I would judge also a bright one. I don't imagine she'd have found it too difficult to find someone suitable. Then all she has to do is admit the young man discreetly into her arms – swearing him to secrecy, naturally – and go on doing so until he's done the trick for her and she knows herself to be pregnant. Then comes the really clever bit!'

Helewise, who had already guessed, did not want to spoil the infirmarer's moment and so she said encouragingly, 'Yes? And what is that?'

'The lass begs to come here, to Hawkenlye, she takes the waters, prays a bit and goes off armed with a couple of Sister Tiphaine's concoctions. She hurries back home, where she encourages old Ambrose into her bed as often as he's willing to be persuaded, then, before a month's passed, says, oh! How wonderful! I've missed my courses, my breasts are swelling like ripe fruit, I must be pregnant! Thank the Lord for Hawkenlye!'

Helewise nodded slowly. 'And if the baby were to arrive a few weeks early she would merely say, as doubtless many a woman does, that the child was a little premature.'

'Exactly!' The infirmarer folded her arms, her face triumphant. 'What do you think, my lady?'

'I think it is entirely possible and quite likely,' Helewise said. 'But tell me, Sister, do you have anything to support this interpretation of events?'

'Nothing whatsoever,' Sister Euphemia replied cheerfully. 'Other than two decades of experience of human beings.'

Helewise gave her a warm smile. She both admired and loved the infirmarer; for her skill, her tender care of her patients, for her wisdom. Most of all for the fact that, although she had seen the depths to which people could sink and the terrible harm they were capable of doing to one another, she did not condemn. She was happy to leave that to God and, even so, Helewise thought, Sister Euphemia would always expect God to understand that sometimes men and women just couldn't help themselves and hope that He would not deal with them too harshly.

'I never underestimate your experience, Sister,' she said. 'But I do not know how we should set about proving this theory of yours, though.'

'I'm not sure we should try,' the infirmarer replied. 'The poor girl's dead. Perhaps we ought to let her secrets die with her.'

'Yes,' Helewise said slowly. 'It is only that I am thinking of whoever it is whose child she carried. If we are right and there *was* a lover, what will he be thinking now? Will he be waiting for her, expecting her return, worrying that, having got her pregnant, he is now to be dismissed totally from her life?'

'He may not have wanted anything but to bed her,' the infirmarer said shrewdly.

'That is, of course, possible. Still, I cannot but help picturing him.'

'You've a kind heart, my lady,' Sister Euphemia said. 'If you're right, news will spread to the young lad soon enough, I would guess. Anyway, how on earth would we set about finding him to tell him?'

'You are quite right, Sister, it would be impossible. And, indeed, we may have imagined it all wrong; Galiena may have been innocently pregnant by her husband and just not realised.'

'Hmm. It's always possible, as I said at the time.' Disbelief was written all over the infirmarer's face but she managed not to express it.

'Thank you for bringing your thoughts to me,' Helewise said. 'As always, you reason soundly.'

'That's kind of you, my lady. Now, if you'll excuse me, I must return to my patients.'

'Of course.'

Helewise sat deep in thought for some time after Sister Euphemia had gone. Then, making up her mind, she went to seek out three people.

First she found Ambrose. After burying Galiena, he had gone down to the Vale with Brother Firmin; he seemed to find comfort in the old monk's kindly and undemanding company. Ambrose had announced that, together with his two servants who were attending him, he would like to stay on at Hawkenlye for a few days and he was welcomed as a guest with nobody

asking him for an explanation. He had been offered
the comfort of a bed up in the Abbey guest quarters,
but he preferred, he said, to put up in the simpler
accommodation down in the Vale with the monks and
the pilgrims who had come to take the waters. A space
had been found for him with the lay brothers, while
Aebba and the young manservant were lodged in the
pilgrims' shelter.

When Helewise went to see Ambrose, he was sitting
beside Brother Firmin and the carpenter, Brother
Urse, while Brother Urse mended a rickety bench
and Brother Firmin helped by handing him the tools.
Seeing her approach, Ambrose got up and came to
meet her.

'My lady Abbess, were you looking for me?' he
asked.

'Indeed. I was thinking, my lord, that nobody has
yet informed your household of your wife's death.
Perhaps you would like to arrange to do this?'

'It is a charitable thought, my lady,' he answered
gravely. Thinking for a moment, he said, 'I could send
the lad, I suppose, although I hesitate to make him the
bearer of such bad news, for he is rough in his ways.'

'I will ask two of the brothers, if you would prefer,'
Helewise offered, ashamed even as she spoke of her
duplicity. 'Safer, in any case, for two to ride together
than for you to send your lad by himself.'

Ambrose studied her closely. Keeping her expression
wide-eyed and innocent, she stared right back. Then
abruptly he nodded. 'Very well, my lady. Thank you.'

Then, as if such brief consideration of matters he

preferred not to dwell on were more than enough, he gave her a brief bow and returned to the bench-mending.

Helewise next sought out Brother Saul and Brother Augustus. 'Come with me,' she said to them, 'I have a job for you.'

As they walked either side of her back up to the Abbey, she explained.

'I have told the lord Ambrose that I am sending you to his manor of Ryemarsh to inform his household of his wife's death,' she said quietly; there was nobody else on the path but, all the same, she felt the need to keep her voice down. 'But in fact I want you to act as my eyes, if you will.'

'What do you wish us to see for you, my lady? Saul asked.

She paused, trying to think how to phrase it tactfully while not giving away her suspicions; nobody but herself, the infirmarer, Sister Caliste and Josse knew that Galiena had been pregnant and she intended to keep it that way.

'I wish,' she said eventually, 'that you try to gain an impression of the sort of life that was lived at Ryemarsh when Galiena was alive. Whether Ambrose and his wife were happy together, whether they entertained many visitors, whether either of them had close friends. Men or women.' She tried to sound casual. 'That sort of thing,' she added lamely.

'You want us to ask some clever questions of the servants and have a bit of a nose around?' Augustus asked.

Saul began a reproof: 'Gus! You must not—', but Helewise put a hand on his arm to stop him. Giving Saul a smile, she then turned to Augustus and said, 'Yes, Gus. That is precisely what I want.'

Josse returned to Hawkenlye the next day. He left New Winnowlands early and was riding through the Abbey gates as the community were in church for Sext. Leaving Horace in the stables – a young lay brother rather nervously took the big horse's reins in Sister Martha's absence – Josse decided that, while he waited, he would stroll off down to the Vale to stretch his legs.

There was a group of pilgrims in the shelter or, more accurately, just outside it, sitting in the shade of the chestnut trees. The noon sun was strong and all of them – there were five men, seven women and four children – looked exhausted by the sultry heat. Josse nodded a greeting and walked on to the monks' shelter.

There he found Ambrose. The woman Aebba was with him; it seemed that she had just brought him fresh linen. She gave Josse a quick and, he thought, somewhat furtive glance then, at a nod from Ambrose, she hurried out of the shelter and off up the path towards the Abbey.

Josse said straight away, 'I have visited your late wife's kinfolk, my lord, and told them the news. They were greatly saddened, of course, and they send their condolences to you.'

Ambrose studied him. 'Thank you, Josse,' he said

quietly. He sighed. 'She is buried now, my poor young wife. The nuns will pray for her soul.'

'God will hear,' Josse said softly. 'Rest assured of that.'

'Hm.' There was a pause, then Ambrose said, 'I am staying on in the Vale for a few days. I find that it is peaceful here.'

And, Josse thought, you are loath to return to a home where there will never again be the light tread of Galiena's swift feet. 'I understand,' he murmured. 'I, too, always find solace in the very air of Hawkenlye. Especially down here in the Vale, where the pace of life seems less urgent.'

Ambrose smiled faintly. 'It is the Abbess Helewise, I judge, who drives the ship forward,' he remarked. 'Down here, the monks have but to pray, care for the small needs of the pilgrims and perform what light duties crop up.'

Josse, too, smiled. 'Aye. The Abbess told me when I first met her how dear old Brother Firmin once famously announced that the nuns were the Marthas and the monks the Marys. I am not sure,' he added, lowering his voice, 'that the Abbess, in her heart of hearts, entirely approves of a division of labour whereby the women do the work and the men gaze in rapt adoration on the wonders of the Lord.'

'It's the way of the world, Josse,' Ambrose said. 'Within the home, anyway, a good wife will work quietly and unobtrusively while her husband idles away his day in activities that really only serve to pass the time.'

He was, Josse was sure, describing his own life. His tone was ironic and, Josse realised, probably concealed grief. No wonder the poor man did not want to go home.

He said tentatively, 'My lord, there is no limit on the length of stay here, you know.'

Ambrose looked up at him sharply. 'You are suggesting I become a monk, Josse?'

'No! I merely meant to imply that nobody here will urge you to leave until – unless – you are ready.'

Ambrose's harsh expression softened. 'Thank you. I did not mean to be offensive.'

'You did not offend.'

They sat in fairly companionable silence for a few moments, looking out at the peaceful scene before them. Then, as a group of monks appeared in the Abbey's rear gateway, setting out on the path down to the Vale, Ambrose said, 'The Abbess has sent two of the brethren to Ryemarsh with instructions to tell my household of my wife's death.'

'A kind gesture,' Josse observed.

'Indeed. Most considerate.'

Was anything to be read in Ambrose's strangely expressionless tone? Josse wondered. Did he suspect – as Josse, who knew the Abbess so well, instantly did – that there might be more to the offer than its superficial purpose?

I need to speak to her, Josse thought . . .

He turned to Ambrose. 'I see that the community have finished Sext,' he said. 'If you will excuse me, I will go and report to the Abbess.'

'Please, do so.' Ambrose looked at him briefly, then resumed his silent contemplation of the view down the Vale.

With a hurried bow, Josse left the shelter and hurried away.

He tapped lightly on her half-opened door and her instant 'Come in, Sir Josse!' told him that, once again, she had known it was him.

'It is the sound of your spurs, as I have told you before,' she said as he entered the room; her head was bent over a heavy ledger and she had not even looked up.

'Good day to you, my lady,' he said.

She raised her head and her grey eyes met his. 'Good day, Sir Josse. How are Galiena's parents? Are they prostrated by the dreadful news?'

'They are, my lady, although there is a rare strength in Audra, her mother, that I am sure will see them all through their grief. But there is much that I have to tell you.'

Drawing up the stool that was kept behind the door for visitors, he sat carefully down – it was rather a small stool – and told the Abbess all that he had learned.

'Adopted!' she breathed when at last he had finished. 'Well, I suppose it is not so rare an occurrence. Raelf and his first wife were desperate for a child and, presumably, found some fecund family with a baby to spare.' She sighed. 'It is a tragic irony, is it not, that Galiena should have come to us for treatment for the same complaint, in Raelf's first wife, that led to the girl's adoption?'

'Yes,' he said slowly, following her line of thought, 'except that Galiena was not barren.'

'Yes, I *know*,' she began, 'I just meant . . .' But, apparently deciding that line of discussion was not worth the bother, she said instead, lowering her voice, 'Sister Euphemia postulates the existence of a young lover, who was engaged to do Ambrose's work for him.'

'Does she?' Josse raised his eyebrows. The infirmarer's suggestion was uncomfortably close to suspicions he had entertained himself and, after a moment's thought, he decided to share them with the Abbess.

Getting up, he went to the door, opened it and looked outside, then closed it again. Then, stepping up to her table and leaning across it so that he could speak in a whisper, he said, 'My lady, as I believe I told you, it was my neighbour, Brice of Rotherbridge, who took me to Ryemarsh.'

'Yes, you did tell me. I thought I recognised the name and later I recalled from where. He, too, lost a young wife, did he not?'

'Aye. When first I came to this region, his young wife Dillian had recently been killed by being thrown from a horse. They were involved, if you remember, in that business of the nun who died in the Vale.'

'I remember,' she said shortly. 'So, Sir Josse, you were saying, this Brice introduced you to Ambrose and his wife?'

'Aye. We dined at Rotherbridge and afterwards I

was quite surprised when Brice said there were some friends he wanted me to meet. It was they who wanted to meet me, if I may say so without seeming to brag, because of my knowledge of Hawkenlye, but whatever the reason, I noticed that Brice was acting strangely.'

'Strangely?'

'Aye. He was tense, excited, as if he were expecting some thrilling event.'

'And was he?'

He wondered if she were being deliberately obtuse; for sure, she was not helping him to put his vague suspicions into words. 'Well, I'm probably guilty of accusing the innocent – and one of them is dead, so I'm speaking ill of the dead as well – but I did think that Brice might be behaving like a young lad in love because he was going to see Galiena.'

'I see.' Her expression gave away nothing of what she was thinking. 'And when they were together, what did you think then?'

He shook his head. 'I really don't know. They seemed totally at ease with each other and, as far as I could tell, they spoke of everyday matters. Still, they might have been acting. After all, Ambrose was present, as well as me.'

'I always thought,' said the Abbess in a small voice, 'that Galiena Ryemarsh was a woman quite capable of dissimulation.'

'Did you?' He was surprised at her words. 'I can't say that I did.' But, as he spoke, he remembered – she had said something once before to the effect that men and women reacted differently to Galiena.

Now she was looking down at her hands as if she did not want to meet his eyes. 'I have sent Brother Saul and young Augustus over to Ryemarsh,' she said, 'to—'

'Aye, I know,' he interrupted. 'I have been to see Ambrose and he told me.' He hesitated, then said, 'I felt, my lady, that possibly you had some ulterior purpose in sending them?'

'I did,' she admitted. 'Having had my discussion with Sister Euphemia, I wanted to see if they could discover what sort of a life went on at Ryemarsh.'

'And whether anyone happened to notice the clandestine presence of a virile man such as Brice of Rotherbridge?' he suggested.

She looked shamefaced. 'I should not be suspecting such a thing, I suppose, but somehow we have to account for her pregnancy. I am *sure* that she knew she carried a child,' she said with sudden vehemence. 'She was, as we all keep saying, a skilled herbalist and an intelligent woman. And we must not forget that she utterly refused to have a physical examination.' There was a short pause. Then she went on more quietly, 'I hope by sending Saul and Augustus off on this enquiry – and it is with this that I justify my actions to myself – to discover who could possibly have wanted her dead.'

Her words reminded him of Sister Tiphaine's potion. 'My lady, I quite forgot to ask, and I deeply apologise. You are well?' He peered anxiously at her. 'You have suffered no ill effects from the remedy?'

She laughed, quickly suppressing it. 'Sir Josse, I am fine,' she assured him. 'As I was quite sure I would be.'

'It was a rash act,' he grumbled.

'I disagree,' she replied, and he thought her tone was slightly frosty.

'But—' he began. Then he made himself stop. He did not want to argue with her. Anyway, she was Abbess here. He reminded himself that she was not accountable to him. 'I am sorry,' he said again.

And, more kindly now, she replied, 'You are forgiven.'

'So,' he said after a slightly awkward pause, 'we wait for Saul and Gussie to report on what they may find at Ryemarsh.'

'Indeed.'

He moved away from her table and resumed his seat on the stool. 'There is one final thing to tell you of my visit to Readingbrooke,' he said. Strange, he thought, how the very thought of what he was about to say sent a faint shiver of dread through him.

'What is it?' She was staring at him curiously. 'Sir Josse, you look quite worried! Whatever is it that you would tell me?'

'Oh – my lady, I can't say why it affects me so, but they told me the place where Galiena originally came from.'

'And?'

'It's some small settlement over to the east of the Marsh and it's called Deadfall.'

'Deadfall?'

The name, he observed, did not seem to hold any fears for her. 'Aye.'

'And for some reason this disturbs you?'

'Aye. The trouble is, I can't understand why.' He frowned deeply. 'I have puzzled at it constantly and I know that, at some time, somebody told me something about the place. Something terrible.'

Her tone brisk, she said, 'You have kin in Lewes, have you not?' He nodded. 'And I believe you told me that you spent some of your childhood there?'

'Aye.'

'Could it be that you heard tell of Deadfall then? Since the name appears to frighten you, perhaps somebody told a tale by the fireside on a winter's night, a tale of ghosts and demons?'

He began to smile at her somewhat simplistic explanation but then, out of the shadows of the past, suddenly he remembered.

Had she not been an Abbess, he might have kissed her for having jogged his memory.

'My lady, how clever!' he exclaimed. 'But it was not exactly as you suggest.'

'It was only a flippant guess,' she muttered.

'It was my aunt's maid,' he said, hardly hearing her. 'Or, in fact, the maid's young man. He'd been at sea and he had stories of all sorts of places. He told of Breton kings and drowned cities, of Welsh dragons and wizards who could tell the future, of heroes battling for the hand of beautiful maidens. He told of raids on England's east coast and of the ancient people who were here before the Romans came. He came from one of the ports on the edge of the Great Marsh and he knew of the old, deserted salt workings there. He'd picked up some colourful local tales, some of which

I think, with hindsight, were based on much older legends. There was one about a Roman soldier—' He broke off. 'But no. It is Deadfall in which we are interested.'

'Well?' She was, understandably, beginning to sound impatient.

But still he was reticent. He'd been a child back then and the sailor's over-graphic tale had turned his stomach. No wonder he had reacted to the mention of the name; he'd lost his dinner the last time he heard it.

The Abbess was waiting.

He drew a breath and said, 'There was a pirate captain, so the story went, who caught a king unawares, slaughtered him, stuck his head on a pole and raped his daughter. Excuse me, my lady.'

'It's all right, Sir Josse, I asked you for the tale. Go on.'

'Well, the king's people gave him a fitting farewell, in a long ship buried in the sands of the foreshore, but that was not enough. They set a trap for the pirate and, when he sprang it, they found him and took him away.'

'And?'

He swallowed. 'They told him that they were a people who always avenged a wrong done to one of their own. Then they flayed him alive and impaled him on a pole at low tide. He did not die until several hours later, when the sea at high tide finally covered his face.'

'A triple death,' she murmured.

He wondered what she meant. 'What did you say, my lady?'

'Oh – nothing. And this event took place at Deadfall?'

'Aye.' One more thing suddenly came to mind. 'The king that the pirate murdered was a Saxon.'

And, with a nod, the memory of the ancient tales and legends told to her long ago by her grandfather filling her mind, she said, 'Yes. I thought he might have been.'

I I

'I think,' he said, 'that I should go there.'

'To Deadfall.' She wanted to be sure that she understood. 'Even though the very name holds dread for you?' That it really did was clear to her; he had appeared to be genuinely affected by the tale he told her. It was often the way, she thought; as children, we are very ready to be frightened out of our wits and sometimes the things that scared us then still hold power over us when we have grown up, despite our adult comprehension and rationalisation.

'Aye.' He sighed and, she reflected, did not look any too eager for his mission.

'Would you like someone to accompany you?' she asked. 'You have ridden out with Brother Saul and Brother Augustus before now and I am sure that either would be more than willing to go with you again.'

He gave her a sketchy smile. 'A kind offer, my lady, but I feel I should conquer my demons on my own. The good brothers rode with me when there was a possibility that we went into danger, but I cannot see that there is any peril in visiting Galiena's original home to inform her blood kin of her death.'

As he spoke the words *blood kin,* she felt a frisson

of fear run down her back. But why? It was just a phrase and, for someone like Galiena who had been adopted, an accurate and surely innocent one? 'I hope that they will be grateful for your trouble,' she said, the mundane remark helping to put that strange moment behind her. 'Your reminding them of the daughter they gave up may not be tactful, Sir Josse.'

'Aye, I know.' He met her eyes, and the expression in his was candid. 'But, as you and I both realise, my lady, my purpose is not simply to tell them that she is dead.'

She smiled. 'I cannot make any accusations, since I am as guilty as you, having sent Saul and Augustus on a similar mission to Ryemarsh. If there is truly a need to excuse our actions, then it is that by our subterfuge we hope to discover why Galiena died.'

'And who killed her,' he added.

His face, she noticed, had darkened angrily. 'Sir Josse?' she said enquiringly. 'You have a theory as to who that might be?'

Approaching her table once again, he said quietly, 'Aye, but it is for your ears only, my lady, since, if I am wide of the mark, I shall be accusing the very last person on whom suspicion should fall.'

'Go on.'

'Well, the evidence is slight, and that's probably an exaggeration, but it is this. When I was with Galiena's parents – her adoptive parents, that is, Raelf and Audra de Readingbrooke – I mentioned that we had thought it possible Galiena had gathered berries or mushrooms in the forest and that eating one or the other had poisoned her. But instantly Raelf refuted the suggestion because, apart from the fact that it is not the season for berries and too warm and dry for fungi, Galiena was a skilled herbalist and would never have made such a mistake.'

She nodded. 'As we ought to have thought out for ourselves and – oh!' Suddenly she understood. 'You are saying that Ambrose, who on his own admission has good reason to know of his wife's skills, should also have remarked upon that?'

'Aye.'

'And the fact that he did not makes you wonder if he welcomed these putative berries and such like as a convenient scapegoat for the poison that he himself administered to her, and— Oh, no, Sir Josse! I cannot accept that!'

He did not speak, merely stood watching her. And, as her instinctive protests – Ambrose loved her! He was grief-stricken when he knew she was dead! – slowly faded, she wondered if he could be right.

'Why would he want her dead?' she whispered.

'She was carrying another man's child,' he replied.

'But Ambrose did not know! Why, he arranged for her to come here to be treated so that she could *become* pregnant! He even consulted you first to see if you thought we could help!'

'I know,' said Josse. 'Moreover—'

She felt tension in him, as if he wanted to tell her something but was reluctant. 'What?'

Not meeting her eyes, he said, 'Something Ambrose said. When he was confiding in me about her – er, her problem, he said, *my lassie goes on bleeding*.' Raising his head, he muttered, 'I remember particularly because the phrase struck me as moving. And now—' He broke off.

She stared at him. 'You are saying that all that was an act? That he deliberately spoke to you in the intimate way that he did to persuade you that what he said was the truth? That he planned the whole sequence of events with the deliberate purpose of deceiving us?'

Josse shrugged.

'And all the while he planned to kill her for her infidelity?'

After a short pause he said, 'It is possible.'

And she had to admit that he was right.

He announced that he would set out for Deadfall that afternoon. He did not expect to reach his destination that day but, as he said, it was ideal weather for sleeping out under the stars and he looked forward to doing so. Helewise, watching him, wondered if the decision was so as to ensure that he reached Deadfall in the bright light of morning rather than late at night. Well, if the very name of the place truly held dread for him, then he was, she decided stoutly, brave to go there at all, never mind by night.

She came to the gates to see him on his way and, as she had done so many times before, wished him God's speed and safe return.

Watching Horace's dust slowly circling in the warm, still air, she had the sudden rebellious thought: *I* should be the one to ride out! The girl died here, in the Abbey over which I have charge. It should be I who informs the relatives and who uses my eyes and my wits to discover the truth. But yet I stay here, and I send others to act for me.

For a wild moment she thought of calling out, Wait, Sir Josse! Wait while I have the golden mare saddled, because I'm coming with you!

But time passed, and she did not.

When the dust had settled and there remained no sign to tell of Josse's passing, she turned and walked slowly back to her room.

In the late afternoon, Sister Ursel tapped on the door to tell her that Brother Saul and Brother Augustus had returned. They had ridden hard, she reported, and were washing off the dust and sweat of their journey before presenting themselves to their Abbess.

'They have indeed ridden hard!' Helewise exclaimed, 'for they have been to Ryemarsh, carried out their mission there, presumably, and returned, all in little over a day!'

She did not say so to Sister Ursel – who had been known to speculate quite wildly enough without anyone actually encouraging her to do so – but it occurred straight away to Helewise that Saul and Augustus must have something important to tell her to have made such haste to come back to Hawkenlye . . .

She dismissed the porteress and then sat with outward serenity while she waited. Inside, however, her mind seethed with questions and possibilities. Disciplining her thoughts was difficult but not, she discovered, impossible; by the time the two brothers arrived – both wearing clean robes and with wet hair – her outward poise was reflected by inner silence.

She accepted their reverences with a brief inclination of her head and then said calmly, 'What did you find at Ryemarsh?'

Saul and Augustus exchanged a glance and then Saul said, 'We rode up at dusk, my lady. We feared we were too late to seek admission and were planning to find a sheltered spot to camp out till morning but there was a manservant out in the courtyard doing the locking-up round and he heard us.'

'Suspicious sort, he was,' Augustus put in. 'Picked up a pitchfork when he caught sight of us and brandished it in our direction while he challenged us.'

'He did,' Saul agreed, 'but he calmed down when we told him who we were.'

'By then he'd caught sight of the habit we wear,' Augustus put in. 'He reckoned he'd less to fear from his visitors than he'd thought.'

Helewise smiled. Augustus was probably right; the habit of religion did tend to disarm people. 'Then he invited you inside?' she prompted.

'Aye,' Saul said. 'We said we were from the Abbey with news from their master, the lord Ambrose, and that it was bad tidings.' He exchanged a look with Augustus and went on, 'It was strange, my lady, because the old servant and the woman who was in the kitchen both seemed very worried even *before* we told them about the poor young lady.'

'I see.' She would, she decided, return to that remark

in a moment. First she asked, 'How did they react to the news of Galiena's death?'

'They were most distressed,' Augustus said. 'No doubt about it, was there, Saul?' Saul shook his head sadly. 'They loved her, my lady, that's for sure, and they were genuinely heartbroken to know she was dead.'

'Did you—' She paused, thinking how to phrase her question tactfully. 'Were you able to gain any impression of how the household servants viewed their master and mistress? Did they, would you say, think that Ambrose and his wife were happy?'

'Without a doubt,' Saul assured her. 'They said she made the sun shine for him, which I imagine you'd readily understand, what with her being so young and pretty. But they insisted that she cared for him deeply too, even though he was so much older.' He turned to the younger man. 'Wouldn't you say so, Gussie?'

Augustus nodded enthusiastically. 'Aye. The old kitchen woman said she – Galiena – had been a shy girl when she came to Ryemarsh as the lord Ambrose's wife, and they all jumped to the conclusion that she was an unwilling bride. But they had to accept they'd been wrong because she blossomed, according to the manservant, and turned from someone who was reserved with them and hardly spoke into a happy and outgoing young girl who made the sap rise in old Ambrose and only needed a baby or two to complete her happiness.' Saul dug him in the ribs and he said, with some indignation, 'Saul, I'm only repeating what they said!'

'It's all right, Brother Saul,' Helewise said. 'After all, I did ask you to report anything that struck you as relevant.' There was something else that she was very keen to know; again taking a moment to word her question, she said, 'And what of visitors? Did they entertain family or friends? Were there any that came regularly?'

'The lord Ambrose doesn't have kin, they're all dead.' Augustus spoke matter-of-factly. 'The lady went visiting her folks at Readingbrooke from time to time, often with the lord Ambrose, and the family there would return the visits. She had several sisters, they told us, and an aunt to whom she was devoted who has young children of her own. The family's a close one, it seems.'

'I see.' No need, Helewise decided, to reveal the details of Galiena's adoption by the family at Reading-brooke. 'Anyone else?'

'Well, that neighbour of theirs, from Rotherbridge,' Saul said. 'He's a friend of the lord Ambrose and calls by when he's passing.'

'I see,' she said again, trying hard not to let her sudden excitement show in her voice. 'And the household – er – they liked all these visitors?'

She knew even as she spoke that the question was absurd. Both Saul and Augustus looked surprised and Augustus, more forthright than Saul, said, 'I don't see as how it was for them to have likes or dislikes, my lady, since they're servants and do as they're told.' His comment – possibly a little forthright for a young lay brother addressing his Abbess, but entirely justified, Helewise thought – earned him another dig in the ribs and, casting down his eyes, he muttered, 'Sorry, my lady.'

'It's all right,' she said. She could not see a way to find out what she needed to know other than a direct question so, after a moment, she asked it. 'Did you receive the impression,' she said carefully, 'that there was any gossip concerning Sir Brice and Galiena? Oh, I know what you said about Galiena being so devoted to her husband, but you both know how servants love to chatter!' She gave what even to her sounded a totally unconvincing little laugh.

Saul and Augustus looked at each other, then back at her. Then, in unison, they shook their heads and said firmly, 'Oh, no.' Augustus added, as if for emphasis, 'There wasn't anything like that. Was there, Saul?'

And Saul said, 'No.'

Well, she thought, that was not necessarily relevant. After all, if Josse had been right and Brice had been Galiena's lover, he'd hardly have ridden up to the door proclaiming it to the world.

The more she dwelled on it, the more it seemed to her that the very strong denials of 'anything like that' were in themselves suspicious. Wouldn't it have been more natural for Brice and the beautiful Galiena to have engaged in a little harmless flirtation?

But her train of thought was interrupted; Saul was addressing her. 'My lady,' he said, 'there is something else.'

'Indeed? Go on, Brother Saul.'

'You remember that we said they seemed upset even before we told them the news?'

'I do.'

'Well, it seems there was a young stable lad called Dickon. He was sent to escort the lady Galiena over to Hawkenlye, together with the woman Aebba.'

'But he didn't arrive here!' she exclaimed. 'Neither did Aebba, not until she rode in with the lord Ambrose. Galiena arrived alone.'

'Aye, my lady. It seems that Aebba returned from the trip with her young mistress by herself and when the lord Ambrose asked what had happened to the groom, she said he had gone on with the young lady.'

'Here to Hawkenlye?'

'That's what Aebba said.'

If that were so, Helewise thought, then Galiena had been lying, because she had said that she had dismissed both Aebba and the groom just before reaching the Abbey gates. 'So, according to the servants at Ryemarsh,' she said slowly, 'Aebba and this Dickon set out to escort Galiena to Hawkenlye, only Aebba turned for home some time before they reached here' – something occurred to her and she amended her words – 'some time between setting off from New Winnowlands, where Sir Josse left the three of them, and here. Leaving Dickon to bring Galiena on to Hawkenlye, after which he was meant to return to Ryemarsh. Yes?'

'Yes,' Saul agreed, and Augustus nodded.

'Whereas, according to Galiena, both Aebba and Dickon saw her almost to the Abbey before she sent them both home.' She would have to speak to Aebba.

Now that Galiena was dead and Dickon missing, she was the only one left of the party. Which, Helewise realised, meant that Aebba could say whatever she liked and nobody could contradict her.

'There has been no news of the lad?' she asked.

Again, Augustus and Saul exchanged a look. This time it was Augustus who spoke. 'There hadn't been, no, my lady. But we—' He stopped, drew a breath and resumed. 'Saul and I left early in the morning. We passed the turning up to New Winnowlands, then thought we'd stop for a bite to eat. It was hot by then and we sought some shade, which meant we had to ride some way up a sheep track leading up into a copse of willows. We'd just dismounted when the horses started acting spooked and we noticed this terrible smell.' His eyes wide, he said quietly, 'We looked around and we found a body, wrapped in a bit of sacking and lying in a shallow ditch with leaves and branches and that over it. Over him, I should say.' He looked at Saul who, with a brief touch on the younger brother's sleeve as if to say, it's all right, lad, I'll tell the rest, took up the narrative.

'We weren't much more than a mile or so past New Winnowlands so we rode back there for help. I know Sir Josse's man Will, he's a sound fellow. Anyway, he finds a cart and comes back with us to where we found the body and he says straight away, soon as he sees the face, that's the groom as rode by with the master and the company, just a few days back.'

She was struggling to take it in. 'You mean that Will recognised the dead man as poor Dickon?'

'Aye,' Saul said heavily.

She said quietly, 'Could you tell how he died?'

'Blow to the back of the head,' Saul said shortly. 'Looks as if someone crept up on him and took him unawares.'

'Could it have been an accident?' she asked.

Saul gave a faint shrug. 'Possibly, my lady, I suppose. Only if so, would someone not have gone for help, just as we did when we found him? Innocent people don't see a man take a mortal blow then leave him to fend for himself.'

'Indeed not,' she agreed. 'But could he not have been thrown from his horse? You did not find his horse, I take it?'

'No we didn't,' Augustus said. 'But, my lady, if it happened like that, who put him in the sack and buried him?'

'No, no, of course, it would have been impossible.' Impatient with herself, she could not think why she was being so slow; shock, perhaps. 'So for some reason Aebba turned for home first,' she said slowly, trying to make sense of events. 'Dickon rode on with Galiena, although we do not know how much further; she lied about Aebba coming to the gates with her so she may also have lied about Dickon. Anyway, he set off back to Ryemarsh by himself and was attacked about a mile this side of New Winnowlands. The blow killed him and he was put in the ditch.'

'That about sums it up,' Saul agreed.

Helewise put her hands to her head as if pressure from her palms could somehow stop the whirl of thoughts and impressions flying wildly around in her mind. 'I do not understand!' she exclaimed.

Then a portion of the picture suddenly became clear. She saw a young woman riding with her servants, in the middle of acting out a plan that had to be made to work if her undeclared pregnancy were to be attributed to her elderly husband. But the young woman's thoughts were not with her husband at all but with her handsome lover. Whom she just had to meet once more before riding on to Hawkenlye where, in time, she would dutifully be reunited with her husband and present the conception to him as the fruits of his lovemaking.

So perhaps, just *perhaps*, thought Helewise, she dismisses both of the servants so that she can enjoy a final idyll in her lover's arms. The woman Aebba does as she is told and rides home to Ryemarsh. But perhaps the young groom, anxious for his mistress's safety, turns back to check that she is all right. He sees the lovers together and, in order to ensure his silence, the man – Brice of Rotherbridge, according to Josse – strikes out and the lad is killed. Perhaps Brice only means to render him unconscious but, in the heat of the moment with Galiena sobbing and crying beside him, he panics and hits too hard.

The poor young groom is dead and Brice bundles him up, covers him with leaves and the lovers run away. Galiena hastens on to Hawkenlye, Brice goes . . . where?

Where was Brice?

She would have to ask Josse.

Josse.

Somebody was speaking his name; pulling her attention back to the present, she listened.

'. . . ought to know about this,' Saul was saying.

'Sir Josse?' she asked.

'Aye, my lady.' Saul, she thought, was eyeing her curiously. 'Are you quite well?' he asked quietly.

'I am, thank you, Brother Saul. You were saying?'

'Oh. Aye.' He frowned. 'Merely that, what with Will being involved and the poor dead lad's body now at New Winnowlands awaiting burial, me and Gus thought we ought to inform Sir Josse as soon as we could, after telling you, that is.' He gave her a brief bow.

'Quite right, Brother Saul,' she agreed. 'I wish I could help you, but I'm afraid that telling Sir Josse will have to wait. You see, he's just this afternoon set off for the north-eastern reaches of the Great Marsh.'

'Where has he gone?' Augustus asked.

'He is looking for somewhere called Deadfall,' she said.

Yet again, she watched the two of them exchange a look. But this time, both men looked more than anxious; they looked fearful.

Thinking that perhaps Josse's aunt's maid's young man was not the only one to have known dreadful tales of this strange place that had the power to strike fear into the hearts of grown men, she rested her chin in her hands and said, not without a tinge of resignation, 'Very well, then. You had better tell me what *you* have heard about Deadfall.'

'It's not really either of us, although the name was already familiar to you, Gussie, wasn't it?' Saul said.

'Aye,' Augustus said heavily.

'Already familiar?' said Helewise.

'Aye, when old Brother Firmin told us the tale,' Saul replied. 'A party of pilgrims came from the Marsh and talking to them seemed to remind Brother Firmin of legends he had long forgotten. Or so he said. It was last winter, wasn't it, Gussie?'

'Aye,' Augustus agreed again.

If the younger man were to be asked for confirmation at every turn, thought Helewise, then this story would take the rest of the day to tell. 'So Brother Firmin scared you all with an old ghost story at the fireside?' she prompted.

'Aye, my lady.' Now Saul was frowning, as if trying to decide whether the story were fit for a lady's ears.

'I need to know it, Brother Saul,' she said gently. 'As you say, Sir Josse has ridden off to Deadfall and if there is danger there, then we must send help.'

'Oh, I don't reckon as how it'll be dangerous, not to a man of Sir Josse's quality,' Saul said. 'I don't see him as someone who is afraid of the dark!' He laughed nervously.

'I am sure you are right.' Then, putting her full authority into her tone, 'Now, the story, please.'

But Saul glanced at Augustus, who, picking up his cue, told her what she had to know.

'Brother Firmin knows those parts where the sea and the land merge,' he began. 'Seems he grew up thereabouts. He said there were such tales told as to keep children safe in their beds at night, else they might have wandered off and been drowned in a creek that wasn't there yesterday, or put their feet on to boggy ground that would suck them down easy as a stone falling in a pond.'

'Cautionary tales,' murmured Helewise. 'Go on, Augustus.'

'Then there was another reason to keep safe indoors, because the heathen men came from over the seas and killed any who stood in their path. They took their long boats up the creeks and the inlets looking for fertile fields and pastures, because their own lands had been drowned.'

'But that was hundreds of years ago!' Helewise protested. 'The Northmen do not come now.'

'No, my lady, but it seems—' Augustus paused. Then, in a rush, went on, 'They left a presence, so Brother Firmin says. They did terrible deeds and the Marsh holds memories.'

The story was, she thought, beginning to sound very like Josse's account. Fear of the ferocious fighting men of the past seemed to be a long time dying.

'They attacked the monasteries,' Augustus was saying. 'Stole the treasures, killed the monks and ra— er, did harm to the nuns.'

'I know what they did to the nuns,' Helewise said softly. 'I, too, have learned of the east coast's violent past.'

'When they launched a new boat, they took a virgin to sacrifice,' Saul said, eyes round with wonder. Entranced by the tale, he seemed to have forgotten about whether or not his Abbess ought to hear it. 'Seems their god of the sea and the storm needed a blood sacrifice in payment for keeping the craft and her crew safe from the waves.'

'And when they were betrayed, they took the traitor and tore his lungs out of his living chest,' Augustus whispered. 'They called it the blood eagle.'

As if all three of them were picturing that horror, there was silence in Helewise's room.

Breaking it – with difficulty, since she knew she must speak normally and was not sure she could – she said, 'We speak, my brothers, of tales told by the hearth, of ancient legends rooted in folk memory. Oh, yes, I am sure they tell of things which really happened, but these things are past.' She fixed both men with a direct glance, Saul first, then Augustus. 'It will, I am sure, reassure you when I tell you that Sir Josse is not ignorant of Deadfall's fearful reputation. However, when offered company on his visit there, he declined and said he did not see that he would be in any danger.' Forcing a smile, she said, 'We must, I think, abide by Sir Josse's decision and agree with him.'

Then, before either brother could protest, she thanked them and dismissed them.

12

The long June day kept its light late and Josse did not make camp until dusk was at long last falling. He had covered many miles that afternoon and he reckoned he could not be far from his destination. The riding had been easy for much of the way, for he had taken a route that ran along the southern edges of the northern High Weald and the track was level and reasonably well maintained. The long dry spell, however, meant that the surface of the road had been pulverised to fine dust, which clouded up around him as Horace's big feet repeatedly struck the baked ground. As he had saddled the horse prior to leaving Hawkenlye, Sister Martha had watched his preparations.

'You'll need more than those two blankets of yours to keep you comfortable if you're planning to sleep in the open,' she had observed.

Turning to her with a smile, he said, 'Will I?'

'Aye. There's rain coming.'

He had stared at her for an instant in total disbelief; he had rarely known a spell of such relentlessly fine, hot, dry weather. 'Are you sure, Sister?'

'Quite sure.' She held out a square of some folded material, loosely wrapped in sacking; it was quite heavy and decidedly malodorous. 'You'd better take this.'

He took it from her gingerly. 'What is it?'

'Linen treated with tallow. It'll keep the wet out.'

'Er – thank you, Sister.' Even as he spoke, he was wondering where he could pack it so that its aroma would not be constantly under his nose.

As if she knew perfectly well what he was thinking, she laughed. 'Aye, I know it's none too sweet, but you'll be grateful for it, Sir Josse, you mark my words!'

Faced with such certainty, he had conceded defeat and stowed the stinking cloth behind his saddle.

Now, settling for the night, he put the cloth package as far away from him as possible. He soon had a small fire going – there was plenty of kindling and dry wood about, there on the edge of the woodlands that cloaked the northern hills – and everything was bone-dry. For safety's sake he made a hearth of stones to contain the little blaze. He put water in a pot and in it threw some strips of meat and some root vegetables. When his makeshift stew was ready, he began his meal by dipping chunks of dry bread into the rich, hot gravy.

He was so hungry that he could have eaten virtually anything but, fortunately, the Hawkenlye victuals were as usual very good and his meal was delicious.

As he settled for sleep – under a darkening sky still entirely innocent of cloud – he went over in his mind the plan for tomorrow. Now that he was nearing his goal, the directions that Audra had provided were beginning to seem a little paltry. The Saxon Shore, she had said – well, that was relatively easy. As a military man, Josse had been taught about the Romans and the line of forts they had built to defend England's east coast from marauding bands coming over the seas from the north and the east; those forts had been known as the Forts of the Saxon Shore. Audra had mentioned a place where men of old had built a fort, and Josse was almost sure she must have referred to one of the Saxon Shore forts. She had said that Deadfall lay beneath an inland cliff, in a place that used to be sea but was now marshland.

It had sounded so simple when she said it, he reflected as he twisted and wriggled on the hard ground, trying to find a comfortable spot. And, indeed, he had found the line of the inland cliff, or thought he had; for the latter part of the evening he had been riding along the top of a ridge that overlooked the marsh below. With a little imagination, he could see that the mysterious, shadowy land that spread out at the foot of the cliffs could once have been under the sea. Sometimes, indeed, as he had stared down half-hypnotised at the secret land below, the lowering sun painted images and fleeting patterns on the salt flats and he had almost thought he could see the ripple of water . . .

Turning his mind deliberately from that strange, seductive and vaguely disturbing memory, he made up his mind that all he had to do in the morning was ride along the cliff top until he saw below him the ruins of the old fort. Then, somewhere on the marsh below, he would surely find Deadfall.

There! Now he had a plan; he had made up his mind. All he had to do now was to go to sleep.

But sleep did not come. He lay first on his right side, then on his left, then on his back, hands linked behind his head and eyes wide open staring up at the stars. Finally, after what seemed hours, he drifted into a doze.

He dreamed he saw a giant hand upraised before him. It was dense black against the navy blue sky and its wrist was the width of a tree trunk. It had seven fingers and they were curled menacingly towards him as if they wanted to grab him, choke the life out of him, feed him into some unimaginably vast and terrible mouth that shone with fresh red blood and had teeth as sharp as knife blades . . .

His eyes flew open and he shot upright.

As the terrified beating of his heart began to subside, he told himself, it was a dream. Just a dream.

Then he saw the tree. It was dead and its skeletal branches reached up into the sky like a grasping hand.

Smiling at his own fear, he deliberately turned his back on the dead tree, closed his eyes and went to sleep.

In the early morning of the next day, there was a freshness in the air that encouraged him to get up and be on his way. He ate a hunk of bread standing up; then, having checked one final time that his fire was properly dead, covered the cooling ashes with the hearthstones. He packed up his blankets and his cooking pot, tacked up Horace, tied the smelly cloth in its sack once more behind the saddle – only his reluctance to hurt Sister Martha's feelings prevented him from chucking the wretched thing away – then mounted and rode off along the cliff top.

He followed the track for some time. In places it turned away from the edge of the cliff and appeared to join a wider, better-built road, cobbled, regular in width and bordered with stones. He would have preferred to follow this more sophisticated road, if only because it was not nearly as dusty as the narrow track, but he feared that if he strayed too far from the cliff top he would miss his destination.

After a time the track wound its way to the north around a low hill. Then, on the far side of the hill, the track branched, one fork heading off eastwards, the other descending a steep slope that led southwards towards the marsh.

Logic said to proceed on the cliff-top track. But instinct said otherwise; clucking to Horace, Josse turned the horse's head to the right and began carefully to descend the hill.

Halfway down a large bird got up out of the under-growth and flapped noisily over Josse's head and away over the marsh. Unreasonably startled, Josse told himself not to be stupid; it was only a heron.

But Horace was alarmed too. Most unusually, the big horse was sweating and clearly uneasy.

'Come on, old friend,' Josse said encouragingly. 'We've seen worse things, you and I, and lived to tell the tale!'

But on the steep, shadowed track, bordered as it was by encroaching trees and tangled undergrowth, there was no air and Josse's words died away echoless.

It was almost as though some invisible, malign presence were aware of him. Aware and unwelcoming.

Desperate suddenly to get out into the open, Josse ignored the steepness of the gradient and kicked Horace into a trot. The horse, eagerly responding as if he too could not wait to see sky and open land again, managed to keep his feet and soon they were stepping out of the dimness and into the hot sunlight.

There was another track down there, Josse saw, that seemed to lead off to the east along the base of the cliff. A narrow stream ran alongside it. Peering that way, Josse could at first see no sign either of any ruined building on the side of the slope or of any dwelling down on the marshland. He kicked Horace and they set off along the track, keeping the stream on their right. After a short while a clutch of low, ruined buildings came into view on the opposite bank and, with a word of encouragement, Josse put the horse at the slight obstacle of the stream and they jumped across.

The ruins, such as they were, were deserted and appeared to have been so for some time. Little remained except some stunted walls and a sole lonely doorway, with no door on the hinges and no inviting view of some cosy room beyond. Nothing could be seen through its gaping space, in fact, but more marshland.

Josse sat for a moment, thinking. He remembered being told that, of old, men extracted salt from the creeks that ran from the sea inland into the marsh. Perhaps that was what had gone on here; with a little imagination he could picture the narrow stream as a wide creek, regularly filled by the tides so that the precious salt could be taken from the ever-generous sea. Only the land had encroached, the creek had dried up to this meagre trickle and, with no salt to extract, the men had gone away.

Suddenly depressed, swiftly Josse turned Horace and set off at a canter back the way they had come.

Passing the place where they had emerged from the slope leading down the hillside, he rode on westwards along the track beneath the cliffs. Then, once more drawing rein, he stopped to look ahead.

But it was difficult to focus on the marshland, for it seemed to shimmer in the light and hide itself beneath wavering mirages, as if it shied from close scrutiny. Holding Horace quite still, Josse stared out across the flat expanse before him. There were few trees – only the occasional clump of stunted willows that looked as if they were on the point of giving up the struggle against winter winds and brackish water – and little else to break up the monotony of the creek-crossed salt flats. Perhaps it was that very monotony that made the eyes play tricks, for one moment he would think he saw something – a low dwelling, the gentle rise of smoke from someone's morning cooking fire – but, when he looked more closely, it would be gone.

He tried not to think about how he was ever going to find Deadfall. It did not do to be discouraged before he had properly started.

He turned back to the cliff and stared along the slope that ran away westwards. The streamlet seemed to come from that direction and so, with no other plan suggesting itself, he set off to follow it.

He had not gone far when, through the trees, he caught sight of stonework. Dismounting, he pushed his way through the branches of alder and willow and peered out at the hillside.

Scattered across it, as if some vast building erected in antiquity had finally given up and allowed itself to be borne away down the slope, were huge clumps of masonry. They were of pale stone, into which had been inserted courses of reddish tiles.

And, understanding the aptness of the name now that he had seen the place, he said out loud, 'Deadfall.'

If he had found the right place – and he was sure that he had – then the house he was searching for must lie under the cliff, behind him to the south. Mounting again, he crossed the track and set out across the marsh.

He searched for most of the day. He found nothing.

The light began to fail early and at first he did not understand why, unless his fruitless and increasingly frustrating search had gone on for longer than he realised.

Then he glanced up at the sky.

His intention had simply been to see how low the sun was. But he could not see the sun, for it was covered by a huge bank of thick, dark, menacing cloud that had steadily been creeping across the sky from the south-west.

The temperature had dropped alarmingly; Josse realised that both he and his horse were shivering.

Biting down the fear that, out of nowhere and for no apparent cause, began coursing through him, he tried to think. Be practical, he told himself sternly. If there is a storm coming – and only someone with a totally unrealistically optimistic outlook could believe there was not – then we must have shelter.

He thought of the massive ruins he had seen earlier up on the hillside. He thought some more, but could think of nothing better. So, kicking Horace into a canter, he headed back towards the cliff as fast as the marshy, uneven ground would allow.

They took the stream in a soaring leap and then had to slow down to pass under the trees that lined the track. Finding a way through the undergrowth and out on to the hillside took precious time – Josse was aware of the approaching storm now almost as of something terrifying and alive that was steadily stalking him – but finally he discovered a place where the brambles grew less thickly, and bodily he and Horace forced an opening through them. He felt his skin tear as a sharp thorn dug into the back of his hand and, sucking at it, tasted his own blood.

The slope was steeper than it had appeared from below and soon Josse dismounted, leading Horace, trying to run over the uneven grass, the breath rasping in his throat and chest as he urged the horse on towards the ruins.

There was not much time. Now the black cloud covered almost all of the sky.

Looking frantically around, Josse sought out the best place. There, where a tall pile of stones stands alone? No, not wise. There, in that shallow dell? No, not enough shelter.

Then he saw it. Aye, over there, he thought, where two massive walls meet and there are the vestiges of a roof. Pulling at Horace's reins, he ran to the shelter. Cold hands fumbling with buckles and straps, he got the saddle and bridle off the horse and stowed them under the walls. He put on Horace's rope head collar and fastened the end around the corner of a very heavy stone lying on the ground. Horace was still sweating and hastily Josse rubbed him down, covering him with the piece of sacking that had held Sister Martha's greased cloth. Then, blessing the sister for her weather lore, he stretched out the cloth and, using stones to weigh it down, fastened it across the angle between the two walls of his shelter so that it was supported by the struts that had once held up the roof. He set it so as to form a slight downward slope that led out and away from the walls; with any luck, the rain ought to run off it and drip harmlessly at the perimeter of Josse's inadequate camp.

That was his hope. For there could no longer be any doubt at all that there was going to be rain, a great deal of it; the first drops had already begun to fall and they were as heavy as if it were their intention to compensate for several months of drought in a matter of hours.

He wrapped himself up in his blankets. Then, with Horace beside him, his head hung in misery, Josse settled down to watch the storm.

The thunder came with a ferocious opening salvo that took Josse entirely by surprise and set his heart pounding. Then there was a sudden flash of lightning that seemed to plunge a trident of brilliance down into the marshland below and, a little later, another crash of thunder. Despite the discomfort and his increasing sense of unease, for a time Josse lost himself in wonder at the spectacle. Peering out for a brief instant from his shelter, he saw that the black clouds now covered the entire sky, as if some sorcerer's cauldron had made smoke enough to plunge the whole world into premature night. And the cloud seemed to be lying low, just over his head, as if, with only a small effort, he could reach up and grasp some of that deep darkness and hold it in his hand.

Shivering, he withdrew his head inside the shelter, shook the worst of the water from his hair and sat down again. Horace, a shadowy bulk beside him, lowered his head and blew soft, warm breath against Josse's neck; it was very comforting.

The storm was getting closer. Now the gap between lightning and thunder was steadily lessening and soon the two were virtually synonymous: the fury of the heavens was right overhead.

It was the moment of greatest danger, or so Josse believed at the time. Into his mind poured images of tall towers made by proud men being struck by vivid

forks of light and tumbling to ruins. He saw again a
scene he had once witnessed, where a fellow soldier
standing on guard on an elevation had been thrown
twice his own height into the air by a lightning strike.
He remembered, against his will, the smell of singeing
hair and flesh.

I am safe here, he told himself firmly. I deliberately
chose to shelter beneath stonework that was well down
the slope and that did not stand up in relief on the top
of the high ground. These old walls have stood here
solidly for a thousand years and they are not going to
tumble down tonight.

He almost believed himself.

He fell into a light doze. The storm had eased and, in
the calm that followed, his sleep deepened. He began
to dream.

He saw a figure in white holding a tall staff, from the
head of which gleamed a mighty jewel that caught the
light and magnified it, sending back brighter flashes
to the black sky from which the lightning came. A
deep voice called on the ancient gods and the dreaming Josse *knew* that Thor the Mighty walked the
earth. Then the scene changed and fair-haired men
dragged a long ship down the foreshore towards the
waiting sea. But there were cries and screams of
agonising pain and terror, for the ship's keel ran over
human flesh.

Moaning in his sleep, Josse twisted his head as if to
turn his eyes away from what he was seeing. But the
screams went on, accompanied by the sound of the

rasping shingle as the hungry waves reached out for the new ship.

Then there was the smell of burning and, on another shore – or perhaps the same one under a different light – a long ship set out across the smooth water with smoke pouring from its deck. Josse was in the water helping the craft on her way and then, with the magical, all-seeing vision given to dreamers, he was high above, looking down on to the ship. He saw the tall, broad-shouldered body of a king, pale hair bound beneath a helmet with cheek pieces and nose guard, deep eyes closed in death. His belt was fastened with a great buckle, decorated with interlaced running lines in which were twined the graceful, stylised shapes of snakes, birds, bears and wolves. The warrior's spear and battleaxe lay beside him and his shield was at his head. To his left was a giant whetstone, the mask of the god and strange runic inscriptions etched into the stone and the delicate figure of a stag standing proudly on the circle of bronze that topped the stone. Laid on his body, his long hands clasped on its hilt, was his broadsword, decorated with garnet-studded gold. From the shore came chanting as the king's people honoured his passing.

And, in time, there came the stench of burning flesh.

Josse woke with horror in his mind. Sweating, breathing as hard as if he had just run up the slope again, he sat up, eyes wide, trying to see into the night.

Behind him Horace gave an uneasy nicker. Josse reached out a hand and gave the horse a pat. It was meant to reassure but Josse was not sure he had reassurance to give.

The darkness was so total that he could not see a thing. He sat quite still, listening. There was scarcely a sound except for the steady drip as rainwater fell from the eaves of his shelter. Drip, drip, drip.

But then there was another sound: somewhere out there a stone had been disturbed.

He listened.

Nothing.

But there *had* been a sound, he thought, feeling the goose bumps of fear start on his flesh. And stones do not move by themselves . . .

Some small animal, he told himself. Now that the rain has eased, the little creatures of the night will be about their business. The concept was quite comforting and he began to imagine some stoat or weasel nosing around in the wet grass.

Then he heard breathing.

He shot backwards until he was pressed up into the corner formed by the walls of his shelter. He eased his dagger out of its sheath on his belt and, with his other hand, felt across to where he had placed his sword. Then, quite still again, he listened.

Nothing.

His heartbeat gradually slowed down. He took a steadying breath, then another. The ears play tricks, he thought. Just as fear can make a man see things that are not there, so the same can happen to the sense of hearing. There *was* no breathing, he told himself firmly. It would be quite impossible.

After quite a long time, he wrapped himself up in his blankets again and lay down.

The rain had stopped. But in the distance, from the south-west out across the marsh, thunder growled menacingly over the sea.

Josse lay, eyes staring out blindly into the blackness, waiting.

He had not been asleep. He *knew* he hadn't, afterwards; despite the suggestions that it had been a dream, that the very real dangers of his situation had sent him a fear-induced nightmare, he knew it was not so. He had been wide awake.

His senses alert, he sat listening, skin prickling with apprehension. The disturbed stone and the breathing he thought he had heard earlier had not recurred; the night was silent and, for the moment, the sky gods were resting and even the thunder had abated.

He began to relax. He laid his sword down beside him and flexed his right hand. His left hand was still on the hilt of his dagger but now he no longer gripped but only touched it, as if to reassure himself it was still there if he needed it. His back against the solid stone, he folded up a corner of blanket and put it behind his head, resting the tension in his neck and shoulders.

It was still totally dark. Never before had he experienced the sensation of literally not being able to see his hand in front of his eyes. He was just experimenting, wriggling the fingers of his right hand to see if he could make out the movement, when it happened.

There was no warning, not one single sound to put him on guard. There was just the one flash of bright light and, right there in front of him, a face staring intently into his, so close that he could look into the silver-grey eyes and feel the cool breath on his cheek.

Then darkness closed in again.

Sweat breaking out on his cold flesh and his heart in his throat, Josse fought for control. His body remembered its training even while his horror-struck mind was in shock and he was on his feet, sword in hand, lunging forward out of the shelter, before he knew it. Then his voice came back and he shouted in a great roar, '*Who's there? Show yourself!*'

Nerve endings tingling as he subconsciously awaited the blow, he twisted from side to side, his sword making great deadly sweeps in a wide arc in front of him. 'Show yourself!' he cried again. 'I am armed and I will attack if you approach again without warning!'

But I cannot see him, he thought. How can I attack what I can't see?

He waited, listening.

There was nothing.

Presently the rain began to fall again.

13

Helewise was still pondering on the wisdom of her decision not to send Brother Saul and Brother Augustus chasing after Josse when she woke the next morning. She had been quite sure she was right when she had dismissed the brothers last night; a strong part of her mind told her that they were passing on pagan horror stories and that she should set a good example by giving the frightening old legends no credence.

And, as she had told the brothers, Josse had been offered their company but had declined it. He did not believe he was going into danger. Why, then, should she?

But I do believe it, she thought as she went into the Abbey church for Prime. Although it appears irrational, I fear for him. And, she told herself, fears are none the less real just because we do not perceive the reason for them. Just as this day, dawning so fair and so warm with the sky above clear and blue, holds the promise of rain.

She did not know how she could be so certain it would rain that day, any more than how she was sure that Josse was in danger.

And she did not know what to do.

But, she thought as she entered the great church, I am going to the right place to ask for help.

She went straight back to her room after the office, forgoing her breakfast as an offering to God in return for his guidance. She still did not know what to do.

She had half expected to see Ambrose at Prime; it was not unusual for visitors staying more than a day or two to slip into the habit of worshipping with the community. However, he had not appeared and Helewise concluded that he preferred to remain down in the Vale with the monks. Well, if he found comfort in the company of those good souls and their simple little shrine, then that was fine. As far as Helewise was concerned, the poor man could stay as long as he liked.

Putting her anxiety about Josse firmly to the back of her mind, she reached for the ledger she had been working on yesterday and resolutely set to work. If there were going to be any heavenly guidance, it would arrive in its own good time. Feeling calm for the first time in many hours, she bent her head and picked up her stylus.

Late in the afternoon she was disturbed by Sister Martha, who announced that there was a visitor wishing urgently to speak to the Abbess. Suppressing a sudden excitement, Helewise waited a moment, then said composedly, 'And who is the visitor, Sister?'

'He *says* he's Brice of Rotherbridge,' Sister Martha

replied, as if she had cause to doubt that the man spoke the truth.

Brice! The man whom Josse suspected of being Galiena's lover! If Josse were right – and Helewise realised that she believed he was – then Brice was also the man whom she herself had been pitying so deeply because he did not know that his young love was dead.

And I, she thought, shall have to tell him.

She said quietly, 'Ask him to come in, Sister Martha.'

After a few moments, Brice of Rotherbridge strode into the room and stood in front of her.

She had not met him before, although she had known his late brother. There was a resemblance between them, she thought. She remembered – just in time – that, after the matter concerning his dead wife and her sister, Brice had made a generous donation to Hawkenlye Abbey. As she looked up into his brown eyes, the memory served to provide an opening remark.

'Some years ago, Sir Brice,' she said, 'you gave us a handsome gift. Please be assured that we have used it well.'

'Of that I have no doubt, my lady Abbess,' he replied, giving her a graceful bow. Then, a wry expression crossing his face, he added, 'How very long ago that all seems now!'

'Four years,' she murmured. What a lot, she thought, has happened in that time. 'You wish to see me, Sir Brice?'

'I do.' He paused and then said, 'I am neighbour

and, I hope, friend to the lord Ambrose Ryemarsh and his wife. I visited their household with Sir Josse d'Acquin a while ago and I was there when Ambrose and Galiena decided they would visit you here at Hawkenlye, Galiena going on ahead. Although Sir Josse was unable to join them straight away – and I had pressing matters of my own to attend to – the three of them agreed that they would meet here when they could.' There was a strange light in his eyes, as if, she thought, he were speaking of something weightier than this innocent reunion of friendly neighbours. 'I have decided that I will join them. I should like, if possible, my lady, to see my friends as soon as possible.'

She made herself hold his glance. Then, speaking quietly and gently, she said, 'Sir Brice, I deeply regret to have to tell you this, but there has been tragedy here. The lady Galiena did indeed arrive in advance of the lord Ambrose, but, soon after his arrival, Galiena became sick.'

'She's sick?' Something had leapt into his face, some fleeting expression that was there and gone before she could identify it. Now he looked stern. Almost – could it really be? – accusing.

'She is dead, Sir Brice,' Helewise said softly. 'I am so sorry.'

'Dead.' He repeated the word in a whisper. 'Dead.' Then, a hand before his face hiding his eyes, he said, 'How did she die?'

'We think she might have been poisoned,' Helewise said. 'By accident, of course. Something she picked up in the woods, some—'

But Brice, who apparently knew of Galiena's skills as well as her father did, protested straight away, 'No. She walks the fields and woods of her home and there is no plant that she does not know. It is impossible that she would have been so reckless as to taste something that was poisonous.' Then, removing his hand and fixing Helewise with an angry stare, he added, 'Unless it were something growing in Hawkenlye's herb patch.'

Biting down her instinctive reaction to the dismissive – and inaccurate – use of the word *patch*, she said, 'It is, of course, a possibility, although my knowledge of Sister Tiphaine, who is our herbalist, tells me that she is far too careful even to think of growing poisonous plants where incautious visitors could pick them. If indeed she grows anything that is poisonous, I am quite sure that it is kept under her strict supervision.' Already, she noted, the anger was fading from his face. But, to emphasise the point that she was prepared to consider anything, no matter how unlikely, she said, 'I will ask Sister Tiphaine if she thinks it possible that Galiena could have taken harm from the herb garden.'

'Oh, don't bother,' he said brusquely. 'I am sure you are right. I spoke in haste and without due consideration. Forgive me, my lady.'

'Of course,' she said instantly. 'You are, I dare say, not yourself.'

'Not myself,' he murmured. Then, rubbing at his jaw, his face puzzled, he said again, 'She's dead. That lovely, loving young girl is dead.' Then, his face crumpling with emotion, he said, 'I'm sorry, my lady, but I just can't seem to take it in.'

'I know,' she said, wanting to comfort him. 'It is always so hard to understand the ways of God when the young are taken.'

'She was *good*!' he cried suddenly.

The echoes of the word rebounded in the small room. Good, good, good. And Helewise thought, despite herself, despite her sympathy for Brice, *was* she good? In the eyes of the church she was an adulteress, if not with this handsome fellow standing before me, then with somebody. For if the child she carried were in truth the fruit of Ambrose's seed, then why had Galiena planned and acted out that elaborate deception?

But it was for God to judge her. And, whatever he had done, Brice needed comfort, that was for sure; he looked shocked and pale and she was worried for him. Standing up, she said, 'Sir Brice, sit down in my chair here. I will call for a restorative for you.'

Dumbly he did as she said. She went outside into the cloister, summoned a nun with a brief beckoning gesture and, in a low voice, told her to fetch spiced wine from Sister Basilia in the refectory; Sister Goodeth had sent up a cask of a good French wine and the best, Helewise reflected, was only suitable for this man who had once been a benefactor of the Abbey.

While they waited for the wine, she stood staring at him. He had leaned his arms on her table and the dark head was bent over his folded hands. He was well dressed, she noted, in tunic and hose that were plain and undecorated but clearly of good quality. And, she had to admit, he was an attractive man. And he had lived on his own – or so she presumed – since the death of his young wife. A sudden worldly thought intruded and she realised that it was no surprise for him to have taken Galiena as his lover.

But I must not believe Josse so unquestioningly! she berated herself. It was only an impression, he said as much himself, and—

There was a timid tap on the door and a young novice from the refectory came in with a tray, a jug and two mugs. Her hands were rough and red; presumably part of her training involved doing incessant pot-scrubbing. 'Pour wine just for our visitor,' Helewise commanded quietly, and the girl did so. She then stood back and waited, head bowed, for further instructions.

'You may leave us,' Helewise said. Cross with herself, she could not remember the novice's name . . . then, with an effort, she brought it to mind. 'Thank you, Sister Arben.'

The nun gave her a brief, blushing smile, then hurried away.

Brice observed the exchange over the rim of his mug and briefly his well-shaped mouth twitched into a smile. 'You have just made that young person very happy, my lady,' he remarked. 'To be thanked by so grand a presence as her Abbess – who, what's more, remembered her name – is a great honour.'

Helewise opened her mouth to make a dismissive remark but, keenly aware that Brice was watching her as closely as she was watching him, changed her mind. Inclining her head slightly, she said, 'They work hard, our novices. They deserve thanks.'

There was silence as Brice sipped his wine. His colour was improving, she noticed; presently she said, 'Sir Brice, the lord Ambrose is still here. He lodges with the monks in the Vale where one of our older monks is, I understand, giving him care and comfort. He was quite unwell when he arrived, and—'

'Unwell?' Brice's interruption was stark.

'Yes,' she said. 'Although he rallied, I am told, after some rest in the infirmary and—'

Again Brice interrupted. 'But Ambrose is hale and hearty. What ailed him? Why did he need to be treated in the infirmary?'

'I do not know,' she said, a degree of frost entering her voice. 'I was on the point of asking you' – before you interrupted me, was the implication – 'if you wished to see him.'

'Ambrose? No.'

Good Lord above, she thought, is that response relevant? Does this abrupt refusal to comfort a bereaved neighbour imply that Josse is right?

'It might be a kindness,' she persisted. 'Ambrose has lost his wife. The condolences of a friend and neighbour' – deliberately she used Brice's own words – 'could be of comfort to him, do you not think?'

He stared at her. 'I cannot see Ambrose,' he said.

Because you were his wife's lover and you feel guilty? Helewise wondered, but she kept her peace and waited.

'I must go to Galiena's kin and take them the terrible news of her death,' he said heavily.

'There is no need,' Helewise said. 'Sir Josse was here and he has already fulfilled that sad mission.'

There was a moment's silence, then Brice said, 'They will be broken hearted. Especially – They all loved her well.'

She had not realised that Brice knew Galiena's adoptive family and, fleetingly, she wondered if he was aware that they were not Galiena's blood kin. But then, she supposed, country families did tend to be familiar with each other, and it was probably only natural that Brice, a friend of Ambrose and his wife, should also be acquainted with her family. 'Yes. It is to be hoped that they may take comfort in each other.' And in their faith in the Lord's mercy, she would have added, but for some quality in Brice that suggested he would not want to hear the words.

'You mentioned Josse,' Brice said. 'Is he here now?' Suddenly he seemed more animated.

'No.' Should she tell him what Josse had discovered, and what it had led to? Where he now was, God protect him?

'Then where is he?' Brice demanded.

She stared at him, her mind racing. Something was telling her to confide in this man, that it was not only sensible but imperative.

And, indeed, why should she not?

She took a breath and said, 'He discovered at Readingbrooke that Galiena is not the true daughter of the family there but that she was adopted as a baby.' Brice's face was impassive, giving no clue as to whether or not this was news to him. 'They told Josse that she came from a place out on the far reaches of the Marsh, over on the Saxon Shore. It was a place called Deadfall.'

'Who told him that?' Brice demanded. 'Was it Raelf?'

'No.' She tried to remember exactly what Josse had said. 'No, not Raelf. Her mother – her adoptive mother – came out as Sir Josse was leaving and explained. She spoke with Sir Josse and told him about Deadfall.'

'Aye, I know the lady Audra,' Brice said, with a degree of impatience. He was frowning deeply, apparently thinking hard on matters that did not please him.

Helewise decided that, strong man that he was and, without a doubt, suffering deeply from the news of Galiena's death, still it was time to remind him where he was. And, more importantly, who she was; his habit of speaking dismissively might be all very well when he was addressing servants but it was not appropriate when conversing with the Abbess of Hawkenlye.

Pride, she thought ruefully. Still I have pride, for all that I tell myself that it is not myself whom I defend but the office that I hold.

She said quietly, 'Are you feeling better, Sir Brice? Has the wine helped you to recover yourself after the ill tidings?'

Instantly he was on his feet, out of her chair and coming round the table to stand before her. 'Aye, my lady, your cellarer keeps a fine wine and it has indeed helped. I apologise for my bluntness,' he went on disarmingly, 'I spend too little time with women of quality and I forget how to conduct myself.' Now for the first time he smiled properly at her and she was surprised at the difference it made to his face; she was right, he was handsome. Very handsome.

She inclined her head. 'I understand,' she murmured. 'And bluntness, in its place, is no bad thing.'

He stood staring down at her; tall though she was, he stood half a head taller. 'I don't like it,' he said.

'You don't like what?'

He gave a brief exclamation of impatience but it was, she realised, with himself. 'Again, I apologise. Despite your intelligence, my lady, there is no reason why I should expect you to be a mind reader. I am not happy that Josse has gone alone to Deadfall. He *has* gone alone?'

Fighting her own private battle against the pleasure it gave her to have a fine, good-looking man praise her intelligence, she said, too brusquely, 'Yes he has. I suggested he take two of my more reliable and useful lay brothers with him but he said he did not see that there was danger in his mission and preferred to ride alone.' Suddenly picturing Josse's face with vivid intensity, she said softly, 'He was afraid, Sir Brice, but he was fighting it. He had a childhood fear of the very name and he said he must fight his demons alone.'

'Demons,' Brice murmured. Then he said, 'He has good reason to fear the place, my lady Abbess. And, forgive me, but I can't see that two feeble old monks could have been much help to him.'

'Brother Saul and Brother Augustus are neither old nor feeble,' she said roundly. 'Would I have suggested them had they been so?'

He grinned. 'No. Of course you wouldn't. They are handy with a sword, are they? Able to spot an ambush and take necessary avoiding action?'

'They do not bear swords,' she said with dignity. 'But they would defend Sir Josse to the death if necessary.'

He looked shamefaced. 'Again, I apologise. If it is any consolation to you after my rudeness, I believe that you were right to propose that Josse did not go alone. It is a pity that he refused to take your advice.'

'You think he is in danger?' She could not keep the anxiety out of her voice and she noticed that Brice gave her a very considering look.

'I – Deadfall is a strange place,' he replied. 'It is, as you understood, on the fringe of the Great Marsh, over on the east coast where the land has built up behind the shingle barrier. It lies under the inland cliff where men of old built a fort, above an inlet that gave access to a wide, safe haven that was not reached by the angry seas.' He was still looking at her but seemed to be focusing on something far away. 'The inlet filled up and the people went away.'

'The people in the fort, do you mean?'

'No, not them. Later, long after they had gone, men built dwellings on the marshland in the summer, when it was relatively dry, and they extracted the salt. But the creek silted up and there was nothing to keep them there. It became a lonely, desolate place. Not a habitation for the good and the godfearing. I—' But, with a very apparent effort, he broke off.

'Yet Galiena's blood kin lived there,' she said, frightened without knowing why.

'They did,' Brice agreed, 'and I believe that they do still.'

She sensed impatience in him, restlessness that was spurring him on. 'Will it take you long to get there?' she asked.

Now he laughed aloud. 'I was wrong, my lady, when I said I could not expect you to be a mind reader! It is a day's ride, even on a fast horse. I will be there tomorrow. I will find him and, if it is required and it is in my power, I will help him.' He took her hand and, bowing over it, added, 'You have my promise.'

Speechless – for too many conflicting thoughts and emotions were flying through her head – she let her hand drop to her side and watched as he paced out through the door and, with a clink of spurs that reminded her poignantly of Josse, hurried away.

It was only long after he had gone that she thought to wonder how it was he came to know so much about Deadfall.

14

It was late in the day when Brice set out from Hawkenlye Abbey. After a short time he realised what he should have realised sooner: there was a storm brewing and, from the ominous bank of black cloud that was blowing up from the south-west, it looked as if it was going to be a bad one.

He had not long passed the fork in the road where a track led down to Tonbridge. He could, of course, turn back to Hawkenlye and seek shelter there, but somehow he did not like to think what the Abbess Helewise's reaction would be when she heard that the gallant, bold fighter who had set off full of his promise to go to Josse's aid had turned back because it was going to rain.

He understood something about himself that came as a slight surprise: the Abbess Helewise was a woman whose good opinion he was quite keen to maintain.

Deciding, he reined in his horse, turned and headed down to Tonbridge. It was not far off his route and he would set off very early in the morning to make up the lost time.

Apart from anything else, an evening spent in the taproom, with a jug of ale and a hot bite to eat, would perhaps take his mind off his grave preoccupations.

She was dead. Dear God, but he still could not believe it!

Kicking his horse to a canter, he hurried on his way.

The storm struck in the small hours. Burrowing down under the covers on his narrow bed in the inn, Brice listened to the wind howling around the old building, rattling a loose shutter and making it bang against the wall in an irregular rhythm that was too disturbing to make further deep slumber likely. The rain was falling as if a vast vat of water had been upturned overhead.

Relieved that he had taken the sensible decision not to risk being caught out in the open this night, Brice made himself relax and waited for the drumbeat of the shutter to lessen sufficiently to allow him to slip back into a doze.

The new day was fresh and washed clean by the heavy rain. Outside in the inn's courtyard, stable lads and house servants were sweeping up water and storm-brought detritus, working hard with their brooms to push it all through the archway and into the already flooded and muddy street beyond. Brice, awake soon after first light, ate a quick breakfast, paid for his night's accommodation and, ordering his horse to be prepared, set out before anyone else in the inn who had a choice in the matter was even out of bed.

★　★　★

Once he was up on the ridge he made good time. Men of old had first made a track there, preferring to walk or ride on the chalky uplands instead of down in the heavy clay soil of the valleys; for one thing, the higher ground gave a better view of the surrounding land and, for another, you were more likely to arrive at your destination with dry feet. Brice, kicking his sleek and well-fed mount into a canter, told himself that the swiftly passing miles made up for his overnight delay and he began once more to see himself as the Abbess's loyal knight and champion, engaged on a vitally important errand to find her missing warrior . . .

In the early afternoon he was on a lonely stretch of track to the north of Readingbrooke. To his right and a little behind him was the steep slope that led from the great tract of woodland on the high ground down to the marsh below. He was on familiar territory now and his thoughts strayed to the place not far from here where they loved best to dwell.

Then, bringing him abruptly out of his reverie, he saw a horseman approaching from the east. The man's mount was a big warhorse, its feathered feet falling heavily on to the chalky ground as it trotted swiftly towards him. The rider was slumped in the saddle, hardly paying attention, it appeared to Brice, to where his horse was taking him.

'Halloa!' Brice cried out. 'Watch where you're going!'

He recognised the horse before he could get a proper look at the rider. As the big animal came up to him he jumped out of the saddle and, holding his own reins in one hand, grasped Horace's in the other. Then, looking up at Josse, he said, 'Dear God! What has happened to you?'

Brice had summed up the position with his usual incisiveness. The nearest place where he could be sure of help was at Readingbrooke; somebody of that household must surely be about and willing to give assistance, even if it was only one of the servants. On consideration, one of the servants might be the best to be hoped for since Raelf did not employ ineffectual wastrels but efficient, hard-working men and women.

Leading Horace – in fact Brice realised that there was no need for this since Horace was such a well-mannered horse that, in the absence of contrary commands from his master, he would have followed along behind Brice anyway – Brice carefully rode back along the ridge and then down the slope that led to Readingbrooke.

In the courtyard at Readingbrooke, Raelf himself came out to meet them. He had, in fact, been standing out there anyway, having just seen his wife, his sister-in-law and his three eldest daughters off to hear mass for Galiena's soul.

Raelf was not yet ready for the comfort of prayer.

Stepping forward to meet the visitors and staring curiously at the still-slumped Josse, he called out, 'Brice! What is the matter?'

'I met Sir Josse riding towards me on the road,' Brice said, dismounting. He did not see any reason for a fuller explanation; for one thing, he did not want to share his business with anyone else and for another, the most urgent thing was to help Josse. 'I think he must have been caught out in last night's storm, for his cloak is soaked and he seems feverish.'

Instantly Raelf called out for help and, as two strong-looking lads emerged into the courtyard, he issued orders and very soon the horses were being led away into the stables and Josse was being helped into the house.

There was no fire lit in the great hall – the day was warm and close – and so they put him in a chair in front of the fire in the kitchen, spreading out his wet outer garments in the warmth to dry. One of the kitchen women made him a hot drink that smelled spicy and another wrapped him in a blanket. After quite a short time, Josse shot up his head and, over-bright eyes staring around him suspiciously, demanded, 'Where am I?', the question instantly followed by *'Where's my sword?'*

'Your sword is by the wall there, Josse, you are at Readingbrooke and we're looking after you,' Brice said soothingly. 'I found you up on the high ridge and as you were clearly unwell, I brought you here for help, it being the nearest house where I knew the inhabitants.'

Josse was glaring up at him as if this reasonable explanation were somehow highly suspicious. 'Readingbrooke?' he repeated doubtfully. 'But I was at—' He broke off. 'Aye,' he murmured, 'aye, I remember.' A shudder went through him. Then, mastering himself with an obvious effort, he managed a weak smile and said, 'I was caught in the rain. I got a good soaking and it seems to have made me shivery.'

'The good blaze here will soon remedy that,' Raelf said from behind Josse's chair.

Turning round, Josse said, in something much closer to his normal tone, 'I thank you for taking me in, Sir Raelf, and for your care. But I will not trouble you long – there is an urgent errand that I must fulfil.'

'Dry yourself and your cloak thoroughly first,' urged Raelf, 'and take some nourishment. Surely your business is not so pressing that you must set off again before you are fully recovered?'

'It—' Again, Josse seemed to be battling with the pressure of whatever emergency had possessed him and Brice suddenly realised that he did not want to reveal his mission.

'I will ride with Josse, as soon as he is ready to leave,' he said smoothly. He met Josse's eyes and tried to make his own expression reassuring. 'Entrust yourself to me, Josse, and I'll go with you, wherever you wish to go, if you will have me.'

Josse stared at him. Whatever mental calculations he was making, soon he had made up his mind. 'Aye, that I will,' he said. 'It is a gallant offer and one that I readily accept.'

'Where are you bound?' asked Raelf. 'Is it far?'

After the briefest of pauses, Josse said, 'To Hawkenlye Abbey. It is some half a day's ride.'

There was no need of the swift glance that he gave Brice for Brice to know that he was lying; Brice had already guessed where Josse wanted to go in such a hurry and it was in the opposite direction from Hawkenlye.

Josse endured the fussing and the enquiries as to whether he was feeling any better yet for as long as he could; Raelf and his household were kindly and they meant well. Also, the warmth of the fire was very welcome and the drink that the serving woman had given him wonderfully restoring. She had followed it up with bread and a thick slice of ham, and he had surprised himself by a sudden appetite that had made him wolf down the good food as if he had not eaten for a week. He had stopped shivering and now felt reasonably confident that he could stand up without that dreadful spinning sensation in his head that made the very earth beneath him appear treacherous and uncertain.

He watched the people around him. The household servants, now that the small drama seemed to be over, had melted away to resume whatever duties they normally carried out in the late afternoon. Raelf was talking quietly to Brice.

Am I right to trust the man? Josse wondered, eyes on Brice. I suspect him of having been very close to Galiena – indeed, such is his familiarity with her family here in their home that my suspicions grow. He and she were lovers, of that I am certain.

But a man succumbing to the temptation of making

love to another man's wife did not make him an unwelcome ally, Josse thought, especially when no other ally offered himself.

And Josse needed an ally. There was no doubt of that.

He unwrapped the soft enfolding blankets – he was now far too hot – and tentatively got to his feet. So far, so good. The clothes he was wearing – his shirt and hose – were dry and, feeling the wool of his tunic and his cloak, he found that they were almost dry too. Swiftly he put them on then, stepping quietly over to the wall and picking up his sword on its heavy belt, he fastened it around his hips.

Brice and Raelf were watching him.

'You are sure that you feel well enough to get up?' Raelf asked.

'Aye, thank you,' Josse replied. Then, raising his eyebrows in enquiry at Brice, he said, 'Shall we be on our way?'

'You are leaving now?' Raelf's tone was incredulous. 'But it will soon be evening – will you not eat with us? There are beds in plenty for guests, I have but to give the word and—'

'You are kind, Sir Raelf, but my mission cannot wait,' Josse said, trying to be firm and polite at the same time.

'But my wife will be back soon and she—'

Then it is even more important that I leave now, Josse thought, for the well-meant but time-consuming enquiries of a group of women are to be avoided at all costs.

'I must go, Sir Raelf,' he said gently. 'Brice?'

'I am ready,' Brice said.

Josse, watching closely, saw him go as if to speak to Raelf but, whatever he had in mind, he decided not to say it. Instead he put a hand briefly on the older man's arm and muttered something that Josse thought was, *I will come again soon.*

Josse was sure that Brice had wanted to make some comment about Galiena. To give his condolences to her father, perhaps, to ask to be of the company when next the family heard mass for her.

Then he suddenly thought: but maybe Brice does not know that she is dead!

He stared at Brice. Had he the air of a man who had just lost his beloved mistress? Josse could not say. Brice seemed edgy and he was surreptitiously peering around as if he expected someone's arrival. Was it Galiena? Was he hoping to meet his lover in her father's household? Had the two of them met here before?

No, no, no, Josse thought, angry with himself that, just when he needed his wits, they were fuddled by his recent fever. Brice cannot hope to meet Galiena here, even if he does not know of her death, because he thinks she is at Hawkenlye taking a cure.

Oh, dear God, he prayed silently, if it has to be that I break the news to him, please let me do it with kindness.

Raelf came out to see them off. He went out through the gates and looked up the track, then, shaking his head, remarked that his wife and family were taking their time and had probably stayed to have a comforting word with the priest.

'Give them my greetings,' Josse said courteously.

'And mine,' Brice added softly.

Then the two men mounted and rode out of the yard.

When they were once more up on the high ridge, Brice drew rein and said, 'I believe that I know where you are going, Josse. I was at Hawkenlye with the Abbess Helewise, and she told me where you were bound.'

'You were at the Abbey? When?' Josse asked.

'Yesterday evening.'

Then he must know, Josse thought. The Abbess would have told him. He said quietly, 'You know, then, the dreadful news?'

There was a long pause. The light was dim beneath the trees that shaded the track and Josse could not read Brice's expression. After a while, he said heavily, 'Aye. I do.'

He said no more and Josse, hearing over and over again those three brief words, could not say whether or not they came from a heartbroken man just beginning to become accustomed to the loss of his lover.

Then Brice said, 'What happened at Deadfall?'

I must wait, Josse thought. I must be watchful, but I do not believe I shall discover the truth by rushing at it. 'I found the ruined fort,' he said briefly, 'but of the place where Galiena's kin live I saw no sign.'

'I am not surprised,' Brice remarked. 'When I heard

you were looking for it, I did not believe that you would succeed. They hide themselves well, I am told.'

Who told you? Josse wondered. Galiena?

And another part of his mind answered, who else?

'Will you help me find them?' he asked. 'I have undertaken to inform them of her death and I cannot return to Hawkenlye until I have done so.'

'You were riding back towards the Abbey when I found you,' Brice observed.

Josse grinned. 'Aye. I had little option, having failed so miserably, but to seek help. I hoped to come across some traveller who knew the area. But—' He shrugged. 'I was not quite sure what I was doing, earlier.' The grin widening, he added, 'It seems I found exactly what I wanted. It was my good fortune to encounter you.'

'I will take you to Deadfall,' Brice said. 'But we must go carefully and prepared for . . . We must be on our guard.'

'Why?'

'They – the people there – do not welcome strangers,' Brice said slowly. 'They prefer to live apart. To keep themselves to themselves, as people are wont to say.'

'You believe there is danger for us there?' In the light of his experiences over the last never-ending night, Josse thought grimly, he would not be at all surprised.

And, watching him, Brice said simply, 'Yes.'

The intimate companionship of two men alone on the road increasingly made Josse feel that he must speak. He argued with himself for some time but finally, almost to his surprise, heard himself saying, 'Brice, I believe that I have guessed your secret.'

Spinning round in the saddle, his face pale, Brice said, 'How? We have always been so careful!'

Josse shrugged. 'I watch. I keep my eyes open. And sometimes I guess, and then on occasions I feel instinctively that I have guessed right.'

'And I,' Brice said softly, 'have just given myself away by what I said in response to you.' He frowned, his whole face taking on a threatening air. 'You will keep silent, Josse?'

'I – aye, I will.' There was hardly any point, he thought, in telling anyone what he knew now. Not when the poor lass was dead. He murmured, 'I am sorry,' but he did not think that Brice heard.

They rode back to Josse's campsite on the slope above the marsh. To his relief, this evening the sky was clear and the salt flats spread out below had taken on a different appearance from the shadowy and vaguely threatening look they had worn the previous evening. Now a golden light shone down on the quiet land as the westering sun sank in the deep blue sky. It was, Josse thought, unfastening his pack and setting out his gear, a place of enchantment . . .

'These old stones must have sheltered you well last night,' Brice said, breaking in on Josse's dreaming thoughts.

'Aye,' he replied. 'And one of the Hawkenlye nuns provided me with an oiled sheet that kept off the worst of the rain.'

'Yet still your soaking made you feverish,' Brice said.

I do not believe, Josse thought, that the fever came entirely from the rain.

But he was not yet ready to tell Brice about the macabre visitor who had come out of the darkness. Perhaps he never would be.

Brice had brought abundant provisions and they ate well. Then, with a moon rising over the marsh and making flashes of silver on the flat land as its beams shone down and sought out stretches of water, they settled in their covers and slept.

In the morning Brice led the way down the slope and out on to the marsh. They rode here and there across the soggy ground for some time, Brice going ahead, Josse following. After a while, Josse realised that they were covering ground that they had already ridden over and he said, 'Brice, let us return to the high ridge. It is difficult, surely, to pick out any landmarks that will help you find your way when we are down here on the levels. Do you not think you would find the task easier from a vantage point up there?' He waved an arm in the direction of the inland cliff, rising steeply behind them.

Brice frowned. 'I do not know, Josse. I thought – I believed, from what I was told, that I would find the place without difficulty.' He stared out across the featureless marshland where, as far as Josse could discern, there was little to be seen but some trees and a long line of hedge in the distance and some sheep dotted around like pale flowers fallen from a basket.

Making up his mind, Brice spurred his horse and set off towards the cliff. 'Let us try out your suggestion,' he called back to Josse. 'It can hardly be of less use than the sum of my efforts so far!'

Following him, Josse had to agree.

They rode up the track that Josse had ridden down the previous day. This time the heron must either have been absent about its business or else had decided to stay safely hidden in the undergrowth. At the top, Brice turned to his right and rode a few yards down the road to where a gap in the trees allowed a view down over the marsh.

They sat side by side for a long time. Josse was aware of the sound of hooves on the track away to the west; it was clearly a well-used route, however, and he paid the approaching rider, whoever he might be, little heed.

Then Brice said, 'I think I may have spotted something, Josse. I remember being told of a long hall, before which there is a corral for the animals, and behind that ought to be a long line of ancient willows that run along beside a little stream.' He stared out over the lands below them, frowning. 'Oh, but I am not sure. If I am right and it *is* the place we seek, then it is not where I expected it to be. I thought it would be simple,' he added again. Then, with a rueful laugh, said, 'You would have done better, Josse, to seek further and find someone who knew what they were talking about instead of a man such as I, who has more confidence in his own ability than is justified.'

About to deny the self-deprecating comment, Josse heard the rider approaching and, turning, saw him come into view; he had just emerged from an over-shadowed stretch of the track out into the sunlight.

Brice had turned too.

Neither of them spoke; they both sat on their horses watching the rider. He was of slim build, he was dressed simply in a long tunic and he wore a soft, wide-brimmed hat that shaded and concealed his face. His horse was a pretty bay mare and on his left wrist, which wore a heavy gauntlet, sat a hooded hawk.

The man, clearly, had been hunting.

But there was a new element in the air; Brice, Josse realised, was sitting quite still and the tension in him seemed to sing through the air.

'Who are you?' Josse called, preparing to ride to meet the newcomer, but, swift as light, Brice shot out a hand to detain him.

'It's all right,' he said quietly. 'I know who it is.' Then, turning to Josse – who was beginning to feel distinctly apprehensive – he added, 'I was only just now wishing for someone who knew their way, my friend. Well, now we have our wish.'

And, in the midst of tension and anxiety, Brice let out a laugh. It was so unexpected and, in that moment, so alarming that Josse, thrown on to the defensive, reacted instinctively.

I have been betrayed, he thought, feeling for the sword at his side. I have admitted to Brice that I know his secret and he is desperate that I keep my silence. He has brought me here with the sole purpose of joining forces with some ally of his, some man of this secretive, dangerous family from which Galiena came. This huntsman, who even now is approaching. And, fool that I am, I fell right into his trap.

They will not take me without a fight!

Not pausing to think further, not even asking himself why he was so sure that Brice meant him harm, he drew his sword and, kicking Horace, shot forward to meet the hunter.

15

But Josse had reckoned without Brice's swift reactions. Just as Horace lunged forward towards the slim man on the bay mare, Brice spurred his horse and, coming in hard from Josse's right, leapt towards him, his right hand waving what Josse thought was a short sword in the air above him.

Horace took an instinctive avoiding step to the left.

It was not Horace's fault.

He had been trained for war. He recognised an armed man advancing on him and he knew what to do so as to avoid the killing blow to his rider's body. And in that moment of drama, he had not the time to look down and check on the ground beneath his large feathered feet. Why, indeed, should he? He was on a track, and tracks did not normally fall away to empty space under him.

Except that this one did.

Although the three people up on the road could not have known, the place from which Brice had elected to gaze out over the marsh was very dangerous. There were some stunted bramble bushes along its outer edge and they hid a spot right at the edge of the cliff where, in the spring rains, fast-flowing rainwater had eroded the chalk from around a huge boulder, which had tumbled away down the escarpment to the flat land below.

In dodging the threat from his right, Horace had put his forefeet right in the place where the boulder used to be.

Pitched forward alarmingly, the big horse tried to gather himself. But the momentum of the fall was too great for him to step back and his hind feet were borne over the edge of the cliff. Frantically scrabbling for purchase, Horace lurched forward down the steep slope and Josse, his left hand firmly grasping a hank of the horse's mane, clung on as tight as a burr on a hound's back and tried to throw his weight backward in a desperate attempt to help arrest their downhill flight.

He quite thought that it was the end of both of them and he spared a brief pitying thought that this wonderful animal who had served him so well for so long should be brought to his death by Josse's mistake; he who should have paid more attention to that well-used, well-worn track up there!

But the slope was steepest right at the top of the cliff; after perhaps twenty paces – which felt to Josse as if he were falling totally out of control – the gradient eased. Horace, still travelling far too fast for a big, heavy horse going over treacherous ground, began to slow down.

And, as he took a final leap from the lowest slopes of the escarpment on to the flat ground below, Josse began to think that he wasn't going to die after all.

There was a shout from above and Josse, turning,

saw Brice at the top of the slope. The huntsman was beside him and both men were waving; Josse thought they were calling out to summon their companions down on the marsh. Hurriedly looking around him, he realised that he could still be surrounded if a party of riders approached from out on the marsh; making a swift decision, he turned Horace to the left and, spurring him on to a gallop, thundered off eastwards along the base of the cliff. He reasoned that in that direction lay the sea, and the sea meant ports and people. It might, he sincerely hoped, also mean safety.

After about a mile, he slowed down and stopped. As Horace's fast breathing gradually calmed, Josse sat listening.

Other than the peaceful, natural sounds of a marsh in early summer, there was nothing to be heard.

And, now that the surging alarm of the flight down the cliff and the fear of armed men hunting him had abated, he wondered if he had judged the situation correctly.

Brice drew his sword! he reminded himself. He rode right at me.

But another interpretation had occurred to him. Brice had said, hadn't he, that he knew who the newcomer was? And then Josse had drawn his own sword and ridden straight at the man on the bay. Well, if Brice did indeed know the man, then was it not perfectly reasonable to have defended him from Josse's sudden onslaught?

'I think, old friend,' Josse said aloud, patting Horace's sweaty neck, 'that I have been a fool.'

And the worst folly of it all, he thought glumly as slowly he began to ride back the way he had come, is that I cannot now recall why it was that I should be so certain the newcomer meant me harm . . .

By the time he had returned to the place where he had slipped down the escarpment, there was no sign of either Brice or the huntsman. I am on my own again, Josse thought, and, thanks to my own recklessness, no further forward in my search than I was yesterday or the day before.

But there had been something, hadn't there? Standing up above the marsh, Brice had said he thought he might have found the place they were looking for, only – what had he said? – it wasn't where he expected it to be.

Well, Josse thought, if he could only picture in which direction Brice had been looking when he spoke, then that might provide a pointer. Staring up at the cliff top, he tried to remember.

And all at once an image slid into his mind. Just before Brice had raised his head to look along the track at the approaching huntsman, he had been staring straight down at the base of the escarpment beneath his feet.

He had mentioned a line of willows that ran along beside a stream. Slowly turning his head, Josse thought in amazement: and there they are! And the stream is there too; I have been jumping to and fro across it for two days.

Could it be? Was Brice right?

No, he couldn't be because he had mentioned a corral and a long hall. There was no corral, unless that line of old, worn stumps had once supported a barricade. But, even if it had, where was the hall?

He was looking straight at the escarpment when he saw it. Half concealed by a copse of willows – they grew on the cliff side of the stream as well as on the marsh side – he thought he had seen something that did not belong there. It was the edge of a thick, reed-thatched roof.

Going stealthily nearer, he realised that he had been right. It was a roof, some fifteen or twenty paces long, and it covered a building so worn by wind and weather and so stained by the camouflaging lichen that he was quite certain he would never have made it out unless he knew exactly where to look. It had, he thought in wonder, so thoroughly taken on the aspect of its surroundings that it blended in completely.

The building was made of wood. And, Josse had to admit, it looked as if it were a long hall. Beside it he could just make out the outlines of a handful of small outbuildings.

Ignoring the prickle of apprehension that flew up his spine, he nudged Horace with his knees and walked slowly forward. This was the place where Galiena's kin dwelt, the place from which she had been taken as a baby to be given to Raelf and his barren first wife. Well, then it was to here that Josse's mission must lead him, whether he was apprehensive or not.

As he rode steadily over the springy ground, something strange happened. The day was fine, with strong sunshine beating down from a deep blue sky and neither a cloud to be seen nor any hint of moisture on the slight, warm breeze. Yet, as if from nowhere, strands of mist seemed to curl up out of the marsh as if some invisible being had set fire to the sparse, dry grass and it was sending a soft smoke up into the air.

But it could not be smoke, because Josse could detect no smell of burning. Checking Horace, he watched. And the tentative first tendrils of vapour quickly grew until the scene ahead of him – all around him, he realised, looking round with a start of alarm – was concealed behind a shifting, flowing, nebulous film of white.

He could no longer see the hall beneath the cliff. Neither could he see the willows or the stream alongside which they grew. In the sudden sea fret that had floated across the marsh – as it not infrequently did, although Josse was not to know it – he was as a blind man on unfamiliar territory.

It seemed unwise to ride on. Speaking reassuringly to Horace, who did not appear to like the mist any more than Josse did, he sat and waited for it to clear.

The silence was total. It was as if the fog were muffling all the normal small, everyday sounds that are taken for granted until they are no longer there.

First blind, now deaf, Josse thought grimly. Then: if they're out there and they are familiar with this ground, then I'll never be an easier target than I am now.

So closely did the sound follow on the thought that he thought for an optimistic moment that he had imagined it. But then it came again: the clear ring of metal.

It sounded like a horseman, approaching unseen through the brume. The sound came from Josse's right . . . but then it came again from his left. Not one but two of them.

Putting his hand on his sword hilt, Josse strained to see them. And presently they materialised out of the mist: four men, all armed, on short, sturdy ponies.

They were pale, as if they lived their lives in the shadows, and light-eyed. Three were hooded; the fourth wore some sort of round helm on his blond hair. Forming themselves into a semicircle facing in towards Josse, they stared at him in intent silence.

Then the man in the helm said, his words carrying a peculiar accent, 'What do you want here?'

Josse had been staring, half hypnotised, at the brooch that fastened the man's cloak. It was round and bore a design of a running wolf chasing its own tail. It shone in the opaque light with the unmistakable brilliance of gold. Looking the man in the face, he replied, 'I am searching for a place called Deadfall.'

There was a murmur from one of the other men and what sounded like a brief, humourless laugh. The man in the helm said, 'This is Saltwych, or so it is known to us. Men do call it Deadfall, or so I am told.'

Again, one of the other riders made some comment. Josse heard it, quite clearly, but he did not understand it; the man had spoken in an alien tongue.

The helmed man said, a hint of menace in his voice, 'What is your mission at Deadfall?'

I am here on an honest quest, Josse told himself. I have done no wrong, have not even trespassed on private land, as far as I am aware. I will not be intimidated.

'I have come from Hawkenlye Abbey with news of a death,' he said quietly.

'Hawkenlye Abbey?' The man frowned. 'I know it not. Why should a death in that place be news that you have to bring to us here?'

Josse was reluctant to explain. He did not know whom he was addressing; the man might be an important figure in the community who dwelt in this penumbral place, and therefore entitled to hear first of what had happened to the daughter whom they had given away. He might equally well be nothing more than a guard whose job it was to give the alarm when strangers came too close. 'It is a delicate matter,' he said. 'I would tell of it first to—' To whom? And how could he express himself without causing offence? But the four men were close upon him now and he realised he had no option but to speak his mind. 'I wish to speak first to whoever leads your community,' he said firmly.

There was more muttering but the man in the helm gave a curt nod, as if he understood the etiquette that demanded grave tidings be given first to the head of the group.

'Wait here,' he commanded. 'I will announce you and ask if they will receive you.'

Putting spurs to his horse, he trotted off into the mist.

The remaining three riders were now very close to Josse and Horace was uneasy. Murmuring to him,

Josse put a calming hand on the horse's neck. Then suddenly the man on his right said haltingly, 'You are – fit to go to hall?' One of the others laughed as if at a private joke. 'It is great honour,' the man went on. Reaching out, he brushed at Josse's tunic, which was showing all too many signs of nights spent in the open. 'Must not go inside in dirty clothes!' the man said. 'Must tidy hair, clean mud from boots!'

Now all three men were laughing, but quietly, as if they did not want to be overheard. Glancing swiftly at the man on his left – he was young, little more than a boy – Josse was quite sure he saw fear in the pale eyes.

Dear God, Josse prayed silently, what sort of a place have I stumbled into?

There came a sound from the midst of the white fog before him; it was faint and, again, suppressed by the mist, but it sounded as if someone had blown on a horn. The three men leapt to attention, all amusement wiped from their faces, and formed a line beside Josse, one man on his right, two on his left.

The man who had spoken to him gave him a nod and said, 'We go.'

Then, moving as one, Josse included, all four of them began to go forward into the blind whiteness.

As they went, it seemed to grow thinner until it was no more than a thin veil that confused sight. Then, through its silvery sheen, Josse could once more see the hall and the huddle of outbuildings.

His attendants – he hoped that was what they were, although in fact they seemed more like guards

– pressed close on either side of him. As they neared the collection of buildings, he saw, dismayed, that there were more men standing on either side of the hall and all of them were armed.

His guards rode with him right up to the wooden hall. Then they fell away, the man who had spoken to him making a gesture that said plainly, go on!

Feeling very vulnerable in the open space between the horsemen at his back and the swordsmen in front of him, Josse rode on alone. When he was only a few paces from the hall, he spied what he thought must be the door, although its presence was only indicated by a small gap in the wooden planking of the wall, as if it had been opened just a little to admit fresh air.

One of the men standing by the door approached and indicated that Josse should dismount. He did so, putting Horace's reins into the man's outstretched hand. Then, eyes holding the other man's, he straightened his tunic and put his right hand on his sword hilt. With a faint smile, the man said, 'Nobody carries arms when he is admitted into the company in the great hall. Your weapons, please.'

With reluctance, Josse unbuckled his sword belt and handed it over. The man nodded at the dagger in its sheath, and Josse passed that to him as well. Then, the smile broadening until it seemed to hold a tiny amount of genuine warmth, the man said, again in that strange accent, 'Your sword and dagger will be safe. I will guard them for you.'

With a brief bow – it seemed wise to reply to courtesy with courtesy – Josse said, 'I am grateful.'

Then the man pushed the door open and, extending a hand palm uppermost, indicated that Josse should go inside.

He did not know what to expect. The light was poor; the long hall was tucked away beneath the cliff and the willows, and not much light penetrated through the partly opened door. Josse could see little but, to judge from the presence of the guards outside and from the remarks of the three horsemen, he thought that the hall might be a place of splendour. Long tables groaning beneath food and drink, splendid tapestries on the walls to keep out the draughts, the crossed swords and shields of defeated enemies and the heads of noble creatures felled in the hunt as decorations. The home, perhaps, of a rich lord who valued his privacy and maintained his borders by a show of arms. And there was the man with the helm to consider too – that brooch he had worn on his shoulder must be worth a fortune . . .

Stepping forward, Josse's foot slipped and he stumbled into what seemed to be a shallow groove cut in the floor. The stench of animal urine rose around him, hardly what he had thought to find in this place. But perhaps the hall was built in the old style; he wondered if this first area were a stable or a pen for livestock. Men had always lived alongside their animals when they believed that there was a need to keep the creatures safe; many men still lived that way. Withdrawing his foot – his boot made an unpleasant squelch as he pulled it from whatever substance made up the noisome slurry – he moved on.

He went through a wood-framed doorway set in a wattle screen that appeared to be some sort of internal division and decided that he had been right about the first space inside the door being for the animals. This second area smelt strongly of smoked meat and, above him, he could make out bulky shapes hanging suspended from the beams that held up the reed thatch.

As within the first area, there was nobody there.

And if the lord whom Josse had been imagining did indeed live in the luxury that wealth bestowed, then there was still no sign of it.

He went on through another partition and now he felt warmth. Abruptly there was light as whatever dark material had been before the hearth, blocking its glow, was removed.

Before Josse had a chance to do more than have a swift glance around him – bare walls made of planks that were warping so that gaps had begun to appear between them . . . smoke-blackened rafters and cobwebs hanging down from the reed thatch . . . bare floor thick with dirt – someone spoke.

And a voice that demanded instant attention said, 'You have penetrated to the depths of this hall. You have come with news of a death. Why do you bring it here to us?'

Looking across the hearth, firelight after darkness rendering him almost as blind as he had been outside in the mist, Josse made out shapes, forms. Beyond the fire, set against the far wall of the hall, was a raised dais. Standing upon it, darker patches in the darkness, were two tall wooden chairs, the taller of the two splendid and resembling a throne. Both seats were occupied.

In the hearth, a log fell with a shower of bright sparks. As the sudden brightness lit the dim interior, Josse was staring towards the figure in the lower of the two chairs. Light fell on the face – the man was leaning forward to study Josse as curiously as Josse was studying the outlines of the pair in the wooden seats – and Josse recognised the bright eyes.

With a start of horror he recoiled, stepping back involuntarily from the hearth as memory made the sweat break out across his back. Catching his foot in something on the dirty floor – he had a fleeting impression of softness, as if he had tripped on a tattered fur rug – he fell heavily, banging the back of his head hard against the beaten earth.

A blazing trail of stars seemed to flash across his vision, then everything went black.

16

He opened his eyes to see someone staring down at him. It was a small child – a girl child – and, as soon as she saw that he was conscious, she called out something that he did not understand then, leaping up, rushed away.

He turned on to his side – he had, he discovered, been flat on his back – and stared after her. She wore a tunic in some sort of rough fabric that looked like sacking and her long plait of pale hair hung down to her waist. The delicate white skin of her bare feet was begrimed and filthy.

A recollection floated into his head. He had opened his eyes once before, he was almost sure of it, and seen someone . . . Not the child but an adult. A woman. And there had been something odd about her . . . He frowned, worrying at the image until it began to clear. Aye, that was why it was strange, because if he *had* seen who he thought he had, then she should not be there because she was at Hawkenlye Abbey.

He was still staring in the direction in which the little girl had run away. He seemed to be lying in the middle section of the hall; he could see the joints and haunches of smoked meat hanging from the blackened rafters above. The child had run off towards the door and he shifted his position slightly so that he could peer round the wattle screen.

Aye, that was where she'd been, the woman who ought not to be there! She had been standing in the outer area of the hall and looked around the screen at him, tentatively, as if ready to draw her head back swiftly if he saw her.

As he recovered from having knocked himself out, he began to wonder. Maybe it had been part of a dream, for why on earth *should* she be here? Deciding that all he could do was to keep his eyes open and see if he spotted her again, he resolved to put the matter out of his mind. Instead, he turned his attention to sitting up – which made his head ache more fiercely – and seeing if he could attract anyone's attention.

But in fact there was no need, for soon the little girl came back with an older woman – her mother, presumably, for there was a likeness between them – who, with a solicitous smile, asked Josse how he was feeling and offered him a drink.

He was about to take it from her when he stopped. Was it wise, to take food or drink from suspicious strangers? As if the woman perceived his doubt, she said, 'It is a concoction made from the willow. It will help your sore head.' Putting out her hand, she touched the bump on the back of his skull with gentle fingers. 'You fell hard, stranger, and the floor is unforgiving.'

Still he was uncertain. With a soft sound of impatience, the woman gave the mug to the child, said something to her and both she and Josse watched as the little girl took a mouthful, swallowed and made a face.

The woman smiled at Josse. 'It is bitter to the taste. But I will give her a honey cake to take the effect away.' Then, her face straightening, 'Now will you drink?'

It seemed foolish not to, so he sipped at the drink – it was indeed very bitter – until it had all gone. He was not sure whether it was merely his imagination, but he had a fancy that the throbbing in his head began to lessen immediately.

The woman was watching him intently. 'You feel better?'

'Aye. I do,' he agreed.

'Ah. Then,' she said as gracefully she rose to her feet, 'I am ordered to take you before the clan chieftain.'

She helped him to stand and, understanding without being told, waited at his side until his head stopped spinning. His eyesight was a little blurred, he noticed. He blinked hard a few times and it seemed to help. Then he nodded to the woman and she led him through the doorway and into the end chamber of the hall.

Now only one seat was occupied; in the larger of the two wooden chairs sat a tall, fair-haired man. Although Josse had not studied him closely when he had first entered the room – he had had eyes only for the other man, in the lower chair – he was almost certain that this was the same man who had sat on the throne-chair then. His long hair was fair and bound with a narrow circlet of gold above his brow. He was bearded and the tails of a moustache hung down either side of his firm and generous mouth. He was broad in the shoulder, his muscular strength displayed by the sleeveless tunic that he wore. Around both upper arms he wore gold arm-rings.

The light blue eyes fixed on Josse, he said, 'You have news for me, stranger. Since you have taken pains in the bringing of it, let me hear now what tidings you bring.'

Standing on the opposite side of the hearth, Josse tried not to think about the figure who had previously sat in that other chair – perhaps he had dreamed that, too – and, straightening his back and squaring his shoulders, gave his credentials. 'I am Josse d'Acquin and I have come from Hawkenlye Abbey. I am constrained to inform you that a kinswoman of yours has recently met her death there.'

Watching the chieftain, Josse had no doubt that Galiena had indeed stemmed from here; everyone he had encountered so far shared her pale skin and colouring and the man in front of whom he now stood could easily have been her true father.

'My kinswoman?' the chieftain asked. 'You are certain?'

'My lord' – Josse was not sure if that was the correct form of address, but it would have to serve – 'I speak of a woman known as Galiena of Ryemarsh. She was adopted as a baby by a family that dwells at Readingbrooke; the lord's name is Raelf. I went to them to tell them of Galiena's death and, although they grieved for their daughter, they told me that she was not of their blood but that she had been born in a place known as Deadfall. And this community of yours, I understand, is known by outsiders as Deadfall, although your people tell me that you speak of it by a different name.'

'Yes, we call our dwelling place Saltwych,' the chieftain agreed. 'Of old, men extracted salt from the flood plains of the marsh. But the shingle bank that guards the salt marsh from the sea has grown with time and now the tides come no more to flood the land. The name, however, is a long time dying.' He gave Josse a smile. Then, as it faded, he said with sudden sharpness, 'Galiena, you say? And how old was this woman?'

'Er – seventeen. No, eighteen, I think. I do not know for sure,' Josse said. This man, he was thinking, was perhaps in his late thirties or early forties and could certainly be her father. Feeling the tension in his neck and shoulders, he tried to relax. It was not, after all, as though he were in danger!

Was it?

The chieftain's hand was on his belt buckle and, as he sat staring down at Josse, his hand played over the intricately carved design that stood out in relief from the bright metal; the buckle, too, looked like gold or possibly silver gilt. Then he removed his hand and Josse saw what the design represented. It was a naked man with a headdress of eagle heads and in each hand he carried a long spear.

Then the man spoke. 'You believe, Josse d'Acquin,

that we are in the habit of giving away our children?' Then, as Josse hesitated, he commanded curtly, 'Speak!'

'I do not know, my lord.' Josse had decided that diplomacy was the wisest choice, bearing in mind the many armed men who stood within earshot. 'I only report what others have told me.'

'Of course you do,' the chieftain said, mild irony in his voice. For some time there was silence and then, as Josse was beginning to feel distinctly uneasy, the man on the throne appeared to make up his mind. 'You are mistaken,' he stated flatly. 'This woman who has died at the Abbey is not of our blood.'

'But—' Josse began. Then he stopped and, with a bow of the head, waited for the chieftain to continue.

'You have come far to bring us the news and, although whoever sent you to us has in fact misled you, still your intention was good. And in addition you have suffered hurt here.' Breaking off to raise a hand and call out some swift commands, he turned back to Josse and said, 'Please, eat and drink with us before you go on your way. The day is still young and you can be on the road well before nightfall.'

There seemed no point in argument. Josse bowed again and told the chieftain that he would be honoured to accept the proffered hospitality.

A trestle table was set up and a carved wooden chair set at its head for the chieftain. A bench was put along one side and Josse was invited to be seated. As the chieftain took his place he said, 'It is not right that a man should share my board and not know my name. I am Aelle, son of Aethelfrith of the line of the Iutae, who of old trace their lineage back to Woden. You are welcome, Josse d'Acquin, in my hall.'

While Josse was still absorbing this remarkable statement, food and drink were brought and quickly his host filled a rough earthenware mug with ale and thrust it into his hand. Bread still warm from the oven was placed on trenchers and a steaming black pot of some stew was dumped on the table. A brawny-armed woman stepped forward and ladled out portions for Josse and the chieftain. Obeying Aelle's injunction to eat, Josse tried the stew and found that, despite the appetising smell, it consisted mainly of cabbage, onions and leeks, with a background of turnips to provide ballast. There was the smell and the faint taste of meat – pork, Josse thought – but he guessed it was only in the stock in which the stew had been cooked.

Eating and drinking as Aelle had commanded, he realised a profound truth about these strange people. They might be descended from kings – from gods, if Aelle were to be believed – and they might wear still the proud treasures of their past; Aelle's circlet and arm rings, the shoulder brooch of the guard who had apprehended Josse. But their long hall was dirty and in ruins, their bare feet trod in their own filth and they subsisted on vegetables. The very guards who had detained Josse outside had made what he now appreciated to have been joking references to the need for him to brush the mud off his tunic before entering the hall, as if its squalor were a fact that had grown acceptable – even ironically amusing – by long familiarity. In short, they were deep in poverty.

Josse wanted more than anything to leave. He could have understood why a girl babe such as Galiena might have been given away; indeed, it would have been a brave and humane gesture to place her with a barren woman who longed for a child of her own and who could offer more than a life in this run-down, desolate and forgotten corner. But Aelle had denied all knowledge of her, and that appeared to be that.

Without any appearance of haste, Josse finished his food and drained his mug. Then, bowing to his host, he voiced courteous thanks and appreciation for the victuals and announced that he would be on his way.

Aelle walked with him to the door and watched as he reclaimed his weapons. Horace was brought and Josse mounted up. Then he said, 'Farewell, Josse d'Acquin. I wish you success in your efforts to find the kinfolk of this dead woman and I regret that we were unable to help you.'

Repeating his thanks, Josse kicked Horace to a trot and rode away.

They would be watching him, of that he was certain. He set off towards the track leading up to the good road that ran along the cliff top and he resisted the urge to turn round. An innocent man would not keep checking to see if he were being followed. He found the steep track and set Horace to climb it and it was only when he was in the concealing shelter of the trees and the undergrowth that lined the upper road that he drew rein and, dismounting, found a vantage point from which he could look down on the marsh.

He could not see a soul.

Had they gone back to their dwelling? Forgotten all about him?

If they *were* innocent, he reasoned, then aye, that was what they would have done. But they were not. For all that Aelle denied the giving away of a child eighteen years ago, Josse did not believe him. There was far more going on at Deadfall – or Saltwych, as they called it – than it appeared on the surface. For one thing, there was that figure who had sat in the second chair. Unless Josse were imagining things – a possibility, he acknowledged, given that he had suffered a blow to the head – then who, or what, was he? And the fall was not relevant, Josse thought, with a sudden realisation that would have been exciting had it not been so frightening, because he had seen the man *before* he fell and knocked himself out. And that had not been the first encounter; Josse had seen him on the night of the storm.

It was the eyes, he thought. He had never seen eyes like that. Silvery, luminous, as if they were lit from within by some unearthly radiance.

Why had the man disappeared? Why had he been there at first – and, what was more, in a position of honour beside the chieftain – and then gone, disappearing without trace or mention, as though he did not exist?

He *does* exist, Josse thought.

And the silver-eyed man was not the only oddity;

there was also the matter of the woman who should not be there. Josse had kept a surreptitious lookout for her while he was entertained at Aelle's board and his vigilance had been successful. She had been careful – very careful – and he had only caught a rapid glimpse of her as she stood, behind two other women, and peered between them into the chamber where Josse and Aelle were eating.

He was sure she had not seen that he had noticed her; he had been facing away from her and seen her from the very edge of his field of vision.

It *had* been her, he knew it. She was not a handsome woman but she was a striking one. And what in God's holy name was she doing in Saltwych when the proper place for Aebba, serving woman of the late Galiena Ryemarsh and now in attendance on the lord Ambrose, was surely at her master's side?

He was going to have to return to Saltwych. He would go by night and he would be very careful not to be seen.

Aelle had said that Galiena was not of his blood. He claimed that his kin did not give up their children for adoption. Well, he might be telling the truth. But if so, if the people who lived at Saltwych were nothing to do with Galiena, then what was Aebba doing there?

There *was* a connection; there had to be. Frowning, Josse puzzled away at it. Aebba had set out in the party that had escorted Galiena to Hawkenlye and Galiena had dismissed her and sent her back to Ryemarsh when they came into view of the Abbey gates. Then the woman had gone with Ambrose when he went to join Galiena at Hawkenlye, this time arriving at the Abbey and staying there. Then Galiena died – Josse had a sudden vivid memory of Aebba's expression as she stared down at her young mistress's face – and Aebba, in the absence of any other duties, set about caring for Ambrose. Josse himself had seen her when she brought clean linen down to her master staying in the Vale.

How, then, did she come to be here at Saltwych?

Perhaps, he mused, Aebba knew of Galiena's true lineage and, on the girl's death, had come on the same mission that Josse had tried to carry out: to inform Galiena's people that she was dead. But there was something amiss with that reasoning . . . After quite a lot of puzzling, Josse worked out what it was. Galiena had not liked Aebba; he was sure of it. He recalled the girl's mutinous expression when Ambrose had suggested that Aebba be one of the party to escort Galiena to Hawkenlye Abbey, and he also remembered his own surprise that Galiena did not dismiss the woman and find herself a servant more to her liking. Was it reasonable, then, to assume that Galiena had entrusted the secret of her true birth to this serving woman whom she had disliked? No. It was not.

Something occurred to Josse that he had not thought of until now: did Galiena actually *know* her true parentage?

He stood deep in thought for some time. He finally concluded that it was a question that he could not answer. Ambrose did not appear to know, for he had sent Josse to Readingbrooke, to break the news to the people there whom he believed to be his late wife's family.

But Ambrose, he reminded himself, had cause to do harm to Galiena, for she bore another man's child and jealous husbands had been known to kill their wives for less. So perhaps he *had* known about Saltwych but had chosen to keep his knowledge to himself.

I am fumbling in the dark, Josse thought in frustration. There is so much that I do not know – that, I believe, is being deliberately obfuscated and kept from me.

He would go down to Saltwych as soon as it was dark. He would leave Horace securely tethered at a safe distance and he would creep up on the settlement as cautiously as he knew how. He would spy on the inhabitants, eavesdrop, search around those outbuildings to see what was kept in them. Audra had told him the truth, he was sure – why should she not? – and Aelle had lied. They did know about Galiena at Saltwych and the more Josse thought about it, the more convinced he became that they were somehow involved – implicated? – in her death.

They had herbal knowledge, that was plain, for had he himself not been treated with a remedy that was swifter and more effective than anything that he had been given before? And, for an old soldier who had sustained his share of wounds and sundry hurts, that was saying a lot. So could one of those strange people have made up a poison designed for slipping into something that Galiena would consume? And, not having succeeded at Ryemarsh, followed her to Hawkenlye and put the poison into Sister Tiphaine's potion?

No. Not there, for the potion had not harmed the Abbess Helewise when she so bravely – so recklessly – drank from it.

And, anyway, why? *Why* should Aelle's people want Galiena dead? Ambrose was a very wealthy man and the Saltwych community lived in dire poverty, but how could they expect to benefit from Ambrose's wife's death if the lord did not even know of the connection? But then perhaps he *did* know . . .

Oh, it was hopeless!

Smacking a fist furiously against the trunk of a birch tree, Josse tried to stop the whirling thoughts. I cannot solve the puzzle until I find out more, he thought, massaging his bruised knuckles. And find out more I shall.

He sat down, made himself as comfortable as he could against the birch tree and waited for darkness.

17

It was night, and Josse had crept right up to the long hall. The Saltwych community appeared to be asleep and, as far as Josse had been able to ascertain, they did not post a guard during the hours of darkness.

He had left Horace some distance away, in a hawthorn brake where the stunted, twisted trees had provided both concealment and a stout trunk to which to hitch the horse's reins. The sky was clear and Josse could see the stars, whose faint light was the only illumination; the moon had not yet risen. As he had made his stealthy way from the thorn brake to the Saltwych settlement, silver strands of mist had risen from the marsh to twine around his legs and feet as if they were silken bonds that tried to hold him back.

He stood in the shelter of the long hall's thatched roof for some time, perfectly still, listening. Other than the calming sounds of animals' and humans' snores and deep regular breathing as they slept, not a sound. Finding a gap in the warped planks of the wall, he peered through it and, by the last glow of a torch set in the wall that was slowly spluttering to extinction, made out the sleeping forms of men and women. If one of the women were Aebba, there was no way of knowing. The chieftain's area had been closed off by a hanging that had been drawn across the doorway; presumably he and his immediate circle – including, no doubt, the man with the silvery eyes – were within, but Josse did not think it necessary to confirm it. Necessary or not, it was far too dangerous; the very idea of sneaking inside the hall and peering around the heavy hanging made sweat break out on his back. If he were to be caught, there would be no mercy and he was beginning to think he had made a bad mistake in coming.

It was not a good thing to think. Still, he was here now and he might as well try to accomplish what he had set out to do. Moving silently along the length of the hall, he stepped out from under the thatch and made his careful way to inspect the huddle of outbuildings. There were four of them, as far as he could see, and all were circular in shape, quite small – about three or four paces in diameter – and in an even worse state of repair than the long hall. One smelt of woodsmoke – the bakehouse? – and another seemed to be a workroom of some sort; Josse thought he could make out a workbench through the partly open door. He stepped inside and felt along the rough wood of the bench. His fingers touched the cold metal of tools, then something that gave a faint clink as his hand knocked against it, the tiny sound magnified by his fear. Feeling the links of a chain, he waited for his heartbeat to slow down.

The last hut, furthest away from the hall and set apart from the others, was empty. Or so he thought, stretching up to look through a knothole in the planking. But it was dark inside and he went round to the door to see if he could open it. The door was bolted on the outside with a heavy wooden bar that had been thrust through four iron hoops, two on the door and one on each of the walls on either side.

He was turning away when it occurred to him that you only bolt a door on the outside to keep somebody in.

It could, of course, be livestock; a sickly hound, a farrowing sow. But there was no animal smell and Josse did not think that whatever was inside walked on four legs.

Standing right up against the door, as if he hoped to muffle any sound he made by his body, he took hold of the wooden bar and slid it slowly and carefully to the right. Despite its weight, it moved easily, as if this action were a frequent occurrence. When it was clear of all four hoops, Josse placed it very carefully on the ground. He had, he was almost certain, made not a sound.

He pulled the door towards him, opening it just enough to cast a little of the night's soft radiance within. The light fell upon a beaten earth floor – not very clean – and upon a dark shape, perhaps a bundle of old sacks, lying against the wall on the far side of the hut. He was just wondering why it should have been thought necessary to bolt the door on a heap of sacks when the sacks gave a low, mournful groan.

His heart gave a great lurch of alarm. As the shock subsided, he knelt down and put out a hand . . .

. . . and touched a bare ankle, around which was the chill clamp of a shackle attached to a chain. Following the chain upwards, Josse found its other end, securely fastened to a ring set in the wall.

Whoever the prisoner was, he – or perhaps she, for the ankle felt slender – was clad in sacking and lying on the bare floor. Muttering quiet words of assurance, Josse felt for where he thought the shoulder ought to be and gave it a gentle shake. There was a wad of some rough cloth beneath her head and, stuck to her cheek, it moved with her.

There was no response and so he shook her a little harder and, hating himself, gave the soft flesh quite a hard pinch. Again, nothing, other than a soft moan. Getting his arm round behind the girl's back – he was sure now that it was a girl – he propped her up and said, right into her ear, 'Can you hear me? Do not be afraid, I wish only to help you.'

The head lolled heavily forward and sticky rats' tails of ill-smelling hair fell across the face. Was she unwell? Was that why she had been isolated in here? Suddenly fearful that he had done something foolishly rash that might result in some dread sickness developing in his own body, he cursed under his breath. Then reason came back; for one thing, you did not normally chain up a sick person – unless they were mad and dangerous – and for another, she was cool to the touch with no hint of fever.

Why was she chained there all alone? And why, if she were not ill, was she so unresponsive?

The thought came to him that she might be drugged.

Carefully he laid her heavy head back down on the hard earth. How was he to get her out? The first problem would be how to get that shackle off her ankle and he remembered the workroom with its array of tools. If he could find something that he could use, then he—

From somewhere quite close, somebody coughed. Josse froze.

Dear God, he had left the door of the hut ajar! There was a watchman after all and he was doing his rounds, would any moment now be outside the hut!

But then there came the blessed sound of water falling on the earth. There was a grunt of satisfaction – a deep grunt, so it was a man – then he must have finished urinating for there was silence once more. Then, faintly, there came the sound of a wooden door closing.

Josse crouched for some time, utterly still. Then, when his cramped legs could stand it no longer, slowly he stood up.

He stared down at the girl, who had not stirred. There was nothing he could do for her just then, he realised that now. Any attempt to free her would make a noise, and then he would probably end up chained in there beside her.

I won't leave you here, child, he told her silently. I don't know what you've done but, whatever your crime, it's inhuman to chain a child away in the darkness and drug her to insensibility. I will come back for you.

Then he crept out of the hut, carefully closed

the door and replaced the wooden bar and hurried away.

As he ran, crouching, back to the thorn brake, he realised that the mist had thickened considerably while he had been at Saltwych. He could make out the hawthorn trees – just – but they were disappearing fast into the milky whiteness. Breaking into a sprint, he raced over the last fifty paces and gained the shelter of the trees. Horace, moving his feet in restless unease, gave a soft whicker of greeting; patting his neck, Josse unfastened the reins, swung up into the saddle and said, 'You are not near as relieved to see me as I am you, old friend.' Then, giving the horse a cluck of encouragement, they hurried away towards the track that led up to the top of the escarpment.

The way up through the trees was even more sinister by night and darkness reduced the visibility almost to nothing; Josse and Horace went by instinct alone. Reaching the top, it was a relief to emerge into the relative brightness of the starlight. Dismounting, Josse was about to find himself some sheltered spot in which to sleep away what remained of the night when they jumped him.

There were at least two of them, he knew that because he saw someone grasp Horace's reins just as another man threw a length of cloth of some sort over his head and flung him to the ground. He opened his mouth to yell out his protest when a large hand was clamped across his lips and a voice – a man's – hissed in his ear, 'Do not make a sound! They are abroad and they must not find us!'

Josse gave an almighty lurch and the man pinning him down almost lost his grip. But, powerful though Josse was, his assailant had the strength of desperation and Josse realised after a moment that he was not going to escape the man's hold. Relaxing, Josse gave a nod, which he hoped the man would take for assent, and waited.

The man got off him. The cloth was pulled off his head and he found himself face to face with Brice.

'I am sorry, Josse,' Brice whispered, 'but we had to stop you making any sound. We have been waiting for you to warn you. They are looking for you.'

'Why? What—' Josse began, but Brice shook his head.

'Not now. We are not safe here. Come with me.'

Horace, Josse saw, had been led away by Brice's companion – was it the huntsman? It looked as though it was – and was already some distance down the road. He was heading eastwards, along the cliff-top road and towards the distant sea. Of Brice's and the huntsman's horses there was no sign. Urging Josse to hurry, Brice set off at a run after Horace and the huntsman.

Soon the man turned off the road and led the way up a narrow and overgrown track that wound through thick undergrowth into a copse of ancient beech and oak trees. They came to a small clearing and the man led Horace over to a makeshift corral where two other horses were tethered. Brice said, 'Do not worry – your horse will be fed and watered,' and, taking Josse's arm, led him into a rough shelter made of woven branches and roofed with bracken. Motioning him towards a seat made from a length of log, he said, 'Please, sit down. I will fetch food and drink for us as well.'

He was gone for only a short while, returning with bread – rather dry – and some strips of dried meat. He also brought ale in a flask. Setting these offerings out neatly on the grassy floor of the shelter, he said, 'Again, I apologise, Josse, for treating you so roughly and I thank you for coming here with us. You had only my word that there was danger in remaining exposed out there on the cliff top.'

Josse studied him. Then he said, 'I have no reason to doubt your word, Brice. I do not now believe that you mean me harm.'

Brice dropped his head. He said quietly, 'Thank you for that.'

'But,' Josse went on, 'be that as it may, I need an explanation.'

'Of course, of course.' Brice sounded distracted. Getting up, he went to the entrance of the shelter and looked out, returning with a glum expression. 'I had hoped to have help in this tale that I am about to tell you,' he murmured, 'but it seems that it is to be left to me.' He grinned suddenly. 'Which I suppose is only fair, since much of what has occurred has come about because of my own insistence in having that upon which I had set my heart.'

'Ah,' Josse said, and even to him the brief syllable sounded knowing. He was beginning to think that he understood.

Brice looked up at him sharply. Then he said quietly, 'Aye, Josse d'Acquin. They do say that little escapes your notice.' Then, after a short pause as if he were gathering his words, he said, 'You are aware, I know, of the tragedy that befell my wife.'

'Aye.'

'Well, I felt much guilt over the manner of her death and, until I did penance with the good monks at Canterbury, I was near to drowning in remorse and self-pity, neither of which was going to bring Dillian back. Did you ever wonder how I picked myself up and got on with my life, Josse?'

'I—' The truth was that Josse had barely spared Brice's private life a thought. They had met from time to time, as neighbours tend to do, exchanged greetings, made small talk. 'No,' he said honestly.

Again, Brice smiled. 'Well, men are not in the habit of searching their souls concerning their own or one another's emotions. We consider, do we not, that sensitive and complicated things of that nature are best left to the womenfolk?' Not waiting for an answer, he plunged on, 'I did mourn my wife, sincerely and for a long time. But then I met someone else and I fell in love with her.'

You met Galiena, Josse thought, although he did not speak.

'She was – matters were delicate,' Brice went on. 'We were not free to be together, to enjoy a steady fostering of our feelings for each other; in short, not free to admit our love. We could only meet by careful arrangement and we were helped in this by a sympathetic friend who did us the great kindness of relaying messages between us. She – my lady – liked to ride and it was known that she often set off alone to hunt with her falcon.'

'Indeed?' Josse had not known that Galiena enjoyed such pastimes but then, he thought, why should he have been told?

'Indeed,' Brice repeated. Misunderstanding Josse's query, he said, 'It sounds unlikely, perhaps, for one who does not know her, and I suppose that it is unusual for a woman to hunt alone. But that is her way.'

He spoke of her, Josse noticed, as though she were still alive. It touched him profoundly for, even though the man's love for her had been adulterous, it also appeared to have been deep and sincere.

'We spent many happy hours out in the wild country together,' Brice was saying, 'and our urgent need not to be seen caused us to find lonely places where men do not go.' He raised his eyes to Josse, his own naked with the emotions that were driving him. 'We became lovers, Josse, for we could not wait for matters to work out so that we could ask the Church for her blessing on our union. We—'

But Josse could not contain himself. Even if the two of them had truly loved each other, Galiena was wife to Ambrose; what of him? Were his feelings not to be considered at all? 'And just how were you expecting this working out of matters to be accomplished, eh?' he demanded. 'Were you waiting for Ambrose to die so that you could marry the mistress whom you had already impregnated?'

Brice stared at him, his mouth open. He shook his head as if in disbelief, then said, 'Ambrose? Why should we wish that Ambrose—'

Then light appeared to dawn. He said, and the anger was audible in his voice, 'You believe I loved Galiena? Josse, you make a foul accusation!' He was on his feet, looming over Josse, large hands clenched into fists.

Quickly Josse got up too. 'I make the accusation because I have followed the hints and the suggestions that led me to it!' he shouted back. 'From the first, when you took me to Ryemarsh, I observed the tension and the suppressed excitement in you as we rode towards your love! Man, you were like a boy in the throes of calf-love!' Ignoring Brice's menacing expression, he ploughed on. 'And then, when we rode out together from Readingbrooke just yesterday, I said that I had guessed your secret and you did not deny it!'

'Yes, but I thought you—'

But Josse was too agitated to let him speak. 'You were not of the party that escorted Galiena from Ryemarsh on her way to Hawkenlye, for you had left Ryemarsh the previous evening to return home. Or so you said. Then, after we reached New Winnowlands and I left the group, you met up with her somewhere on the road! I went to your house, Brice, I went to call for you when I set off for Hawkenlye and you were not there! And then she died, your mistress Galiena, and she was poisoned!' He paused, breathing hard. 'Good

God, I have even found myself wondering if it was you who poisoned her!'

Anger seemed to have drained out of Brice. His face dark with sorrow, he said gravely, 'Why should I have wished her dead?'

'Because she carried your child. It was meant to be a pleasant diversion, your lovemaking, and yet it resulted in her pregnancy, she who was married to another.'

But even as Josse said the words, he knew that he was wrong. Terribly wrong.

There was silence in the shelter. Slowly Brice sat down again and, after a while, looked up at Josse. 'I am horrified that you should believe me capable of such dreadful callousness,' he said, dropping his head and burying his face in his hands. 'You know of my past, aye, and I suppose you think that a man whose hot temper led to the death of his wife might similarly lose control and bring about the death of his mistress.' Removing his hands, eyes firmly on Josse's, he said, 'But I swear to you that you are wrong this time. I knew Galiena, of course I did, and I honoured her for her kindness and her generosity, aye, and for her beauty.' He gave a faint smile, there and gone in an instant. 'I admit that, had she been free and had my heart not already been engaged elsewhere, I might well have courted her. Under those circumstances, what man worth the name would not have done the same?'

'Aye,' Josse agreed. 'She was comely, aye.'

'Ambrose is my friend,' Brice said simply. 'I did not seduce his wife and become her lover, Josse;

I give you my word. And I certainly did not poison her.'

Josse did not know what to say. He had been wrong, he knew that, and he thought he should go back along the misleading, treacherous track that had led him to accuse an innocent man of the fell deed of murder to see if he could discover where he had gone so badly astray.

But Brice took his silence for doubt.

'You *shall* believe me, Josse d'Acquin,' he raged, leaping to his feet again. 'Wait and I will give you proof!'

Before Josse could protest, Brice had run from the shelter. Going to the entrance to watch, Josse saw him vault the makeshift rail around the horse corral and approach the huntsman, who was still engaged in tending to Horace. Brice bent down to say something – his very stance gave away his tension – and the huntsman nodded, wiped his hands and stepped over the rail beside Brice. Side by side they walked slowly back to the shelter.

Before Brice spoke; Josse realised what, had it not been for his having leapt so confidently to a totally wrong conclusion, he might have realised before.

Brice, the anger gone from his handsome face to be replaced by a very different, softer emotion, took the huntsman's hand. And as the young man threw back the wide-brimmed concealing hat, Josse looked into a woman's face.

A woman whom he recognised.

Brice, still smiling, held out her slim hand to Josse

and he took it in his. Then Brice said to her, 'My dearest love, I believe that you have already met Sir Josse d'Acquin. Josse, here is my lady.'

And Josse, burning with embarrassment, looked down into the sea-green and faintly amused eyes of Isabella de Burghay.

18

She stood in the entrance to the shelter, still regarding him with that cool expression. After a moment – a highly awkward one for Josse – she said, 'Brice tells me that you have interpreted the situation slightly erroneously.'

Bowing briefly, he said, 'So it would seem, my lady, and I am sorry to have caused you distress.'

'It is not I who am distressed,' she corrected him gently. Glancing across at Brice by her side – Josse noticed that they were hand in hand – she went on, 'Brice has never quite managed to convince himself that he was not responsible for the death of his wife, Dillian, despite what he says.' She turned to give Brice a loving smile. 'It is not kind, Sir Josse, to have disturbed old hurts by accusing him of poisoning Galiena Ryemarsh, whom he cared for deeply *as a friend*.' She emphasised the last three words. Then, her expression grave, she said, 'As did I, for she was always kind to me and offered her strength for me to lean on when I was in sore need.' The shadow of some past sorrow crossed her face. 'And she was our messenger,' she added softly. 'She knew of our love and she understood why we cannot yet declare it openly. She offered to relay our communications to each other and that, Sir Josse, is why Brice seemed excited and eager when he took you to Ryemarsh: he was expecting Galiena to pass on to him the place and time of our next meeting.'

Now both of them were looking at Josse and he felt himself to be standing before his accusers and judges. 'I am sorry,' he said humbly.

'And that day when you went to visit Brice when you were bound for Hawkenlye Abbey,' Isabella went on relentlessly, 'Brice was away from home, yes, but he was not chasing after Galiena. With our beloved messenger's absence, we had nobody to relay word from one to the other and so, knowing my habit of hunting in the early mornings, he had gone to look for me, although without success.'

Once more, feeling even worse, Josse mumbled his apologies.

Brice began to speak but, with a gentle touch of her hand to his cheek, Isabella stopped him. 'Perhaps you are wishing to know the answer to the obvious question, Sir Josse? Why it is that we have need of secrecy and private, unobserved assignations?'

'Well, aye, I am,' he said haltingly, 'although in truth, my lady, there is no call for you to explain yourselves to me.'

'No, there isn't,' she agreed. She paused, then smiled and said, 'But I see no reason why we should not satisfy your curiosity. What do you think, my love?' She turned to Brice.

'I would like Josse to know,' Brice said firmly. 'If

only to convince him that I have not acted in the dishonourable way that he accuses me of doing.'

'I have already apologised!' Josse cried, stung.

But Isabella's calm voice murmuring words in Brice's ear was clearly more persuasive than Josse's outburst, for, with a curt nod, Brice said, 'Very well. I accept your apology, Josse.'

Isabella looked from one to the other and, with a faint sigh of exasperation, muttered something under her breath. Then, facing Josse, she said, 'When I was seventeen, I was married to a fine man named Nicholas de Burghay. It was an arranged marriage and I had little say in the matter, but fate was kind and gave me a husband whom I could honour, care for and, over the months and years, come deeply to love. In time our union was blessed with children; first a son, Roger, who is now nine years old, and then, two years later, a daughter, Marthe.' She paused, then drew a shaky breath. Brice disengaged his hand from hers and put his arm around her, pulling her close to him. She flashed him a brief smile and then said, 'Nicholas and I loved to hunt together. Nicholas was permitted to hunt with the falcon and he passed on his skills to me, teaching me to raise the eyas from the nest and train her to fly from my wrist. It was ever our habit to ride out early in the morning, when the field and the woodland were quiet, and fly our hawks together. We believed that few were aware of our regular outings but—'

Again she paused. Then, apparently altering what she had been about to say, she went on quietly, 'One morning there was an accident. Nicholas was badly hurt and, although he lived on for three days, in great pain, he died.' Tears formed in her eyes, making the green colour suddenly as vivid as emeralds, and, quickly blinking them away, she whispered, 'Marthe was but a month old. She does not remember her father at all.'

Then, overcome, she turned to Brice and for a while he hugged her to him. Looking at Josse over her blonde head, he said quietly, 'It is an unhealed hurt, Josse. And she—'

But at that Isabella raised her head, wiped her eyes with the back of her hand and said, 'Let us speak of happier times. Sir Josse, you have met Audra de Readingbrooke and Raelf, her husband.'

'Aye.'

'Audra is Nicholas's younger sister. She and Raelf met in our house, soon after Raelf lost his wife. He and Audra had been wed for some ten years when Nicholas died and they already had three little girls of their own who are my nieces by marriage, since they are the daughters of my husband's sister. Also, of course, there was Galiena, whom Raelf and his first wife had adopted as a baby, Matilda being barren.'

'Aye, so the lady Audra told me.'

'Did she indeed?' Isabella raised a narrow, dark eyebrow. 'She must have taken to you, Sir Josse, for normally she is reticent over divulging private family matters to strangers.'

He sensed a rebuff and felt unreasonably guilty.

'I did not force the words out of her, my lady,' he said stiffly.

Isabella smiled. She was, Josse could not help noticing, a very lovely woman. 'I am sure that you did not,' she said smoothly. Then, picking up her tale: 'They took me in, me and my two little children, and we found comfort in that kind, open-hearted and affectionate family. Galiena and I became particular friends. She was thirteen years my junior but the gap always seemed less than that, for she was a mature girl. She was but fifteen when she made up her mind that she wanted to marry Ambrose and, although there was some consternation because of the age difference, Galiena insisted that he was the only man she would have and that was that.' She smiled again, this time a soft, reminiscent expression as though her mind was on some happy occasion in the misty past. 'She had been used to kindness from the family who had adopted her and she recognised its importance in a marriage. She always said that she could look all her life and never find a kinder husband than Ambrose. They were wed in the early spring of 1191 and, as I believe you know, Sir Josse, she then spent the next two years trying to conceive a child.'

Something was tapping insistently at Josse's mind and he knew he should stop and isolate what it was; it was something important, something he should not ignore. But Isabella was still speaking and he was entranced by her storytelling. She had the gift of keeping the attention of her audience, that was for sure.

'It was in Ambrose's hall that I first met Brice,' she was saying. 'I had gone to stay with Galiena and Ambrose at Ryemarsh and Brice, being Ambrose's friend and neighbour, had been invited to join us. We fell in love very swiftly.' Again, the brief look at Brice, who still had his arm around her slim waist. She contrived to look very feminine, Josse thought, even dressed as she was in man's clothing.

'But I do not understand why you could not declare your love,' he said, trying to turn his attention from Isabella and her femininity. 'Will you now tell me at last?'

Isabella dropped her head and did not speak. Instead Brice said quietly, 'It is on account of young Roger, Isabella's son.' He hesitated, as if speaking of this ongoing hurt pained him. 'Roger does not like me.' It was flat, bald, and clearly hurt Isabella as much as it did Brice, for she seemed to wince and looked at the ground. But Brice went on, 'It is, as you will appreciate, a delicate matter because Roger's poor father died when the boy was only two years old and in his imagination he has made up a detailed and, I am sure, accurate picture of the father he lost. Naturally he does not welcome the idea of another taking Nicholas's place, usurping his position as Isabella's husband and father of her children.'

Josse wanted to ask why not, or, at least, why Isabella could not persuade her son to adopt a more reasonable stance. He opened his mouth to speak but Isabella shot him a look and, almost imperceptibly, shook her head.

'That is our sorry position, Josse,' Brice concluded with an unconvincing attempt at a carefree laugh. Then, looking suddenly puzzled, he began, 'It is strange, all this, because—' But then he stopped himself. 'Ah well, there it is. Until Roger's hostility lessens a little, we are stuck with being secret lovers.' He hugged Isabella and added quickly, 'Do not think that I am complaining, Josse, for I would have Isabella's love in any way that I could, so precious is she to me.'

Josse did not know what to say. The boy was nine, he thought, so presumably would soon be sent for training to some other household. Could not Isabella and Brice quietly be married then? But no, she surely would not agree to that; he had the feeling that Isabella de Burghay would not take Brice as her husband until such time as her son was fully reconciled to the match.

'I am sorry for you,' he said eventually. 'It is, or so it would appear, an insoluble problem.'

'It is,' Brice said with sudden bitterness. Then, as if he regretted the upsurge of emotions that he could not control, he stepped away from Isabella, gave both her and Josse a brief bow and, hurrying out of the shelter, went across to the corral.

Into the tense silence that he left behind him, Isabella said, 'There is more to this, Sir Josse. I have had to be—' She paused as she thought. 'I have had to be less than truthful with Brice, for what I entreat you to believe are very good reasons. But my sorrow is that, in making up this tale of Roger's dislike, I harm and misrepresent both my lover and my son. Brice adores

Roger and cannot understand why I keep telling him that Roger resents him, for Roger is also very fond of Brice and, as a child will, he shows it.'

'Now I understand Brice's comment about the strangeness of it all,' Josse said. 'You are telling him that Roger dislikes him, whereas his own senses tell him that the opposite is true.'

'Yes!' she agreed eagerly. 'Brice asks me why Roger does not display the enmity that he really feels and I have to lie and say oh, because he is too well-mannered.' Her face full of self-disgust, she added vehemently, 'I *hate* myself, Josse.'

His sympathies engaged by her frankness, he said, 'You cannot go on like this, my lady. If there is no true impediment to your marriage to Brice, then surely it should be celebrated as soon as possible.'

But she whispered, 'Oh, Josse, there *is* an impediment.'

'Can we not remove it?' he whispered back.

She looked at him, affection in her face. 'Thank you for the *we*,' she said. 'It heartens me to have such a man as Sir Josse d'Acquin offering me his help. If that is what you are doing?'

The look in her greenish eyes – comprised of anxiety in case he wasn't and a touch of prickly pride, as if to say, I don't need you anyway! – was hard to bear. So he just said, a little gruffly, 'Aye, lady. What aid I can give you is yours to command.'

And she said quietly, 'Thank you.'

But Brice was coming back, and she said no more. Whatever this problem – this impediment – was,

Josse decided, it was to be kept from Isabella's lover.

Well, that decision was hers alone to make. Josse could only wait.

As the three of them settled down to sleep in the small shelter – the men lay a discreet distance from Isabella and Josse could not help but wonder if this observance of the proprieties were merely for his benefit – he tried to put a halt to the seething thoughts running wild in his mind.

He closed his eyes. No good – all he saw was Isabella's face.

Think of Saltwych. Oh, hell's fire, he remembered, he'd meant to ask Brice why the people from the settlement should have been out hunting for him. And he also must honour his promise to that poor girl imprisoned in the outhouse and try to find a way of helping her. Well, it would all have to wait until morning since Brice appeared to be asleep.

There was something else bothering him. Something that he had been worrying about when Isabella had told him about her friendship with Galiena.

Aye! That was it! Now that he had called it to mind, he could not see how he could have possibly forgotten.

Lying on his side, shoulder hunched into the folded cloak that he was using for a pillow, he thought about it again and still he could see no answer.

Aye, it was a poser all right. He yawned, feeling his eyelids grow heavy. Perhaps inspiration might come if he went to sleep on the problem . . .

Which was this: if Brice and Galiena had not been lovers, then who had fathered her baby?

In the morning, Josse awoke to find that the others were up and about before him. A small fire was burning in the lee of the shelter and Isabella had made some sort of hot drink. Brice stood looking out at the day and eating a heel of bread, which he had softened by dunking it in his drink.

As Josse emerged from the shelter, Isabella handed him a mug and another hunk of bread. 'It is dry, I fear, and the drink not as tasty as I would like, but better than nothing.'

'Aye, lady, and I am grateful even for this.' Josse toasted her with his mug; the drink, on trying it, had a reviving, slightly medicinal taste and he thought he detected rosemary.

Brice said, 'We should get on the road and be away from here as soon as we can. They do not usually pursue trespassers by day but it is always possible.'

'Why do they deem us trespassers?' Josse asked. 'And why were you so insistent last night that I was in danger?'

Brice frowned, then, after a quick look at Isabella, said, 'The people of the Saltwych community do not like strangers. They keep themselves to themselves and they foster their own isolation by spreading fearful rumours of ghosts and hauntings that threaten any who wander down there under the inland cliff.'

'I cannot believe they threaten armed men!' Josse protested. 'They have a few gold treasures but I saw nothing to persuade me that they can command a fighting force.'

'Oh, but they can,' Brice said. His hand was on his sword hilt as he spoke. 'They have lived in poverty since the salt workings failed – and *that* wasn't a recent calamity, I can tell you – but they retain a sense of their own worth. In full measure.'

'It is often the way where wealth has evaporated,' Josse observed. 'Nothing left but stiff-necked pride.'

'Exactly,' Brice said.

A thought occurred to Josse and without thinking he voiced it. 'Think you that it was for that reason – their poverty – that they gave Galiena up for adoption? Because a baby girl was one more mouth to feed and she would likely enjoy a better life elsewhere?'

'No,' Isabella breathed quietly. Both men turned to look at her and, in some confusion, she said, 'I mean, I don't think that's the way Galiena looked at it. She – er – she did not know where she came from but I think she imagined that she was the child of some young girl whose chances of marriage would be badly affected were it known she had borne an illegitimate baby.'

Passing over that – Josse wondered if Brice had also noticed that Isabella's explanation was given with such a lack of conviction that it seemed she couldn't make herself believe it either – Josse asked her, 'How did Raelf know that there was a baby up for adoption at Saltwych? If the people there are so secretive, why should anyone come to know of their business?'

'I believe it was done through the mediation of a priest,' Isabella said. 'Someone of importance among the Saltwych folk put out word and the priest under-took to try to find a family of wealth and influence who would welcome a child and treat her as their own.'

'A family of wealth and influence?' Josse repeated. 'The wealth I can readily understand, for to send her to a poor family would not provide any advantage over staying with her own kin. But why did they specify influence? And influence with whom?'

'Oh, *I* don't know!' Abruptly Isabella seemed to tire of the discussion. 'We waste time here. Let us pack up and be on our way.' And, not waiting for the men to agree or disagree, she ducked back inside the shelter and began packing her few belongings into a soft leather satchel. Josse noticed her pick up her thick gauntlet and he wondered what had become of Isabella's hawk.

Josse looked at Brice. 'You have found out much about these strange people,' he said.

Brice smiled wryly. 'I have found out nothing. I merely pass on what Isabella told me.'

'Oh! But I thought she said Galiena knew nothing of her own background, so where has Isabella gained her knowledge?'

Brice looked bemused. 'I couldn't say.' His eye-brows went down in a worried frown. Then, his expression clearing, he said encouragingly, 'But let us pursue the question when we are safe.'

Josse stood where he was. 'You, of course, must go if you so wish,' he said. 'For my own part, I must return to Saltwych.'

Isabella, overhearing, shot out of the shelter again. 'You can't!' she cried, just as Brice was asking, 'Why?'

'I can and I must.' Josse gave them both what he hoped was a reassuring smile, the look of an old soldier for whom riding alone into a community of hostile strangers holds no fears. 'You ask why, Brice, and indeed, since you both demonstrate such concern for my safety, you are owed an explanation.' He paused, searching for the words to deliver his message so that they would understand the urgent need. 'For one thing, Galiena's serving woman, Aebba, is down at Saltwych and I believe she may have important information concerning the events leading up to Galiena's death. For another, there is a girl chained in an outbuilding and I have promised myself that I will help her.'

Neither Isabella nor Brice spoke for some moments. Then Brice said, 'But I thought that Aebba rode with Galiena to Hawkenlye. Did she not remain there to care for Ambrose?'

'She cared for him at first, aye,' Josse agreed. 'But she is not there now. She is at Saltwych.'

'You are sure?'

'Quite sure.'

Again, silence. Then Isabella said, 'There may be a good reason for the child to be locked up. Perhaps she is being punished, or perhaps being kept apart from the community because she has a fever.'

'She has no fever,' Josse said evenly, 'and, for my part, I can see no crime that a young girl could commit that would deserve being chained in a filthy hut with no light, no warmth at night and nothing to lie on or with which to cover herself.'

But Isabella was not satisfied. 'Josse,' she said, her face urgent, 'we should leave this to the Saltwych kin. It is not for us to say how they should treat their own!'

Josse stared at her, eye to eye, and, after a short time, her glance fell. 'Isabella,' he said gently, 'how do you know so much about them? Why do you defend their deeds?'

'I'm not defending them! They are cruel, and—' she began hotly. Then, breathing hard, she said more calmly, 'I do not think we should risk our own lives to save a child who may not even *need* saving. That is all.' And, as if she knew how weak her argument was, she hung her head.

'We will go down on to the marsh,' Brice said eventually. 'We will wait for cover of darkness or, if the mist descends during the day, we will descend under its blanket. I do not see how we can seek out Aebba, Josse, without everyone else seeing us. But we can at least try to release the girl and take her away with us.'

'She may not want to go!' Isabella shouted. 'Even if they are punishing her harshly, the Saltwych folk are her kin! What do you propose that we do with her, Brice?'

He looked at her, and the love in his face softened her harsh, angry expression. 'I do not know, my sweeting. Perhaps we should ask her what *she* wants.'

'She's drugged,' Josse said baldly. 'Or anyway she was last night.'

He was uncertain what they should do. Isabella's protest was a valid one – what, indeed, *would* they do with the girl once they had managed to rescue her? – and he was troubled too at the prospect of leading Brice, and possibly Isabella too, into danger.

'I'm going alone,' he announced firmly. 'I do not believe that they will harm me if I go openly by day. I will ask to speak to Aebba and I will find a way to help the poor chained girl.'

'You can't. We must all go in together,' Brice said, equally firmly. 'We—'

But Josse held up a hand. 'Let me finish,' he said. 'It is unwise for us to move as one for, should we encounter difficulties, there would be none of us left to bring help. I would like you, Brice, to act as my reserve force. Watch for me from a safe distance. If I do not return by a certain prearranged time – by nightfall – then perhaps you will ride down in the dark and see what has become of me.' He said it with a laugh, as if to suggest he was joking, but it was no joke.

Brice looked at Isabella, who shrugged and then nodded.

'And if Isabella will agree to wait for us up here on the cliff top,' Josse went on, 'then she could go to Readingbrooke for help should—' No. He stopped himself from saying *should neither of us return* because it was far too pessimistic. 'Well, in case it proves necessary,' he finished instead.

There was a pause. Then: 'It makes good sense,'

Brice said. With a wry grin, he added, 'And I do not think that Isabella and I will change your mind, Josse, if we argue for the rest of the day. Very well. So be it. When will you go?'

And Josse replied, 'I shall not wait for cover of mist or darkness. I shall go right now.'

19

For the third time, Josse rode down the track and across the marshland to Saltwych.

This time they knew who he was and they were waiting for him. Two of the guards who had apprehended him on his first visit rode out to meet him and, grim faced and silent, fell in on either side of him and rode with him into the settlement. There were few people about; the place appeared almost deserted. One of the guards took charge of the horses; the other man took him to the long hall. Josse expected to be faced with Aelle, but it was not the clan chieftain who waited for him across the hearth.

The strange silver eyes contemplated him for some moments before the man spoke. Then, in a neutral voice, he said, 'You have returned, Josse d'Acquin. By day now and not sneaking through the dark on your belly like a whipped hound.'

Josse straightened his shoulders. 'I was told quite definitely that the woman of whom I spoke, Galiena Ryemarsh, came from this community. I came back because I wish to establish the truth.'

'The truth,' mused the man with the silver eyes. 'A dangerous commodity, Josse d'Acquin. Are you quite sure you wish to know it?'

'I am,' Josse replied.

'Even more dangerous,' went on the man, still in the same quiet, contemplative tone, 'is your implication that the clan chief lied to you. Aelle does not care to have his word doubted.'

'But I was told by Galiena's family that this was where she was born!' Josse said forcefully. 'I believe that they spoke true.'

The man said nothing. He stood on the far side of the bright fire in the hearth, and Josse could not see him clearly. He wore a long robe of some light colour and its outline seemed to shimmer in the flickering light. Unaccountably, Josse felt heavy-eyed as he tried to focus on his adversary.

The man held up a long hand and beckoned. Josse stepped around the hearth and went over to stand beside him. 'Aelle is away hunting,' the man said softly. 'He has taken the strong men of the clan. They will not be pleased to see you back here, asking your questions. Oh, no.'

'Then tell me what I need to know and let me leave before they return!' Josse urged. 'I have come in peace, it is not right to threaten me in this way.'

'You perceive a threat?' The man's eyes opened wide with false innocence. Or was it false? Josse could not decide. 'Well then, we shall have to reassure you.' He glanced around and, seeing that he and Josse were alone in the far section of the hall, stepped back to the far wall and, lifting the corner of a ragged hanging, revealed a small door. 'Come,' he ordered. 'We shall sit in my own private chamber and I shall attempt to tell you what you wish to know.'

Josse hesitated. The guards had not relieved him of his weapons – perhaps because their chieftain was not in the hall – and he felt the weight of his sword at his side. The silver-eyed man gave a soft laugh. 'You will not need your sword,' he said. 'You would not attack an unarmed man, and I, as you see, carry no knife or broadsword.' He opened his arms wide and the long, full sleeves opened out gracefully. But he was right; as far as Josse could see, he bore no blade.

'Will you come?' he asked.

'Aye,' said Josse.

The man carefully closed the door after them and led Josse to a small building that he had not noticed before. It consisted of a shallow cave in the cliff face, out from which walls had been built so as to increase the space within. The man opened a low door in the outer wall and ushered Josse inside.

The chamber was in near-darkness, the only light coming from glowing embers in a small iron brazier. The man put some small pieces of wood on to the embers, blew up a flame and then added a bundle of what looked like dry, twiggy sticks and dead leaves. Then, having drawn up a simple stool for Josse to sit on, he said without preamble, 'Galiena did come from here. She was known by a different name and she was of high birth among our people.' Watching Josse closely, he murmured, 'Iduna was her given name. She was called for the goddess who guarded the golden apples of youth, for it was hoped that her birth was an omen and that she would put new vigour into the chieftain.'

Goddess. Apples of youth. Good God above, Josse thought, these are pagan things.

'She was the chieftain's daughter,' the silver-eyed man was saying, 'begotten by him upon a woman of the bloodline and born to him in his dotage. We hoped she would heal him, for he was sick at heart and in despair.'

'It cannot be that you speak of Aelle?' Josse said.

'No. Of Aethelfrith, the father of Aelle, who was chieftain before him.' The man sighed. 'Aelle saw the responsibilities of a chieftain differently. His father had encouraged us to look outwards, to mix with our neighbours and to end our long self-imposed and inward-looking isolation. He did not think it healthy for us to preserve our secret ways and to keep others away by the fostering and the propagation of frightening legends. That, he considered, was the old way. The unenlightened way.'

'The old ways worked efficiently,' Josse murmured, remembering the tale that had so distressed him as a child.

'Yes, they did, didn't they?' The silver-eyed man looked pleased. 'But then it is very easy to frighten uneducated and superstitious folk out of their wits.'

It was nothing to be proud of, Josse thought. But he did not say it aloud.

'The baby girl whom we knew as Iduna was healthy and she thrived.' The man picked up his tale. 'But the name that we hoped would bring good fortune failed us, and her father died when she was but a few weeks old. With his death there was no choice but to hail Aelle as chieftain. He turned his back on the outside world, shutting out the light just as it had begun to penetrate our life here. And his first act as our chief was to send his little sister away.'

'Why?' Josse asked.

'Why? For two reasons. One, because she too was the daughter of a chief and when she grew to adulthood, she might have thought as her father did and so challenged her brother's rule of secrecy. For another—' He paused. Then: 'Josse, what did you think of Aelle? A clever man, would you say? A wise and worldly one?'

'I cannot say,' Josse admitted. 'I did not study him sufficiently well to judge.'

'A fair answer.' The man gave him a nod of approval. 'Aelle is wise, and also worldly, for all that he lives isolated out here on the marsh and has little contact with the world. But he understands power, you see. He wants power, as it is understood in the wide world. Therefore he placed his baby sister in a place where he believed power was to be found.'

'But Raelf of Readingbrooke is but a country lord!' Josse protested. Smoke from the newly stoked brazier was floating through the chamber and prickling his eyes. It had quite a strong smell; somehow it caught at the back of the throat. He coughed, then said, 'He lives comfortably, aye, but his prime concern is for his family!'

'Yes,' the silver-eyed man said patiently. 'But I

do not speak of Raelf de Readingbrooke. I speak of Ambrose Ryemarsh. Wealthy, indeed, very wealthy, would you not agree? And of a certain influence with those who rule over us?'

'Aye,' Josse agreed, remembering Ambrose's swift and generous response to Queen Eleanor's ransom appeal and the implied closeness to Plantagenet power circles, 'but—' He was struggling with what he was being told. 'But she was not placed with Ambrose, she was adopted by the family at Readingbrooke!'

'Yes, but she was married to Ambrose Ryemarsh.'

Again, Josse felt incredulity. 'You are telling me that Aelle *knew* she would marry Ambrose if she were to be adopted by Raelf?'

'Aelle did not know. But I did. I saw it.'

Josse slowly shook his head. 'I can scarce believe it.' It was more than that; he actively *dis*believed it, but it did not seem prudent to say so.

'She married him, did she not?' the man enquired. 'You will have to take my word for it, Josse d'Acquin.'

Abruptly Josse stood up and began to pace up and down in the small space. His head was swimming and he was finding it hard to concentrate. The other man watched him, and his unusual light eyes following the restless movement held a hint of amusement.

'I don't know for sure that Ambrose has influence, not with the King,' Josse said after a time.

'He has already given a very large sum towards the Lionheart's ransom,' the man said. 'He plans to give a great deal more. He is a stout supporter of the King and when Richard returns, those who gave most generously to his cause will not be forgotten.'

'So King Richard will return?' Josse demanded.

'Yes.'

'I suppose you've seen *that*, too?'

'Oh, yes,' said the man with silver eyes.

Josse threw up his arms in exasperated confusion. 'I believe I must be dreaming!' he cried. 'I see nothing but confusion!'

'It is quite simple,' the man said. 'Aelle wanted rid of a sister who might grow up to encourage the people in the old chieftain's ways, with which Aelle strongly disagrees. But if he had to give her away, why not ensure that she found a place where she could influence the tides of men? If she bore Ambrose a child, what might not be that child's future as the son of a man who stood high in a king's favour?'

'But in giving her away, surely all her ties with her people here were severed!' Josse argued.

'You forget one thing: she carries our blood, and so would her son. You overlook the bloodline.'

The bloodline. Stunned, Josse sank down once more on to the stool.

Was the man telling the truth, or was it all an elaborate story told by a master whose words convinced even as he spoke them? Josse could not decide. There was a certain logic to it, he had to admit, assuming that Galiena would have been open to an appeal by her blood kin for assistance of some sort in this future time when she and Ambrose – and their son – were to ride high in Plantagenet favour. Ambrose had indeed given generously towards the ransom, or so he had told

Josse, and apparently intended to go on doing so. Was he close to the King? If he were, Josse was not aware of it, which was not to say that it was untrue . . .

But Galiena is dead, he thought suddenly. So all this careful planning, all this miraculously accurate foresight, has been for nothing.

He was about to say as much to the silver-eyed man when the man spoke. Very softly, he said, 'It will not help to make you believe what I tell you, Josse, but Iduna was not the first child to be given away. The same thing was attempted before, when Aelle gave away his dead sister's daughter.'

'And what became of her?'

'She married . . . unwisely. Her husband turned out to be a man who did not care much for those circles of power which rule our destinies, preferring the quiet life of the country.'

'So you failed there, too.' It was a provocative comment and, as Josse had expected, it was met with a shaft of anger.

'Failure is not a term I like to use,' the man said, the cool tone denying the sudden heat in his eyes. 'The matter was dealt with.'

Dealt with. There was a sinister quality to that. 'There is a girl chained in one of your outbuildings,' Josse said. 'Is she too to be given to a powerful husband?'

'She?' The anger was gone and the man was smiling. 'Oh, no.'

'Will you let me see her? She has been drugged, I believe.'

'Yes, she has. No, I will not let you see her.'

The man was staring at Josse. His fascination for the tale that had been woven for his benefit wavered for an instant and for the first time Josse felt fear.

He put a hand down to his sword but with a snort of laughter the silver-eyed man raised his arms. Josse's sword hand suddenly felt as heavy as if it were tied to a solid block of iron and it fell uselessly to his side.

Still holding Josse's eyes with his, the man said, 'The smoke that you have been inhaling has, I believe you will find, robbed you of your resistance. It used to have the same effect upon me, but long usage has inured me to its powers.' Gripping Josse's wrist with a firm hand, he added, 'Come with me.'

And, hypnotised, unable to stop himself, Josse followed him out of the hut.

In Hawkenlye Abbey, the sunny day was nearing its end.

As Helewise emerged from the Abbey church after the penultimate office of the day, she set out on the first of the two missions she knew she must complete by the end of the day. It concerned Galiena's serving woman, Aebba, and they had told Helewise three days ago that she was missing. Nobody had reported whether or not she had turned up and Helewise, preoccupied by so many other matters, had forgotten to ask.

She asked now. Aebba was still missing.

The only person who seemed the least concerned was the young lad who had arrived at Hawkenlye with Ambrose and Aebba. When Helewise ran him to ground – behind the stables, where apparently he spent most of his time – he said Aebba hadn't even said goodbye and he was worried about her, even more worried that nobody had given him any orders for ages and perhaps it meant he had been dismissed from the lord Ambrose's service and so didn't have a home any more.

'What is your name?' Helewise asked him gently; he seemed a pathetic boy and none too bright.

'Arthus,' the boy replied.

'Well, Arthus, I will remind your master that you are still here and I will ask him if he would care for you to attend him. Would you like that?'

Slowly the boy nodded. 'But Master don't know 'oo I am, not really,' he said, looking at Helewise with childlike eyes.

'He will remember that you rode here with him,' she said.

'Don't reckon 'e will,' Arthus said. ''E's normally pretty sharp, if you take my meaning, specially for one as don't see too well. Ain't comfortable, sometimes, and that's the truth. But 'e were proper poorly when we came 'ere.'

His naïve comment set off a vague alarm in Helewise's mind. It recalled something that someone else had said, someone with a more enquiring, acute brain than poor young Arthus . . .

She thought about it. Then she remembered. Clear as day, she saw Josse, face wearing a deep frown, saying, *I do not understand this talk of Ambrose as a doddering dotard.*

Josse had perceived him quite differently when the
two men had met previously. And now here was
Arthus, implying that, when he came to Hawkenlye,
Ambrose had temporarily lost his usual keen percep-
tion. They were right, both of them, she realised.
Ambrose had been deeply affected by his young wife's
death, yes, but, despite his grief, he had never again
reverted to being the dazed, uncomprehending, vague
old man that he had been when he had arrived.

So *why* had he been like that?

Her next mission might well provide a clue. Thanking Arthus, reassuring him once more that he would
not be either forgotten or homeless, she set off down
to the Vale to look for Ambrose.

He was sitting on a low bank that jutted out over the
lake that filled the Vale's lower reaches. He had a small
pile of stones beside him and he was skimming them
across the flat surface of the water.

She sat down beside him. 'Seven,' she remarked,
counting the bounces. Reaching for a stone, she had
a try.

'Eight,' Ambrose said. 'I cannot in truth see that
well, but if I listen intently I can count the splashes.
You win, my lady Abbess.'

Helewise returned his smile. 'My sons taught me,'
she said. Then, addressing the matter uppermost in
her mind, she said tentatively, 'Ambrose, you are a
different man from the one you were when you rode
into the Abbey. You have lost your wife, but that is
not what I mean. I refer to your own health and, I

confess, I am at a loss to understand how it was that you were so weak when you arrived and yet now you are strong.' She looked at him, willing him not to take offence at her enquiry.

He did not. Instead he frowned, as if the question puzzled him, too, and said, 'My lady, I have thought long and hard about the same thing. I conclude that probably I had picked up one of those brief summer fevers that are there and gone swiftly but, while they rage in the blood, can turn a strong man into a mumbling fool.'

'I do not believe,' she said carefully, 'that you were febrile.'

'Well, then, the only other explanation is that my late wife's serving woman, who was then attending to my food and drink, had drugged me,' he said lightly.

Helewise was uncertain whether he spoke in jest. 'Why should she do that?' she asked.

And, with a shrug and an unreadable look in his face, he answered, 'You tell me.'

There seemed little more to say. In the silence that followed she studied him. Ambrose's face wore clear signs of his grief, but behind them she sensed that the man was returning to himself. 'Ambrose, would you like to go home?' she asked gently. 'I will ride there with you, if it is that you dread returning to an empty house. I will stay for a time, if it would help.'

Ambrose looked down at his hands; he was flipping a stone from one to the other, catching it deftly each time. Then, raising a hand to rub at his near-sighted, slightly watering eyes, he said, 'It is a kind thought, my lady, and it is true that I long to go home. But—'

She waited, but he did not go on. So she said, 'You are welcome to stay with us here as long as you wish. Many folk do, when they lose the person they love best in the world. Sometimes by staying here, where they perceive themselves to be watched over by God who loves them, they believe they have found a heavenly replacement for the one they have lost.' Thinking of one monk in particular – Brother Erse, the carpenter – she added, 'Some even hear the call of God and decide to spend the rest of their lives in His service as monks or nuns.'

Ambrose was looking at her, an intelligent interest in his eyes. It struck her that he was a powerful man and, despite his years, still a handsome one; Galiena, she thought, had been a young woman with a mature and a discerning eye.

He was asking her a question: 'Was it that way for you, my lady? You spoke just now of your sons; did you lose your husband and seek solace with the Lord?'

It was a very long time since anyone had asked Helewise that. Pausing to gather her thoughts, she said, 'Not exactly. Ivo and I – I loved my husband dearly, Ambrose, and grieved when I lost him. But—' Should she say what was in her heart? She had never done so before, not in this matter, but somehow she felt it was not only right but also actually quite important to do so now, with this sympathetic and generous-hearted man beside her.

'I had grown used to a position of authority in my marriage,' she said quietly. 'My husband was a man of some influence and he delegated many of his concerns to me.'

'A man is lucky indeed if he has an accomplished and educated wife,' Ambrose observed.

She shot him a grateful glance for the implied compliment. 'When I was widowed, the options were few and little to my liking,' she went on. 'I had not thought to take the veil, for I had no desire for the limited life that I believed would be my lot behind convent walls. But then I heard of Hawkenlye Abbey, and I learned about the principles upon which it was founded, and I thought that it was where I wanted to be. I was admitted to the congregation, I grew to love the place, I learned the meaning of a truly satisfying day's work.' She smiled suddenly, a wide, happy smile that seemed to well up straight from the joy in her heart. 'I discovered that God had had a plan for me all along,' she finished, 'and ever since I have done my utmost to follow it.'

'With no small success,' he remarked, and she smiled again at his lightly ironic tone.

'I never expected this,' she said softly. 'To become abbess.'

'No. I understand that.' Then: 'You are not the first to speak in this manner to me. But I do not wish to become a monk, my lady. Although I am grateful for the kind thought behind the suggestion.'

'I did not in truth believe that you would see your future with us,' she agreed. 'That was, in fact, what I was leading up to. I wanted to say that I do not think, Ambrose, that you are destined for this life; I think you are, and must remain, a man of and in the world.'

He sighed heavily. 'I cannot but agree, since what prompts me to go home is the thought of the promise I made to our sovereign lady, Queen Eleanor, concerning the King's ransom. I have already given what I could immediately give, but I must do more. We must all work without cease until we obtain his release.'

Helewise, who did not quite share his fervour, nevertheless was not surprised to hear him express it. 'Then will we ride to Ryemarsh together, you and I?' she asked. 'Your wife's serving woman appears to have left us, but up behind the Abbey stables there is a forlorn and forgotten lad named Arthus who is homesick and longing to be of service to you again. Shall we ask him to ride back with us?'

Ambrose studied her. 'You are subtle, my lady, so to remind me of my obligations,' he murmured.

'I meant no reproof,' she said quickly.

'I did not detect one,' he replied. Then, with a surprisingly boyish grin, 'And had I done, it probably would have been justified.'

In the sudden closeness between them, she ventured to say something that she might otherwise have kept back. Putting aside the vague dislike that she had felt for Galiena, she reminded herself that it was Ambrose whom she now must comfort. She reached out to touch his arm lightly and said, 'The house will be empty without her, Ambrose, but you will learn to deal with your loss, of that I am certain, for you are a strong man.'

He put a hand on hers and gave it a squeeze. 'I am grateful for your confidence, my lady, for I confess that mine is at a low ebb. She – she—' But whatever image of his wife he held in his heart was too much for him and without warning he began to weep.

'She was so young, too young to die!' he sobbed. 'And still we do not know how it happened! That in itself would be a comfort, of sorts, and yet the matter appears insoluble.'

She took his hand in both of hers. 'It may be that we shall never know,' she said gently. 'If that is the case, you will have to find a way to accept it.'

'I know.' He wiped his eyes with his free hand and took a deep breath. 'I know. I shall try, my lady.'

They went on sitting there on the bank, side by side, hand in hand. Helewise, open to the message that all her senses seemed to be sending her, was thinking that, if it transpired that Galiena had indeed been killed by another's hand, then there was one person who Helewise was quite certain was innocent.

Josse, she remembered, had wondered if Ambrose, the cuckolded husband, might have poisoned his young wife. Josse had been suspicious because Ambrose had failed to mention the objection that Raelf had made to the possible explanation that Galiena had accidentally poisoned herself by eating berries or fungi in the forest, yet the girl's husband must have known as well as her father of her skill with herbs and plants.

Well, Josse was an astute man but in this case he

was wrong. Helewise knew that Ambrose Ryemarsh had not killed his wife; he had not been himself at the time of Galiena's death, which would explain why he had not challenged the poisonous berry theory, and his sadness was genuine, she was quite sure of it. So, thank the kind Lord, was his ignorance that she had been pregnant.

Tomorrow, she thought, we shall set out for Ryemarsh and Ambrose will take the first steps in resuming his life at home. I will help him if I can, and I will ask God in His mercy to support him as he learns to live without her.

With a sort of peace descending on her which she prayed that Ambrose felt too, she stared out at the setting sun's reflections in the quiet water.

20

The silver-eyed man led an unprotesting Josse out of the rock chamber and along to the outbuildings behind the long hall. When they came to the middle of the three round huts, the one in which Josse had noticed a workbench and some tools, the man opened the door and beckoned to Josse to go inside, relieving him of his sword as he passed.

'Are you going to render me senseless, as you have done that poor child who sleeps so deeply in the next hut?' Josse demanded. He had intended his voice to sound strong and threatening, but to his consternation, he sounded as feeble as if he had been abed with a fever for a week.

'No,' said the man. 'I have already done enough. And she lies sleeping until we manage to reach agreement upon her fate.' He frowned briefly, as if that disagreement were a continuing and pressing anxiety. 'This is to be your prison, Josse d'Acquin.'

'Why do you have to imprison me?' That was better – he thought he sounded a little more menacing now. Perhaps the effects of that foul smoke lessened as soon as you stopped breathing it in. He fervently hoped so.

'You have far too much curiosity,' the man answered with a faint grin. 'We are a private people. We obey our chieftain's dictates and keep to ourselves.'

'But you are so few!' Josse protested. 'How do you breed? Do you take wives from your own kin?'

It was a devastating accusation and Josse half expected that the man would find some way to punish him for his audacity in having made it. But instead he merely said mildly, 'We have enough people to avoid incest. In the past it has sometimes occurred that half-brothers and sisters have mated, but that has not happened in many years.'

'You broke the church's strict prohibition when you did that!' Josse cried, horrified.

The man murmured, 'Not *our* church. The gods we serve are wider minded and comprehend that sometimes necessity makes demands that cannot be ignored.'

The gods we serve. Aye, thought Josse, it seems I was right. 'You are pagan,' he said. He did not frame it as a question.

'Of course,' said the man. 'We came to these shores with the religion of our forefathers and we have held fast to our gods.' With a weird light in his strange eyes, he added softly, 'We shall be rewarded for our loyalty.'

'This is why you choose a life of isolation?' Josse asked. 'So that you may continue to worship as you see fit?'

'In part, yes.'

'But—' Josse was not sure how the law of the land

– or indeed of the church – stood on the subject of paganism. There were, of course, the persistent legends that spoke of the Norman kings maintaining a foot in the Old Religion, but what kings did was, in Josse's experience, their own business and had little to do with what they permitted in their subjects. 'Does your parish priest not condemn your practices?' he finished lamely.

It was no great surprise when the man burst out laughing. 'Oh, Josse, I had not expected such a naïve question!' he said, still chuckling. 'In answer, yes, probably he does. But his condemnation is his own affair and has little bearing upon us.'

I am to be left here a prisoner, Josse thought. I must keep this man talking as long as I can.

He was not sure what purpose that would serve, but suddenly another question occurred to him.

'You have a woman here, Aebba,' he said. 'She was serving woman to Galiena Ryemarsh – your Iduna – and was with her mistress and her master Ambrose at Hawkenlye Abbey. But I saw her in your hall.'

'It was careless of her to allow herself to be seen,' the man observed. 'She was told not to go anywhere near you but I suppose that, like you, her curiosity overcame her. What of her?'

'She is one of your people,' Josse said. 'Is she not?'

'Yes. She was related to Iduna's mother.'

'And sent to Ryemarsh to watch over Galiena.'

'Yes.'

'But why did Galiena allow her to be a member of

the Ryemarsh household?' Josse demanded. 'It was apparent that she did not like the woman!'

'Iduna understood her obligations to her blood kin,' the man said. 'We sent Aebba to her with a tale of dire need – Aebba, we said, had lost her man and had young children depending on her, and so needed the small wage that Ambrose Ryemarsh paid her to send back to Saltwych for her family's keep.'

'So she knew that she came from here!' Josse cried. 'Galiena was aware of the identity of her true family.'

The man said slowly, 'At first, no. But once she was wed to the lord Ambrose, it was necessary to inform her who she was and to tell her what she must do.'

'To share Ambrose's wealth with her family, you mean!' Josse shouted. 'But, as I said before, her family gave her away! Why was she obliged to do *anything* for your people?'

The man shrugged. 'It was always a possibility that she would refuse to recognise the obligations that she owed to her blood kin,' he said. 'It has happened before,' he added in a murmur.

Aye, Josse thought, the other woman he spoke of. But, his mind still firmly on Galiena, he said, 'And what did she think of these plans that you had for her child? Did she agree to her and Ambrose's son being pushed into a position of influence?'

'She appeared to accept it, yes,' the man replied calmly. 'But, all the time that she did not conceive, it was a plan that remained hypothetical.'

Josse wondered suddenly if that was why Galiena had not become pregnant. She was a herbalist, they all said so, and so perhaps, knowing what her child's destiny would be if her blood kin had their way, she had made sure he would never be born . . .

No, that could not be right. Because she had gone to Hawkenlye to ask for help in conceiving. And anyway she had already been carrying a baby when she died.

With a sense of defeat, Josse leant his back against the wooden wall of the hut and slowly sank down to a sitting position. He had done so much, he thought miserably, to trace Galiena. He had even found the very place where she had been born and discovered who her father was. But, despite all that, still he was no nearer to solving the mysteries of who had fathered her own child and who had poisoned her.

He put his face in his hands and rubbed hard at his eyes, which were still smarting from the smoke. But the silver-eyed man must have misinterpreted the gesture, for he said in a hypnotic voice, 'Soon you will sleep, Josse d'Acquin. And sleep will bring dreams and oblivion.'

Peering through his fingers, Josse saw the man walk stealthily to the door, which he pushed closed behind him. There was the sound of a latch of some sort being dropped home.

And Josse heard the soft thump of the man's footfalls as he strode away.

He found a spy hole in the plank wall and sat for some time breathing in the sweet air from outside. The swimming sensation cleared and his eyes, nose and throat, although still feeling red and raw, began to smart less.

After a time he stood up and went to try the door. It was firmly fastened. He had his short knife in his belt and, inserting the blade in the crack between door and frame, he eased it upwards until it encountered the latch. I believe, he thought with excitement, that I could get out of here.

But there seemed little point at present, for surely someone – the silver-eyed man – would instantly put him back inside again, possibly more firmly secured and perhaps even chained like the poor girl in the other hut was. No. It seemed better to wait for darkness. Or, if providence looked down kindly on him, a nice, thick, concealing blanket of mist.

In the meantime, the best he could do was to go on breathing in the mind-clearing fresh air in the hope that by the time he was called upon to anything more active, he would be fit and ready.

He could hear voices. There had been the sound of a fast horse arriving, then the rider had called out to someone in the settlement. A voice had answered – Josse thought it sounded like the silver-eyed man – and then there had been an exchange which finished with something about the hunters being engaged on the far side of some boggy ground and held there by the mist.

Providence, it seemed, was on Josse's side.

He waited to hear if the rider would leave again but there was nothing. Maybe he was seeing to his horse – he had come into the settlement at quite a pace.

He put his eye to the knothole and peered through it. Aye, he could see the mist for himself now, swirling up from the marsh and beginning to obscure the trunks of the trees and the feet of the scrubby undergrowth. Soon, he thought. And silently he spoke to Brice: come soon.

He stood up and went back to the door. He inserted the knife blade again and this time went on pushing steadily even after he began to feel resistance. There was a sudden clank – too loud in the silent encampment! – and, as the latch came free of its holder, the door opened.

Holding the edge of the door tightly, Josse pushed it open just a crack. The mist was inching around the buildings now and growing deeper by the minute; he watched a woman on the far side of the enclosure pulling a child by the hand, urging it to hurry up and get indoors. The woman appeared to be wading in creamy milk and the only part of the child that was visible was its head.

Josse waited until there was nobody about outside. Then he opened the door more widely and edged carefully through the gap. Naked without his sword, he looked around in the hope that the silver-eyed man had stowed it somewhere near. He thought at first that his luck had failed this time but then he saw the sheath, lying across the top of a wooden barrel placed a short distance out from the end wall of the hall, presumably in a spot where rain water channelled down off the reed thatch.

With a quick prayer of thanks, Josse tiptoed over and

carefully retrieved both sheath and sword, buckling on his sword belt and clasping it for a moment, as if for reassurance.

I must act quickly, he thought. If Brice has taken his cue from the mist's descent and is on his way, then I need to be ready for him.

He made for the other hut and, as he had done before, eased the wooden bar out of its supports. He opened the door and went inside. The girl lay in almost the exact same position that she had done before; with a stab of alarm he put his fingers to the place in her neck where there should be a pulse and, relief flooding him, felt a faint beat. There was no time to check further on her condition; he bent instead to examine the shackle on her ankle.

His enforced spell of waiting in the other hut had allowed him to have a look around at its contents. It had indeed been a workroom and he had helped himself to a stout pair of pincers and a small adze. Calculating that a girl with a shackle on her ankle was not as much of an impediment to freedom as a girl still chained to the wall, first he attacked the chain. Using the adze, he flattened the chain across a large stone on the floor and brought the thick iron blade down hard on a link of the chain. It bent, but did not break. Josse hammered away at it repeatedly and, at last, it gave. Hastily he pulled the crushed ends apart with the pincers, then turned his attention to the shackle.

It consisted of a wide bracelet of iron, hinged on one side and fastened on the opposite side by a bolt thrust through two pairs of loops. The bolt was firmly bent over at each end to hold it fast and, without the pincers and Josse's strong hands, it would have been quite impossible to remove.

The atmosphere seemed oppressive, somehow. Alert to every small sound, he had to concentrate hard in order to keep his hands steady. The providential mist could disappear as quickly as it had crept in and then—

No. He must not think about that.

He worked on the bolt until both ends were straight enough for it to be slid out from the loops. When at last it gave, he was distressed to see that the girl's narrow ankle was raw from where the iron shackle had bitten into it. It looked, he thought, as if she had been chained in the hut for several days, an impression that was heightened by the full bucket of human waste that stood on the far side of the hut. Someone must have been coming in regularly to help her squat over the bucket to relieve herself. Had the same person fed and watered her, putting another dose of whatever was keeping her comatose into her drink?

It was no way to treat a girl.

Putting his pity aside – that emotion was no help to her now, when what she needed from him was action – he extended his arm behind her shoulders and lugged her into a sitting position. Her head lolled forward and the dirty, tangled hair fell like a curtain, concealing her face. 'Come on, my girl,' he whispered encouragingly, 'I'll get you out of here!'

She stirred, mumbled something, then slumped against his chest. 'Can you not stand up?' he muttered.

'No' – he answered his own question – 'I will have to do it for you.'

He straightened up, still holding her to him, and got her on her feet. But her legs were like rope and seemed to fold up beneath her, so he picked her up, one arm round her shoulders, one under her knees, and carried her out of the hut.

The mist was heavy now and small droplets of water settled on Josse and the girl, soaking into the rough sacking of her single garment and the filthy hair. Every inch of her flesh left exposed by the makeshift smock was as dirty as her hair and she smelt dreadful. She was going to get very cold, he realised, and that might be dangerous to her in her semi-conscious state. Slipping back inside the hut, still with the girl in his arms, he stretched out a hand and picked up whatever it was that her head had been resting on and shook it out. There was a strong aroma of wet dog but he could ignore that; he wrapped the old blanket securely round the girl like a hooded cloak, covering her head and face. It would have to do. Then he fastened the door of the hut and, trying to look in every direction at once, he crept away.

He knew where the guard had taken Horace and, skirting the boundary of the settlement, steadily he edged his way around to the rail where the horse was tethered. He did not believe that his run of luck would extend to permitting him to get the girl on to Horace's back, mount up and ride away, which was just as well as it didn't. He had got as far as freeing Horace's reins from the hitching rail and flinging the girl across the horse's back when the guard leapt out at him.

There was not much time for consideration. Josse believed that both his own and the girl's life were in danger – there had been an ominous ring to *until we reach agreement on her fate* – and Josse drew back his right arm and punched the guard in the face without pausing to think about the predictable results of a large, strong man hitting someone much younger and slighter as hard as he could. There was a sharp click of breaking bone, a brief gasp from the guard as he fell, and then nothing.

Josse leapt up behind the girl, put spurs to Horace and they flew out of the settlement and away across the marsh.

He had not taken the poor visibility into consideration. At a walk, it would have been possible to look ahead and make out enough detail of the ground to move on safely. But Horace was cantering, breaking into a gallop, and very quickly both the horse and his rider realised that this was sheer folly; they could have hit disaster before they had the time to register that it was there.

Reluctantly they slowed to a walk.

Josse thought he heard something. Another horse. No, horses – more than one animal, and voices calling out.

Was it Brice and Isabella? Or was it Aelle's hunting party making their way home?

Out of nowhere came a brief flurry of wind. The mist tore apart briefly and Josse saw that it was both.

Brice was riding towards him from the escarpment, which was over on his right and behind him; Isabella sat on her horse a short distance up the track leading to the cliff top.

Ahead of Josse, riding in hard from the left, came Aelle. He had drawn his sword and he was whooping like an animal. Behind him rode five other men, their fair hair streaming as they galloped over the marshy ground.

Josse did not hesitate. Rough ground was the lesser threat now and, in any case, the rent in the mist was still there and, for the time being anyway, he could see. Heels digging into Horace's sides, he urged the horse round to the right and, trying to steady the girl's motionless body with his left hand, rode as fast as he could for the track up the cliff.

Brice galloped to meet him, wheeling around in a circle and coming in to ride close to Josse's left side. Josse spared a moment to be thankful that Brice knew better than to take up his position on Josse's right flank, since this was his armed side. Neck and neck, they flew towards the inland cliff.

Josse spared a glance behind them. Aelle had outrun his men and was gaining on Josse and Brice. Dear God, but he moved fast! His teeth were bared and he looked as if he were half out of his mind.

Josse reached the track a bare nose ahead and Brice reined in to let him set off up it first. He urged Horace into the shade of the trees and up the dark tunnel that their branches formed over the path, hearing the sounds of Brice starting out on the ascent behind him.

Horace plunged valiantly up the track, moving quickly until he reached the very steep section right at the top, where he checked, then went on at a slower and more careful pace. Now Josse could see Isabella, who had gone on ahead up the path and was waiting for them on the road above. Her hawk was on her wrist.

Turning hastily, Josse had time to register that Brice was just riding out from the concealing trees when a stumble from Horace drew his attention back to more crucial matters. Steadying the horse, he leaned his weight forward across the inert girl, encouraged Horace on and very soon they were safe on the road.

He was saying something to Isabella – he could not later recall what it was – when he saw her face change. A look of horrified recognition twisted her features and with a quick, decisive gesture she flung her fist in the air and her hawk took off in swift, graceful flight. The bird gained height and then, falling like a dead weight from the summer sky, dived down on Brice.

Watching helplessly, Josse called out a warning . . .

But it was not Brice who rode after them up the track. It was Aelle.

He was on the steepest part of the slope now. The hawk shot down straight at his face, her talons outstretched for the kill, and there was a sudden flash of scarlet as she opened up deep cuts through his eyes and down his cheeks. Then she flew up again and fell on the horse, and a sudden shrill whinny of pain and terror made a discord with Aelle's screaming.

Aelle's horse reared and then shied so that its forefeet came down slewed over at an angle and missed the track. In alarm it tried to find firm ground but, panicking now, it failed. Overbalancing, it fell off the path and dropped down over the almost sheer cliff. Aelle, blood pouring down his face and frantically trying to get his feet out of the stirrups, did not release himself in time. The horse fell on its side straight on to the rock-strewn ground at the foot of the cliff with its master beneath it.

Aelle was dead. He had to be; no man could survive when his head had been burst open and the white and red matter of his brains was already mingling on the short grass.

Now Brice came thundering up the track, eyes only for Isabella. She sat on her horse, the hawk once more on the heavy gauntlet. Meeting Brice's anxious look, she nodded and said, 'I am unhurt. So, I believe, is Josse, and he has the girl with him. But what of you?'

'Aelle outmanoeuvred me at the foot of the track,' Brice said grimly. There was a vivid mark on the side of his head that would soon turn into a spectacular bruise. 'I could not stop him — he was possessed.'

Brice nudged his horse with his knees and the animal stepped off the track and on to the level ground of the road. Josse, still feeling the shock, said, 'What of his men?'

'The mist has closed in again,' Brice said shortly. His eyes had followed the direction in which Isabella was staring and he, too, took in the sight of the chieftain's dead body. Then he looked from that grisly spectacle to Isabella, and Josse did too.

To his amazement, she was smiling. 'It was necessary,' she said. 'I will explain, but not now.' Then, her smile widening as if at some secret joy that was spreading like sun's warmth through her whole body, she cried, 'Oh, Brice, my dearest love, at long last all shall now be well!'

Then, without another word, she put her heels to her mare and led the way off along the road into the west. She did not stop – and neither did Josse, burdened with the unconscious girl, nor Brice – until they reached Rotherbridge.

21

At Rotherbridge, Josse, Brice and Isabella hardly spoke as they saw to the horses and then went inside. The girl seemed to be recovering a little. She had been muttering during the ride from Saltwych and Josse had moved her so that, for the latter stages of the journey, she had sat astride in front of him, leaning back against him. He hoped that perhaps the fresh air, and being outside in the beautiful day after her long confinement in the hut, had helped her. She had suffered bouts of shivering, and Josse had contrived to fasten the old blanket more securely around her.

Inside Brice's hall, it was cool and shady. Brice headed straight for the door to the kitchens and hollered for wine and, as soon as it was brought, poured out deep mugs of it for himself and for Josse. Isabella had declined; she insisted on first attending to the girl and so, helped by Josse, the two of them took her through into a smaller room that led off the hall. Brice was sent to fetch warm water, washing cloths and towels; Josse was commanded to collect Isabella's saddlebag, in which she said she had spare clothes. The sacking garment and the blanket, Isabella said firmly, she would throw out to be burned.

Josse and Brice were on their second mugs of the cool wine when a sudden cry shot them both to their feet. Brice in his alarm threw his mug on to the flagstones and rushed for the door of the little side room.

He yelled, 'Isabella! *Isabella!*' And, with a shout of alarm, flung his weight against the door.

On the journey to Ryemarsh and in the course of the day and a half that she had spent there with Ambrose, Helewise felt that she had learned a great deal about him. He was, as she might have predicted, unfailingly courteous and considerate and, as soon as they were ensconced in his house, he was revealed as a man of authority who knew exactly what he wanted and usually got it instantly. His household seemed to be both deeply in awe of and genuinely fond of him which, in Helewise's experience, was rare enough to be noteworthy.

She had not known how wealthy he was. His house spoke loudly of his means, from the finely carved wooden furniture in his hall and the richly worked tapestries on the walls to the high standards of his board.

But all the money in the world could not help him in the moment when he first set foot into the home that no longer included his wife. Helewise, walking beside him, felt him falter and she heard him mutter something under his breath. He dropped his head and put a hand up to his face, as if to conceal his emotions from the servants who stood in the hall to welcome their master home.

She waited, uncertain whether or not he would want her to intervene. But in the end she was glad she did not for, from the front rank of the household staff, an elderly man stepped forward and said gently, 'We are glad to have you home, my lord. We too mourn her and it is good that you are here with the folk who loved her best.'

It was perhaps over-familiar, but Helewise realised that the little speech was just right. Raising his head, Ambrose gave the old man a sketchy smile and said simply, 'Thank you, Julian.' Then, turning to Helewise, he said, 'My lady, may I present Julian, who is the head of my household staff. Julian, this is Abbess Helewise of Hawkenlye. Please give orders for the best guest chamber to be prepared.'

Then, squaring his shoulders in a gesture that went straight to Helewise's heart, he went into his hall.

In the morning following their arrival, visitors were announced. Helewise, who had been outside strolling in Galiena's garden, heard the call go up from the courtyard and soon afterwards there came the sounds of a group of horsemen. It is none of my business, she told herself, and resumed her quiet walking. Later Ambrose sought her out and said, with a wry expression, 'My lady, you have just missed the Queen's couriers.'

'Indeed?' Momentarily having forgotten about King Richard's humiliating captivity and the huge ransom demand – which she guessed must be the sole pre-occupation of the court and its members just now, if not indeed that of the entire country – she wondered what message Queen Eleanor should wish to send to Ambrose Ryemarsh. 'All goes well with the Queen, I trust,' she said.

'I believe so.' Ambrose paused and then said delicately, 'I have sent a certain sum already towards the King's ransom and I am engaged in raising more. The Queen has sent me a letter expressing her thanks for my generosity.'

Still the odd smile remained on his face. Curious, Helewise said, 'Why, my lord Ambrose, does that amuse you?'

Ambrose's smile widened. 'They tell me, my lady, that you are personally acquainted with the Queen?'

'I have that honour and pleasure, yes,' Helewise said, a little stiffly.

'Oh, I share your high opinion of the lady,' Ambrose assured her. 'I think, however, that you too will understand why I smile when you read her note.'

He handed to Helewise a roll of parchment bearing the Queen's distinctive handwriting. Swiftly scanning the note – it was not long – Helewise did indeed smile. The Queen, so clever in her use of words, managed in five short lines to convey her gratitude, her admiration for the speed with which Ambrose had rushed to contribute to the appeal and her heartfelt delight that this was to be but the first of his donations. 'With the continuing generosity of his most loyal subjects such as you,' she finished, 'it surely cannot be long before my precious son our King is once more free.'

'Had you in fact promised her that you would send

more?' Helewise asked, returning the parchment to Ambrose.

'Not exactly,' he replied. 'Our beloved Queen, it appears, is adept at reading between the lines.'

Helewise studied him. The Queen's message had come at a good time, she thought, for it gave Ambrose both a pleasant distraction and also reminded him that he had an important job to do. Giving him a brief bow, she said, 'With such a summons, my lord, you had better get on with your task.'

Returning her bow, he turned and hurried away back to the house, leaving her to reflect on the implications of having discovered quite how high her host rode in Plantagenet favour . . .

They had finished supper – a light but delicious meal taken at a small table in a cosy corner of the great hall – when, once again, there came the sound of horsemen. Julian appeared from the doorway leading through to the kitchens and, at a nod from Ambrose, went out to see who had arrived.

There was some excited talk, a cry, then nothing.

Ambrose, listening intently, shot to his feet. There was an expression of strain on his face that made it appear that he was suffering in some way.

Helewise, suddenly anxious for him, said calmingly, 'Ambrose, I am sure it is nothing; will you not sit and finish your meal?'

But he did not appear to hear. Moving slowly, as if sleepwalking, he walked across the hall to the wide doorway. It was a mild evening and the sky was still

light, so the door had been propped open to let a soft
and sweet-smelling breeze flow through the house.

She got up and followed him.

Standing beside him at the top of the steps leading
up from the courtyard, she saw that three horses
were being received by the Ryemarsh stable lads.
Dismounting from the horses were three – no, four
– people.

One was Brice of Rotherbridge, standing beside a
woman whom Helewise did not know and who was
dressed in a man's tunic and hose. She wore a wide-
brimmed hat pushed back from her face. Another was
Josse, and he was supporting the slim frame of a young
girl. She too wore man's clothing and the garments
were too big for her. Her face was concealed by the
deep hood of a light travelling cloak.

Ambrose was trembling.

Helewise put a hand on his arm and said softly,
'Ambrose, I am sure that—'

But he shook her off.

He ran down the steps and, to her amazement,
threw his arms around the girl in the cloak who, at
his approach, stepped away from Josse's supporting
arms and threw herself at Ambrose. There came the
sounds of muffled sobs, but Helewise did not know
from whom.

Amazed, shocked, she did not know what was happening. Josse must have read her confusion in her
face for, hastening across the yard and bounding
up the steps, he said, with a huge smile, 'My lady,
we have found her! We have brought her home to

him and, other than a weakness which will pass as soon as she begins to eat again, she is fine! Quite unhurt!'

Not daring to believe the sudden hope that flared up in her, Helewise whispered, 'Who is it?'

And Josse said, 'It's Galiena.'

They took her inside and the woman with Brice – presented to Helewise as somebody called Isabella de Burghay – led her away to be washed and dressed in her own clothes. The maids of Galiena's own household all offered their help but Galiena seemed to prefer Isabella. Judging by the brief impression that she received as the girl was helped across the hall, still in her hooded cloak, Helewise thought that this Isabella must have been important to Galiena in the first moments after whatever ordeal she had been through. For the time being, the younger girl appeared to depend on the woman.

Well, thought Helewise, it is good that she has someone she can turn to.

Ambrose, both bemused and at the same time so happy that he kept throwing his arms around them all, ordered fresh food and drink. Then, while they waited for Galiena to reappear, he pressed them all to eat and drink.

Helewise sought out Josse. 'You too are unharmed, my friend?' she asked quietly.

'Aye.' He gave her a grin. 'What joy to find you here, my lady Abbess, the one person with whom I wished to share this triumph! I had envisaged having to wait to give you the good news until I reached Hawkenlye, but here you are!'

'I rode home with Ambrose because – er, because—' She found that she was at a loss to explain without either making Ambrose appear weak or herself sound self-important.

But Josse, bless him, said, 'I think I understand. You helped him to face a home without her.'

And thankfully she whispered, 'Yes.'

After a moment she said, 'What happened?'

Josse replied, 'We do not know the full story yet. Galiena refuses to tell us; she begged our indulgence but said it was only proper that she reveals it first to Ambrose.'

'So you have had to contain your impatience,' she murmured. 'How very trying for you.'

He gave her a sharp glance. 'Indeed, my lady.'

'The dead girl whom we buried at Hawkenlye,' Helewise asked softly, 'do you know her true identity?'

'Not so far,' he whispered back. 'Galiena implies that she may be able to tell us. You think of her grave, I imagine?'

'I do. She is buried in our plot as Galiena Ryemarsh but clearly that is not who she was.'

'Hm.' He thought for a moment. 'My lady, if it is necessary I will press the matter for you. It may be that it is overlooked in the excitement of Galiena's return, but I know that it is important to you and I will help if I can.'

'Thank you.' She touched his arm lightly with her

fingers. And she thought, dear Josse. Dependable as ever.

When Galiena reappeared, it was obvious that she had taken great trouble over her appearance. Her clear skin shone with cleanliness and her hair had been washed and was still damp; as it dried, its white-blonde colour reappeared. There was a bruise on her forehead and her deep blue eyes seemed overlarge in her pale face. Before she had time to say more than a few words of greeting to the company, Isabella led her firmly over to the table and stood over her while she ate a plateful of food and drank some rich red wine.

Then, with Ambrose holding her hand, she went to sit beside him on one of the benches that Brice and Josse had drawn up before the great fireplace. Brice and Isabella sat on another, Josse and Helewise on the third.

As they settled themselves, Helewise studied the girl's face. Yes, there was a strong resemblance to the woman who had taken her identity and ridden into Hawkenlye Abbey. But Galiena was lighter in build, shorter in stature and her face was finer-boned. She was also younger, by quite a few years, Helewise guessed. And she had a – how to describe it? An altogether *softer* quality, she decided. An air of kindness, of generosity, as if anyone approaching her would know instinctively that they had found a friend.

It was no wonder, Helewise thought, that she and the Hawkenlye nuns had formed such a very dissimilar impression of the woman they knew as Galiena

Ryemarsh from that which Josse had gained; the Hawkenlye nuns and Josse had unknowingly been talking about two different women.

At last Galiena was ready to speak. Looking first at Ambrose, she said, 'My dearest, it is through the efforts of three very dear people that I am here returned to you, and I would first give them my heartfelt thanks.' Standing, she bowed to Josse, to Brice and to Isabella, who in turn got up to return the courtesy. Then, looking at Helewise, she said, 'My lady Abbess, you and I should have met some days ago, and I wish that it had been so, for many people would then have been spared pain, heartache and death.' Death! Helewise thought. Well, there was the dead woman at Hawkenlye and also the poor young groom, Dickon, whose body Brother Saul and Brother Augustus had discovered.

Hoping very much that the death toll was not to be any greater, she said, 'Galiena, I too wish that you had made your way in safety to Hawkenlye and found the help from my nuns that you had hoped for.'

Galiena's eyes were firm on Helewise's. 'I shall come, my lady,' she said. 'If I may.'

'Of course,' Helewise said. 'We shall look forward to it.'

'Sweetheart, will you now proceed with your tale?' Ambrose prompted gently.

And with an obedient nod she did so.

Some time later, in the soft darkness of the midsummer night, Helewise again walked in Galiena's garden.

Ambrose had taken his wife off to bed some time ago; the young woman was clearly exhausted and had wanted nothing more, once her story was told, than to lie in her husband's arms and seek the comfort of a long sleep. Isabella had been given a guest chamber next to Helewise's, and she too had retired, as had Josse and Brice to their own chamber. The three of them had been almost as tired as Galiena and, despite the many things she burned to talk over with Josse, Helewise had seen that it would have been cruel to keep him from his rest.

The only wakeful person in the house, she had waited till all was quiet and then slipped outside. Now, walking alone in the soft, scented night, she went right back to the start of Galiena's extraordinary story and went through it all over again . . .

She had had such high hopes of the Hawkenlye nuns. Had known, somehow, that they would be able to help her. And, oh, how she wanted to be helped! To give her beloved Ambrose a child was her dearest wish. And she wanted children too, for her own sake, she who had known such love in her childhood from those generous, big-hearted people who had taken her in and who, in all but the blood, were her true kin. A boy first, she hoped – and, with Ambrose's permission, we will call him Raelf – and then a little girl. Two little girls. The first we will call after my beloved Isabella, closer to me than any sister, and the second, Audra for my mother.

They set out for the Abbey as soon as they could. Dear Ambrose had not been able to ride with them, preoccupied as he was with the business of the King's ransom. But it did not matter because Josse d'Acquin offered to escort her part of the way, and young Dickon and Aebba would accompany her on the remainder of the road to Hawkenlye.

She had never liked Aebba and did not welcome her company. She did not care for Aebba to be with her even when she was about her normal daily round and to have her there, a silent and oppressive presence, on this particular journey, with its precious and above all private purpose, was depressing. But Aebba had a claim on Galiena and Galiena did not feel that it was right to send her away.

It happened only a few miles after they had passed New Winnowlands, where they had left Josse. The three of them, Galiena, Aebba and Dickon, were riding on a stretch of track that was shady and dark beneath overhanging trees. Dickon – poor Dickon! – was in the lead, Galiena behind him and Aebba in the rear.

Five men in rough cloaks, their fair hair long and plaited, jumped out on to the track. Four leapt on them, the fifth – who had a woman riding pillion behind him – sat on his horse watching. Dickon was dragged to the ground; Galiena was grabbed by two men who rushed up on either side of her. Spinning round, she screamed to Aebba to help her.

But Aebba just sat there.

Dickon was on his feet, wrestling with the man who had thrown him down, and he managed to cripple his assailant with a knee to the man's groin.

'Yes, Dickon!' Galiena had yelled, wildly struggling

with the two men holding her arms. They had pulled her from her horse and she kicked out hard, trying to catch them on their shins. Dickon, hearing her cry, spun round to look at her.

He shouted back, encouraging her — 'Aye, that's right, my lady, fight dirty! That's the way! A heel in the bollocks if you can, then—'

But then the fifth man, who appeared to be the leader of the band, rushed at him, a club in his upraised right arm. He brought it crashing down on the back of Dickon's head. And Dickon neither fought nor cried out any more.

They wrapped him in some sacking and rolled him in a ditch. They made an attempt to cover him with leaves and branches, but it was not a proper burial. And nobody said prayers for him except Galiena, who said the words silently, for God's ears alone, as the tears flowed down her face.

In her grief and her shock, they thought to overcome her easily. But as Aebba curtly ordered her to control herself, because there was a long way to go, something in Galiena woke up again. Waiting her moment, she stood drooping until the chance came.

Then, grabbing an unguarded moment, she leapt back into the saddle and, shouting 'Help! Help!' at the top of her voice in case some blessed traveller should be within earshot, she raced away. They were after her instantly and, half-turning, she grasped her riding whip and launched a savage, cutting slice at the face of the man nearest to her. As he cried out in pain, the man behind her kicked his horse and came up on her other side, so she

slashed at him too. Then she set spurs to her mare's sides
and flew off up the track.

But the two men she had attacked were not badly hurt
and there were still three more men and Aebba. Galiena's
resistance did not last long; the men's horses rode down
her gallant mare and soon they were upon her. They took
her down from the mare and, as she stood held fast in their
firm grip, the woman got down from the fifth man's horse
and swung up into Galiena's saddle. Then, after a quick
exchange with the leader, she and Aebba rode off up the
track, westwards towards Hawkenlye.

Galiena was still wondering why the woman was
dressed in garments that should have been hanging in
Galiena's own bedchamber when the two women disappeared around a bend in the road.

Now the men took no chances. Her hands were bound
behind her back and, to stop her shouting again for help,
they stuffed a cloth in her mouth and tied it in place with
a length of cord. Then they put a heavy cloak around her
and pulled its hood over her head, securing it with more
cord until she was trussed so tight that she could hardly
move. Then they slung her across the saddlebow of the
leader of the band.

Throughout the endless journey to Saltwych, she bounced
helpless before him, the cloth in her mouth making it hard
to breathe and the hot cloak making the sweat pour off her.
They must have passed along secret, hidden byways, for
she heard no sounds of any other horses and the only
voices she heard during her long ordeal were those of her
captors.

Her pride kept her going. She would not give them the

satisfaction of hearing her muffled sobs. Biting on the gag, she kept her resolve. And she survived.

They got to Saltwych in the night. Hands on her hips and her shoulders dragged her down from the horse and the cloak was untied and taken off her. In her silk gown, soaked with her own sweat, she stood shivering in the cool air. With her hands still tied behind her and the gag in her mouth, she was taken into the long hall. Past the animals, restless at being disturbed from sleep, past the gawping people who stared at her, bound and captive, until she stood before a blond man in a throne and a man with silver eyes who sat beside him.

The man in the throne wore a circlet around his brows. He said, 'I am Aelle. You know what I am and what you are to me, for you were told long ago. But you seem to have forgotten us, your blood kin, and we sent Aebba to remind you.'

She could not speak and refused to try. With an impatient curse, Aelle ordered one of her guards to remove the cloth. Her mouth horribly dry, she tried to form words. The silver-eyed man got up, poured water in a cup and, coming to her side, held it to her lips, tipping it carefully so that she could drink without choking.

She drank her fill and then said, 'Thank you.'

He gave her a grave bow and returned to his seat.

'Well?' Aelle's tone was curt.

Sipping at the drink had given her precious thinking time. Now she said, 'I know that I am the daughter of the last chieftain and that you, Aelle, are my brother. I know that our father wished to end our long isolation but that you, as soon as he was dead, took our people

*straight back to the old ways. You sent me away because
you feared I would take after our father and, as I grew
up, would persuade the people that our father was right
and you were wrong.'*

Aelle said, 'You have been well schooled in your own
history.'

'She taught me well,' Galiena flashed back. Aelle knew
whom she meant by 'she'.

'And she also told you of the obligations that you owe to
your blood kin? How, in return for our having placed you
in a position of wealth and influence, you must support us
and advance our status via your son?'

'I have no son!' she shouted, using anger to disguise the
torment. 'And the wealth that my husband owns is his to
disperse as he sees fit!'

'He disperses it now to bring back the king they call
Lionheart!' Aelle said with icy fury. 'His wealth that
should be yours and your kin's to share will instead fill
the coffers of some foreign duke while we slowly starve!'

'Ah, now I see!' She gave a harsh laugh as she understood. 'I see why you had to do all this, why I have been
brought here now to face your threats and insults. Because
Ambrose chooses to answer the King's appeal and you
don't like it! Well, it has all been for nothing because I
will not help you!'

There was a short silence; she could almost hear the
collective intake of breath of the people nervously listening
all around them.

'Yes, yes,' murmured Aelle, 'it is true what Aebba told
me. You have strayed too far from your kin, Iduna, and
you forget where your true allegiance lies. But you will not

leave here until you have not only been reminded of what you owe to us, but you have also managed to convince us that you will mend your ways.'

'I will not. I will never do as you command me!'

'Brave words,' Aelle said, *'but mere bombast. You know, Iduna, how we treat those who disappoint us.'*

She hung her head at that, for it recalled to her another's pain and the memory hurt. But then she stiffened in horror for suddenly she understood exactly what it was that Aelle was threatening.

Her eyes met his and she breathed, *'No. You would not.'* Tears running down her cheeks, she whispered, *'Not Ambrose.'*

'Why not?' Aelle said silkily. *'Think on that, Iduna, in your confinement!'*

He beckoned to the guards and they advanced on her, one of them still holding her gag in his hands. She cried *'NO!'*, kicking, screaming, trying to bite the hands that came at her. Then someone had hold of her head in a grip that felt like iron and her mouth was forced open. A mug was crushed against her lips and liquid poured into her mouth. But this time it was not pure, refreshing water; Galiena was a herbalist and she knew what it was for she recognised the taste.

It was the poppy solution that brings deep sleep and oblivion. As, against her will and choking, she was forced to swallow, she realised that it was strong; very strong. Then her legs buckled and the world went black.

When she woke she was lying in a round hut and the man with the silver eyes was sitting beside her. Her hands *were free but there was an iron shackle round her ankle, and a long chain led from it to a bolt set high in the wooden planking of the wall. She was naked but for a loose garment of sacking. Her skin felt foul and itchy where mud from the beaten earth floor had stuck to her drying sweat.*

She urgently needed to pass water. He must have realised, for he pointed to a wooden bucket beside the wall and he stepped outside whilst she used it.

He came back inside, closing the door. 'This is kept barred on the outside,' he remarked. 'You will not escape, Iduna, even if by some miracle you manage to remove the shackle.'

'I will be missed!' she cried. 'I am expected at Hawkenlye Abbey and they will look for me when I do not arrive!'

'But you have arrived,' he said smoothly. 'A woman of your family who strongly resembles you has gone to the Abbey in your place.' And, horrified, Galiena remembered the woman dressed in stolen clothes; stolen, no doubt, by Aebba from Galiena's room. 'She will tell the good nuns that she dismissed her groom and her serving woman as she reached the gates and, to everyone there, she will be Galiena Ryemarsh, come to seek the help of the nuns because she wishes to conceive. Nobody there knows what you look like, child, but, as I say, in any event your replacement resembles you sufficiently to convince the casual observer.'

She will not convince Ambrose, Galiena thought, with a stab of optimism. And they do not seem to know that he also is bound for Hawkenlye and will arrive there soon. And I, she resolved, shall not tell them; it is my only hope that my dear lord will instantly see that this woman who passes herself off as his wife is no such thing.

She wondered for a moment why they should have bothered with the deception; why was it necessary to send an impostor to Hawkenlye? She could see no reason why she should not ask the silver-eyed man, so she did.

'Ah, because your friends Josse d'Acquin and Brice of Rotherbridge both know that you are going there,' he said with a sigh. 'Word may spread that you are expected. If by mischance they too arrive at the Abbey, then your replacement will have to be very careful that she does not let them approach too closely until she has modestly covered her face with her veil.'

Then he gave her water, then another draught of the poppy potion. She slept once more.

The next time she woke it was Aelle who stood before her. He was furious.

Crouching before her, he said, 'Aebba has returned. She has told us something that has surprised us and that you, little sister, knew all along.' He pushed her shoulder with some force and she fell back on to the floor. 'You knew full well that Ambrose was going to follow you to Hawkenlye!' Aelle shouted.

'And just why should I have told you?' she shouted back, as furious as he. 'It was my one hope that Ambrose would recognise the impostor and raise the alarm!'

Aelle gave a cruel laugh. 'Well, you hope in vain, Iduna. Aebba is cleverer than you think and, predicting that your replacement's disguise would readily be *penetrated by your husband, she took steps to prevent the unmasking of the deception.'*

Cold suddenly, Galiena whispered, 'How? What did she do?'

'She drugged him,' Aelle said, an unpleasant smile on his face. 'She has been caring for her lord in the absence of his wife and she managed to slip a certain potion into his drink. His bad eyesight combined with a sudden severe mental confusion meant that he would have been persuaded that almost any fair-haired young woman was you. But Aebba, cunning Aebba, took an extra precaution. Do you want to know what it was?'

Slowly Galiena nodded. She could not help herself.

Leaning confidingly towards her – she could smell his rank sweat – Aelle said, 'She told your replacement to visit the doddering old fool. She instructed her to take some of the special ointment that you had just made for the pains in his joints and told her to sit at his side and lovingly rub it into his hands. Had he entertained any doubts that it was his own beloved wife who crouched there, then he certainly forgot them then. It was your very own potion that she used – Aebba gave it to her – and very few others know the recipe.' He touched Galiena's hand, rubbing the skin as if he too were massaging sore joints. 'It has a very distinctive smell, I believe?'

It did. Oh, dear God, he was right. Even if Ambrose had entertained any doubts – which seemed very unlikely, since they had drugged him – then the arrival of a woman who looked like her and bearing her own secret remedy would surely have driven them away entirely.

Aelle was looking at her and then he said softly, 'No one will look for you here.'

I am lost, she thought.

The next time they came to force the poppy sedative down her, she did not resist.

22

It was pleasantly cool in the garden and Helewise, who had been sitting on a wooden bench as she went in her mind through Galiena's tale, got up and began to walk up and down across the short grass. It was a clear night and she could see the quick flit of bats. Somewhere owls were hunting, calling to each other.

The poor girl must have thought there was no hope left, she thought. Which was exactly what Aelle wanted because, had he wished to, he could have told her just why it was that Aebba had come running back to Saltwych in such a fluster. He had kept that knowledge from his sister, though. The moment of despair in the little hut had been the last part of the story to be told by Galiena, for, giving in to the strong sedative, she had known no more until she came to her senses sitting in front of Josse astride Horace.

It had been Brice and Josse, but primarily Isabella who had provided the rest of the tale.

It appeared that Isabella had been a skilful and adept spy, for she had managed to work out the detailed lie of the land around Saltwych and she had hidden herself away where she could watch the comings and goings in the settlement. Helewise was still not sure what Isabella had been doing at Saltwych. Brice and Josse appeared to think that she had joined them there only after their visit to Readingbrooke. Helewise, however, had a suspicion that Isabella knew more about the place and its inhabitants than had been revealed and she wondered if it was possible that Isabella had been there *before* either Josse or Brice had discovered it. Before Galiena had been imprisoned there. But why? What lay at the root of her interest in the place? That, she decided, was something to be discussed in the morning.

The fact remained – she went back to her recall of the story – that Isabella had witnessed the fury that whatever it was Aebba told him had aroused in Aelle. Although Isabella had not been close enough to overhear what had been said, it was possible now to surmise that Aebba must have come straight from Hawkenlye to tell her chieftain what had just happened there. She must have reported a death: not that of Galiena, as everyone had believed, but of Galiena's replacement. Perhaps, too, she had told Aelle of the discovery of the groom Dickon's poor murdered body. As Helewise had been able to verify, Aebba had done her best to keep out of everyone's way at the Abbey but she had seen the body in the infirmary. Her instinctive reaction – Helewise could still picture Josse's surprised expression as he had watched the woman – had been fury because all the careful planning had gone so badly wrong.

Helewise took several more turns around Galiena's sweet-scented garden. That was the end of the story, as Galiena and Isabella had told it.

Isabella had mentioned that the name of the woman who had replaced Galiena was Fritha. Helewise wondered now if Fritha had known she was pregnant. Helewise almost hoped that she had not, for it surely would have been worse to suffer that agonising death in the knowledge that her unborn child was dying with her.

Who poisoned Fritha? Helewise asked herself the question for the twentieth time. And why?

I am too tired to puzzle over it any more now, she thought, turning at last back towards the house. I shall sleep, as I trust everyone else is doing. In the morning, perhaps our refreshed minds will manage to find some answers.

It appeared that others had also appreciated the need for answers. As they convened for the morning meal – Isabella was now dressed in women's clothes and Helewise noticed in passing both that she was a remarkably handsome woman and also that she bore a resemblance to Galiena – Ambrose announced that Brice had something that he wished to tell them all.

'Brice,' Ambrose said commandingly, 'please, enlighten us as to what it is you would have us know.'

With a quick glance at Isabella, standing by his side, Brice took hold of her hand and said, 'Isabella has consented to become my wife. It is something I have prayed for since I met her and, at last, my prayers have been answered.'

There was a sudden babble of excited congratulations and delighted exclamations; Galiena went to hug her friend and whispered something in her ear that made Isabella smile broadly.

Then Josse said something which Helewise did not understand: looking both pleased and slightly perplexed, he asked, 'But Isabella, what of the matter we spoke of? What of the – er – the *impediment?*' His voice dropped to a whisper for the last word but, since Josse had never been very good at whispering, Helewise heard it clearly, although she did not think that anyone else had done.

With an affectionate look at him, Isabella replied quietly, 'Wait, Josse, and I shall explain.'

Ambrose, once again master in his hall, said loudly across the noise, 'There is another tale to tell here, unless I am mistaken. We would hear it, Brice, if you please.'

'It is Isabella's tale primarily,' Brice replied. 'I will speak when asked but, for the main, let us listen to her.'

Isabella paused for a few moments, looking down at the floor. Then, raising her head and staring out through the open door towards the bright sunshine beyond, she began to speak. 'I was married, as all of you except the Abbess know, to a fine man, Nicholas de Burghay. When our second child was but a baby, my husband was killed. Galiena's family, by which I mean her adoptive family at Readingbrooke, took me in because Audra de Readingbrooke is my sister-in-law; Nicholas was her brother. Then Galiena met and married Ambrose, and here in his hall I first met Brice. We fell in love but there was a powerful reason why I could not agree to follow my heart and marry him.'

'Roger,' Brice interrupted. 'Isabella's boy,' he explained to Helewise, who nodded.

But Isabella put her hand to his face and said gently, 'No, my love. Roger was not the reason and my heart has pained me every time I have had to endure your sad puzzlement, for you believed me when I said he disliked you. In fact he does like you, very much.'

Brice's face was a study. He looked, Helewise thought, hurt, bemused and, not very far beneath the surface, angry.

Isabella must have perceived the rising anger too for she hurried on. 'Hear what I have to say, Brice, before you judge me. My refusal to wed you was out of fear for your safety, for I believe – no, I know – that Nicholas was murdered and I was terrified that, if my love for you were to be made public by our marriage, you would suffer the same fate.'

'No, I cannot believe this!' Brice, deeply disturbed, shook his head. 'Nicholas was murdered? By whom?'

Again Isabella paused. Then she said, 'You may have wondered how it was that I came to know so much about the community at Saltwych.' She glanced at Brice, who shrugged and muttered something about having supposed that Galiena had told her.

Helewise, who had been wondering that very thing, waited for an answer.

'But I knew little of the place until quite recently!' Galiena protested. 'It was Isabella who told me much of what I know!'

There was a tense silence. Then Ambrose said commandingly, 'Isabella, if you please. Go on.'

She gave him an anguished look and then said, 'Like Galiena, I too am a child of the clan at Saltwych. My mother was Aelle's second cousin and she died giving birth to me. I do not know who my father was – there was some mystery about it and I was half-afraid to know the truth, even had it been offered to me.' She tried to laugh, but it was a feeble attempt. 'It has been known for close kin to marry and bear children, and I did not—' She made herself stop. 'I was raised in the community until I was almost seventeen and then they found a husband for me. They thought they had selected a man who was close to the powerful circles that rule our land, but they were wrong. I do not know how they came to make such a fundamental error – perhaps the source of their information was mistaken over the name. Anyway, as far as my people were concerned, I was married to the wrong man. It was never explained to me.'

'And they were not pleased when the man whom they had chosen proved not to be the influential person they had believed him to be?' Helewise put in softly.

Isabella spun round to look at her, wide blue-green eyes taking on a bright shine in the light streaming through the open door. 'No, my lady. They were not.' She hesitated, then, swallowing, voice cracking on the words, said, 'Aelle killed him. They made it look like an accident – we were out hawking and, as we rode through a stretch of woodland, a heavy branch came crashing down out of a tree and knocked Nichola from his horse. He suffered a grave wound to his head and it became inflamed and he died in torment.'

Josse said, after a short respectful pause, 'Isabella, are you certain Aelle was responsible?'

She looked at him, tears in her eyes. 'Oh, yes. I saw him, and he had other men from the settlement with him. He pretended to be there to help me but there was no reason, other than an attack on Nicholas, for him to be in that vicinity; normally he rarely leaves the marsh.'

'But it *could* have been coincidence,' Josse persisted. Helewise, watching him, wondered why he was pursuing the point.

'No,' Isabella said firmly. 'There is something else: later, when Nicholas was buried and I was about to move in with the family at Readingbrooke, Aelle visited me. And he said they would find another husband for me who would better advance the cause of our blood kin.'

Josse sat back with a smile, increasing Helewise's puzzlement. But Isabella, who had also noticed, gave a quick laugh and said, 'Are you happy now, Josse? Now that you understand that I truly had a reason?'

And he said, 'More than happy, Isabella. Thank you.'

There is a small mystery there, Helewise thought to herself, that I will pursue another time . . .

Brice, who no longer looked angry, said, 'Isabella, my love, you should have told me this long ago! I would have done something, I could have—' He topped.

'What would you have done?' Isabella asked. 'What happened to Nicholas could so easily have happened to you. In the case of an active man, a man who loves to hunt as much as you do, it is all too easy to feign a fatal accident.' Then, holding one of his hands in both of hers, she said, 'I did not want to be the cause of the death of another man I loved.' Then, passionately, 'I did not want to lose you too!'

At which Brice put both arms around her and hugged her to him as she wept.

When, after some moments, she moved a little distance away from Brice and, giving him a grateful smile, wiped her eyes, Josse said, 'Was that why, Isabella, you tried to dissuade us from going down into the Saltwych settlement to rescue Galiena? Because you feared for Brice?'

'I feared for you too!' she said. 'I knew what they are capable of; you did not. And I did not know the identity of the girl in the hut. I was sorry for her, of course I was, but I felt that for your sakes, we should leave well alone.' She looked at Galiena, then back at Josse. 'I am so glad,' she added, 'that you ignored me.'

'Just how long,' Helewise asked cautiously, 'had you been watching the Saltwych settlement, Isabella? Days? Or was it weeks?'

Again, Isabella turned her remarkable eyes on to her. 'You guess accurately, my lady,' she said.

'The Abbess does not *guess*, she reasons,' Josse interrupted pontifically, and his tone broke the tension in the hall, allowing them all a moment of laughter.

'It *was* a guess, really,' Helewise admitted. 'Yo

gave the impression last night, Isabella, that you knew the place much better than Josse or Brice, which, of course, you have just explained to us by saying that you were born and brought up there. So it follows that you would have known of a good place to hide while you watched and listened to all that went on.'

'Yes, I have been going there on and off since Nicholas died,' Isabella said. 'My family all know that I love to hunt alone which, as well as allowing secret meetings with Brice, also meant I could slip away and see what was happening at Saltwych. Try to hear, for example, if any plans were being laid for me.' Looking across at Galiena, she said, 'I am only sorry that I did not learn of the threat to you, dearest. Aebba must have slipped away from Ryemarsh the very night after you had announced your visit to Hawkenlye, in order to tell Aelle that the perfect opportunity had arisen to snatch you and substitute a woman who looked like you. Had I seen Aebba in the settlement then, I might have been suspicious. But I did not.'

There was a silence as they all considered the implications of that. Then Ambrose said, and from his tone Helewise thought he was giving a final summing-up of the discussion, 'Well, that cannot be helped. Galiena is safe now, back where she belongs, and, with Aelle's death, it appears that there is no longer a threat to Brice if he becomes Isabella's husband. You do not think that his successor will carry on his policy of marrying selected girls of the kinfolk to important outsiders, Isabella?'

'No,' she said firmly. 'There is not another like

Aelle. He has no child of his own and his successor is his cousin's son, a weak-minded fool who wishes nothing more than to hunt fowl in the marshes by day and whittle wood in the evening.'

'I pray,' Ambrose said gravely, 'that you are right.'

'I am,' Isabella said firmly. 'The Saltwych community has had its time and will degenerate to nothing.' Then, as if surprised at her own prophetic words, she said 'Oh!'

Ambrose got up and embraced both her and Brice. 'I will send word of this happy news to your kin at Readingbrooke,' he said, with a warm smile for Isabella. Then, delight flooding his face, 'And, indeed, we must also impart the miraculous tidings that Galiena is returned to us. But for now we will drink the health of the newly betrothed couple!' Turning towards the door that led to the kitchens, he shouted, 'Julian! Bring us the best wine!'

As the day reached and passed noon, Helewise felt that she should set out back to Hawkenlye. The revelries at Ryemarsh were clearly going to continue for quite a time and, she thought, why not? Both couples had something to celebrate; a betrothal in one case and a joyous and unexpected reunion in the other. She hoped that Josse might offer to ride with her but, failing that, that Ambrose would supply an escort from his household.

She had spoken quietly to Ambrose and he had asked that the Hawkenlye community say masses for the soul of his groom, Dickon. To her surprise, he had added, 'And, for all that she was a pagan and set out to do me great harm, please also pray for the woman who impersonated my wife.' He paused, then whispered, 'Now let her be buried under her own name.'

Guessing that he probably felt a superstitious dread at the thought of the Hawkenlye grave that was marked with his wife's name, Helewise nodded.

Josse must have guessed that she wanted to be on the road for, as soon as they had finished the midday meal – which took a long time – he approached her and said, 'I am ready to leave as soon as you give the word, my lady. We can be back at the Abbey by nightfall.'

Ambrose, Galiena, Brice and Isabella all came out to the courtyard to see them off. Helewise was helped on to the golden mare, Honey, and Josse swung up into Horace's saddle; both horses looked sleek and well fed from their brief stay in the Ryemarsh stables and Josse muttered to Helewise that they had a lively ride ahead of them.

'I will visit Hawkenlye soon, if I may,' Galiena called out.

And Helewise, understanding, called back, 'You will be welcome, you and your lord.'

But Josse, looking down at the radiant girl and her dignified husband, his lined face filled with a luminous joy that took years from him, muttered, 'Perhaps it will not prove necessary.'

They did indeed have an exciting ride. Sensing the mare's impatience, Helewise held her in; there was one more thing she wanted to ask. 'Sir Josse,' she said when they were out of sight of Ryemarsh, 'why did you question Isabella so closely concerning the murder of her husband?'

'It seemed cruel to you, my lady, that I pressed her hard?' he asked.

'Yes,' she admitted. 'But I am sure you had your reasons.'

He said, after thinking for a few moments, 'I saw her deliberately fly her hawk at Aelle. He was chasing us and he would doubtless have harmed some or all of us had he caught up with us; he had already given poor Brice that alarming bruise on his face. Isabella's intention was clearly to defend us. But still, it was a calculated act and it is certain that the hawk's attack probably blinded Aelle and caused him to fall to his death.'

She understood. 'And you wished to reassure yourself that she acted out of what she saw as necessity,' she commented. 'She was, in short, not only protecting her friends but also, and perhaps more crucially, avenging her late husband.'

'Exactly,' Josse replied.

And, despite her own misgivings, Helewise decided from his set expression that it was probably best to say no more about it.

The lively horses were eager to run and at first Josse – who, as always, had been displaying his usual uneasiness in the company of the golden mare – seemed anxious in case Helewise could not stand a full gallop. But now she was impatient to be home.

I'll show him, she thought gleefully, I'll prove that, although I'm a nun, I haven't forgotten how to ride!

With a cry of delight, she kicked her heels into Honey's sides and felt the mare leap off. Flying, feeling the wind of their fast passage tear at her veil, she heard Horace's thundering hooves beat against the hard ground as Josse came after her. And she found herself laughing from sheer happiness.

She had been back at Hawkenlye for a day when Isabella came to speak to her. Helewise had spent some time thinking back over the impostor's time at Hawkenlye and several things that had puzzled her about the woman whom she had believed to be Galiena Ryemarsh were now clarified. Why she had been so heavily veiled all the time, for example. Why she had refused to pray in the Abbey church but instead spent her time crouched in the corner of the shrine down in the Vale. Why she had shouted at poor Saul when he went in to clean the steps. Why, too, the serving woman, Aebba, had slipped away to the forest; she must have been looking for her accomplice, desperate to speak to Fritha so that the two of them might find a way to deal with the unexpected arrival of Ambrose.

And now that poor young woman – that pregnant young woman – was dead. It was, thought Helewise, all very sad.

It was a relief when Isabella was announced. She had brought her two children with her and Brice had escorted them all to the Abbey. She wished, however, to speak to Helewise alone and so Brice was going to take the children off down to the Vale to see Josse. Josse was about to return to New Winnowlands and now, Helewise thought, feeling pleased for him, he would have company on the road home because Isabella's party had only come for a brief visit and would ride away with him.

The children had been brought in to be presented to Helewise. The handsome young son had nice manners, she thought, and she noticed in passing that Isabella's daughter had her mother's wide eyes, although their colour was different . . .

When the others had left the two women alone in the privacy of Helewise's room, she turned to her guest and said, 'Now, Isabella. What can I do for you?'

'It is a question of what *I* can do for *you*, my lady Abbess,' Isabella replied.

'Indeed? Please, go on.'

'I have been speaking to Ambrose about the woman who pretended to be Galiena,' Isabella said. 'I knew her. Fritha was also a child of the Saltwych community, as no doubt you realised, and she was closely related to Galiena. She was her half-sister, born to the same mother but by a different father.'

'She resembled Galiena quite closely,' Helewise said. 'As you do too.'

Isabella smiled. 'I am related by blood to Galiena but it is not such a close tie. She is my second cousin. There are few families at Saltwych and most of the people are distantly related. But, if I may return t the reason for my visit, it is to ask you whether y and your nuns have resolved the question of how Fritha died.'

'I regret to say that we have not,' Helewise admitted. Watching Isabella's calm face, she decided not to mention the fact that the dead woman had been pregnant. If Isabella did not know – and it was difficult to see how she could have done – then there did not seem any need to tell her. 'Poison was administered,' she said, 'of that my infirmarer is reasonably certain, for there seems no other way to explain Fritha's terrible, fatal symptoms.'

'There *is* another way,' Isabella said quietly. 'According to Ambrose, Fritha included in her impersonation of Galiena a session of massaging Galiena's special cream into his hands?'

'Yes, indeed she did.'

'The ointment had a base made of hazelnut oil,' Isabella said. 'I know the recipe. It is one that I was taught as a girl and I showed Galiena how to make it.'

'I see,' Helewise said, although she was still mystified as to why Isabella had ridden over to tell her all this.

'Only a very small number of us were taught to be healers,' Isabella went on, 'because our people believed that such skills are precious and not for the many. But those of us with the knowledge learned caution with the fruit of the hazel because, for a few people, the oil of the nut can act as if it were poison.'

'A hazelnut can kill?' Helewise was incredulous.

'Oh, indeed it can, my lady. The sensitivity appears to run in families.'

'And you know of somebody related to Fritha who has this sensitivity?'

'Yes. Her elder sister – her full sister, not a half-sister like Galiena – went gathering nuts when she was a young girl and, disobeying the instructions to bring her basket home without eating any of her harvest, she returned to Saltwych in a dreadful state. Her face was grossly swollen and the swelling seemed to extend down her throat, for she could hardly breathe.'

'Did she die?'

'No. The wise man has a small silver tube that he uses to blow the ritual incense into life on his brazier. He snatched it up, forced it down the child's throat and it allowed her to take in breath until the swelling went down again.'

Helewise realised, to her shame, that she was surprised. She had dismissed these strange marshland people as backward and barbaric yet their healer – if that was what Isabella meant by wise man – had managed to save a life when all the skill and devotion of the Hawkenlye nursing nuns had failed.

It does not do, she thought sombrely, to be proud.

'Thank you for telling me this,' she said to Isabella after a moment. 'It seems that you have solved for us the mystery of how she died. And, since it was by pure mischance, there is no necessity to search for her killer.' Something occurred to her. 'But surely this cream for Ambrose's painful hands would not be something that Fritha would have eaten?'

Isabella smiled sadly. 'It smells delicious, my lady. Appetising. Did you not remark on it?'

'Oh – yes, I suppose I did.'

Still with the same smile, Isabella said, 'Fritha would not be the first person to lick the residue off her fingers.'

Helewise told Josse later, when he came to take his leave of her. With a whistle of surprise, he said, 'It would be wise, my lady, to mention this business of the nuts to Sister Euphemia and Sister Tiphaine.'

'I have already done so,' she said. 'Sister Euphemia said she would bear it in mind. Sister Tiphaine said, oh, of course, and why hadn't she thought of it?'

'She already knew?' he said.

'So it seems. But then nothing surprises me any more about our herbalist.'

She went with him to the gate, where Isabella, Brice and the two children were patiently waiting for him. The children were laughing at something Brice had said and already, she thought, the four of them looked like a real family. She went up to them and said her farewells.

Then she went over to Josse. 'Goodbye, my friend,' she said to him. Then, on an impulse, 'Be *careful*.'

As he swung up on to Horace's broad back, he too was laughing.

She stood in their dust as the five of them rode away and out of sight. Then, smiling, she went back to her duties.

Postscript

September 1193

Deep in the great forest, a solitary traveller had made a temporary camp. He had been living there for a little over two months and, although he knew he would have to move on soon, he was as yet undecided where to go.

Perhaps he would make his way north-west to Mona's Isle.

His old life was finished and he could never go back. For one thing, there was no future in that place, not for him, not for any of them, or at least not for long. For another, he had given away too much of himself there and did not want the constant reminder of what was lost and could not be reclaimed.

As evening came down, he did as he often did and prepared a small fire. In its soft light, he poured water into a black iron pot and stared into its inky depths.

After a while, the pictures began to form.

He saw a young woman, tall, slim and very fair, walking in a garden. She was happy; she sang as she walked. She had placed a jug of water on a small pile of rocks and beside it there were flowers and a tallow lamp. She lit the wick and the lamp's light shone out into the twilight. As the moon ros in the deep blue sky, softly the woman began to chant.

There was a bump in her belly, below the waistline of her closely fitting gown, and her breasts were swollen with early pregnancy.

Ah, she might have been raised in the ways and the beliefs of the new religion that came from the east, the man thought, but the blood of her people runs true in her veins. She remembers. She knows who has granted her this, her heart's desire.

With a sigh of pleasure, he watched as Galiena gave thanks to the spirits whom she still honoured for their gift of new life.

Time passed.

There was another whom he yearned to watch over but he knew he had forfeited the right. He would try to resist the temptation. Getting up, he went to the branch and bracken shelter that he had made and selected food for his evening meal. Having something to do with his hands might act as a distraction.

He ate his simple food and thought about the place he had left. They had been numbed by Aelle's dreadful death and finding themselves suddenly leaderless had unhinged them. It was Aelle's fault; he should have made better provision for his succession. There was only the witless son of his cousin and, in truth, the lad was not much of an heir. But, had he been given the proper schooling and training that was his right, he youth would have done. He would have been no

Aelle but then, despite his charisma and his undoubted strength, Aella had been far from perfect. As it was, the youth had reacted badly to his suddenly elevated status and he had wept and pleaded for pity, support, for another's shoulders to help him to bear the heavy burden of leadership.

It was my shoulders he wanted, the man thought. And, by the gods, I have had enough!

The silver eyes glittered in the firelight and, against his will, he saw again in his mind the scenes he had despaired over when he had first sat watching them flitting to and fro in the black scrying water. The Saltwych community was doomed, of that he was sure. They would live on there in their isolation and their increasing squalor for another generation, perhaps more, but already others were encroaching on the marshland. The incomers were beginning to live there all the year round now that the land was drying out. They were planting trees and hedges, these new marshmen, building their churches, turning the salt wilderness into a pattern of small, neat fields, careful cultivation and tidy little dwellings. The Saltwych people would face strong and resolute competition for the marsh that they regarded as their own. It would be a case of adapt or die and, because the Saltwych folk had for so long looked inward and kept themselves to themselves, they did not know how to adapt.

They would die.

He knew because he had seen it.

Oh, they would not go dramatically, all togethe

some final battle! No, they would become demoralised, interbred, desperately poor, weak, helpless and, in time, sink down into starvation. And Saltwych, that place that had been so wonderful, the haunt of kings descended from the very gods, would fall, forgotten, in the dust.

It had begun so proudly, thought the silver-eyed man. The men from over the water had been fine people, strong, healthy, with the courage to seek out a new place for their people when the villages of their homeland were threatened by the rising seas. They had flooded in to fill the rootless, leaderless land that was left behind when the Southerners departed and, for generations, they had ruled in triumph. Their leaders had been great men and the greatest of them had been cast adrift on the seas in his flaming longboat; the people still sang of him around the fireside.

Then the new order had come, ruthless, powerful, relentless. And those who did not – could not – bend their proud necks became outlawed, marginalised, a people dwelling on the fringes where nobody else wanted to live.

It could have been so different, the man mused. In a sense, Aelle had the right idea in wedding our young women to outsiders, although he did it for the wrong reasons. We should never have expected our women to render to us the extremes of love and faithfulness that Aelle demanded. He did not understand how a woman gives her loyalty to her husband and her children when she marries, leaving her family – her – to take second place. He did not understand women at all and that failing played a large part in his doom.

Ah, well, Aelle would not listen to the voice of moderation and in the end it killed him.

His thoughts did not want to go down that path. Instead he contemplated the happy prospect of Galiena's baby. It will be a son, he thought, and ironically he will become the man of influence that Aelle wanted. Not with this warrior king who now rules us, not even with this king's errant brother but with the brother's son who will rule after him. This man will be a weak king and his very weakness will allow stronger men to seize power. With them, of them, shall be Raelf de Ryemarsh.

The blood would not die out. Aelle's line, the line of the Old Kings, would continue . . .

Exhausted by the Sight, he lay back, sipping from the drink he had prepared.

He dozed for a while, then woke. He would not be able to rest, he realised, until he had followed his heart and looked where he knew he should not look.

Resignedly he got up and, kneeling once more over the iron pot, stared into the still water.

There she was, his Elfgifu, waiting as she always was on the edge of sight. She too was happy, as happy as Galiena, and in part for the same reason for, although she did not yet know it, she too was pregnant.

And so she should be happy; she deserved it. S had known hardship – an upbringing such as hers demanding for a woman – and she had known

He wondered if she had yet discovered her gift. He had known of it since her birth, for he had cast her natal chart and it had been foretold in the stars. He guessed she must have begun to suspect.

He went on staring into the water. Now there was someone with her – ah, it was her little girl! Not so little now, for she must be almost eight years old. She was so pretty, he thought fondly, and she had those strange eyes that, in his experience, had always exerted such power over people. Those who had the eyes – and he should know – were awesome in their very appearance, even before they had uttered any words of prophecy. Would this girl too inherit the gift?

It seemed likely.

He returned to the woman. Oh, Elfgifu, child, I am sorry! he said silently. Forgive me, now that you have found happiness, for my sin against you, for it was I who chose Nicholas and hence it was I who brought you such pain. But I acted for the best, my love, for, although I knew full well he was not the man of power and position that Aelle wanted for you, I also knew that he was kind and good. These qualities were not, however, enough for Aelle and so your man was killed.

You will have joy now, my daughter. I have looked and I know it is true. Forgive me.

He bowed his head as the tears came. She *would* forgive him. He knew it and it was not that which ⸺sed his pain.

⸺ was the loss of her, for he would never see ⸺ain.

He lay down on the grass, his head thrumming with the deep, dark ache that always followed a long session of Seeing. I loved you, Elfgifu, he thought, as I loved your mother. He smiled grimly. Only once did I break my lifelong celibacy, my daughter. Your mother, Aelle's kinswoman Wilfra, was a woman in a thousand and I could not resist her, for she loved me even as I loved her. To lose her as she gave life to you was an ending for me too, for never again would I look at a woman and seek to make her mine.

Then I watched you grow, my dearest, and my joy in your beauty and your intelligence was marred only by the fact that I could not claim you as mine. I was the clan's sage, their magician, the chieftain's seer, and for me to lie with a mortal woman was forbidden. Wilfra died with my secret untold and, when my time at last comes, I must do the same.

He began to grow drowsy. He saw her again, Wilfra, his dead love. Then he saw Elfgifu, although the man who now spoke softly to her in the night with such love in his voice called her by another name.

He saw her children. He saw the ones that would come; he saw the son and daughter that she had borne Nicholas, the brave boy and the quick, silver-eyed girl.

My daughter's daughter, he thought with a grandfather's fondness, will not only inherit the gift that comes to her via her mother from me. She is also going to be a beauty . . .

Then, smiling, he fell asleep.

The Readingbrooke Family Tree

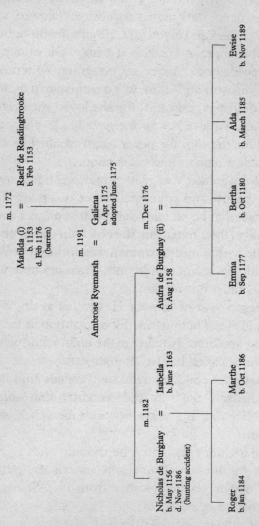

m. 1172

Matilda (i) = Raelf de Readingbrooke
b. 1153   b. Feb 1153
d. Feb 1176
(barren)

Galiena
b. Apr 1175
adopted June 1175

m. 1191

Ambrose Ryemarsh = Audra de Burghay (ii)
                            b. Aug 1158

m. Dec 1176

Emma   Bertha   Alda   Ewise
b. Sep 1177   b. Oct 1180   b. March 1185   b. Nov 1189

m. 1182

Nicholas de Burghay = Isabella
b. May 1156   b. June 1163
d. Nov 1186
(hunting accident)

Roger   Marthe
b. Jan 1184   b. Oct 1186